I AM KLINGON

Counselor Deanna Troi leaped around the corner, phaser ready, and blasted the Klingon by the door to engineering. The warrior fell, and his half-raised disruptor pistol flew from his grip, skittering down the corridor. An acrid stench filled the air of the *Enterprise* as the lavender blood flowed.

"Freeze." Deanna aimed her phaser at the other Klingon.

This warrior had both hands buried in the ripped-open access panel, no doubt trying to rig a bypass to the computer-locked door. Caught with her disruptor holstered, no weapon in hand, the warrior looked at first surprised, then angry. She growled, teeth bared and eyes blazing defiance at the phaser pointed at her five meters away . . .

STAR TREK®
STRANGE NEW WORLDS
II

Edited by
Dean Wesley Smith
with John J. Ordover and Paula M. Block

POCKET BOOKS
New York   London   Toronto   Sydney   Singapore

This book consists of works of fiction. Names, characters, places and incidents are products of the authors' imaginations or are used fictitiously. Any resemblance to actual events or locales or persons, living or dead, is entirely coincidental.

Originally published in trade paperback in 1999 by Pocket Books

POCKET BOOKS, a division of Simon & Schuster Inc.
1230 Avenue of the Americas, New York, NY 10020

This book is published by Pocket Books, a division of
Simon & Schuster Inc., under exclusive license from
Paramount Pictures.

ISBN: 0-671-02693-3

First Pocket Books mass-market paperback printing January 2000

10 9 8 7 6 5 4 3 2 1

POCKET and colophon are registered trademarks of
Simon & Schuster Inc.

Printed in the U.S.A.

Contents

STAR TREK®

Introduction

Dean Wesley Smith

It seems that in *Star Trek*, miracles just keep happening. You hold in your hand one of those miracles—volume two of *Star Trek: Strange New Worlds*. And coming next year is volume three, with submission rules here in this book. Let me give a little history of how these miracles came about.

Last year, for the first volume, Executive Editor John Ordover and Paula Block at Viacom moved heaven and earth to get the approval for a fan-written anthology of *Star Trek* stories. There were more than a few hurdles to climb over, but they got it through, only to be faced with the next level of problems—would the fans respond, could we find enough good stories to fill the anthology, and ultimately would the book sell?

I'm happy to report that combined with those business miracles pulled off by John and Paula, you fans did it again. Last year over three thousand stories poured in, making my job of picking the contents of the first volume both wonderful and painful at the same time. (If you want an outline of the process of picking the stories in that first book, find a copy and read my introduction. Then read the stories.)

This year over four thousand stories came in for me to

consider for volume two. I somehow managed to get the stories down to a top twenty-five. So I sent to John and Paula the twenty-five stories I considered the best picks, and the three of us worked into a final shape the anthology you now hold in your hand. There are seventeen top-notch stories here. Five of the winners are returning authors from the first book, some making their final appearance in *Strange New Worlds* because they have now sold too many stories. (See the rules here in this book for qualifications.)

As with the first volume, I am very proud of the content and professional level of this anthology. Not even the professional-writer fans who do the novels could have done such an original job, in my opinion.

But there is one more part of the miracle that I haven't touched on. On top of sending in stories—good stories, professional-level stories—you fans went out and bought the book, too. And because you did that, the final element of the miracle occurred. The anthology went to a second volume. And next year a third volume. And this wouldn't have happened without the support of you, the fans and readers.

So tell your friends to buy a copy of this book, and maybe even order a copy of volume one. Then sometime this year, before the October 1 deadline, sit down and write that *Star Trek* short-story idea you've always wanted to do, follow the rules, and mail it to us. Who knows? Just maybe next year you'll hold in your hands a book with your story in it. A *Star Trek* story—and you will be a *Star Trek* author. Trust me, you will consider that a miracle, too.

But in *Star Trek*, miracles happen.

STAR TREK®

Triptych

Melissa Dickinson

I

Twilight, on the city's lower east side.

As the first stars appear in the eastern sky, a man and a woman in love cross a street. The two figures merge against the light of a streetlamp; a third watches them go, thinking of tragedy to come.

It is an old story—perhaps the oldest story. Love binding, love wounding, the Fates watching: Clotho with her hand upon the wheel, Lachesis measuring, measuring the threads of lives inextricably woven, patient Atropos with her shining scissors poised to snip . . .

At the far curb, Edith Keeler turned toward the man she loved and spoke the words that would seal her fate. "If we hurry, maybe we can catch the Clark Gable movie at the Orpheum. I'd really love to see it."

Her companion gave a questioning look, as if not quite

3

sure he'd heard correctly over the bustle of the evening traffic. "The what?"

"You know, Doctor McCoy said the same thing!"

"McCoy—! *Leonard* McCoy?" As if the name were a curse, Kirk's smile vanished, leaving a hunted look in its wake.

His intensity was frightening. She fell back a step. "Well, yes. He's in the mission—"

At that, all the blood left his face. "Stay right here." It was an order, and for an instant she froze in simple reflex. His hands tightened painfully on her shoulders; he was already turning. "Spock!" He released her and started back across the street. "Stay right there—Spock!"

The Vulcan had already turned and was hurrying back down the sidewalk. He reached the pool of lamplight even as Kirk did, and gripped the captain's forearms to steady him. "What is it?"

"McCoy!" A few feet away, the door of the mission opened. "He's in— *Bones!*"

"Jim!"

The weeks of tense waiting broke in one joyful moment of recognition. Kirk pulled his old friend toward him, enveloping the doctor's spare frame in an awkward bear hug. Even Spock could not quite stop himself from reaching out to confirm the reality. In their stunned delight, none of the three saw the woman start across the street.

Then, one of them did.

It was the look of alarm in the doctor's face that reached Kirk first—but he knew, even before he turned, that it was now, this moment—that there would be no turning from his fate.

From hers.

Spock's "No, Jim!" followed the captain as he turned, as he took one reflexive step toward her. McCoy made an incoherent sound behind him, and Kirk met her eyes, and then everything began to move very slowly.

Afterward, he would remember it in too much detail. Each stop-action flash of motion seemed to take a small forever, each frame imprinting in his memory with scarring, indelible accuracy. By the time he turned, she was already halfway across. Her eyes were asking him a question, a tiny, puzzled frown gathering between her brows.

"Edith . . ."

She was looking at him. Right at him. He felt more than saw the truck, felt McCoy beside him and Spock at his back, the pressure nearly crushing his heart. The rumble of the oncoming vehicle came up through the pavement, the soles of his feet, rooting him in place. She was looking right at him.

She would know.

Kirk knew what he had to do. He knew it. But he had lost too many times, had made too many choices that had taken too much of his soul. Her eyes were on his, widening suddenly as at last she sensed the motion of the truck bearing down on her, perhaps seeing it out of the corner of her eye. She knew.

Beside him, McCoy started forward.

Unable to take his eyes from hers, Kirk moved. It cost something deep inside him, at the very heart of him, something that burned like acid. And still he paid the cost and moved.

But Spock was already moving, and in his blind grief, Kirk was slower.

* * *

Three men in motion—one in fear, one in sorrow, one in love—and it is Spock's hand on the doctor's arm, Spock's grip that tries to catch him back, and in the end it is Spock who has miscalculated, underestimating the doctor's determination and thus his inertia. A bare ripple in the flow of time, his miscalculation slows McCoy's motion for a crucial instant.

In one moment a few scant inches become an infinity; in the next McCoy has slipped past his friends, into the street.

James Kirk was not in his body. He was somewhere outside himself, somewhere far away where this could not touch him. He heard Spock breathe, "No . . ." from close by, and then reality came unglued.

Edith in the street. The truck. And McCoy moving, moving fast with the surge of adrenaline, very fast, too fast—

Fast enough. He plowed into Keeler full force, his momentum knocking her back, hard, carrying him with her to the pavement, out of the path of the grinning steel grille of the truck. It roared past and skidded with a screech of tires, slid sideways and slammed into a parked car not ten feet from where Kirk stood, frozen, his mouth open in what might have been a shout if there were any sound. The car rocked against the curb, squealing, struck the pavement with a screech of metal on metal. The truck shuddered to a halt, and then was still.

For an instant nobody, and nothing, moved.

That frozen moment made a snapshot in Kirk's memory. Then time itself rushed forward, tidal surge through the keyhole of the present.

The street was suddenly full of people stepping forward from the curbs to see. More brakes squealing, as cars stopped to avoid the tableau in the middle of the street. Angry drivers shouting, a rising murmur of delayed reaction from the onlookers. Someone said, "Is she okay?"

She was. McCoy rolled off her stiffly, and the two of them sat up, looking back across the street to where the truck had careened into the parked car. Kirk breathed again as he saw her move and realized that it was over, that she was all right, she was alive. McCoy had saved her.

Which meant—

"No . . ." The sidewalk lurched under him, and suddenly there was a hand at his elbow, steadying him. Spock. Kirk turned instinctively toward the Vulcan, as he had in so many moments of crisis. Sick realization tightened in his stomach when he saw the answering dismay on Spock's face.

McCoy, reaching the curb, saw that look and knew that his attempt to prevent tragedy had somehow gone disastrously wrong.

Kirk stood at the window of the cheerless little room, gaze fixed on the pool of yellow light cast by the streetlamp below. McCoy knew he wasn't really seeing it. Kirk had alternated staring out into the night with bouts of viciously controlled pacing, leaving it to Spock to fill the doctor in on the havoc he'd inadvertently wreaked.

"It's not over yet," McCoy said at last, feeling as if he had to say something to break Kirk's fixed stare, his unnatural stillness. "We're still here. . . . There's gotta be something we can do." Captain and first officer exchanged a glance, and something in it chilled McCoy. "C'mon, Jim, we're acting like we're helpless here. We can still change things. Spock said 1936. That means we've got six years before the headline you all saw about Edith and the president. So we can still change things, right?"

Spock's tone was patient. "I do not think you understand, Doctor."

"Well then, explain it to me, will you!"

"Aside from other . . . obstacles, there are very real practical difficulties involved in tampering with the subsequent timeline—"

"Wait a minute, Spock. Pretend you're talking to a regular human being. You know, words of less than four syllables."

Spock blinked at him. After a moment's stare that managed to communicate the Vulcan's opinion of his language skills quite eloquently, Spock went on.

"In the flow of time, there are a billion possible futures, a billion points of decision. We have images in our tricorder of only one possible set of these divergent points—only one possible reality. The very fact of our presence here makes my tricorder's data unreliable at best. This unreliability will increase logarithmically as time passes."

As it often did when he was stressed, McCoy's mouth got ahead of his brain. "No wonder you look so glum, Spock. All those little tubes and wires, and nothing but one poor confused tricorder to talk to!"

Kirk shot him a quelling look, and McCoy managed to control the hysteria. "Well dammit, Jim, we've got to try at least."

"Of course we've got to try! Don't you think I *know* that?" Kirk caught himself. McCoy looked from him to Spock, sensing something they weren't telling him.

"All right, out with it, you two."

But Kirk pressed his lips together and turned away. At last Spock gave a nearly inaudible sigh and steepled his hands together. "There is another, more serious problem." His eyes flicked briefly to McCoy's, then away. "Perhaps you should be seated, Doctor."

McCoy knew he wasn't going to like this, but he sat, on the edge of the bed that wasn't covered by Spock's home-made Frankenstein machine.

"I'm listening." Spock took a deep breath; McCoy forestalled him. "In English, if you don't mind."

Perplexed, the Vulcan looked to Kirk for help. Kirk sighed and left the window at last, straddling a chair that faced the doctor. He pursed his lips as he searched for a way to explain.

"You know the old story about the time traveler who goes back in time, meets his own grandmother, and accidentally kills her?"

McCoy nodded. "Sure. Go back in time, kill your own grandmother, thus assuring you're never born. Paradox."

"Right. Logic says that killing your own grandmother is a paradox. It can't happen. Unfortunately, when it comes to time travel, logic doesn't apply." Putting the problem into words seemed to provide Kirk with a focus he sorely needed, and he warmed to his task. "In the early days of speculation about time travel, scientists suspected that traveling into your own past might be impossible. Or that if you did travel into your own past, you'd find yourself unable to change anything of importance. But as it turns out, the universe has no problem at all with you killing your own grandmother."

"Grandma might have a problem with it."

Kirk didn't smile. "The real problem comes further down the line, when you find out that by killing her, by changing history, you've in effect put yourself into another timeline—with no way to get back to your own."

"This stuff makes my head hurt."

"Look, try thinking of time as a river. Each time a decision is made, another little stream splits off and goes its own way." Kirk used his hands to illustrate. "The water itself keeps flowing, always in the same direction, and you can't swim upstream, see. But you can climb out of the river, walk back up the bank, and jump in again. If you change something—say, if you knock off your own grandmother—you'll find yourself swimming down a different branch of the river, with no way to get back into the first branch except to get out and walk back upstream to a spot before the split occurred. Time travel."

Kirk and Spock were watching him with identical expressions of sober intensity. Understanding began to gel, and a chill made McCoy's short hairs stand up. "But we don't have a Guardian here. We can't get out of the river."

Spock nodded. "Essentially correct, Doctor. It is still theoretically possible to divert this timestream back toward its original course. If we are very, very fortunate, we might yet succeed in creating a distant future where the *Enterprise* exists once more—for some other Spock, some other McCoy, some other James Kirk."

McCoy instinctively looked to his captain, but all he saw in Jim's face was the same bulldog resoluteness the man always showed when the going got toughest. Kirk put a hand on McCoy's arm, the grip strong and sure. "The Guardian gave us one chance, and we failed." Spock started to say something, but Kirk shook his head sharply, cutting him off. "We. Both of us, Mister Spock." His tone gentled. "I'm sorry, Bones. We're trapped here, in this time, this place. We can try all we want to change our own future, but we'll never know if we succeeded, and we'll never get back to the *Enterprise*."

Across a gray plain scattered with the ruins of a dead world, a steady wind mourned the lost millennia.

Uhura ran through the frequencies, as carefully as she had the first two times. She was excruciatingly aware of the three men's eyes on her. At last, as she reached the top of the band again, one of them broke the tense silence.

"Anything?"

She looked up, trying not to let her despair get the better of her. "I'm sorry, Mister Scott. No response on any frequency."

He met her eyes for a long moment. At last, straightening his shoulders as if to bear an unexpected weight, he nodded. "That's it, then. We have to assume that the captain and Mister Spock have failed."

Michael Jameson, security officer and ensign of only two months, had the look of a young man who was scared to death and trying not to show it. "How do we know if we've waited long enough? Maybe—"

Scott shook his head sharply. "No maybe about it, lad. When McCoy went through, the change was instantaneous. If they'd succeeded, the *Enterprise* would be up there right now." He met their eyes in turn, weighing responsibility and choosing in the space of a few seconds. "The captain's orders were very clear." His gaze settled at last on Uhura, whose courage was contagious. "I'll go next, and I'll take Ensign Jameson with me. Lieutenant Uhura, you're to continue monitoring for fifteen minutes. If we don't reappear in that time, then you and Ensign Worsley will try."

Her gaze met his steadily, and Scott wished for a moment that he could take her with him. If they were to be exiles, then at least it might be exile shared with a friend. But she must know as well as he that splitting up the officers in the party would increase their chances if he, too, should fail.

She nodded, showing nothing but confidence. "Yes, sir. I understand." She wanted to wish him luck, but it stuck in her throat, an unwelcome reminder of his words to Kirk only a few minutes before. "When you're ready," she said instead.

He turned to the youngest member of the landing party. "Ensign?"

"Ready, sir." The young man's voice betrayed him, but he stepped forward and locked his hand around Scott's wrist. As the captain had not, they said no farewells.

"Time it for us, lass?"

She did, counting down for them, her eyes on the tiny display screen of her tricorder. In another moment, the four *Enterprise* crewmen were only two.

II

Kirk squinted at his handiwork. The leaky pipe seemed to have stopped dripping, so he put the tools away, dusted himself off, and went to find Edith.

As he climbed the steps to the second floor, he tried to make himself believe that tonight would be the night Spock would finish, the night they would know for certain what to do. He tried to hope that they still had a chance. But they had been in the city almost a month, and Kirk's confidence in Spock's "river of time" theory was wearing thin. There had been no sign of McCoy.

He found the two of them conferring over a ledger in Edith's office. The Vulcan straightened, seeing Kirk in the doorway. "Shall we continue in the morning, Miss Keeler?" At her bemused nod, Spock made himself scarce.

Kirk came into the room, moving to the narrow window that overlooked Twenty-first Street. Outside, the streetlamps were just coming on.

"He's such an enigma," Keeler said, coming to stand beside him.

Kirk had to smile. "He is that."

"To you, too?"

"As long as I've known him."

She folded her arms beneath her bosom and tilted her head, a self-conscious gesture that touched him with a little pang. It kept taking him by surprise, that feeling. "Have you known each other a long time, then?"

He realized it had been less than two years. "Not really. But we've been through a great deal together."

"It shows. He worries about you, you know."

"Why do you say that?" Kirk wasn't used to anyone noticing that but him.

She turned to put away the ledgers. "Oh, just a feeling I get." The questions she never asked were between them, filling quiet spaces. "Whatever you're hiding from . . . I feel better knowing you have him to look out for you," she said seriously. "It eases my mind."

"Mine too," he admitted.

And again, she didn't ask, only smiled and came to put her hand into his. "Let me buy you dinner?"

As if they had ever gone to a restaurant, as if either of them could have afforded it. As if they were just a man and a woman who could share dinner and maybe a life together. As if.

He made himself answer her smile with one of his own. "What did you have in mind?"

He was just about to bring her hand to his lips when Spock reappeared in the doorway, wearing a look as troubled as any Kirk had ever seen on that impassive face.

The chief engineer of the *Enterprise* was with him.

An hour later found the four Starfleet officers gathered around the makeshift computer in the cramped one-room flat. The newcomers had been briefed on the situation, including the likelihood that Edith Keeler was the focal point in time they had been looking for. Spock and the engineer worked on the burned-out interface as they talked, installing the newly purchased replacement components.

Some whim of Fate had landed Scott and Jameson in the city three days before the arrival of Kirk and Spock. It had taken Scott a month to find them; he had been systematically searching the shelters and soup kitchens for McCoy, and tonight, it had paid off. Kirk was still finding the enormity of failure difficult to grasp. Every time he looked at Scotty or the Jameson boy, it hit him again what was at stake here, and how insignificant their chances really were. The fact that he'd overlooked something so stunningly obvious as searching the city's soup kitchens brought home how easily failure could come again. He couldn't let himself think about the scope of it for too long, or he'd drive himself to distraction for sure.

Just then Scott looked up from the tangle of tubes and wires. His amazement at Spock's synthesis of stone knives and bear skins had done a great deal to erase his obvious fatigue. "Captain, I'd not have believed this if I hadn't seen it with my own eyes."

Kirk managed a grin for him. "Makes the case for Vulcan ingenuity, doesn't it?"

"Aye. So you think I did right, leavin' the other tricorder with Lieutenant Uhura?"

"Yes, I do, Scotty. Let's just hope she doesn't have to use it." Kirk included young Jameson in his look. "Each one of us has got to be ready to act at any moment."

Scott nodded, securing a last connection. "There, that's got it. Are ye ready to give it a try, Mister Spock?"

"Affirmative. Captain, I believe we shall have our answer on this screen. . . ."

The answer was plain enough, but two days later they were no closer to knowing when the moment would come. And so they waited, tension mounting by the day while, for Keeler's benefit, they pretended business as usual. One of them remained in her presence as much as possible.

This afternoon Scott had stayed with her at the mission, ostensibly repairing the cranky boiler, which was acting up again. He had helped design antimatter warp engines, but this was the first time he'd ever laid hands on a vintage 20C boiler, not to mention one with an attitude like this one. It was with no small satisfaction that he coaxed the old dinosaur back to life.

Keeler appeared at the top of the stairs just as he was wiping his hands on a rag. "Well, well! It seems you've earned your right to the name 'miracle worker.' "

"You flatter me, madam. But she seems to be obliging, for the moment."

"You have my sincere thanks. And anything else I can offer you—which at the moment is a hot meal and not much else, I'm afraid." She glanced at her watch, a small frown gathering on her face. "Have you seen our Mister Kirk, by any chance? I'd hoped we might make the seven o'clock show."

He started up toward her, looking apologetic. "I havena seen him, nor Mister Spock."

She sighed. "Well, I suppose they'll turn up eventually." A smile. "Don't suppose you'd care to keep me company while I wait?"

Beaming, he reached the top of the stairs and offered his arm, which she took. "It would be my pleasure, lass."

In the front room, she sat with him while he ate. He longed for a hot shower, but coal dust and grease would have to be scrubbed off. Hot water was not easy to come by. Self-conscious, he apologized for his appearance.

She scolded him. "I won't have any of that, Mister Scott. You look just fine."

He chuckled. "Aye, for a coal miner. I'm not fit to be seen with."

"And here I was thinking chivalry was dead."

"Never in the presence of a true lady, Miss Keeler."

"Now I think *you* are flattering *me,* sir."

He pretended outrage. "Not a bit of it."

She grinned ruefully. "I can see I'm going to have to watch my step around here. Between you and Doctor McCoy, a girl could easily—"

The spoon fell out of Scott's hand with a clatter. "What did you say?"

"What is it? What's the matter?"

"McCoy!" He'd risen to his feet before he knew he'd done it. "Miss Keeler—*where is he?*"

She started to rise, too, expression bemused and questioning. "He's upstairs, in the back room. But what—?"

Scott was temporarily frozen to the spot with uncertainty. How had this fallen to him? His eyes went to the front window. Across the street, the glow of a streetlamp and a gleam of fair hair caught his gaze. As if in answer to his panic, the captain and Mr. Spock were standing on the curb, waiting to cross.

Scott stumbled for the door, leaving a surprised Edith Keeler in his wake.

"Captain!" The door slammed back with the force of his exit.

On the opposite curb, Kirk's head snapped up. "Scotty?" His voice was small over the rush-hour traffic.

"Doctor McCoy—he's here!"

Shock flickered briefly over his captain's face, then froze into grim determination as Kirk started toward him.

He never saw the truck. It came around the corner, too fast—and Spock, slow by seconds, was too late to shout a warning.

Spock is supremely aware of just how late he is. He perceives the rumble of the oncoming vehicle, the chaos of sound and motion, the flash of red beside him, with perfect clarity. And then the woman's scream.

Spock believes he has moved, or cried the name. But all he hears is that last, surprised intake of breath and then the other sound, the one he knows he will hear for all the rest of his life: the smack of steel impacting flesh and bone.

The truck roars past and skids with a screech of tires. Slides sideways and slams into a parked car not ten feet from where Edith Keeler stands, frozen, unable to scream again because her lungs and heart have seized in clenching horror. The car rocks against the curb, squealing. Strikes the pavement with a screech of metal on metal. The truck shudders to a halt and then is still.

More brakes squealing, as cars stop to avoid the crumpled form in the middle of the street. Angry drivers shouting—but her gaze is riveted to James Kirk, fallen and not moving, his neck twisted at an angle she does not want to see, cannot bear to see—

The one called Spock kneels beside him, his face telling everything she needs to know. She turns away, the warning she cried too late cooling to ash in her throat. It is at that moment that Leonard McCoy appears in the doorway, in time only to witness the unraveling of all that he knows.

Too much blood—far too much. Spock knew before he saw the angle of the neck, but he knelt anyway. Hands reached out, seized the broken form, and pulled it into his lap. Were they his hands?

He saw the open eyes then, the absolute surprise.

"No—"

Spock doubled over, instinctively sheltering Kirk with

his body though it was all too clear that no one could protect him now. Faced with that truth, he made a second, wordless sound of denial, and hid his face against the dead man's hair.

It seemed the longest fifteen minutes of Uhura's life. She and Worsley watched history flicker like hypnotic dream images in the mist, both their communicator channels open, both sounding only silence. At the end of the designated waiting period, she scanned once more with her tricorder and ran through the whole band one last time.

There didn't seem to be anything that needed to be said, so when she shook her head and held out her hand, the young *Enterprise* crewman took it wordlessly. In another moment, only footprints in the dust remained.

III

There'd been no work at the docks that morning. Kirk had let Edith convince him she needed more help at the mission, even though he knew that she could ill afford even the meager wage she paid him. But Spock needed five more meters of wire and a number of other bits and pieces, so he'd let himself be convinced. The downside was that after last night, after what Spock had shown him, he had found it nearly impossible to face her and smile as if everything were fine.

After the evening meal they walked as usual, but tonight the air felt pleasantly mild, and they didn't stop at their usual corner. Tonight they kept going past Seventeenth Street and Sixteenth, and after a while she started to tell him about the neighborhood before the war, about ragtime in its heyday, about Tin Pan Alley as it had been before the music and the glitter had moved north to Broadway.

Her voice sounded wistful, and he asked how long she had lived in Manhattan.

"Oh, since before the war. That reminds me—" She stopped under a streetlamp and patted her pockets, coming up with a soft bundle of fabric. "I almost forgot. I thought you might have a use for these."

He looked at what she'd handed him, smiling quizzically. Gloves, a good pair made of tightly knitted wool, and a soft matching scarf.

"For your friend. I noticed he doesn't stand the cold well. The gloves should be an improvement over the ones he has, yes?"

They were lined, he saw, hand sewn, and almost new. "A considerable improvement." They had to have cost dearly.

"They were my brother's. He had musician's hands, like Spock's. They should be a good fit."

He searched her gray eyes, understanding now a part of the sorrow he had seen there so many times. "The war?" he asked softly.

She sighed, confirming his guess. "Stephen loved his music. He was never meant for guns, and killing." She curled her fingers around his, closing the material in his hand.

"I . . . don't know what to say."

"Thank you is more than enough."

"Thank you, then. From both of us." He tried to find something more. "I have a brother who . . . I haven't seen in a very long time. I'm sorry, Edith."

She just patted his hand and nodded, letting him go. "So am I." And just then, the wind off the river changed direction slightly, and the sound of lively music drifted to them from what sounded like the next block over.

A delighted smile lit Keeler's face, and it was catching. Kirk held his elbow out for her to take. "Shall we?"

"Let's!"

They followed the music until they saw a set of stairs leading down to an open door. A sign over the door proclaimed the name of the club, *After the Ball*, and as they drew near they could hear the rich mezzo tones of a woman's voice singing, "To my heart, he carries, the key. Won't you tell him please to put on some speed. . . ."

To Kirk's surprise, Edith gave him an uncharacteristically impish grin and pulled him along the sidewalk. She sang along with the next line, "Follow my lead, oh how I need . . . someone to watch over me." Her off-key, accented rendition was so charming he had to laugh, though his heart hurt with the irony.

They were halfway down the steps when it hit him that, as impossible as it seemed, he recognized the singer's voice.

When Kirk saw her, crooning on the tiny stage in a white evening gown that almost did her justice, he couldn't hide his shock. He could only stare, as his communications officer finished the song and the audience erupted in noisy appreciation.

"What is it?" Edith cried over the noise. "What's wrong?"

"I know her!" he yelled back, when he could find the words. Oblivious to the jostling of the club's patrons, he stood on tiptoe and tried to catch Uhura's eye. For a moment he thought he wouldn't be able to, and he'd have to force his way through the crowd, or wait until the set was over. But finally, thankfully, she saw him, her shocked recognition as obvious as his own. *Backstage,* she mouthed at him, and he nodded and grabbed Edith's hand, pulling her toward the side door.

Kirk tried to think logically, tried to come up with some explanation he could give Edith for how he and Uhura knew one another. Tried to think what it could mean, that she was here, and what was to be done about it. But when they found her pacing nervously backstage, logic deserted him and he found himself throwing his arms around her, selfishly glad to see her no matter what it might mean. After a startled moment and out of sheer relief, she hugged him back.

Both officers were overflowing with questions, but they couldn't talk in that place, with an audience. Kirk scribbled the address of the rented flat on a cocktail napkin, adding *"Tonight, after the show"* for Uhura's eyes only. She obviously didn't want to let him out of her sight, but he smiled encouragingly and she managed to wave after them without blowing their cover, or her cool.

When she came to the door much later that night, Worsley was with her. Kirk lit the stove and made coffee, and the four officers related their experiences since coming through the Guardian.

"It's been difficult for us," Uhura admitted, glancing at the security officer. "A light-skinned man and a dark-skinned woman together . . . you wouldn't believe some of the things we've seen."

"And heard," Worsley added, his lip curling. "I had no idea people could be so ugly."

"Ignorance is always ugly, Ensign," Kirk said quietly. He rubbed his hands over his face tiredly. Spock had agreed that chances were good Scott and Jameson were already in the city somewhere, searching for McCoy even as they were. But Kirk could see they were all too tired to tackle that additional complication tonight. "All right," he said, "let's get some shut-eye. We'll see about locating Mister Scott in the morning."

Uhura insisted that Worsley take the single bed. He had been working odd jobs wherever he could find them, sometimes fourteen or sixteen hours a day; glad to oblige, he began snoring almost immediately. Kirk, curled up on a blanket on the threadbare carpet, soon followed.

Uhura wasn't surprised when Spock made no move to quit for the night. The Vulcan had been working steadily as they talked, hooking up Uhura's tricorder to his jury-rigged interface. Kirk had related the troubling discovery they had made three nights before, and the subsequent burnout that had prevented getting a definitive answer about Keeler's fate. Spock had advised against making another attempt for at least another day, but the acquisition of Uhura's tricorder, with its precious record of three divergent timelines, had prompted Kirk's decision to risk it.

Accustomed to working nights at the club, Uhura found that sleep eluded her. She lay curled on her side, watching Spock unobtrusively through half-closed eyes. Locked within her tricorder's memory were images of the original timeline prior to McCoy's intervention and the one after, the one Kirk and Spock had created, and even the one created by Scott and Jameson. They were now existing in yet a fifth reality—their last chance to repair the ever-widening rift between the future-that-should-have-been and the future-that-was.

Time travel had always fascinated Uhura, but it was easy to get lost in the twists and double-backs of temporal logic.

She began to drift, aware of the soft snores of Kirk and Worsley, aware of the dark head bent under the dim yellow light of the room's one bare bulb.

Then, after what might have been minutes or hours, she found herself suddenly wide awake. She sensed that something had woken her, some sound, but the captain was dead to the world and she could still hear Worsley's even breathing. Her eyes went to Spock.

He had gone very still, a stillness so profound that for a moment he didn't even appear to be breathing. Other than that, she could see nothing amiss. His face was expressionless, his posture exactly the same as it had been the last time she'd looked at him, hunched over the tiny screen. But something about the way he sat there, not moving, made her get up and go to him.

He said nothing, did nothing to acknowledge her approach. It was only when he moved to clear the screen that she saw the way his hands trembled.

"Mister Spock?" she murmured involuntarily, suddenly feeling the chill in the room. "Is everything all right?"

For a moment he didn't answer. But then he seemed to pull himself together. "Yes, Lieutenant. Quite all right."

He started to disconnect the tricorder unit—and stopped, startled, at the touch of her hand on his shoulder. He looked up.

She nodded toward the kitchen. "Break time, sir," she said, still almost whispering. "You've caught a chill." Her eyes held his. "Come on, let's go warm up."

The tiny kitchen was barely big enough to permit them to stand side by side, leaning against the cracked sink. The warmth of the stove gradually seeped through the pervasive cold of the room, though Spock suspected he might never rid himself of this particular chill.

He stood facing the doorway, where he could see the sleeping man curled on the floor. Uhura seemed content to share the silence, and Spock was both shamed and shamefully grateful that his involuntary gasp had woken her.

One thing, to understand intellectually what forces they manipulated, what kind of power the Guardian wielded. Another to see it, in black and white on a three-inch screen. The grainy photograph felt permanently imprinted on his optic nerves.

"You saw something, didn't you?" she said quietly, after a time.

He didn't look at her, but studied a spidery crack in the ancient baseboard.

"Yes." Despite his best efforts, the word came out a hoarse whisper.

"One of us?"

Time passed, inexorably.

"Yes. One of us," he said at last.

Out of the corner of his eye he saw the direction of her gaze, toward the captain, who slept on. "He loves her, doesn't he?" Spock glanced at her, surprised. He didn't answer, but she nodded sadly, as if he had. "It's going to be hardest on him."

"I would spare him that decision, if I could."

She sighed. "I wish I could believe Fate will be that kind. But all you can really do is be there afterward, to pick up the pieces."

Spock didn't know what it was, exactly, that made him speak, what made him tell her the thing that had been troubling him for the past three days. But something about this moment—here with this remarkable woman in this dingy, drafty kitchen in 1930—made the words come easily.

"I am afraid," he confessed, seeing the image again, flashing starkly behind his eyes. "I fear he will not be able to let her die." Spock immediately wanted to take the whispered words back. Too late—they had taken shape in the tiny room, inescapable.

But Uhura steadily met his gaze, and illogically, he was reassured.

"I don't know how anyone could make a decision like that," she said. "I don't know that I could. But he is the captain. We just have to do what we always do, Mister Spock."

He raised one eyebrow, questioning.

"We just have to trust him."

Scott mounted the stairs from the basement, making a futile effort to wipe his hands clean on a rag. He longed for a hot shower, but coal dust and grease would have to be scrubbed off. Hot water was not easy to come by in this time and place.

The captain and Mr. Spock were standing with Keeler in the dining room, and saw him come up. Kirk smiled, but it didn't do much to hide the strain just under the surface. "Scotty, there you are. We saw Uhura on the way to the post office. She said you might need some help with the boiler."

"Nay, she's working like a trouper. You and Miss Keeler go on now and enjoy your evening." Scott smiled at Edith, then remembered what he must look like after two hours with the boiler. "Forgive me for insulting your nice clean dining room. I'll go wash up."

"You look just fine, Mister Scott."

He chuckled. "Aye, for a coal miner. I'm not fit to be seen with."

"And here I was thinking chivalry was dead."

"Never in the presence of a true lady, Miss Keeler."

"You, sir, are a flatterer."

Kirk leaned closer to Scott and said conspiratorially, "I think she's got your number, Scotty." He gave Keeler a smile and said, "Have to watch this one every minute." He took her hand, and they started toward the door, plainly having eyes only for each other.

Scott watched them go, not wanting to think of what the future might hold for them. He became aware that another pair of eyes watched the young couple with the same thought. "May heaven watch over us all tonight, Mister Spock," Scott said with a sigh.

The Vulcan said nothing about the illogic of his prayer, saying only, "Good night, Mister Scott," in much the same tone.

Kirk called from the door, "Coming, Spock?" and the Vulcan followed them out into the evening chill.

Uhura felt each step throb in the soles of her tired feet. She had been walking most of the day, most recently to check the post office box for possible replies to the classified ads they'd placed in the city's newspapers for McCoy. She had not expected any, nor had the captain, but they were determined that even the smallest possible avenue should be explored. The fact was they were getting desperate.

The light was red at the corner of Twenty-first and Fourth, and she stood on the corner as rush-hour traffic sped by, wondering if she would ever set foot on the bridge of the *Enterprise* again. She had managed to keep her chin up, for the others if nothing else. But tonight she felt afraid, really afraid, for the first time since the captain had found her.

As if in response to her sudden despair, some hundred meters down the block the door to the mission opened and Kirk himself appeared, Keeler on his arm. The sight of them lifted Uhura's spirits, and she felt instantly better. Spock emerged a moment later. The three stood for a moment on the sidewalk, talking. Then Spock headed off down the street, and Kirk and Edith crossed to the opposite curb. Uhura's light changed; she had just started to cross toward them when a stranger's hand snatched her back forcefully.

Not a moment too soon. A battered truck barreled through the red light and turned, tires screeching, onto Twenty-first Street.

Each stop-action flash of motion seems to take a small forever, each frame imprinting in Kirk's memory with scarring, indelible accuracy. By the time he turns, she is already halfway across. Her eyes are asking him a question, a tiny, puzzled frown gathered between her brows.

The rumble of the oncoming vehicle comes up through the pavement, the soles of his feet, rooting him in place.

Beside him, McCoy starts forward.

Beside him, Spock trusts his captain, and doesn't.

Unable to take his eyes from hers, Kirk pays the cost and moves.

Two men in motion, one in fear, one in love. One frozen moment in which a few scant inches become an infinity.

One woman, dead before her time, a thread in the loom.

For an instant nobody, and nothing, moved. Then McCoy, frozen to stillness in the circle of Kirk's iron hold, found words at last for his shock. "You deliberately stopped me, Jim. I could've *saved* her. Do you know what you just *did?*"

Kirk let him go, but did not turn, his back kept firmly to the street.

Spock's words were for the doctor, but his eyes were on his captain, whose fist was clenched tightly against his mouth with the effort not to turn and look.

"He knows, Doctor. He knows."

They appeared on the barren plain in twos. Uhura maintained the presence of mind to hustle Worsley out of the way, as a disoriented Scott and Jameson stepped out of the mist behind them. Scott turned to her in confusion. "What in heaven's name—"

It took Uhura a moment to orient herself, the image of Edith Keeler's death far more real to her than the surreal gray landscape. "There was an accident," she said. Saying it helped anchor her to this reality; she recovered enough to reach for her communicator. As if on cue, it chirped.

Scott fumbled for his own communicator and flipped it open, hope lighting his face. *"Enterprise, this is Mister Scott. Come in please!"*

"Sulu here, sir. Are you all right?"

"Sulu! Ah, laddie, you don't know what good it does me to hear your voice!"

Sulu sounded amused. *"Is that a request for beam-up, Mr. Scott?"*

"Aye, is it ever! Stand by." Scott turned to Uhura, grinning broadly.

But she was already turning back toward the Guardian, scanning it for activity. Scott's grin faded, as he realized the others had not yet appeared. "I was saying good night to the captain and Mister Spock, and next thing I know, I'm here. Did you see—?" Just then, the misty center shifted, and they were there, first Kirk and Spock and, a moment after, McCoy.

Scott searched Kirk's face, plainly not liking what he saw. "What happened, sir? You only left a moment ago." Uhura's gaze, too, went instinctively to Kirk's, but he did not seem to see either of them.

It was Spock who answered, in an even tone that somehow forbade questions. "We were successful."

The Guardian flickered, a hint of promised wonders within. **"Time has resumed its shape. All is as it was before. Many such journeys are possible. Let me be your gateway."**

Uhura broke in, offering her captain the one thing that might bring him back to the present. "Captain, the *Enterprise* is up there. They're asking if we want to beam up."

It seemed to reach him. Kirk's eyes lost their faraway look, regaining focus for the first time. "Let's get the hell out of here."

His officers took up transporter formation behind him. Uhura adjusted the tricorder at her shoulder, mindful of the priceless cargo she carried.

The Quick and the Dead

Kathy Oltion

The air where the landing party beamed down on Theta Tau V held a confusing combination of odors, like rotting compost and spring flowers, and the sky resembled a bowl of thin pea soup. What a disgusting color, McCoy thought, wiping the sweat from his forehead. It was warm, too—warmer by far than the *Enterprise*'s climate-controlled environment.

"Why is it," McCoy said to Kirk, Spock, and Sulu, who comprised the landing party, "all the perfect, Edenlike planets the *Enterprise* has come across are somehow fatally flawed for colonization? Yet a planet that smells like this one has so much more potential?"

"Well, Bones," Kirk said, "maybe we aren't ready for Eden, yet." He kicked at a clump of dirt.

"Maybe Eden flat out doesn't exist," McCoy said. He looked around at the rugged landscape where the transporter had deposited them. They stood on the only level spot on the flank of a small mountain. From here, it was either up or down, and up was a steep boulder scramble. Even where they stood, there were boulders and rocks strewn about, and sparse, bushy vegetation grew between them. Looking down, McCoy could see a brown, dusty basin that stretched kilometers across, surrounded with rocky hills like the one they were on.

The landscape bore the signs of heavy erosion; deep gullies cut into the hillsides, rock debris and boulders forming talus slopes at their bases. Upon closer inspection, McCoy noticed that the hillsides were riddled with dark crevices, some of which appeared to go deep into the rocky outcrops. He could hear rushing water somewhere to the left of where he stood.

Lieutenant Sulu huddled over some low-lying plants while Spock studied geological readings from his tricorder, searching for signs of any desirable minerals. The captain had walked a few steps away from the landing party, looking down a steep embankment. Hands on hips, he peered out over the land.

"Well, Jim," McCoy said as he approached Kirk, "it looks like we got ourselves a real find, here."

"Indeed, Bones," Kirk answered. "There's an indescribable feeling to be the first people, maybe the first intelligent life ever, to step onto this unknown soil."

"Unknown soil, unknown plants, unknown animals." McCoy spread his arms. Overhead, he heard a trilling, and he looked up to see a flock of some kind of animal circling in the breezy sky. "For now, at least, the whole place is one big question mark."

"Yes," Kirk said with a smile, "it is."

"I am endeavoring to identify some of those unknowns," Spock said as he joined Kirk and McCoy. "For instance, there are seven hundred thirty-four different species of animal life alone within the range of my tricorder. The terrain in this area is composed of granite and limestone with forty-seven trace minerals and elements. There are—"

Kirk interrupted Spock with a raised hand. He shaded his eyes and peered out into the basin. "The ground out there," he said with hesitation, "looks . . . greener . . . than when we arrived."

"It could be your eyes adjusting to the weird light," McCoy suggested without much conviction.

"No, the cliffs over there are still the same dusty brown, but the basin floor looks like an irrigated field in spring," Kirk said.

"Captain," Sulu called. He squatted near a patch of dark, green-leafed vines with large blue, bell-shaped flowers. "I've found something interesting here."

"I'm not surprised," Kirk said, smiling at McCoy as they made their way to Sulu's side.

"These plants are growing at a phenomenal rate! The vines have grown fourteen centimeters in the past three minutes." He held up a vine, and McCoy could actually see it stretch out and form new leaf buds.

"Good gods, Jim! Imagine the cellular division that must be going on in that plant."

"The energy readings from all these plants are sky-high," Sulu said. "At this rate of growth, the plant is consuming nutrients at the equivalent of an average Earth growing season in a matter of minutes."

"Any normal plant would burn itself out at this rate of growth," McCoy said. He pulled his own tricorder out of its case, which he carried slung over his shoulder.

"Mister Sulu, make sure you collect some of these— extraordinary—plants for further study," Kirk said.

"Aye, Captain," Sulu said, holding up a couple of fifteen-centimeters-long, cylindrical stasis tubes. "I have two samples already, but I'm having trouble getting an intact root from any of them. Even when I loosen the ground with a trowel, the stems break off more easily than the roots let go of the soil."

"Keep trying," Kirk said. He glanced back to the basin below, then up toward the butte's summit. "I think I'll go see what's on the other side," he said.

"I'll stay here and give Sulu a hand," McCoy said, studying his tricorder. "Besides, I want a look at the mitosis going on with these." He snapped a sprig of leaves from another vine.

McCoy watched as Kirk climbed up the butte. The trilling of the birds, or whatever they were, filled the skies. He wiped sweat from his forehead, turned back to Sulu, and said, "Is it me or is it getting hotter?"

"The ambient temperature of our location is indeed rising, Doctor," Spock said, "as are the humidity and the activity of the local fauna." He pointed to a clump of grass where three white, fist-sized, large-eared, naked-looking herbivores devoured it. One of the little rodentlike creatures stopped eating the grass long enough to give Spock the once-over, emit a sound much like a burp, grab one more mouthful of food, and bound away to disappear into an opening in the ground no bigger around than McCoy's little finger. The rodent's compatriots did likewise, burping all the way.

McCoy turned his attention back to his own tricorder and the piece of plant he still held in his hand.

Spock said, "The oxygen level is increasing, as is humidity. No doubt a result of the increased metabolism of the plants. There are corresponding readings for decay of organic matter. . . ."

But McCoy didn't pay any attention to the last of Spock's findings, for in the doctor's hand, the freshly picked plant had more than wilted. It had disintegrated before his eyes to a black, slimy goo. Alarm raced through McCoy's mind as he read the tricorder's data. Bacteria swarmed over the tissue, breaking down the cell walls and using the nutrients to multiply. Then it hit him, and he felt so stupid. It would be logical, Spock would say, for something that grew so fast to also die off fast. Die off and deteriorate.

"Jim!" McCoy called, interrupting Spock's observations, but the captain was too far up the mountain to hear him. He rubbed what was left of the plant on his pant leg and hailed Kirk on his communicator.

"Kirk here."

"Jim, just a warning." McCoy could see Kirk stop his ascent and turn back to the rest of the party. "Be very careful up there. Avoid getting cut. The bacteria on this planet are just as fast-growing as the plants, and I don't want to take the chance that they'd use us as the next host."

"Understood, Bones," Kirk said. "I'm going to turn back when I get to the next ledge, anyway. The heat—"

"Jim!" McCoy shouted as he watched dirt and rocks give way under Kirk's feet, and the captain lose his balance. The captain slid a short way down the slope, but managed to stop.

Kirk recovered quickly, found his communicator, and said, "Maybe I'll start back now."

"Are you okay?"

"Yes. I'm fine. I—"

"Are you sure? Did you scrape yourself?"

"Not badly, just the top layer of skin on my left hand."

"Well, get back here so I can check it out," McCoy said. He turned to Spock and Sulu. "The same goes for you two, as well."

"Yes, sir," Sulu said. He bent back to digging the roots of the vine. "What the—?"

"What is it, Lieutenant?" Spock asked. He was also digging at the base of a clump of grass, but was having no more luck getting a complete specimen than Sulu.

"This plant has already gone to seed! There were flowers just a minute ago."

"Most remarkable," Spock said. He abandoned his digging to consult his tricorder. "Humidity is leveling off, as is the temperature." He set aside the tricorder and took his phaser from his belt. "I shall attempt a different approach to obtain a specimen with an intact rootball." Spock aimed his phaser at the ground surrounding the grass and used it to cut deep enough to pull out a plug of root and dirt ten centimeters long. "Your plant sample," he said, handing it over to Sulu.

"Where is Jim?" McCoy asked. "He should be down by now." He flipped open his communicator. "Jim! Come in! Are you okay?"

"Up there, Doctor," Spock said, pointing to a large, flat rock, halfway between the landing party and where Kirk had been when he turned around.

"Kirk . . . here."

McCoy could see him, sitting on the rock, bent over, his

elbows on his knees and his hands holding his head. His voice sounded tired.

"Stay put, Jim. I'll be right there." McCoy returned his tricorder to the medkit and indicated that the others should follow him as he raced up the rocky slope.

"Be careful," McCoy warned. "I don't want any more injuries until we're off this rock."

They hadn't gone more than a hundred meters when Sulu said, "Listen."

"I don't hear anything," McCoy said, picking his way around a boulder.

"I believe what Mister Sulu is referring to is the lack of noise. The chirps and calls from the flying creatures have diminished," Spock said.

"So have the creatures themselves," Sulu said.

Being careful of where he stepped on the rocky ground, McCoy took a glance at the sky. It was nearly empty. Only a few stray birds circled above the horizon. At this moment, however, the birds were not his concern.

He made his way to Kirk's side. The captain's breathing was nothing more than shallow panting, and his skin was pale and clammy. Definitely symptoms of shock. A pass of the tricorder confirmed what McCoy feared: single-celled organisms were multiplying unchecked in Kirk's body. They'd reached his bloodstream and it had carried the bacteria systemwide.

"Spock. Hail the *Enterprise*. Tell them—"

Kirk's communicator whistled for attention before Spock could grab his own. "*Enterprise* to landing party." Scotty's voice sounded urgent.

McCoy snapped the communicator open. "McCoy

here," he said. "The captain's been injured. Prepare to beam us up."

"I canna do that, sir. That's why I'm—zzzzzz—We're reading gigantic storms—zzzzzz—all over the planet's surf—zzzz—sprang up outta nowhe—zzzzz . . ." Nothing but static.

While McCoy tried to raise the ship again, Spock surveyed the area with his tricorder. "The local barometric pressure is falling, and there is a dramatic increase in atmospheric ionization that is most likely affecting communications."

"Zzzz—peat—zzzzzz—take cover! Zzzzzz—storm is— zzzzzz—your coord—zzzzzz."

"Dammit, Scotty! Jim's suffering from a raging septicemia! He's in shock and he could die. You've got to beam us up now!" McCoy ordered.

"It's too danger—zzzz—canna get a lock—zzzzz—"

A gust of wind blew through McCoy's hair. The birds were gone.

"Mister Scott is correct. A storm is bearing down on our area," Spock said. "We must find shelter soon."

From McCoy's point of view, they might as well be floating free in space, for all the cover he could spot. He hadn't seen a tree since they arrived, and the rocky face of the mountain looked like it could all slide to the bottom with little provocation.

Spock scanned uphill from their perch, while Sulu worked his way down. Sulu seemed to have lost track of his mission and was instead chasing a horde of rodents over the rocky ground. McCoy was about to shout at him to forget the damned samples and concentrate on shelter, but a moment later Sulu shouted, "Here! There's a cave large enough for all of us!"

"Help me get the captain down there," McCoy said.

Kirk forced his heavy eyelids open, looked blearily at the faces of those helping to lift him, and let the lids slam shut again. He moaned, more than said, "Bones . . ."

"I'm here, Jim. Just hang on and I'll get you fixed up."

The cave's entrance stood behind three large boulders, making it invisible to the casual observer. "How'd you find this place?" McCoy asked Sulu.

"I didn't, but lots of the locals knew about it. I noticed all the animals scurrying for cover and I followed them."

"Ah. Smart," McCoy said, turning away.

The inside of the cave smelled damp and musty. Faint light filtered past the boulder guardians at the entrance, but illuminated only a meter or so in. McCoy couldn't tell how far back into the mountain the cave reached, nor could he see evidence of other cave dwellers. Maybe the landing party had scared the other animals away.

In the few moments it took to get Kirk inside the cave and settled, the storm had arrived in earnest. The wind blew strong, and a fertile-smelling rain pelted the rocks. McCoy heard a moaning sound. At first he thought it was the wind whipping around the mountain, but when Sulu shouted "Watch out!" and an instant later Spock's phaser burst lit up the cave, he knew it wasn't the wind. He whirled around just in time to see a wall of bristly gray fur topple to the cave floor at his feet.

He looked at the two-meter-long, barrel-chested beast. It now lay on its left side, stunned, its flat face in a grimace that exposed sharp, uneven teeth. It took McCoy a moment to find his breath, but when he did, he turned to Spock and said, "Thanks."

"Losing our doctor to predation at this point in time would have been most illogical," Spock said, sticking his phaser back onto his belt.

He had a point. McCoy forgot the creature—and Spock as well—and turned to the captain. It was obvious that Kirk had slipped into unconsciousness, but McCoy kept talking to him anyway. "Jim, I'm giving you a wide-spectrum antibiotic booster," he said as he injected his unresponsive friend with a hypospray from his medkit.

Spock held McCoy's medical tricorder over Kirk's prone body. "The injection appears to have reduced the bacterial population by fifteen percent, eighteen percent, twenty-four percent . . ."

Sulu stood watch at the cave entrance. "Good thing we got in here when we did," he said. "The wind speed is accelerating to fifty kilometers per hour. Seventy. Eighty."

As Spock monitored the success of McCoy's treatment, the doctor took a moment to look out over Sulu's shoulder. The wind blew past the cave's entrance, throwing dirt, rain, and rocks at lethal speeds. Mixed in with the flying mud were pieces of plants and what looked like a small animal carcass.

"Doctor," Spock said, "the bacterial count is increasing."

McCoy spun away from the view outside and grabbed the tricorder to see the data for himself. "Damn," he said. "The booster has worn off already. I'll have to increase the dosage."

Kirk's ragged breathing and pasty color distressed McCoy. The wide-spectrum antibiotics worked to keep bacteria to a minimum while the body's own defense system built immunity to the invaders. Unfortunately, it took the body seventy-two hours to start the process. The accelerated nature of this native bacteria wasn't going to allow for that kind of slow response time. Left unchecked, massive infection could kill Kirk in less than an hour.

"Increased dosages of the medicine could cause damage to his liver and kidneys," Spock pointed out.

"Increased numbers of bacteria in his bloodstream will *kill* him," McCoy said, anger prickling just below the surface. He was hot, sweaty, and stuck on some damn fast-forward planet with the mother of all storms raging just meters from their shelter, unable to get to his sickbay, where he'd have more options open to him. McCoy took the hypospray, clutched it in his hand, and took a deep breath. After a moment's reflection, he said quietly, "I understand your concern, Spock. I also know the limitations and dangers of the only course of treatment I can think of right now."

Spock said, "I understand," and took the medical tricorder back as McCoy injected Kirk a second time. "The bacteria count has leveled off. . . ."

McCoy held his breath while he waited for Spock to continue. If this didn't work, he didn't know what he could do.

"The count is decreasing," Spock said, "but the captain's temperature is rising."

"Dammit!" McCoy said. "Sulu, is there any change in the storm?"

"Only that it's gotten worse," Sulu replied. He hunkered down beside a large boulder that protected him from the storm, yet allowed him to see outside the cave. "Wind speed has increased to two hundred twenty kilometers per hour, and the particulate matter in the air has also increased." He looked up at McCoy and said, "The wind must have scoured the entire area of any plants and loose dirt to get that kind of particulate density. It's thick as mud out there."

"No rescue from the cavalry, then," McCoy muttered. He'd feel much better if he could just get Kirk back to the ship.

"How can a storm like this one just . . . happen?" Sulu asked.

"I suspect that this is not an unusual occurrence," Spock answered. "The terrain shows evidence of harsh weather in the recent past, and the animal and plant life appear to have adapted to the unpredictability of their environment. It is possible that weather patterns like the one we're experiencing can happen multiple times in a day."

"But we were in orbit here for a full ship's day before we beamed down, and didn't observe *any* weather like this," Sulu said.

"Computer simulations of weather have demonstrated its chaotic nature for centuries. An area can experience a long quiescent period, where the weather is calm and stable, but it takes only a minor alteration, such as a rise in temperature of just a few degrees, to cause a major change. Sometimes the new weather patterns can even lock into a repeating cycle of violent oscillation that is as stable as what we consider normal. This is the first planet we have discovered that actually displays these patterns, but they are well understood. It would not surprise me if the storm dissipated as fast as it arose."

McCoy looked out at the storm again and marveled at the power behind something as basic as moving air. It wouldn't surprise *him* if the storm never ceased.

"The antibiotic is not working," Spock said. "The bacteria count is once again on the rise."

McCoy took back the tricorder. "Those bugs have gone through enough generations that they're already resistant to the drug. But that's not the worst part. Jim's blood pressure is dropping and his pulse is extremely fast but weak. He's in shock. If I give him epinephrine, it would counteract the vasodilation, but in his weakened state, it could kill him."

"It would appear that anything we do could kill him, Doctor. It is also apparent that doing nothing will kill him as well."

"You're right, Spock," McCoy said. "Which is no surprise, since that's just what I was arguing a minute ago." He changed cartridges in his hypospray and injected Kirk with the drug.

"I am merely stating the obvious."

From behind him, McCoy heard grunts and groans and scrabbling sounds. Claws scratching a rock surface. "Sulu! Our host is waking—"

A burst from Sulu's phaser flashed past McCoy and hit the bearlike form, knocking it back to the cave floor.

"—up."

Spock continued to monitor the captain. "Doctor," he said, "there is a buildup of an unknown substance in the captain's blood. It is concentrating in the liver."

McCoy looked at the readout. "It's a bacterial toxin. Septicemia was bad enough, but now those damn germs are poisoning his liver, too. What we need is a specific antibody to the bacteria. I just don't have the equipment or the time to synthesize one." He sat next to Kirk, wondering how they were ever going to get out of this mess, stuck in a musty cave with a stunned creature big enough to . . .

"Spock. That thing we just stunned. Its metabolism is accelerated, too, isn't it? Just like everything else around here?"

After scanning the animal with his tricorder, Spock said, "We have slowed it down considerably with our phasers, but your assessment is essentially accurate."

"In the ancient days of vaccines," McCoy said, "people used cows and rabbits to make antibodies for human use. It's barbaric, but it worked." He took a hemosampler from his medkit and withdrew a few milliliters of Kirk's infected blood. Moving cautiously to the prone gray form at the back of the cave, he set his medical tricorder to search for existing antibodies to the bacteria. None existed. He reached for the animal's ear, looking for a vein that would be easy to inject.

The bear creature snorted. McCoy jumped back involuntarily, and both Spock and Sulu aimed their phasers.

"Don't shoot it unless you have to," McCoy told them. "I want his immune system to work on this as fast as possible."

Spock nodded, holding his phaser ready.

With a quick, smooth motion, McCoy injected a drop of Kirk's blood into the animal, then leaped back as the beast twitched one massive paw toward the sting in its ear. He backed away and focused his tricorder on the creature's head, recording the entry of the invading bacteria and the immediate response of the animal's immune system. In less than a minute, the creature demonstrated discrete antibodies to the bacteria and to Kirk's blood components.

"I think we have something here," McCoy said. "Okay, stun it."

Spock fired his phaser, and the creature became a rug again. McCoy took another hemosampler and drew the animal's blood, then ran it through filtration to remove all but the bacterial antibodies. One last scan to determine the safety of the filtrate, and then . . .

"Damn!"

"Problems, Doctor?" Spock asked.

"I've got the antibodies, but there's a toxic peptide chain attached to it." McCoy ran the antibodies through two more filtrations, but the tricorder insisted that the toxic substance remained.

"This is useless. Worse than useless," McCoy said, glaring at the deadly contents of the hypospray.

He was running out of options. This must be the way doctors centuries ago must have felt before the advent of morphine or penicillin, standing by helplessly while their patients suffered and died. McCoy had already faced the specter of incurable disease when he took his own father off life support, only to find that the cure for his illness was just around the corner. Well, he wasn't about to give up on Jim just yet.

"Spock, what keeps the ecology of any planet going? Even one as wacky as this one."

"Doctor?" Spock asked, one eyebrow raised.

McCoy answered his own question. "Checks and balances. All complicated systems have a method of checks and balances to keep them on track."

"Survival mechanisms," Sulu said, sitting down beside McCoy. "Like camouflage, or butterflies that taste bad to hungry birds."

"Or mimicking a butterfly that tastes bad when the one in question tastes fine," Spock said, nodding his head.

"Or even mutating a gene to outsmart a local parasitic disease, like sickle cell syndrome to prevent malarial infection," McCoy added. "In this case, there must be something that keeps the bacteria in this valley, on this planet, from turning everything into goo."

"You are making the assumption that there is a naturally occurring antibacterial substance?" Spock asked.

"That's right," McCoy said. "There are all kinds of examples of that sort of thing happening on other planets. It's a long shot, but it's the only shot we have left."

"In this situation, where we do not have access to anything beyond the confines of this cave, our success is bound to be limited."

"Without trying, our success doesn't exist."

"There are the plant samples we collected," Sulu offered. He handed McCoy the exploration satchel with the specimen stasis tubes in it.

"Excellent," McCoy said. The hemosampler he had used earlier still held enough of Kirk's infected blood to experiment with. Plant by plant, he took a leaf from each stasis tube and quickly mixed it with a few drops of blood, then monitored the bacterial activity before the leaf degenerated. Four of the five plants showed no inhibition of the bacterial growth from Kirk's blood. The fifth showed only a weak effect.

"No good," McCoy said. With a heavy sigh that was nearly drowned out by the howling wind, he handed each stasis tube back to Sulu to be put back into the satchel.

"The captain's condition continues to deteriorate," Spock said. As if to verify this statement, Kirk groaned weakly.

"Least I can do is ease his pain," McCoy said. He held the fifth plant's stasis tube as he reached for a hypospray of painkiller. That was when he noticed that this was the plant that Spock had dug out of the ground with his phaser. It had a root still attached. It was also the only plant that had any effect whatsoever on the bacteria.

"Spock, give Jim a dose of this," he said, handing over the hypo. "Sulu, let's see that 'sampler again."

McCoy tore off a piece of the white woody root and combined it with the blood sample. His tricorder told the story. The bacteria died the instant it came in contact with the root.

"This is it!" McCoy crowed. "This is the inhibitor. I should have thought of this right from the start. The roots are the only permanent part of the plants on this crazy planet; of course they'd be the most heavily protected."

Extraction would be a simple matter. The only problem would be finishing the extract before the bacteria finished Kirk. But after the other close scrapes he and Kirk and Spock had been through, he knew Kirk would fight, was fighting right now, to live.

The root gave off a bitter fragrance as McCoy mashed it. In a way, that was comforting. Many strong medicinal plants did the same. If he'd had the time, he would have purified the extract, making it an injectable liquid, but time was something he didn't have. He checked and double-checked the tricorder readings for edibility and toxicity of the mash. When he was satisfied that the cure wasn't worse than the disease, he slipped a lump of the mash under Kirk's tongue where the capillary-rich tissues afforded the quickest, safest route for the inhibitor to enter his bloodstream.

Spock held the tricorder over Kirk's body. "Bacterial counts are decreasing dramatically," he said. "Toxin production is arrested. . . ."

McCoy stared at Kirk's face, watching the pain leave. "Well?"

Sulu sat silent next to McCoy, and looked nervously between the doctor and Spock and Kirk.

"Fascinating," Spock said in that irritatingly calm manner of his. "The toxin itself is deteriorating to smaller molecular particles, most of which the human body can easily excrete."

"Most? Give me that," McCoy said, grabbing the tricorder back from Spock. Sure enough, there were still some borderline toxins—oxidants and the like—but none would do any permanent damage. Not like the live bacteria, at any rate. McCoy read the vital stats aloud. "Blood pressure returning to normal, kidneys functioning perfectly, liver processing what's left of the toxins. His recovery is phenomenal!"

Kirk groaned, a stronger sound this time, and blearily looked around. "Did someone identify the shuttle that ran me down?"

"Welcome back, Jim," McCoy said. "Now, just sit back and take it easy for a few minutes." He turned to Sulu and asked, "Any change in the storm yet?"

"I'll check." Sulu went over to the cave entrance again and consulted his tricorder, then looked out into the distance. "It does appear to be letting up. The wind speed has decreased to one hundred eighty, and I can see through the rain now."

"That is welcome news, Lieutenant," Spock said. He flipped open his communicator and it emitted its familiar chirp. "Spock to *Enterprise*. Come in, *Enterprise*."

"*Enterpr*—zzzz—here. Can you rea—zzzz—"

"We read you, Mister Scott, but your signal is weak. Can you beam us up?" Spock asked.

"I canna get a lock—zzzz—yet. But the storm is breaking up. Is the captain—zzzzz—"

McCoy helped Kirk to a sitting position, with his back against the cave wall. Jim would recover fully; his heart, liver, kidneys, and lungs all showed no indication of permanent damage. McCoy nodded to Spock, and the Vulcan said, "The captain is out of danger."

"Good. We'll get you out of there the moment we can—zzzz—through the ionization," Scotty said.

"Affirmative. Spock out." He closed his communicator.

"The wind is dying down as quickly as it picked up," Sulu said. "The atmospheric ionization levels are still high, but dropping." He paused, looking out around the boulder that had served as his shield during the storm. "Everything feels . . . fresh. New."

McCoy joined Sulu at the cave's entrance. The air smelled just as it had when the landing party first arrived at the scene: fresh, and at the same time sweetly rotten. He felt a tickling sensation on the top of his right foot, looked down and watched as a pale green, mouse-sized creature scurried over his boot toward the open air. Without thought, he jerked his foot out of the path, just as half a dozen more, a couple of which were juveniles, squeezed out of the crevices of the cave's wall and took the same path as the first.

"It would appear that the natives believe the storm is over," Spock said.

McCoy looked to the predator they had shared the cave with, but it still lay stunned. "Looks like he'll have to hibernate for a season," he said.

Kirk struggled to stand, and Spock helped guide him to

the cave entrance, keeping a firm hand on the captain's shoulder.

"Jim," McCoy said, "you shouldn't be moving around yet. You should be resting."

"I feel fine, Bones. Just a bit of a headache and a nasty taste in my mouth."

"Be grateful for that nasty taste—it saved your life," McCoy said.

"It looks like it's safe to go outside again," Sulu said. He led the landing party back out into the open. They searched the sky, looking for signs of a returning storm. But all appeared quiet, calm. They eased down the rocky slope to the plateau where they had first beamed down.

"Well, Jim," McCoy said. "I guess this time the hot, ugly, smelly planet isn't a prime candidate for colonization after all."

"Maybe next time, Eden will really be paradise," Kirk said.

McCoy glanced at the ground where he and Sulu first examined the hyperactive plants. Already, the first shoots of vines were snaking their way from their solidly anchored roots.

"I don't know about you, gentlemen," Kirk said, "but I feel like I've been on this planet for a year. It's time to get back to work." He flipped his communicator open and hailed the ship.

A year. Hell, McCoy thought as he took up his position next to Spock, it felt like a lifetime.

The First Law of Metaphysics

Michael S. Poteet

Captain Spock sat alone in his darkened quarters at Starfleet Academy, silently watching the fire in the fireplace die. From time to time a log splintered, breaking the stillness, sending a small swarm of sparks up the chimney. Spock could still feel some warmth from the flames, but it was quickly fading away. He considered stoking the fire but decided against it; the day had been taxing, and he would soon be ready to rest. He took a slow sip of lukewarm water from the glass he held, and then set it on the end table next to him. A thick book was on the table, a gift Jim had given him just a few days earlier. Spock picked up the heavy volume, admiring its leather binding and marble-edged pages in the fire's flickering light. The title stood out in gilded letters on the spine: Kiri-kin-tha's *Metaphysics*. Spock carefully opened the book to the first chapter. Although an English translation was on a facing page, he read the work's first line from the original High Vulcan calligraphy: "Nothing unreal exists." The words confronted him with a grim exercise in logic. Jim died today, thought Spock. He ceased to exist. Does that make him unreal? Can one grieve the loss of the unreal?

A beep from his computer terminal interrupted his thoughts. Spock rose and walked to his desk. Sympathy calls had been arriving all day—even one from Klingon Chancellor Azetbur, who said she fully expected Kahless himself to embrace James Kirk in *Sto-Vo-Kor*—but according to the information flashing on the monitor, this was the first message from Vulcan. Spock assumed it was his parents. "Computer," he said, "open visual channel."

"This is a text-only message," the computer said.

Curious, Spock thought. "Display text."

The computer did:

> Captain Spock: I have heard about the accident aboard the Enterprise. I grieve with you and regret that I have not contacted you before now. I ask that you come to Vulcan as soon as possible. One of my students at the Institute, nearing her seventh birthday, lacks a than'tha. Would you serve? Please respond—Lieutenant Saavik.

Spock pondered the white words on the black screen for several minutes. He and Saavik had not spoken with each other since she had requested assignment to the Institute for the Transmission of Vulcan Culture. While it was good to hear from her, he was puzzled that she should contact him about a *than'tha*. The duty of guiding Vulcan children through their first mind-meld on the eve of their seventh birthday was normally that of a parent. Where, he wondered, were this girl's mother and father?

Suddenly, like one of the few glowing coals in the fire, a painfully concrete hope began to burn in Spock's heart. The emotion startled him, but he could not extinguish it. He tried. At first he attributed it to the funereal atmosphere that had hung over the entire day. Then he blamed it on the lateness of the hour. But it would not disappear.

Nor would memories from almost seven years before: forceful winds on the Genesis Planet . . . incessant rumblings from beneath its crust . . . the gentle words spoken to him as his blood boiled: "It is called *Pon farr.* Will you trust me?" . . . the tender way she and he had caressed each other's fingers and hands . . .

The next morning, Spock immediately contacted Starfleet Command to request a leave of absence—an indefinite leave. With Jim's death, little was left for Spock on Earth. But much might be waiting for him on Vulcan.

Including, perhaps, a daughter.

They materialized in the middle of a storm. Spock was no longer surrounded by the transporter beam's gentle, shimmering sparkles, but a swarm of thick, red sand. Blown about by a howling wind, it stung his hands and face. Vulcan's sun burned high in the midday sky with harsh light and beat down with oppressive heat. Spock wondered briefly if the desert's angry welcome anticipated that which he would receive at the Institute.

"Oh, damn!" Spock's escort—a gangly, perpetually flustered young cadet named Walters—coughed as he inhaled a mouthful of sand. "Can we walk it from here?" he shouted.

Spock squinted at the horizon. Among the jagged peaks of the Llangon Mountains, barely visible through the storm, he spotted the valley that was their destination. "We can."

"You lead!" Walters flipped a switch on the antigrav platform at his feet, on which sat a bulky computer case, and pushed it in front of him as he trudged behind Spock. Moments later, the swirling sand settled to the rocky soil and the fierce gale quieted to a soft but still sweltering breeze.

"To think," said Walters, spitting sand out of his mouth, "I used to complain about family vacations on Mars. . . ." He trailed off, glanced sideways at Spock, and added, in obvious embarrassment, "No offense, sir."

"None taken, Cadet." Spock swept sand from his maroon uniform jacket. "You are not the first human to find our climate uncomfortable. The winter sandstorms are wildly unpredictable; even Vulcans think them unpleasant."

Walters's eyes widened. "After a winter like this—" He bit his lip and shut his eyes for a second, shaking his head in an abrupt motion. He was clearly uncomfortable in Spock's presence. "I'm sorry about that beam-down, sir," he finally said. "I'm still not too good with transporter coordinates, I guess."

"Again, no apologies are needed," said Spock. "We did arrive safely."

Walters half-smiled a nervous smile. "Aye, sir."

"Hello there!" a cheery voice called from the valley they had now reached. Canvas tents covered several open pits where members of the Federation Archaeology Council were hard at work, scanning the ground with tricorders and peeling back its strata with specially calibrated phasers. A petite human woman wiped her hands on her pale blue jumpsuit, which was stained with dirt and mud. She brushed a lock of blond hair from her perspiring forehead and raised her hand in the Vulcan salute. "Captain Spock," she said. "It's an honor, really."

Spock returned the salute. "Doctor Tully, I presume?"

Tully laughed. "Afraid so. Welcome to FAC Site V-271 . . . or, as I like to call it, Camp Camelot." She extended a hand to Walters. "You must be Dustan; always nice to put a face with a subspace radio voice. Thanks for bringing the new computer."

Walters set down the antigrav unit and pumped Tully's hand vigorously. "I was thrilled that the *Raleigh* drew the assignment. Your excavation logs from Chi Rho III were some of my favorite readings last semester at the academy."

Tully grimaced. "Great Bird, I'm not old enough to be on some professor's reading list, am I?"

"Despite your youth," said Spock, "you have had a distinguished career."

"Hm. If this is how the FAC rewards its 'distinguished' members, I'm not sure I want to be among that company."

"Indeed?"

"I don't call this place Camelot for nothing. When the director asked me to head up a dig for ShiGral, I honestly wondered what I'd done to make him angry!"

"ShiGral?" asked Walters.

"According to some traditions," Spock explained, "ShiGral was an oasis of logic and peace in the midst of Vulcan's violent past, a village founded by Surak himself prior to the Time of Awakening. Stories about it are common in our nurseries, but the vast majority of Vulcans do not believe it existed. ShiGral is an important symbol of the Vulcan way, but is nonetheless a legend."

"And that's not all," added Tully. "Don't some of the stories go so far as to claim that ShiGral was the only place Surak's ideals were ever fully realized?"

"Yes," said Spock. "There are some who wait for Surak to return to ShiGral, when Vulcan has fallen too far from his teachings. They view the village as a locus of incredible power that could be used to 'purify' our society."

"Well," sighed Tully, gesturing at the arid plains around them, "if ShiGral ever was here it's long since been swept away. The FAC doesn't have the resources to be playing in the sand like this; we've got too many important digs on other planets."

"But this new computer we brought is state of the art," said Walters, sounding puzzled. "If the FAC isn't paying for it, who is?"

Tully lowered her voice to a conspiratorial tone. "I can't prove it, and I wouldn't be crazy enough to risk my 'distinguished' reputation trying, but I'd bet my credits on the Vulture." She chuckled. "Sorry. That's my pet name for the matron up there." She pointed a thumb over her shoulder where, on a rocky outcropping overlooking the campsite on one mountain's side, the wrought-iron gates of the Institute stood watch.

"I see," said Spock, gazing at the Institute. He arched his left eyebrow. "The comparison is not altogether unfair."

"You know the matron?"

"She tutored me during my year at the Institute."

Tully shook her head in mock amazement. "Yet you've led a productive adult life." She resumed a serious tone of voice. "T'Ryth is down here every other day, asking me about our progress. I tell her that if there were anything to find we would've found it, but she doesn't understand.

'Work harder,' she says, 'dig deeper.' She says our presence disrupts the Institute's work, and she's eager for the excavation to end."

"You sound dubious," said Walters.

"I am. I think she's convinced that ShiGral is here."

"Have you suggested expanding the site's boundaries?" asked Spock. "Perhaps she would be satisfied if you investigated the caves around the valley."

"I have suggested that," said Tully, her voice heavy with exasperation. "T'Ryth won't hear of it. The caves are, in her charming words, 'forbidden to outworlders.' "

"But many of your team members are Vulcans," Walters observed.

"Yes," said Tully, "but Vulcans who work for the Federation in any capacity are second-class in T'Ryth's eyes."

"Then her views have not changed," said Spock.

"Not surprising. She's always talking about the past, about how the Institute has held these lands for centuries, and how she's doing us a favor by letting us dig here. But I'm not stupid. There's something about those caves she doesn't want us 'outworlders' to know, and she's doing her best to keep us contained. For someone who says she wants us to leave, she works hard to make sure we stay." She rapped her knuckles on the computer case. "This new toy is the perfect example." Tully looked around the site in disdain. "I don't know what the Vulture's game is, but I do know I don't want to play."

"At the risk of keeping a game going," said Walters, "my job is to get your new toy up and running."

"How about lunch first?" asked Tully. "A big bowl of chilled *plomeek* soup? Captain Spock?"

"No thank you. I have an appointment to keep at the Institute."

Tully frowned. "Give the Vulture my best."

The Institute's lobby still impressed Spock. It bore silent witness to his homeworld's rich, ambiguous heritage. There, just where he remembered it, was an ancient *lirpa*, green bloodstains still visible on the blade. A large gong, intricate glyphs carved on its face, stood in one corner. Beneath Spock's feet, an elaborate mosaic covered the floor: precious stones from all areas of Vulcan joined together in an exquisite rendering of the IDIC symbol. If any room embodied that philosophy, surely this one did.

When Matron T'Ryth entered the room, however, its air of harmony was shattered. Flowing black robes trailed behind her, accentuating her height and severe face. "Live long and prosper, Spock," she greeted him. "You are welcome."

He could tell she did not mean her words. "Peace and long life, Matron."

"So many years gone by, and you address me so formally? You are no longer a boy; you are a Starfleet captain." She glanced at the insignia on Spock's shoulder strap with obvious contempt.

Spock bowed his head slightly, as much to hide whatever irritation his eyes might betray as to show deference. "You are no longer my instructor, but you are still worthy of respect."

T'Ryth raised her chin and pursed her lips. She neither accepted nor declined the compliment, but beckoned Spock to follow her through an arch down a long, stone hallway. "I am told that you became a teacher yourself, after a fashion."

"For the past sixteen years I have served Starfleet as a teaching captain."

"And what have you taught your pupils?" She sounded condescending. "The military tactics of the late Captain Kirk?"

"I need not justify my vocation, Matron," Spock said, each word firm. "I and many others have shown the compatibility of our way with Starfleet. Your continued prejudice is illogical."

T'Ryth turned to face him. "You challenge my logic?"

She acts as though we are still in the classroom, Spock thought. She, the tutor with mind and nerves fashioned of steel; I, her cowering and uncertain "half-breed" student. But those days are past. "I challenge anyone who would characterize James Kirk's service as strictly military. Even my father deemed him a man of high character."

T'Ryth's icy, gray eyes never wavered. "I watched the reports of Kirk's memorial service. I heard the ambassador's eulogy. Remarks on such occasions are often tainted by unchecked emotion."

Spock knew she was attempting to bait him, but he had grown beyond that game, even if she had not. "As you wish." He changed the subject. "Doctor Tully says you have expressed great interest in the dig for ShiGral."

"My only interest," said T'Ryth, "is in seeing the outworlders leave. But the Federation keeps sending more supplies with which to desecrate our world. While I cannot deny that ShiGral would be the greatest archaeological find in our planet's history, neither can I condone the presence of outworlders who seek it. How can they appreciate what ShiGral is? It is the very essence of the Vulcan way."

"Then you believe ShiGral can be found?"

The matron faced him, her eyes wide with indignation. "Of course."

"You used to refer to stories of its existence as mere myths."

T'Ryth turned away again, and her pace increased. "I know the majority of Vulcans would prefer to keep the tales domesticated. But logic dictates that the majority is not necessarily correct." T'Ryth quickly changed the subject. "The lieutenant has proven a competent instructor. I am forced to admit that your service as her mentor has been valuable. Perhaps my pedagogy influenced you more than you realized."

"She would prove an effective teacher no matter who was her mentor. She is a remarkable young woman."

They stopped outside an open door bearing Saavik's name. T'Ryth looked at Spock and asked, "How long has it been since you have seen her?"

Six years, eleven months, twenty-three days, Spock thought. "Too long," he said.

"Then I leave you to your reunion," T'Ryth said. As she walked away, she added, "Be careful. Reunions are also occasions often tainted by unchecked emotion."

Ignoring the comment, Spock looked into the room and saw Saavik and a young girl staring intently at a three-dimensional chess set. Saavik sat poised and calm, hands folded in her lap, the gaze of her emerald-green eyes following every move of her opponent's hand as it hovered indecisively above the various pieces. Saavik looked just as Spock remembered: her noble face with its strong but delicate cheekbones, the locks of her black hair falling gently over her forehead and upswept ears. Unbidden, a couplet from an ancient human poem entered his mind: "For we, which now behold these present days, have eyes to wonder, but lack tongues to praise."

Startled by this thought, he focused his attention on Saavik's opponent. The girl was chewing her lower lip, tugging occasionally at the tresses of her long, ebony hair. She took a deep breath as she picked up her remaining rook—gingerly, as if handling a hot coal. She raised the piece two levels and set it down, exhaling. "Check," she announced. Saavik lowered her own queen one level, placing it between her king and the girl's rook. "I didn't see that," the girl said slowly.

"Only because you weren't concentrating," said Saavik. "I'll take your rook in my next move unless you see how to save it."

The girl's gaze ranged over the handful of pieces left, but kept wandering back to the threatened rook. "There is no way."

"There is," said Saavik. "Look again, Sanara."

"There is no way!" Sanara repeated, raising her voice slightly. She shoved a knight forward, not even looking as she did.

Saavik captured the girl's rook with her queen, then dropped the queen another level. "Checkmate."

"I don't like this game!" Sanara folded her arms. "Can't we play *kal-toh?*"

"You're already an advanced *kal-toh* player," said Saavik. "Chess is your challenge . . . as it was mine." She happened to look up—perhaps, thought Spock, remembering long-ago matches with him—and her eyes widened as she saw him.

She quickly rose to her feet. "Captain!" Spock thought he saw a single tear threatening to escape one of her eyes. "Thank you for coming."

Slowly, Spock entered the room. "I should have returned long ago. It would have been the logical thing to do."

"But you are here now." She gestured for Sanara to stand up; with obvious reluctance, Sanara did so. "Sanara," said Saavik, "this is Captain Spock. He will be your *than'tha* tonight."

Then this girl was the one. "Hello, Sanara," said Spock. The words did not sound right to his ears, but he knew no others to say. Irrational though it was, he felt as if he were back in the desert, under the sun's severe light.

Sanara did not meet his gaze. "Why would you guide a *viltah* like me through First Meld?"

Viltah! Involuntarily, Spock flinched. He had first heard that taunt when five years old, and he had taken years to recover from its sting.

"Sanara," said Saavik in a stern voice, "that word isn't allowed. Your other heritage benefits you as much as your Vulcan one."

"The matron doesn't think so." Sanara sounded bitter.

Spock said, "Then we will prove her wrong."

Sanara eyed Spock with skepticism, then muttered, "May I go, Lieutenant?"

"Yes," said Saavik, "but Captain Spock will visit you tonight at Second Watch to conduct your meld."

"I have other plans," Sanara said. She refused to look at Spock.

Saavik looked back and forth between Sanara and Spock, frustration on her face. "Sanara," she said, "tomorrow is your seventh birthday. Captain Spock *will* be your *than'tha*."

Sanara's eyes were cold. "If he must." She brushed past him as she left.

Saavik sighed. "Your meeting didn't go as I'd wished." Spock thought he saw a smile as she added, "But our meeting pleases me."

"It pleases me also. I do regret not having contacted you."

"Regrets are not logical. You had commitments to Starfleet, as did I."

Spock was thankful for her gracious words. "Then your assignment to the Institute has been well spent?"

"Preparing children for First Meld has been a fascinating experience." She gazed after Sanara. "But part of me thinks that girl will be the true test of whether or not my time here has been valuable."

So many questions clamored for answers in Spock's mind; he chose to begin with the simplest one. "What is the rest of her heritage?"

"Human."

Spock's throat was dry, and he knew it was not because of the sandstorm. "Fascinating," he finally said. "Sanara and I have much in common."

"Which is why I'm thankful you've come."

"You're fond of her."

Saavik nodded. "But I don't know if she is fond of me. Our lessons have always been a struggle."

"She is obviously an exceptional student."

"Yes, in many ways. She has the highest IQ of any student here. She's already earned a B-9 computer rating on the Daystrom scale. And her mental abilities are astounding; her telepathic capacity grows exponentially." Saavik allowed herself a small smile. "Even T'Ryth admits that Sanara is 'highly talented.' " She sighed. "But Sanara's spirit is restless. She insists that she doesn't need this training." Saavik furrowed her brow. "And she often mentions another teacher, though she has never lived anywhere else." A note of barely suppressed anger crept into Saavik's voice. "The matron was opposed to taking her in, but I convinced her that it wasn't logical to waste potential brilliance in any form."

Spock was puzzled. The Institute's program was designed for the sixth year of life only; for Sanara to have spent her entire life at the Institute with Saavik was most unusual. Again, a multitude of questions demanded attention, but he asked only one. "Do you know who her parents are?" He found himself holding his breath as he waited for Saavik's reply.

"Captain . . ." Saavik began. She opened, then shut, her mouth. "I've already said too much. My role as instructor mandates that I respect Sanara's privacy."

"Of course." Spock concealed his disappointment. He marveled that his emotions troubled him so. Was he losing control as he aged, or was the possibility before him so palpable that even a full-blooded Vulcan in his situation could be forgiven such feelings?

"I will tell you this," Saavik said. "I did not ask you to be Sanara's *than'tha* lightly. I know of no one better suited for the task."

"Thank you, Lieutenant." Spock was having trouble finding words. "I . . . trust you will not have occasion to regret your choice."

"I know I won't."

* * *

Later that night, Spock stood outside Sanara's door, hesitant to press its chime. He was wearing the traditional gold robes of a *than'tha*, and they made him feel uneasy. His father was the last person he had seen wearing such robes, at Spock's own First Meld. It had not been a pleasant experience; Sarek had been careless. During the meld his thoughts had drifted back to Spock's birth, to Sarek's initial sight of his "so human" son. He tried to raise a mental screen to shield Spock from the vision, but the scene burned itself into Spock's consciousness. The father's memory became the son's. Spock had always wanted the chance to serve as a *than'tha*, to compensate for his father's failing, but now that such a chance had arrived, a completely illogical but nonetheless powerful part of himself feared it: not for himself, but for Sanara. Would the question that preoccupied his mind damage the girl's?

He rang the chime and heard Sanara's indifferent reply: "Enter."

She sat cross-legged on her bed, bent over a thick, dusty volume, engrossed in a page full of ancient calligraphy. Spock was impressed. Even after years of studying the High Tongue, he made no pretense of fluency in it and had never read samples as complex as what Sanara was reading. "Greetings, Sanara," he said. She did not respond. Spock looked over the room's stark walls. Only one item identified the occupant as Vulcan: a gem-encrusted, circle-and-triangle pendant dangling from a hook. "Your IDIC medallion is beautiful," said Spock.

Sanara's head snapped up. "Don't touch that! That was a present from my other teacher!"

"Who was your other teacher, Sanara?"

Sanara shook her head fiercely. "That's none of your business!" She made a tiny huffing sound. "My other teacher's better than any here. The matron speaks of IDIC every day at morning assembly, but doesn't appreciate how diversity has combined in me."

"I understand."

Sanara looked directly at Spock, her gaze intense. "Do you?"

"Didn't the lieutenant tell you? I am part human, like you."

Sanara's stare softened. "When you were my age, did others call you *viltah?*"

"That insult is not new. I came home from school in tears many times."

"Tears?" Sanara sounded intrigued. "The matron says that tears are not part of the Vulcan way."

"The matron has her own understanding of the Vulcan way. I have forged my own way, whether Vulcan, human, or, as has most often been the case, a diverse combination of both. You will forge your own way as well."

A stony glaze returned to cover Sanara's eyes. "If I must."

"You are overly fond of that word," said Spock. "The life that lies before you is not an obligation, but a gift."

"A gift?" Sanara sounded scoffing, even challenging. "From whom?"

"From whatever powers hold the cosmos together and bring its life to fruition. I have seen too much in my travels to be persuaded that we live in a random universe. That each of our lives has purpose is something I accept on faith."

"Faith?" Again, that doubtful tone. "My parents must not have your faith. If they did, they'd have claimed me by now.

My mother or father would be my *than'tha,* and not a stranger."

Spock was stung by her words, but said, "We are not strangers, Sanara. You and I share a bond. We know what it is to be outcast."

Sanara looked at Spock with skepticism in her eyes. Then she deliberately turned her attention back to the book. "I want to read."

Spock was determined to reach this girl somehow. He moved closer to her. "What are you reading?" She shifted her body to try to block Spock's view, but he had already recognized one of the ancient characters, intricately illuminated and occurring repeatedly on the page. "ShiGral," he said, his voice barely concealing his astonishment. "Fascinating."

"I can read whatever I wish!" said Sanara. "Aren't I supposed to be studying Vulcan culture?" She added, her voice cracking, "Maybe then a *viltah* like me can be accepted."

"ShiGral is a legend," said Spock, "worthy of study, but not here. It will not help you prepare for First Meld." A suspicion began to form in his mind. "Who gave you that book?"

"I found it in the library."

"No. Legends of ShiGral are not part of the Institute's curriculum. Are you lying, Sanara?"

Sanara slammed the book shut. "My other teacher gave it to me! Why do you care?"

"Because if any 'must' applies to you, it is that you must not continue to let others define you as *viltah.* I want to show you another way of life is possible." Spock moved to a glass door that opened onto a small patio. "Let me try, Sanara."

Sanara stared adamantly at the floor for a moment, then pushed herself off the bed and walked out onto the patio. Spock followed her. He had always appreciated the desert at night. Vulcan's sister planet hovered high in the sky; the light it reflected from their shared sun starkly lit up the rocky soil and the craggy peaks of the Llangon range.

"So," said Sanara, a little too loudly, "what do we do?"

"By this point in your training," Spock said, "you should be able to discern the logic that underlies nature." He took in the landscape around them with a sweep of his arm. "Choose something, and tell me about its place in that order."

Sighing, Sanara scanned the ground in front of the patio, and finally jabbed a finger at a thin, limping *aylak*, scraping against a boulder. The palm-sized, mud-colored scavenger was digging around the rock with six scaly claws; its twin whiplike tails twitched violently. "The *aylakim*," Sanara said, intoning the words as though she were weary of them, "exist in futility."

"Yes," said Spock, trying to encourage her despite her evident lack of interest. "How so?"

"They look for water where none exists."

"And?"

Sanara breathed another heavy sigh. "And they are like our ancestors before the Time of Awakening. As the *aylakim* search hopelessly for water in the desert, so our forebears followed hopeless paths before the dawn of logic. Those who forsake logic are as the *aylakim*, fated for destruction . . ." Abruptly, she stopped her singsong recitation and told Spock, "I can give that *aylak* water."

"Compassion is admirable, but you have just told me about the place of the *aylakim*. They live only to die; if we gave them drink, the *le-matya* could not feed on their corpses."

"You don't understand," Sanara interrupted. "I can give that *aylak* water." She stared at the boulder. Within a few seconds a crack appeared in its side. The fissure grew, spreading like a spider's web over the face of the rock. Spock heard the sound of churning water from deep inside it. He watched, amazed, as a clear trickle of water spilled out from the crack, splashing onto the *aylak*. The creature shrieked in delight as its forked tongue began lapping up the water.

"Sanara," Spock said, his voice hushed. He had not felt the force of a mind so strong and yet so undisciplined since Gary Mitchell . . .

The girl shrugged. "I wanted it to have water, so in my mind I told the rock to give it some." The crack in the rock had grown even larger, and water was cascading out of it, soaking the parched ground. Chattering excitedly, other *aylakim* scampered toward the pool of water as it grew bigger and bigger. Sanara watched with enjoyment; Spock saw her smile for the first time. Saavik had told him about Sanara's mental abilities, but he wondered if even the lieutenant knew their full extent.

"Stop this, Sanara," he told her.

"Why?" The smile vanished from Sanara's face. "My teacher would approve."

"I am your teacher and I want you to stop." Yet it had been ten thousand years since any Vulcan had displayed such powers. How could he hope to teach her?

"No!" Sanara shouted. The boulder trembled violently and then burst into pieces. Water washed over the patio, lapping at Spock's feet. Where the boulder had stood, a fountain now bubbled. Its spray was cool against Spock's skin.

"Sanara, stop!" he ordered. Why had Sanara displayed her power to him and not to Saavik? Perhaps to scare him off? To avoid her *than'tha?* Or because they were both *viltah?*

"No, *you* stop! You speak as though you care for me, but you don't! If you did, you would let me be who I am!"

"I do want that," Spock replied, "but not like this. You must control your gifts. . . ."

"They are not gifts," she screamed, "they are *mine!* I did this! I don't need you!" The fountain shot water even higher into the air. The ground trembled, beginning to break open, and the *aylakim* that had been drinking yelped as they tumbled into the cracks. Sanara thrust her hands in front of her; Spock felt a heavy blow strike his chest. He fell backwards; his head struck the patio. Water washed over his face, as if carrying him into unconsciousness.

"Captain!"

When Spock awoke, he saw Saavik gazing into his face with concern. His robes, soaked with water, clung closely to him. A moaning wind chilled his body; another sandstorm was gathering strength. Saavik cradled his head with one hand and supported his back with the other as he struggled to sit up. "What happened?" she asked, pointing to Sanara's still-gurgling fountain.

Spock told her about the girl's display of psychokinetic power. "Is she with you?"

"No."

"What time is it?"

Saavik glanced at her chronometer. "Third Watch has just begun."

Spock frowned. "She has been gone for over two hours."

"I hope she's found shelter from the storm." Saavik watched the sand being stirred up by the increasingly strong gale.

The mention of shelter sparked a thought in Spock's mind—and suddenly answers to many, but not all, questions fell into place. "I believe she has," he told Saavik. "Follow me."

Within minutes, they arrived at the archaeological camp, where Saavik scanned the surrounding caves with her tricorder. "Odd," she remarked, tapping the instrument lightly. "Some kind of energy field is causing interference, but I read two life-forms in a cave fourteen meters to the northwest: one full Vulcan, and one Vulcan-human."

She and Spock ran toward the cave, calling out Sanara's name. The sandstorm's wail grew louder, drowning their voices, and the sand blowing around them restricted their vision. At last, Spock saw the cave's entrance. A soft, warm light shone from within. "Do you hear that?" he asked Saavik.

Saavik listened, then nodded. "Conversation—in the High Tongue!"

"And one of the voices is Sanara's," said Spock.

They stepped quietly into the cave. Its rugged walls glowed with a strange, pulsating light. Saavik aimed her tricorder at the walls. "Captain," she whispered, "this is the source of the interference. The stone seems to amplify psionic energy."

"Then we must be cautious," Spock said.

They carefully crept a few steps forward, staying just inside the cave's mouth, peering at the scene before them. Sanara sat on the ground, eyes shut, at the feet of a young Vulcan male who strummed a simple, seductive tune on a lyre. His back was turned to Spock and Saavik, but Spock recognized the man's multicolored tunic: stripes in various shades of blue, orange, green, and yellow. Only one Vulcan had ever worn such a garment.

"Sanara's other teacher?" asked Saavik. "It can't be . . ."

"No," Spock whispered back, "it cannot. But Sanara apparently believes her other teacher is Surak himself."

Sanara opened her eyes and let out a long sigh. "Surak, I'm tired. Can I go back? I'll return tomorrow; I always do."

"Sanara, we are so close to this discovery, you and I." Surak continued to play his song; its notes filled the air with an almost tangible tranquillity. "You must concentrate. Open your mind further than you have ever dared."

Sanara took a deep breath, contorting her features in earnest concentration, but after several seconds she shook her head in aggravation. "I've worked too hard tonight."

Surak put down his lyre and patted Sanara's head benignly. "I know you are tired, but you must understand what is at stake. Events have taken an unforeseen turn, and our time grows very short. If we do not find ShiGral soon, then . . ."

"Then what?" Spock stepped out from the shadows.

Surak spun around to face Spock. "Spock." He spoke the name as though it were an accusation. "What are you doing here?"

"Sanara," Saavik called from behind Spock, "come here."

"No!" Sanara leapt to her feet. "Surak, don't let them take me!"

"Of course not."

"What is your business with Sanara?" asked Spock.

"I'm helping him look for ShiGral!" said Sanara.

"Indeed," said Spock, moving closer. He felt intense mental energy emanating from this person; it pressed against his own mind, throbbing around him, as thick as the sand in the storm had been. He fought to stay focused against the amplified psychic field "Surak" was projecting.

The other man arched his eyebrows. "You do not seem surprised to see me, Spock. Are you not curious? Why ask about my quest when so many more questions beg for answers?"

"I do not ask," said Spock, "because you are not Surak. But you knew who I was. How?"

The man's gaze wandered for a moment before he said, "Sanara has told me about you. Your attempt to be her *than'tha,* your career in Starfleet . . . I must admit I am disappointed that you have chosen a path which has involved so much violence."

Spock shook his head. "I have told Sanara very little about my service in Starfleet. The answer is quite logical: you are not Surak."

"Sanara," Saavik called again, "please."

"No!" Sanara grabbed the stranger's leg. "You're just jealous because he chose me and not you!"

"Sanara," said Spock, "think logically. Even if the tales of Surak's return to ShiGral are true, do they not claim that all Vulcan will know of it?"

Surak began to say, "I have my reasons for . . ."

Spock did not listen, but continued to move nearer to Sanara. "And do those tales not teach that Surak will return in Vulcan's hour of greatest need? We have had unbroken peace since the Time of Awakening; we are in no hour of need."

Sanara looked confused, and the impostor noticed. "Sanara, he lies to you. He is a fool for focusing only on the external." He spoke to Sanara but stared directly at Spock. "I see the heart. Vulcan's need has never been greater. The threat is real; our culture has become impure. We cannot tolerate so much diversity if we . . ." He stopped in midsentence.

Spock narrowed his eyes. "These words from the man who gave us our creed? That infinite diversity in infinite combination yields beauty and hope? Sanara: did not Surak teach IDIC to our world?"

Sanara looked back and forth between Spock and the stranger; doubt filled her face. "Yes . . . but . . ."

"Sanara!" Spock grasped her shoulders. "What is Kiri-kin-tha's first law of metaphysics?"

Fighting back tears, Sanara quoted, "Nothing unreal exists."

"Good. This is not Surak. He is not real. He does not exist."

Sanara stamped her feet. "You can't accept that he's chosen me!"

Spock glanced at Saavik, who had moved behind the other man. The mental energy continued to oppress Spock; he found it increasingly hard to concentrate. Action must be taken, he thought, and it must be taken now. The risks were great; the potential for damage existed. But ultimately Sanara would face more risk at the hands of this person, whoever or whatever he was. Spock made the decision, and gently but firmly grasped Sanara's face, his fingers instinctively finding the appropriate pressure points. Sanara gasped, but Spock recited in a soothing voice, "My mind to your mind. My thoughts to your thoughts."

Surak raised his hand as if to strike Spock; he crumpled to the floor as Saavik squeezed the nerves between his shoulder and neck.

"Sanara," Spock said, "open your mind. . . ."

And their minds opened, one to the other. Wave after wave of vibrant colors swept over Spock's mind. He carefully navigated through the upper layers of Sanara's consciousness, then descended into the kaleidoscopic maelstrom . . . and the link was established.

Images from Sanara's psyche floated up from the whirlpool. Surak's face . . . chess and *kal-toh* matches played with Saavik . . . Vulcan's blazing sun . . . crystal stars against a black night sky . . . and Sanara's voice drifted above them all: *I'm frightened.*

Do not be afraid, Spock reassured her. *I mean you no harm.*

What is this?

This is First Meld. Trust. Let go.

The images wavered in and out of focus, as if dancing among the whirling colors. The colors exploded violently from time to time like solar flares, but as Spock continued to comfort Sanara, they gradually resembled a smooth ocean at sunset, one hue of the spectrum gently blending into the next. Clarity. Peace. Calm. Spock could now ask the traditional three questions of First Meld.

Who art thou?

I am Sanara.

And whose child art thou?

I know only their faces. And for a moment Spock glimpsed those faces. His most pressing question was at last answered, but he had one more question to ask, one final query to assure that the Meld was successful.

And what art thou?

I am Vulcan.

Spock removed his hands from Sanara's face and opened his eyes. Sanara trembled, but seemed to stand a little taller than she had before. She raised her hand in the age-old salute. "Live long and prosper."

Spock returned the salute. "Peace, Sanara, and long life."

"Captain?" Saavik gestured to the person at her feet, now recovering from the neck pinch. It was T'Ryth. The matron sat up, dazed; then she twisted her face in fury. She rose shakily to her feet, shouting, "Spock, you are an illogical fool!"

"I think not," said Spock. "What you seek is not logical, T'Ryth."

"ShiGral will be found," said T'Ryth, pounding one fist into an open palm.

Spock arched his left eyebrow. "Perhaps. But not by one as blind as you."

T'Ryth glowered at Spock. "You are the blind one: blind to the dangers of diversity. There are more of us than you know, Spock. I am not the only one who sees through the Federation's lies. Its worlds—none more so than Earth— have led our youth astray, urging them to forsake our traditions for others. Rejecting our heritage is not logical!"

Spock asked, "Is it not you who lead our youth astray, by teaching them that strength is found in isolation? You who claim to hand on our tradition betray it at every turn, even as you would have betrayed Sanara." He tenderly placed his hands on Sanara's shoulders. "You saw her strong mental abilities and were threatened. All that power—from a *viltah!*" Now Spock's eyes flashed in anger. "So you lured her here, to these caves, to amplify those powers even more, to abuse them to find an energy source you believe would destroy all 'impurities' like her. Was that not your plan?"

"Our world would be better off without all *viltah,*" T'Ryth said, spitting out every word. She marched toward the mouth of the cave, turning back to add, "Yourself included, Spock." With that, she went out into the stormy night.

Sanara was weeping. Saavik went to her, softly laying a hand on her back. "Let's leave this place, Sanara."

She looked at Saavik and Spock through tearful eyes. "I thought . . . I did want to find ShiGral."

"If ShiGral is the essence of what it is to be Vulcan," said Spock, "perhaps you did."

"Fascinating!" Doctor Tully laughed as she read the communiqué in her hands. "This is from the Institute. It seems the Vulture has resigned her position."

Spock stood with Saavik and Cadet Walters at the archaeological camp. "That is for the best," he said. What he did not say was that T'Ryth's resignation had not been voluntary, and her unbalanced thoughts were now being treated.

"And that's not all." Tully waved a second sheet of paper. "This is from FAC Central. It seems all funding for the ShiGral dig has mysteriously dried up. We've been reassigned to Andoria." Tully grinned as she looked around the camp. "So much for Camelot."

"Captain Spock, are you ready to beam up?" Walters asked.

"One moment." He walked to the edge of the camp, beckoning Saavik to follow. When they were out of earshot, he asked, "How is Sanara?"

"She's resting," said Saavik. "She's still shaken by last night and upset about who her 'other teacher' was. But she will be well. The meld freed her from T'Ryth's illusions. Sanara asked me to thank you."

"Wish her a happy birthday for me." Spock's gaze drifted to the horizon. "Her parents are dead." It was not a question.

Saavik cast her eyes down. "Yes. In the Vulcana Regar quake. I am sorry I could not tell you."

"You were right; your role as instructor left you little choice." Spock turned to face Saavik. "Lieutenant, I want to . . ." He closed his eyes briefly. "I have been remembering our time on the Genesis Planet." Saavik straightened visibly, but remained silent. Spock continued, "I wish to thank you for your kindness. I would not have survived without you."

Saavik turned away for a moment. When she looked at Spock again, a tear rolled down her cheek. "Captain, *I* would not have survived without *you*. I would not be who I am today."

Tenderly, Spock touched Saavik's hand. *"Saavikam,"* he whispered, "should you ever need . . ."

"Captain?" Cadet Walters was calling again, clearly eager to return his legendary charge safely to the starship above.

"Very well," said Spock. He and Saavik returned to the camp, and Spock stood next to Walters.

"Raleigh," Walters spoke into his communicator, "two to beam up."

Saavik was the last sight to fade from Spock's vision as the beam enveloped him. He had not found what he had hoped to find. He had found something better. He had found two extraordinary young women in whom Vulcan's bright future was assured. And perhaps that discovery compensated for the nonreality that he had come seeking.

After all, as Kiri-kin-tha taught, nothing unreal exists.

The Hero of My Own Life

Peg Robinson

"Okay—*fine*. You don't like Handel, you don't like T'Tron, you don't like Bach or Baabaatarma Ka? How about another sort of classic? Let's try Frank Zappa." Gillian Taylor knew she sounded demented as she ordered the computer to broadcast yet another piece of music out into the vast and empty seas. But then, she felt demented.

Darkness was upon the face of the waters of Pacifica. The only light to be found was the dull glow of the planetwide force fields, and the crackling flashes of lightning as storms harrowed Pacifica's seas. From the surface it was as though the Lord God had said, "Hey, Gabriel? Ditch the light thing. I have another idea. . . ."

It wasn't God who had summoned the darkness, but a woman named Carol Marcus. Even without God making an appearance, this was *Genesis:* the birth of life on a lifeless world. The rebirth of a failed project. But no birth is without danger. Lost in the birth-tempest was a young humpbacked whale, named Harpo.

In the observation room of the drift-station *Madrigal,* Gillian searched the waters and swore.

If only he'd answer. Sing to her. Anything.

There was a crackle as the communication system struggled to deliver a message from the *U.S.S. Hermes,* in orbit above. "Doctor Taylor, we can't hold off on the second discharge much longer. Doctor Marcus has been ready to begin the second stage of the Genesis transformation for the past day. If you and your team don't beam up soon, we may have to abort."

Gillian grimaced. "I'm sorry, Captain Uhura, but Harpo still isn't answering. Have your people picked up any trace of him?"

"Nothing. I'm sorry."

"You'd find his body, wouldn't you? If he were dead?" Gillian was annoyed at the quiver of fear in her voice. Her inability to wall off her feelings about "her" whales had always been her downfall. In all the years she'd been "here," in the twenty-fourth century, that hadn't changed. If anything, it had become worse, as her relationships with the great creatures became fuller and more equal. But it was embarrassing to sound so helpless and needy. She was in her fifties. A professional. An officer. Why did she still feel . . . what? Blurry and undefined, as though she'd never quite come into focus after leaving her own era. As though she were just a loose end, a raveled thread flapping in the high winds of time.

Uhura was patient. "We'd probably find him, but not certainly. You *know* that, Doctor Taylor." Her voice moved from the frustration of a busy officer to the sympathetic warmth of a friend. "I'm sorry, Gillian. We'll look as long as we can. But if you haven't found him in another six hours, I'm going to have to make a final call—and the Genesis Project can't wait."

"And when Doctor Marcus sets off the second device? What about Harpo then?"

"I don't know. Doctor Marcus has modified the design and altered the procedure. But no one has ever stayed on planet when the device goes off."

"And no one wants to. As I recall, with the original version, you'd end up very dead—or, shall we say, severely edited?"

Gillian sighed and ran her fingers through graying blond curls. "Sorry, Uhura. I know there's only so much you can do. I have six hours?"

"Six, if you're lucky."

"Understood. I'll have all the nonessential personnel beam up from the *Madrigal* now. I'll stay and keep looking up to the last minute." There was silence on the other end of the link. Gillian gave a wry smile. "Uhura, really, I'll come up on time. I promise."

There was a low chuckle, and the voice of the commanding officer of the *Hermes* said, "I'll hold you to it. Six hours . . . Captain Uhura out."

Then the communication room of the drift-station was filled with nothing but the sound of Frank Zappa singing about "St. Alfonzo's Pancake Breakfast."

Six hours later there was still no sign of her teammate, Harpo.

"What do you mean you can't find him? You have sensors. Scan for his lifesigns, then beam him up to the aquatic deck. Fast. I have to release the second round of energy, or this attempt is going to be for nothing."

Carol Marcus paced the floor at the head of the *Hermes*'s briefing room. Now in her early seventies, her lean body had grown almost Vulcanoid in its elegance. The trials and losses of her life had stripped away all that was frivolous, condensed her personality to a burning core of intellectual passion. She seemed lit from within, consumed by her desire to set Genesis in motion again. "We can't wait. If you don't find him, I have to set the device off anyway."

"It could kill him." Gillian was furious. She rammed her fists deep in the pants pockets she refused to give up to "modern" fashion.

"This is *not* the same device as the original Genesis."

"It may not be the same," Gillian grumbled, "but I don't see you down there on Pacifica, do I?"

"Ladies, this isn't getting us anywhere." Uhura leaned back in the big chair at the head of the table. She studied the two scientists: both strong, both determined, both, in their own ways, desperate. "Doctor Marcus, you need the Genesis Project to proceed. Doctor Taylor, you need to recover your teammate. So, in the immortal words of Mister Spock, cooperation is only logical."

Gillian Taylor frowned and flicked a glance over at Carol Marcus. The other woman's blue eyes met hers, wary amusement lurking in the cool depths.

A sudden spark of shared laughter passed between them.

Marcus smiled for the first time that day. "I suppose we might do that. Only as a last-ditch option, of course."

"Of course," Gillian agreed, soberly. "We wouldn't want to do it for anything less. People might talk."

Resigned understanding passed between the two women. They were, in their own way, celebrities. Each had a colorful past. Each had prestige within her field. And, always, each was associated with the memory of the late James T. Kirk.

People would always talk. And when two of Kirk's women were in the same vicinity, working on the same project, they'd talk even more. Nothing would change that.

Uhura seemed to understand. But then, as one of Kirk's old bridge crew, she would. She smoothed her uniform jacket and suppressed a mischievous grin. "Let them talk, if they have nothing better to keep them busy. *We* have work to do. Now, Doctor Taylor, if you could present your information?"

Gillian nodded, routing her data to the big display terminal at the back of the room.

Pacifica rotated in the screen, against a black backdrop of empty space. The world was water: vast expanses of sterile, saline water, peppered with islands, with only one continent at the northern pole. At the edge of the continent there was a dim red blob.

Gillian cocked her head at the image. "That red area is where we last had a reading on Harpo. Unfortunately he disappeared soon after the first Genesis Device was set off. Once he realized we were out of touch, he'd have stayed put, though. If he's still alive, he's probably still somewhere in that vicinity."

"Can't the *Hermes* do a high-intensity sensor scan and find him?" Marcus asked.

"Not with the storms, and the other effects of the Genesis blast," Uhura answered. "There are the containing force fields to worry about, the ionizing effect of the storms, and atmospheric and oceanic turbulence. And that first energy release you made may not have gotten real life started on Pacifica, but it has created a soup of amino acids. Trying to read through that is like—"

"Trying to read through a pot of gumbo." Marcus grimaced. "I always did say I could cook."

"Don't feel too bad," Uhura said. "Your Genesis effect isn't the only trouble. We've been picking up some other interference in that locale too—something we can't quite pin down and can't factor out. But we can't do a reliable scan in the area."

"Other interference? What sort?" Marcus's voice was sharp, her expression suddenly avid.

"We're not sure," Uhura said. "It could be nothing. A few odd sensor echoes that could just be side effects of Genesis."

"Disrupted energy readings could mean trouble for Genesis," Marcus snapped. "Why didn't you tell me?"

"It's in the report we sent up, Doctor. I suspect you've been too busy trying to get clearance to set off the second device to review our data," Uhura said dryly.

Marcus scowled, then sighed, "Understood, Captain. I apologize. But this could be serious."

"And Harpo isn't?" Gillian muttered.

Doctor Marcus just looked at Gillian, then frowned at the screen. "Have you got any pre-Genesis readings on that area?"

Gillian reduced the first image, and pulled up a 3-D map of the ocean bed. The ground dropped away from the shore in stages, rose up in a bank surrounding the continental shelf, then dropped fast and steep into a rift nearly a mile deep. "This is it. It's a wilderness. There are miles of nooks and crannies. Harpo could be anywhere in that."

"He has to come up to breathe. We could get a probe down to monitor the surface; he'd have to come up for air eventually. And we might learn something about Captain

Uhura's 'unknown interference' in the process." Marcus drummed her fingers on the surface of the table, mind racing to find a solution to their problem.

Gillian shook her head. "Sorry. Good idea, but no cigar. He's rigged with an aqualung oxygen filter. He can stay down till hell freezes over. And we've had probes out for a week and haven't learned more than this."

Marcus stood. "Then there's only one thing I can think of to do, now."

"Ignore the interference, set off the Genesis Device, and let Harpo take his chances?" Gillian snapped.

"No, Doctor Taylor," Dr. Marcus returned. "I suggest we go down in one of the *Hermes*'s amphibian shuttles, and do an on-site search."

"We?"

"This is *my* project, Doctor Taylor. Anything that disrupts it is my concern."

Captain Uhura tipped her head, observing Marcus. "Very well, Doctor Marcus. A two-person team to go down in the *Nautilus*. Doctor Taylor will be in command."

"Doctor Taylor?" Marcus's voice was sharp.

Uhura nodded. "Genesis may be your baby, Doctor Marcus. But Doctor Taylor is the oceanographer, and she has the deep-water experience."

Dr. Marcus weighed the order and nodded. "Very well." She turned to Gillian. "I'll be at the shuttlebay in ten minutes. I hope you'll be ready by then."

When Gillian nodded, Marcus left.

Gillian looked at Uhura. "This isn't going to be easy."

"No?"

"No. She's . . ." Gillian frowned. "If I'd had my way, I

wouldn't have worked this project with her. Not after I heard who she was. Less after I met her."

"Why? She's a forceful woman, I'll admit that. More so than she once was. But she's a good scientist."

"It's— She makes me feel sloppy, and young, and incompetent. And it's always hard being around another of Jim's old flames. Between what people expect us to be, and how we react to that, simple conversation turns into an effort." Gillian groped helplessly, trying to define a feeling that had haunted her for years. "He's a legend . . . and thanks to him, all of *us* are just the legend's women. Afterthoughts. Sidekicks. Everyone defines us in terms of who we were to James T. Kirk, and even our professional status is altered by the connection. People expect more of us, and less." She gave a bitter snort. "Even *we* do it. It's not so bad normally, but when you get more than one of Jim's . . . flames . . . in one place together, between the outsiders peering in at us, and us peering at each other, it can be like waltzing with shadows. In the end you're not sure who you really are, and who's just the image cast by the light of history—and James Kirk."

Uhura laughed. "You are two of the most able women in the universe. The captain seldom settled for less. That's why I requested assignment to Genesis when I heard she needed a ship as a base. And it's why I suggested you and your team when I heard she needed an oceanographic unit. Working with the captain's former associates is always a pleasure."

Gillian was amazed. "You elected to work with Marcus, and then added me to the deal? No, no, no—don't tell me that Jim's women are forming an Old Girls Network."

Uhura raised an eyebrow and quirked a grin across the table. "Old? Girls? Neither, thank you. More like family, if you ask me. Or friends. Or at least women with top-notch references: the captain tended to pick quality, more often than not, and those of you I've met, I've liked. Why not work together?"

"Because people talk. Because it's lonely being stared at. Because sometimes I wonder if that's all I am: Jim Kirk's broad from the past. A curiosity. Enough people think so . . ."

"You shouldn't worry about how people define you—who you are and what you do are more than sufficient."

Gillian smoothed back her unruly curls. "Maybe. Maybe not. When I'm not reminded, it's simple enough. Maybe I just feel it more because Carol Marcus reminds me that so much of my own definition is back there in the past. I have my career, I have the whales—and the connection with Jim. And all the rest is, as they say, history."

Uhura *tsk*ed, and stood, elegant and queenly in her uniform, wearing her rank with dignity and confidence. "No. I don't accept that. The same could be said of me, in many ways. Even without the romance, I'm still seen as one of Kirk's women. And my career has been my life. And the rest is, as you said, history. But it doesn't make it any harder to work around you, or Doctor Marcus. And I refuse to believe I'm nothing more than a . . . what? A supporting character in James T. Kirk's biography?" She snorted. "No, thank you. I prefer to be the hero of my own life."

"But you can afford that kind of confidence. You belong here, and now," Gillian said. "So does she."

"And so do you," Uhura said, firmly. "So you're just

going to have to deal with it. Like the rest of us. Now, get that shuttle checked and ready. Doctor Marcus isn't going to want to wait one second longer than she has to."

"Strap in tight, ladies." Uhura's voice was drowned out as static swept the comlink. Then it surged back in. "If our observations are correct, the weather's fairly violent. It won't be easy sailing."

Marcus and Taylor both started to answer—then Marcus nodded, and yielded to Gillian. "Your ship."

Gillian addressed the tiny viewscreen on the upper console. "Thanks, Uhura."

"My blessings then. We'll be watching. If you're out of touch for more than half a day I'll send down search and rescue teams."

"We'll try not to make you go to the trouble, though, if you don't mind."

"And here I was counting on this to keep my people on their toes. Oh, well." Uhura shook her head. "Maybe another time. Is that all for now?"

"I think so. Wish us well."

"Always. Uhura out."

Gillian and Dr. Marcus had only enough time to exchange nervous glances, then the shuttle entered Pacifica's atmosphere and immediately slewed off-course. The storm snatched at them and spun them away.

Gillian swore and braced herself, forcing the steering control up. "Computer, activate stabilization programs . . . adapt for extreme turbulence."

"Complying."

The shuttle bucked again, tossing the two women against

their safety harnesses. Then the programming cut in and the shuttle stabilized and returned to course.

"Better." She looked down at the navigation readings. "The area we're interested in is due north, Doctor Marcus. We should be at the edge of the search area in five minutes."

Marcus leaned back in her seat. "Good enough. What now?"

"Do a sensor sweep for organics. Pick up what you can, anyway. And I'm dropping a sea probe. I'll start broadcasting from that to let Harpo know we're here, if he can hear us." The shuttle shook again, and Gillian was forced to scramble, her attention on the controls. She scowled. "What do those Genesis things do to the planet, anyway? This weather is like a typhoon."

Marcus's hands moved over the control panels as she took sensor readings. "Do you have time for a course in advanced quantum mechanics, some chaos theory, and a lot of particle physics? Topped off with stable systems of turbulence, organic chemistry, and computer programming?"

"No. Thanks anyway." Gillian scowled. "Those sciences and I never did get along."

Marcus's eyes flicked across the cabin, then back to the controls. "A pity. It's been hard finding enough people to support Genesis."

"Genesis doesn't seem to be lacking support," Gillian said, dryly. "That's one thing that hasn't changed in four hundred years. Physics is sexy—oceans are just a lot of water. The *Madrigal* and its team wouldn't be here, if we weren't needed for your project."

"Genesis is new life." Marcus said it as though that made everything all right.

"It's a big galaxy, Doctor. It's already full of life. Can't we give a bit more attention to what's already there?" Gillian voiced the complaint of the undersupported scientists of history.

Marcus didn't comment.

Gillian dropped a sea probe, then selected a piece of organ music by a Tellarite composer named Fronch. It was nearly two hundred years old—and had been written nearly two hundred years after Gillian had been born. She queued up a prerecorded hail which the computer had translated into the whoops and wails of humpback song. Then she programmed in the Fronch, letting the music play in the shuttle as it was broadcast into the dark, heaving seas. The opening passage swept out, proud and regal. It was music that would have reduced even Bach to tears of awe. The amphishuttle's walls vibrated with it.

After that Gillian concentrated on her flying. The skies were black and sullen. Lightning crackled and spidered around them. Below, lit by the shuttle's floodlights, she could see the waves, high and white. She guided the shuttle lower, watching the course readings, looking for a good place and moment to come down to the ocean's surface, then submerge.

"Why music?" Marcus asked. "I've wondered ever since I heard you played music to communicate with your whale. It seems—inefficient?"

"Whales sing. And we've never found a true language that humans and whales can share. We still depend on telepaths and the universal translator to communicate. But we do share music, song. It's our one great common link. And Harpo?" Gillian's mouth twitched as her heart wobbled between remembered laughter and worry. She began the shuttle descent, concentrating on controlling the little craft, letting the words take care of themselves. "He was singing even when he was in Gracie's womb. So it got to be a thing with us—we'd pipe him music; he'd sing back to let us know he heard us and was still fine. It became almost a secret language—even more of a language once he was old enough to understand that the ideas that the translator passed on with the music were interpretations of the lyrics. He'd sing whole conversations using shared melodies. Or tell jokes with bars of music."

"With David it used to be surprise programs on the computer. Intentional viruses, he called them. Little messages that would pop up in the middle of the day, just to say, 'Hi, Mom.' " Marcus was silent for a moment, as she took another reading. "Two weeks after he died, I got one. He'd put it in as a time bomb . . . it was triggered when I went over some of his old records. It said, 'Just so you know—I love you. Always. David.' I cried for an hour." She leaned back in her seat. Her thin face seemed almost luminous in the dim light of the cabin. "Kids. Don't they just kill you?"

Gillian thought of Harpo as a baby, leaping after Gracie in the open waters of San Francisco Bay . . . and belly flopping. She wondered if he was dead, as Marcus's David was dead. "Yeah. Like a knife in your heart."

Marcus twitched, and Gillian remembered too late how David had died.

Too late to take the words back.

The shuttle touched water, bucked, and dropped as it slid down the crest of a comber, down farther and farther. The seas were higher than Gillian had realized.

Below the heaving upper layers of water, deep where the currents were usually stable, there was turbulence still.

Gillian turned on more of the shuttle's floodlights.

It was like looking through dilute pea soup—greenish, murky, filled with sediment. If it weren't for the navigational computations, and sonar and sensor readings, she'd be lost.

There was a click, and Uhura hailed them. "Ladies, we're losing your signal. Can you hold steady while we try to counter the effect?"

Gillian opened the channel to the *Hermes*. "Can do, Uhura. Let me know when you've finished." She set the amphishuttle's controls to stand in place in the current.

"Doctor Taylor," Uhura said a moment later, "we've been able to clean up our readings—and in the process we've discovered something else: a sensor null area, right in the heart of your search zone. My science officer says that it seems to be related to the effects of the Romulan cloaking device. That moves our 'unexplained interference' into the realm of 'probably caused by intelligent life-forms.' Under the circumstances my advice is to cancel the upcoming stage of Genesis, call the two of you back in, and continue the investigation at our leisure."

"No." The word came from two mouths at once. Gillian and Marcus looked at each other. Then Gillian continued, "I still have to find Harpo—he could be in danger. And we're down already. Let us finish what we started, Captain."

The pause as Uhura considered seemed eternal. Then, her voice a leonine growl, she said, "As you wish. But watch yourselves down there. Do you understand? No grandstand plays."

Marcus snorted. "That was Jim's specialty, Uhura. We're just his shy little shadows. Pale echoes of his derring-do."

Uhura gave a dismissive snort. "In a pig's eye, Doctor Marcus."

Marcus laughed. It was the first time Gillian could remember her doing so. "We'll be careful, Uhura. I promise. Won't we, Doctor Taylor?"

"Oh, yes, Doctor Marcus. Very careful," Gillian agreed, soberly.

Uhura sighed. "I wish I believed it."

"Believe it, Uhura." Gillian laughed. "Now we have to go—the current down here is terrible." In a few moments Uhura had relayed them a course setting for the location of the cloaked area, and they were back underway.

"Thanks," Marcus said.

"For what?"

"For making Uhura let us continue."

Gillian shook her head. "I just fought for what I cared about. But I can't make Uhura do anything she doesn't want to do."

"No. I suppose not. But it's what I wanted, too."

"You treat that damned project like it was your baby," Gillian grumbled. "I have a whale lost, and all you can think of is your schedule."

Marcus looked over at her, as they dropped deeper and deeper into Pacifica's waters. "It's been my life. It was David's death, in the end. It may not be very scientific of me, but I want it to mean something. Somehow, over the years, Genesis has come to define me. If it fails, I don't know what I'll do. Who I'll be . . ."

Gillian didn't comment. She understood too well, and

wasn't ready to admit it, or, more accurately, wasn't quite sure how to.

"You worry about that whale like he was your own child, don't you?" Marcus countered, suddenly.

Gillian felt something ease inside her. She smiled, reluctantly. "Yeah. I do. I've always been terrible, even back when I came from. I overpersonalize. Besides being a teammate, Harpo's as close as I ever came to a child. He is George and Gracie's child—and I love them like family. In a lot of ways they are my family. Having Harpo out there is like having a favorite nephew gone missing."

"I never really thought about it. You're so far out of your own time. Are the whales the only family you have?" Carol Marcus sounded uneasy at the thought.

Gillian swiped a curl out of her eyes. "No. Not just them. You can count some of the people I've worked with over the years, too. And a few special folks like Uhura. I was close to Sarek of Vulcan for some years—he and his wife were good to me when I first came here. But Amanda's dead, now."

Marcus frowned. "Sounds lonely."

"My life's not lonely!" Gillian was startled to hear it described that way. "It's out of kilter in some ways. Making the shift to a new time was harder than I expected. But I'm not lonely—how could I be, with so much to learn and see?" Then Gillian scowled, and pointed to the screen. "What do you think that is?"

"Where?"

"There. Along that rock face." Gillian guided the shuttle closer to the side of the slope, to a sheer cliff that dropped down, and down, disappearing in the green waters.

"I don't know. Could just be a natural vein in the stone. Could be a crack."

"It's too—I don't know. It looks wrong. Like something that's supposed to look natural, but doesn't make it. That edge is too regular, and the irregularities are phony. Like fake rocks in a bad B movie. Like someone printed 'Styrofoam' across the face of the thing. I think we may have found our unexplained interference . . . and maybe my lost whale." It was a relief to move away from personal issues to practical, worldly problems.

"So? What next?" Marcus was tense, her shoulders set. Her fingers drummed the console in front of her, lightly.

"Call Uhura up on the *Hermes*. Arrange for backup." Gillian activated the comlink. "Captain Uhura, this is Doctor Taylor, on the *Nautilus*. We've discovered what appears to be an artificial—"

The console went dead.

Then the entire shuttle went dead.

"Damn." Gillian's hands crept over the controls, trying to find their way by braille. "Oh, hell."

Marcus was struggling with her own controls. "Nothing."

The shuttle jerked and shuddered, then began to move. Gillian thought they were drifting toward the cliff face, but in the absolute black of the cabin it was hard to determine more than a general forward motion.

"I can't tell where we are. Can you?" Marcus said, her voice as tense as a finger on a phaser trigger.

"No. It's like we're nowhere. Nowhen." Gillian swallowed hard. She'd felt this way on deep dives, traveling through black-on-black immensity. But she'd never gone down without knowing she had enough control to get back up, before. This was more like when she'd thrown herself into the glow of a strange, mysterious transporter beam— hoping that she had what it took to cope with whatever she found on the other side. "I didn't know black could be so physical," she murmured. "If eternity had a form, it would look like this."

Marcus laughed, sharply. "Genesis. 'And the Earth was without form, and void, and darkness was on the face of the deep.' I hate it. I do. I absolutely hate it. This is what Genesis is supposed to undo. Endlessness and entropy and death."

Gillian could hear strangled panic in her companion's words.

She couldn't criticize. As the shuttle drifted, her own hands trembled, still looking for a control that would answer to her touch. Another moment and she'd have to give up, open the latches of the safety straps. She and Doctor Marcus would have to grope their way into the diving suits, crank the hatches open manually—and take their chances trying to swim back up to the surface.

It was a long way up.

Then there was a greenish glow, and the crack in the cliff slid open.

" 'And God said, "Let there be light," and there was light.' " Gillian was giggling, as dizzy with relief as if she had the bends.

" 'And God saw the light, that it was good . . .' " Marcus snorted. "I have never been so happy to see light in my life."

The crack was a wide gate, now, leading into the cliff wall. Sediment stirred and swirled in the light. "Why am I so relieved?" Gillian wondered. "It's just light. The controls are still dead. We're being drawn into who knows what, and I'm giggling and shaking and so happy I could sing." The *Nautilus* drifted closer, closer, then passed through, out of the darkness into a blaze of radiance.

"Oh, my God." Marcus leaned forward. The light shone on high cheekbones and polished silver hair, gleamed on the fine, sculpted curves of her eyelids. "Oh, my God. Look at it."

Gillian looked.

The cliff had hidden a cavern—a cavern so vast she could only imagine the existence of a far wall. The water was clear, far clearer than the stew of silt and amino acids the shuttle had just left. And everywhere there were structures, though she was hard put to know what to call them. They weren't houses. The latticed partitions reminded her of lace, and birdcages, and summery gazebos covered with vines.

In and around the structures there were people.

She realized she was leaning forward, the safety straps cutting into her shoulders, her hands pressed flat to force her still closer to the front viewport.

"They're beautiful," Marcus murmured. "Simply gorgeous."

Gillian thought she might be willing to call them humanoid. But there was something as seallike as human about them, and a trace of otterine slenderness and grace. And the frond-fin-feathers of them! A fan-dancer's wardrobe sprouted from spines and crested heads, in colors that would shame a Terran macaw. The beings were small, not much bigger than raccoons. They swam alongside the *Nautilus,* huge eyes peering in at the two women. Their delicate webbed hands brushed the transparent aluminum of the port. The flesh was so thin the blazing light of the caverns shone through, silhouetting bones, and veins of a delicate purple.

Gillian didn't dare move. She didn't even dare smile, or wave. Whatever they were, their technology held the *Nautilus* firm—and they almost certainly had Harpo. She didn't dare risk a single gesture that might be misunderstood.

"What do we do now?" Carol Marcus whispered.

"I think I go out and try to communicate," Gillian returned.

"And me?"

"You wait. Unless *you* want to be the one who goes out. But one of us should stay in the shuttle. Just in case."

"In case of what?"

"You know. 'Just in case'? I'm sure you can think of *something*." She was trying to laugh. She eased a hand up and released the catch of her straps, then stood, cautiously. The strange beings continued to peer in at her, but an uneasy shiver moved through the school. Gillian slip-stepped backwards down the center of the shuttle, reaching behind her until she found the door of the cabinet that held the diving gear. After that she had to risk looking away.

"They don't seem to be too frightened of us," Marcus said.

"They've caught us, not the other way around."

" 'Do not project the social assumptions of your own race onto the aliens you encounter; this is especially true during first contact situations,' " Marcus quoted. "I think I read that in some academy pamphlet I picked up at Jim's place, once." She laughed. "It's a rule he usually broke."

"He broke a lot of rules," Gillian said, dryly. "It was part of his eternal charm."

"Yes, it was, wasn't it?" Carol Marcus said, smiling. "I should remember that."

"Why? You don't break enough rules on your own?"

"No. And the ones I do break, I regret too much."

Gillian frowned. "I suppose I do, too. I regret being one walking broken rule. The chick he brought back from time."

Marcus sighed. "Why the hell are we talking about Jim Kirk, now?"

"I don't know. What else should we talk about?" Gillian had shimmied into the bottom of her suit. She pulled her tunic top over her head, and began to squeeze into the suit jacket. "It's not like we know what to plan for next. And it's the one topic we share in common. What else are we going to chat about?"

"Why did you come to this time?" Marcus asked, suddenly. "It wasn't for Jim—your behavior afterwards made that clear. So, why? It's so dangerous, now. Violent, uncertain. People die for such stupid reasons. The old days were better. One world, one race, one culture. You knew who you were, where you belonged. How could you choose to leave that, and risk everything to come here?" In her voice Gillian could hear the death of a son, the devastation of a career, the loss of a lover, the failure of a dream.

Gillian frowned. "I don't honestly know. It wasn't as good then as you think. That's part of it. The good old days are never as good as people think they were. But—" She zipped the jacket and pulled up the rubbery plastic hood, adjusting the waterproof seals. "I used to collect whale quotes. Lawrence, Nash, you name it. There was one I loved, a poem that ended: 'Lord, if only some fortunate plunge would let me come up into your eternal peace.' I think I threw myself into that transporter beam for a dream of surfacing in some unimaginable peace, where George and Gracie and I could live happily ever after."

"And you ended up here. Surrounded by all of modern life's uncertainties. Some happy ending." Marcus's voice was bitter, even as her awed eyes watched the drift and dance of the beings outside the shuttle.

Gillian frowned, watching the water ballet. "I suppose it is. I certainly hope so." Then she slipped the aqualung attachment over her mouth, cranked the hatch open, and stepped into the chambered airlock.

When she left the shuttle, the water was cold. The aliens clustered around her, close, closer, closest, touching her, tracing her features, exploring. Their hands were like spiders, tickling, prickling, creeping over her face. And there was a hum about them, deep, like the sound of music heard vibrating through the pipes underwater during a bath.

Gillian knew they were trying to communicate, but the results were no better than all the years she'd tried to communicate with George and Gracie, before Spock had melded with them, before they'd all come to a future filled with telepaths and universal translators. She tried to signal her confusion, her regret. Tried to mime Harpo, to mime releasing the shuttle from whatever it was that held it.

She'd never been any use as a mime. She'd once quipped that the reason she became an oceanographer was because she had to do something if she wanted to live and work near the San Francisco shoreline, and she'd never have made it as a street performer. She wasn't any better now than she'd ever been. Her broad gestures to indicate the young humpback only made her wallow, and bump into the delicate little aliens. Desperate waving and pointing at the shuttle, and the exaggerated opening of an upheld fist to signify release, only confused them and made them swim wildly around her.

She was utterly frustrated.

Then a shadow slid beneath her frog-finned feet. It rose up, dark, sleek, and massive, a contrail of silver bubbles streaming from the divided blowhole and rising up to veil her in crystal and champagne sparkle. A second later Harpo was nudging her and humming. She could just make out the melody: one of her old favorites, from her own time. "Octopus's Garden." She laughed, and struggled to hum along through her mouthpiece and the constant rush of air the aqualung forced on her. The results were peculiar and tickled her nose, but they seemed to satisfy Harpo.

Gillian gave a kick, and a twist, and let her hands track along Harpo's skin. He was smooth—far smoother than George or Gracie, as they were smoother than true "wild" humpbacks had been in her own time. It was amazing the difference medical attention and barnacle removal could make. Harpo was a very civilized young whale.

The strange aliens seemed to think so too. They flocked around him, a festive flight of tropical finches fluttering around an elephant. Gillian could hear their hum, moving from single solo passages to the full chords of a choir singing in unison, as they surrounded her friend.

He was communicating something to them. She couldn't tell what, but there was more purpose in their response to him than to her. But she couldn't identify the mode, or grasp the method of exchange.

It was driving her crazy. Under normal circumstances her communication tab would have served as a translation device. But just as the shuttle was still and passive, its technology reduced to the bare mechanical aspects of life support, the translator was silent.

She scowled. There had to be some way to communicate. Harpo seemed to at least be getting by. She dropped down and swam alongside him, listening to him hum and moan.

It wasn't language. Not really. But somehow the creatures seemed to accept it as communication, of some sort. In the time Harpo had been held here, he'd found some way to make contact with these people.

She pulled away and returned to the shuttle, letting herself in through the hatch.

Carol Marcus had released herself from the straps of her seat and was standing in the middle of the shuttle. She made a face as Gillian came in. "I had to move. I was beginning to freeze up solid, just sitting there. So, what did you find out?"

"Harpo's here. He's fine—still has his aqualung, seems to be healthy. Other than that—I don't know." She frowned. "This is going to be a problem. We've been working for years to come up with a functional human-cetacean pidgin, but it's never gotten very far. Whales don't appear to process language in even remotely human ways, and humans are no better off with whale song. Our best solution has been to use the universal translator and depend on telepaths when the translator isn't enough. But that's not going to help now. So I can't communicate with the aliens, because they've shut down our communication system, and I can't talk to Harpo for the same reason."

"Uhura did say she'd send down a search and rescue team if we were gone too long. We don't have to solve this on our own."

Gillian huffed. "No? Another two people who can't

talk, with a neutralized shuttle, will help? Or four? Or more? This could go on forever." She paced to the front port. "We need to find some way to talk to Harpo. He seems to be able to communicate *something* to the aliens. If we can get him to ask them to give us back our power, we could bring the translator on-line—and then we'd be cooking with gas."

Marcus chuckled. "This is exactly the sort of moment Jim was at his best. A problem, a dramatic setting, a first contact—a seemingly impossible puzzle. He'd grin, and pull an answer out of thin air, like a soprano hitting a high C and going for a D as though it was child's play. And the whole thing would be personal to him. I think he found life to be very, very personal."

Gillian nodded again. Then grinned. "Marcus, I owe you for this. You're a genius."

"I know. How did I prove it this time?" Carol asked, as Gillian pulled the hood back over her hair.

"You reminded me of child's play. And Harpo's play was song."

Five minutes later Gillian was clinging to Harpo's fin, shouting music against the whale's broad side. She had to go through "Please Release Me" a good dozen times. But Harpo finally got it.

An hour later Harpo had managed to find some way to tell the aliens what Gillian needed them to know. Whatever had held the *Nautilus* let go, and the power in the shuttle came on.

The first thing Gillian did was call the *Hermes*. The second thing was to test the universal translator by telling Harpo she'd missed him.

After that she was too busy talking to aliens to keep track of what she did next.

On the trip back up through Pacifica's waters, Carol Marcus asked, "What did they want? Why did they take Harpo, and us?"

"They're runaways. They were kidnapped from their own planet by Orion slavers, nearly two hundred years ago. They escaped with a ship and some stolen technology, and hid here, on a dead, sterile planet, where they thought they'd be safe. Then we came. They lay low, and hoped we'd leave. But then you set off the first Genesis explosion, and the storms began, and then Harpo came exploring, and his sonar detected the hollow behind the cliff. And they panicked. I don't think they knew what they'd do, but they were too frightened not to do something."

"Then why didn't they attack us, once they had us?"

Gillian shrugged. "Because they're not that kind of species. We didn't attack them. So they didn't attack us." She pulled the nose of the *Nautilus* up, following Harpo and his entourage of aliens toward the surface. Even this deep she could see a glimmer of light. The effects of the first Genesis explosion were fading. Light was returning to Pacifica. To her that was a joy. To Carol Marcus it had to be a disappointment.

"Are you sorry about how it turned out?" she asked. "Now that we know there are aliens here, Genesis is going to be put on hold for a while."

"No. Of course not. If I'd set off the second device, the accumulated energies might have overcome the aliens' cloaks and shields. They might have died. As it is . . ."

Marcus smiled. "As it is, this may be a godsend. With a new species, one that wants the world to be more habitable, there's some extra push to attempt Genesis here on Pacifica. Uhura's communications team says the aliens will let themselves be moved to an orbiting station while I finish the Genesis conversion—and then they can have first deed and title on the new colony. Or a place on another water world if it doesn't work." She didn't sound as though she thought the second choice would be needed.

Gillian was less sure, but let it pass. Instead she leaned back and watched Harpo's shadow rise up through the waters above them, toward the pale shimmer of the surface. The storm above still raged on, but there was a difference between the dark of storm and the utter dark of the depths. She'd never forget that, now. "So you'll get to finish the Genesis experiments. Is that going to be enough?"

Doctor Marcus shrugged. "Enough? With a thousand things left to learn? It's never *enough*. But it will suffice. For now."

It wasn't what Gillian had really meant to ask. She'd wanted to ask if the other woman was happy. If she'd been recompensed for the loss of a son. The death of a lover. For the pain of her past, and the cool, armored silences of her present. For a lifetime being defined as the woman of a legend.

Kirk's women. Gillian had her whales, her colleagues . . . and an unexpected family made up of Kirk's other women. Those connections, the links that all passed through James Kirk, were a strange family. But in this time they were most of the family she had. She wanted to know that this one was happy.

She wasn't sure. But Carol Marcus was busy, and fulfilled. For now that would suffice.

And, Gillian thought, if her present was not as she had once dreamed, it too would suffice. She'd grabbed on to a transporter beam, a stranger's waist, and a scant hope. She wasn't defined by Kirk, or by history—but by a willingness to dare.

Now she plunged up into the eternal peace of the Federation, to a familiar happily-ever-after she'd once only dreamed of.

It wasn't heaven. It wasn't the Eden of Genesis. But it would suffice.

Gillian Taylor grinned. Then she pulled up an old, old classic on the computer, and spent the rest of the trip up trying to explain Frank Zappa's "Penguin in Bondage" to a woman of the modern world.

Doctors Three

Charles Skaggs

What in blazes are they thinking?

Admiral Leonard McCoy stared through the window of his Starfleet runabout vessel and watched in silent irritation as the ship approached the planet Jupiter. It had been two days since he had learned of the project to construct a holographic medical officer for use in emergency situations, and McCoy was bound and determined to voice his opinion on the subject to practically anyone he could find.

The retired admiral's personal campaign took him to the highest offices of Starfleet Medical, where three separate department heads had the misfortune to encounter the legendary force of nature. Although considerably slowed by his advanced age of 144, McCoy was still a man to be reckoned with if he was upset about something, and the idea of a holographic physician replacing human beings positively troubled him to no end.

Following a clandestine series of private conversations between the department heads, Admiral McCoy was encouraged to visit the Holoprogramming Center on Jupiter Station. It was Starfleet Medical's hope that by learning more about the development of the Emergency Medical

Hologram, McCoy would come to appreciate the project's merit and eventually offer his public support. And just to give more credibility to the visit, a promising young ensign named Debbie Walter was assigned as McCoy's official attaché, with strict orders to keep the admiral from being too disruptive.

One almost had to feel sorry for her.

"We're coming up on Jupiter Station, Admiral," announced Ensign Walter from the pilot's seat of the Starfleet runabout *Hippocrates*. "Do you want me to beam you on ahead or would you like to wait until we dock?"

McCoy smiled at her as he looked out at the orbiting space station coming slowly into view. "They didn't tell you much about me, did they?"

"Sir?"

"Your superiors at Starfleet Medical. They didn't tell you about the infamous Doctor Leonard McCoy and his lifelong hatred for that infernal device called a transporter?"

Shaking her strawberry-blond head, Walter gave her passenger an innocent shrug. "I'm afraid I only received a quick briefing about you before we left, Admiral. However, many of your documented cases are required reading at the academy, and I understand that your neural grafting technique is still the practice."

"Hunh. Is that so?"

"Yes, Admiral."

With a small sigh, McCoy returned his gaze to the approaching station. "Funny how they can fill you kids with all that stuff and still act like it's perfectly fine to have your molecules scrambled all over space just to get from one point to another."

Ensign Walter nodded along politely, despite her lack of sympathy for the admiral's perspective. Checking her control panel once again, she looked back to find McCoy apparently lost in thought. "Sir?" she inquired. "Are you all right?"

McCoy's eyes blinked suddenly. *"Hm?* Oh. Sorry about that. I was just feeling bad about you getting stuck babysitting an old fool off on some damn personal crusade."

"Don't worry about me, Admiral. I think I'll survive the experience. Should I arm myself with a phaser in case you get out of hand?"

"Couldn't hurt." McCoy grinned silently at the young woman's attempt at humoring him. "Not to worry, Ensign. Despite my age, I'm still a Southern gentleman who knows how to behave himself with a lady."

"I'm going to hold you to that. In the meantime, why don't you just sit back and enjoy the ride."

Might as well, thought McCoy as he slowly leaned back into his seat. *I don't expect I'll enjoy my time on the station. . . .*

After the *Hippocrates* docked at Landing Pad B, McCoy grabbed his walking cane and made his way through the airlock with Ensign Walter. Despite the exoskeleton braces he wore on his legs, he had reluctantly taken to using the cane almost two years earlier. McCoy had finally conceded that his frail body was in need of help in order to move about, which was a painful realization for him, a man who prided himself on his health and longevity. However, the more that he thought about the idea, he came to the conclusion that as long as he outlived that green-blooded Vulcan, it didn't matter a damn what he used to get around.

McCoy and Walter emerged from the airlock and found a greeting party of three Starfleet officers waiting for them as they entered the station. Going by the pips denoting rank on each of their collars, Walter turned and faced the most senior officer, a slightly pudgy man in a burgundy-trimmed uniform. "Welcome to Jupiter Station," the officer said in a warm, inviting voice. "I'm Commander David Clarke, commanding officer, and it's a genuine honor to meet you, Admiral."

Glancing around the bustling space station, McCoy eventually returned the commander's welcoming greeting. "Uh-huh."

Clarke was startled by McCoy's apparent lack of interest. "Um . . . These are two of my officers," he continued, motioning to a petite, smiling blonde and a taller, nervous-looking man. "Lieutenant Lynn White, my security chief, and Lieutenant Reginald Barclay, assistant to the Director of Holographic Imaging and Programming."

Lieutenant White merely nodded, while Barclay instantly began to struggle for words to express what he was feeling. "I . . . I can't believe you're here. . . ." he sputtered awkwardly. "You're practically a living legend. . . ."

Looking up at the taller engineer, McCoy gazed firmly into Barclay's face. "It's better than being a dead one, boy. Now, are you the idiot who's responsible for this cockamamie idea about using holograms as doctors?"

Ensign Walter groaned inwardly as Barclay's eyes widened in horror. "Um . . . I . . . No, Admiral," Barclay began hesitantly. "Doctor Lewis Zimmerman is the idi—er, I mean, the *designer* of the EMH program. I'm just his assistant in charge of developing the EMH's interpersonal skills."

"Hunh. Is that a fact?" remarked McCoy, focusing his eyes upon the younger man. "You folks may be in more trouble than I thought."

Not knowing what else to do at this particular moment, Commander Clarke motioned his hand to indicate a nearby corridor. "Admiral, would you be interested in a tour of Jupiter Station?"

"Not right now, Commander. I think I want to go and see what the devil this Zimmerman fella is up to."

Clarke glanced pleadingly over at Walter, who instantly comprehended the commander's silent wish to keep McCoy away from disrupting Zimmerman's work. "Admiral," she spoke in a soothing tone, "perhaps you'd like to get settled into your quarters first? We can arrange a meeting with Doctor Zimmerman for first thing in the morning if you wish."

McCoy shook his head. "There's plenty of time for that later. You know, I've seen and done an awful lot in my lifetime. I've held newborn babies delivered with my very own hands, witnessed entire worlds form and stars collapse, and watched in total helplessness as my closest friends and family were taken from me one by one. If there's one thing I managed to learn through all that, it's that you do things *now*, just in case you happen to wake up dead tomorrow."

A disturbing silence suddenly filled the docking bay at that moment, something which the admiral fully intended to use to his advantage. "Well, don't just stand there, boy," he said to Barclay with extreme casualness. "Let's go see Doctor Zimmerman."

Completely befuddled by this point, Barclay looked over at Clarke for guidance, but the commander could only offer

a resigned shrug. "All . . . all right, Admiral," Barclay nodded. "If you'll follow me . . ."

Walter sighed to herself and gently escorted McCoy to a
nearby turbolift. Clarke, meanwhile, had no desire to experience the confrontation between McCoy and Zimmerman,
so he gave the polite excuse of having to check station operations and left Lieutenant White to supervise things in his
absence. Annoyed, but also jealous of Clarke's hasty depar-
ture, White boarded the turbolift and quietly began muttering to herself. " 'Angels and ministers of grace, defend
us . . .' "

McCoy grinned at the reference.

Passing upward through several levels of the vast
research station, the turbolift eventually stopped on Deck
10. Barclay led the others down a corridor to a rather unas-
suming door labeled "1013—Holographic Imaging and
Programming" and motioned for everyone to wait outside.
"I'll just be a minute," he explained. "Doctor Zimmerman
is . . . very specific about interruptions, so I'll just let him
know that you're here."

After Barclay entered the research room, Walter turned to
Lieutenant White and gestured with her head toward the
door. "Is Doctor Zimmerman usually this hard to see?"

"I'm not sure," the chief of security replied. "No one usually wants to see him."

A few moments later, Barclay emerged from the room
and the sound of someone bellowing *"I don't care who it is!
Tell them I'm busy!"* could be heard coming from inside.
"Um . . ." Barclay began nervously, ". . . this may not be a
good time. The doctor is running through an important diagnostic right now and doesn't want to be disturbed."

"Oh, for crying out loud," McCoy grumbled in extreme annoyance. "I don't have time for these shenanigans. Out of the way, boy. This Zimmerman fella and I are gonna have a little chat."

"Admiral, I really don't think that's wise—"

McCoy pointed a bony finger up at Barclay's chin and glared at him with the spirit of a man in the prime of his life. "No. What's not wise is you getting in my way and making excuses for some fool who wants to let a damn hologram operate on flesh-and-blood human beings. Now, I'm gonna give you two options here. You can let me in, or Ensign Walter and I can go back to Starfleet Medical and report that Zimmerman is being insubordinate by refusing an admiral access to his project."

Taking a moment to gather his thoughts, Barclay looked in Lieutenant White's direction for guidance. "I'd stand aside, Reg," she suggested. "Zimmerman could probably stand to have a little supervision."

"You . . . you may have a point," Barclay conceded, still feeling extremely uncertain about the idea. "I think I'm going to regret this." He sighed and stepped away from the door.

McCoy gave the engineer a pleased nod as he walked past and entered the lab. "Smart boy. There may be hope for you yet."

To Barclay's surprise, he noticed Ensign Walter smiling fondly at him as she followed McCoy inside. It had been a long time since a woman had smiled that way toward him, and Barclay soon found himself returning the gesture in his typically awkward fashion. Lieutenant White, meanwhile, patted him on the shoulder with genuine appreciation. "So,

Reg . . . do you want to bet on how many seconds it takes for Zimmerman and Admiral McCoy to try to kill each other?"

Barclay released a slow, quiet moan and entered the lab once again.

Inside, Dr. Lewis Zimmerman was busy losing himself in his work. Wearing his favorite lab coat over his Starfleet uniform, Zimmerman was regularly going back and forth across the room, checking and rechecking readouts from various control panels. As a result of all this activity, however, he failed to notice that he was no longer alone.

McCoy studied Zimmerman for a moment, watching the programming specialist continue to work while remaining oblivious about the presence of others around him. Before Barclay could get his supervisor's attention, McCoy uttered a sharp cough.

The sound abruptly stopped Zimmerman in midpace, and he suddenly turned to locate the source of the disturbance. His face instantly formed a displeased scowl upon finding Barclay standing behind him with three others. "I thought I told you to tell them I was busy," he snapped at Barclay.

"I did," Barclay explained, "but this is Admiral McCoy and his attaché, Ensign Walter. They've come from Starfleet Medical to look over the EMH program."

"Oh." Zimmerman began to scratch the back of his receded hairline and looked at the elderly McCoy as if he were a bothersome gnat. "I wasn't aware that Starfleet Medical was sending anyone to check up on me."

"Doctor, I told you about it this morning. You . . . um . . . said that Starfleet Medical could just go to—"

"Never mind," interrupted Zimmerman hastily. "Admiral . . . McCoy, is it?" he inquired. "Well, it's wonderful to meet you, Admiral, but I'm afraid that I've reached a crucial juncture in the development of the EMH's personal interaction matrix. I've got to stick to my schedule because Starfleet wants the EMH to be ready for the launch of the . . . What was that ship's name again?"

"*Voyager,*" said Barclay helpfully.

"Right. So, if you'll excuse me, I really need to get back to my work. . . ."

"Hold on a minute there, Doctor," McCoy called out as Zimmerman started to turn his back to the group. "I've got some concerns about this project of yours, and I didn't come all this way just so I could look at your backside."

Zimmerman huffed a heavy sigh and turned around. "Admiral, I'll be more than happy to hear about whatever you have to say some other time. If you talk with Mister Barclay here, he can relay your problems to me and I'll make every effort to get back to you as soon as some time frees up."

"That's not good enough. I need to talk to you before you ship your goddamn computer playtoy off to operate on living beings."

"What . . . what did you say?" asked Zimmerman with outraged astonishment. "A 'computer playtoy'? The Emergency Medical Hologram is the most sophisticated piece of holographic interactive software ever designed, and you want to compare it to a *computer game?!*"

McCoy edged closer to Zimmerman, heightening the tension already present in the room. "If the shoe fits," he shot back. "My God, I've written medical texts that are probably more qualified to be a physician than your blasted program."

"For your information, the EMH has a medical database taken from over three thousand cultures and forty-seven specific surgeons, including *you* if I recall correctly. You can't possibly disregard that kind of potential just because it isn't alive!"

"A chimpanzee with a laser scalpel is still a chimp."

Now fully angered, Zimmerman leaned over and glared right into McCoy's aged face. "Why, you—"

Ensign Walter quickly inserted herself between the two doctors. "Sirs, *please!*" she called out, abruptly silencing the heated argument. Once the young attaché was satisfied that she had their attention, she switched to a softer tone of voice. "I don't think this bickering is going to get anyone anywhere. Doctor Zimmerman, we came here to examine your work, so why don't you just give us a demonstration of the EMH? Perhaps the admiral's opinion will change once he sees what your project has to offer."

"And maybe tribbles can pilot a starship," McCoy grumbled quietly.

Ignoring the remark, Zimmerman mulled over Ensign Walter's suggestion and eventually gave his approval. "All right, Ensign. If a demonstration will get you people out of my lab, I say let's do it. However, I won't promise that everything will be perfect. Mister Barclay and I have had some problems with the personal interaction matrix, so perhaps a little test will help us work some things out. Reg, if you wouldn't mind . . ."

Barclay walked over to a nearby control panel and, after entering a few commands, he waited for Zimmerman to begin. "Matrix diagnostic ready, Doctor."

"Okay," Zimmerman began, rubbing his hands together. "Computer, activate Emergency Medical Hologram AK-1."

There was a momentary pause as the computer

processed the request. A holographic humanoid form soon materialized into view next to Zimmerman, dressed in a Starfleet uniform with the blue shoulder trim of a medical officer. To McCoy's chagrin, however, the hologram looked exactly like Zimmerman himself, albeit with much tidier hair.

"Please state the nature of the medical emergency," said the EMH in a flat, emotionless manner.

Zimmerman nodded in approval. "Well, at least *that* worked," he remarked as Barclay continued to watch the diagnostic readout. "Now, let's see what happens when we introduce external factors. . . ."

McCoy and Walter watched as Zimmerman approached Lieutenant White and motioned for her to move toward the EMH. "You," he pointed. "You've just been drafted as a patient. Stand over there and let the EMH examine you."

The security chief gave him a questioning stare. "Why? There's nothing wrong with me."

"Indulge me, Lieutenant."

"If you say so," White replied, shaking her head at the situation. Walking over to where the holographic physician was standing, she waited for the EMH to acknowledge her, but received no response. With a mischievous look, White then glanced over at Ensign Walter before turning back to the EMH. "So . . ." she asked flippantly, "what's a nice hologram like you doing in a space station like this?"

Zimmerman was seething inside. "Mister Barclay . . ."

"I found a small code error in the response subroutine," announced Barclay while making adjustments at his control panel. "I think I've got it working properly now."

"Presumably, to be treating someone," the EMH finally

answered in reply to Lieutenant White's question. "Are you in need of medical attention?"

White blinked in surprise. "Um . . . I think so."

"AK-1," interrupted Zimmerman. "we're performing a demonstration of your basic diagnostic capabilities. Please examine Lieutenant White for us."

"Certainly, Doctor Zimmerman." The EMH nodded, holding out his hand. "Tricorder."

Barclay hurriedly typed at his control panel. "Right. Sorry."

Instantly, a standard-issue tricorder materialized in the EMH's open hand. Taking one look at the device, both the hologram and its creator turned and frowned at Barclay. "*Medical* tricorder," they simultaneously corrected in the same jaded tone.

The standard tricorder was abruptly replaced with a medical design, and the EMH quickly began his diagnostic scans of Lieutenant White. Everyone in the room was fixated upon the hologram, while Zimmerman simply hoped that the program would function adequately to satisfy Admiral McCoy and Ensign Walter.

A few moments passed before the EMH finished his scans. "You call this a medical emergency?" he remarked in disbelief.

"Just tell us your analysis, AK-1," sighed Zimmerman.

"Well, I'm sure you'll find this terribly fascinating. It seems the lieutenant has a slightly elevated heart rate, increased muscle tension in the lower rear of her neck and right shoulder blade, and a small contusion on her right hand."

All eyes turned to Lieutenant White. "I punched out an

Andorian smuggler earlier today," she explained casually.

"With good reason, I'm sure," quipped the EMH dryly. "I can treat your injury with a dermal regenerator . . . that is, if it's not too troublesome for somebody to replicate one."

Picking up on the hologram's blatant hint, Barclay used his control panel to replace the medical tricorder with a dermal regenerator. The EMH expertly handled the healing device, and within moments, the security chief's bruise vanished from view.

"There you are," the nameless doctor said as he switched off the regenerator. "Try using a phaser next time."

White studied her healed hand, shrugging at the EMH's suggestion. "But where's the fun in that?"

A broad grin instantly formed on Zimmerman's face. Satisfied with his creation's performance, he approached Admiral McCoy, who had been curiously quiet throughout the examination. "Well, Admiral? I realize that this was only a simplistic exercise in the EMH's capabilities, but surely you can see the potential here."

McCoy slowly walked over to the EMH and peered up into its face. "You think this is a doctor, do you?"

"Of course!" Zimmerman replied with total conviction. "You saw how the EMH was able to make a proper diagnosis and then treat the condition. That's what a doctor does."

Turning his head sharply, McCoy gazed firmly at the confident programmer. "Oh, really? I suppose it never occurred to you to try programming some *humanity* into this damn thing."

The EMH arched an eyebrow at the admiral. "Excuse me?"

"And I thought Vulcans and androids were bad.

Zimmerman, I saw more emotion from that dermal regenerator than I did from your damn twin. Instead of offering comfort, he . . . it . . . whatever . . . was too busy being snide and callous to establish the proper rapport with his patient."

"With all due respect, Admiral," began Zimmerman, "I don't think you realize that the EMH is only supposed to be used for short-term emergency situations in which the medical staff is overburdened or incapacitated. It doesn't need to establish a personal rapport to perform its function."

"He's right," added the EMH. "I'm a doctor, not a counselor."

Upon hearing the hologram's disturbingly familiar remark, McCoy abruptly paused and allowed the smallest hint of a grin to creep into his wrinkled face. "Cute. But I still think a doctor needs to try to make his patients feel more at ease. If there's one thing I've learned over the years . . ."

The debate among McCoy, Zimmerman, and the EMH continued for several more minutes, with no man—or hologram—conceding his position. Barclay simply stood back in stunned amazement at the argument taking place before him, while Lieutenant White and Ensign Walter began whispering to one another in mild amusement.

". . . And you came here in a runabout with the admiral?" asked White quietly. "You're gutsier than I thought."

"He wasn't like this in the runabout," Walter replied. "I'm just surprised you haven't hit Doctor Zimmerman before now."

The security chief smiled. "The day's not over yet, is it?"

Shaking her head, Walter sighed heavily as she saw that McCoy was about to raise his cane at Zimmerman. "I suppose I'd better do something before they end up killing each other."

"Want me to stun them for you?"

Deliberately ignoring the question, Ensign Walter took a deep breath and called out to the admiral. "Um . . . Doctor?"

McCoy, Zimmerman, and the EMH immediately turned to face the young attaché. "Yes?" they replied in unison.

"Sorry," Walter apologized. "I meant Admiral McCoy."

"What is it, Ensign?" asked McCoy, irritated at having his argument interrupted.

"Sir, it's starting to get late. Is there any chance that we could continue this . . . discussion . . . of yours tomorrow? I really think that it would be in everyone's best interest."

"You do, hunh?"

"Yes, Admiral."

Pursing his lip in thought, McCoy glanced over at Zimmerman and the EMH and then gave a relenting nod. "Well . . . all right. I should go and get some dinner, anyway."

Walter sighed once again, this time in pure relief. "I'll be more than happy to escort you, sir."

"There's a cafe about two levels down," offered Zimmerman, surprising everyone with his helpfulness. "The food isn't bad, and the waitresses can be quite charming."

"Thank you, Doctor. If that's all right with you, sir . . ."

"Yeah, whatever," McCoy said with a shrug. "As long as I can get a good, stiff drink." Taking another look at the EMH, he turned and exited the lab, followed closely by Ensign Walter.

As the door shut behind them, Lieutenant White appeared somewhat stunned by the whole experience. "He's . . . an interesting man, I'll give him that."

Zimmerman, meanwhile, had a curious look on his face, one that he would be hard-pressed to explain if asked. "Yes, he is, isn't he?" the programmer remarked with an unusual touch of respect in his voice. All at once, however, Zimmerman slapped his hands together and began to rub them. "Well! Mister Barclay and I have a lot of work to do, so if you'll excuse us . . ."

Later that evening, after McCoy had finished his dinner and been escorted to his quarters by Ensign Walter and Lieutenant White, he secretly made his way back to Zimmerman's lab. Using the special security clearance provided to him as a Starfleet admiral, he was able to gain access to the lab and was relieved to find that Zimmerman and Barclay had apparently left for the night.

Earlier, McCoy had made mental notes of how the two men operated the control panels for the EMH database and proceeded to use that knowledge to suit his own needs. "Computer," he announced in a small whisper, "activate the Emergency Medical Hologram."

The EMH rippled into existence once again. "Please state the nature of the medical— Oh, it's you." The holographic doctor frowned upon recognizing McCoy. "Came back to insult me some more, did you?"

McCoy grinned. "Not this time. I wanted to . . . hell, I don't know. . . . I guess I wanted to talk a little."

A puzzled expression formed on the hologram's face. "I'm afraid that I don't understand."

"You're not supposed to, so kindly shut up and let an old man ramble for a bit. You know, I've got a real problem with all of this . . ."

"Really? I didn't notice."

". . . But I never thought about *why* I had a problem until I went to my quarters tonight. There was a mirror by the door, and do you know what I saw when I looked into it?"

"A crotchety old man?" answered the EMH dryly.

"Besides that, dammit."

"I don't know. What?"

McCoy pointed to his own face, weathered with time and the experiences of a full, rich life. "Mortality. That's what motivates a doctor—the awareness that people can die and that your knowledge and skill can possibly prevent that from happening. A doctor has to understand mortality before he can fight against it."

"So how does that apply to medical holograms?"

"Easy. A hologram can't die. If you can't die, you can't understand mortality."

The EMH pondered that for a moment. "But we can be deleted," he countered. "Our systems can degrade and lose the ability to function properly."

"That's not the same thing," replied McCoy. "Deleting a blasted program isn't the same as someone dying."

"Unless you're the program."

The admiral abruptly paused, allowing the hologram's comment to sink in. "Yeah, well . . . maybe from that point of view."

"I'm glad you agree. It certainly took you long enough."

"Oh, brother," groaned McCoy, shaking his head at the EMH's condescending tone. "You're an arrogant thing, aren't you? Just like your creator."

"Is that a problem? My personal opinions should have no bearing on my performance as a physician."

"Let me clue you in on something, hologram. Whether

they realize it or not, Starfleet needs people who can put somebody's nose out of joint. The higher-ups are always acting so damn proper and holier-than-thou that they need a good kick in the pants to remind them about what really matters. If you can do that and not end up getting yourself deleted by the captain, *then* you'll be a good doctor."

The EMH gave McCoy a curious look. "So where do you stand now, Admiral? Are you going to drop your objections about the Emergency Medical Hologram or do you still have more concerns?"

"Oh, I still have some concerns," McCoy answered, looking around Zimmerman's lab with no real interest, "but I've heard enough to keep me from yelling at Starfleet Medical for a while."

"Glad to hear it," came a voice from behind.

McCoy turned around to find Lewis Zimmerman entering the lab from a side door connected to an adjoining room. "Where the blazes did you come from?" McCoy asked gruffly.

"I've been working on some EMH crisis simulations in the room next door," explained Zimmerman. "When my monitors detected you using your clearance to gain access to the EMH, I decided to wait and see what you were up to."

"Hmpf. Sounds like you just wanted to eavesdrop."

Zimmerman suddenly projected a guilty appearance, but the programmer was unable to deny his true motive. "I suppose that goes without saying."

Surprised by Zimmerman's honesty, McCoy gestured his thumb at the holographic doctor. "So this is the future of Starfleet medical officers, hunh?"

Beaming proudly at his creation, Zimmerman gave a confirming nod. "At least in part. I'm not trying to replace living doctors, you know, just help them when they need it."

"Well, I suppose that's all right then." Unable to resist tormenting Zimmerman one more time, McCoy pretended to gaze harshly at the programmer. "However, there's still one very important thing you haven't told me about the EMH."

Zimmerman groaned inwardly. "And what's that, Admiral?"

"Does it drink?"

I Am Klingon

Ken Rand

Counselor Deanna Troi leaped around the corner, phaser ready, and blasted the Klingon by the door to engineering. The warrior fell, and his half-raised disruptor pistol flew from his grip, skittering down the corridor. An acrid stench filled the air of the *Enterprise* as lavender blood flowed.

"Freeze." Deanna aimed her phaser at the other Klingon.

This warrior had both hands buried in the ripped-open access panel, no doubt trying to rig a bypass to the computer-locked door. Caught with her disruptor holstered, no weapon in hand, the warrior looked at first surprised, then angry. She growled, teeth bared and eyes blazing defiance at the phaser pointed at her five meters away. She growled, but she stood still.

"Take your hands out of there," Deanna ordered.

The Klingon looked for options in the bare corridor. Her glance skittered over her comrade's smoking corpse, to his disruptor too far away to reach, to her own holstered disruptor and *d'k tahg* knife, to the phaser aimed at her. Her defiant glare melted to resignation as she seemed to see no way out.

Her shoulders sagged and she took a step away from the panel.

"Now you will—"

Deanna didn't finish the command. A triumphant glint flickered in the Klingon's eyes as she cast a quick glance over Deanna's shoulder. Deanna whirled, crouched, ready to fire.

Nobody there.

Turning back toward the lone Klingon, Deanna got a glimpse of the warrior's boot slamming into her head. The hammer blow knocked her to the floor.

An instant later, through pain-blurred eyes looking up at the ceiling, Deanna saw a *d'k tahg* arc in a smooth, lethal sweep down toward her exposed throat.

"Computer! End simulation!" Lieutenant Worf barked.

The corridor, the weapons, and the Klingon invaders vanished, replaced by stark black walls and yellow holodeck grid lines. Chief security officer Worf appeared and knelt over the dazed Betazoid. "Are you all right, Deanna?"

Deanna, panting, sat up. Worf helped remove her safety helmet. Her sweat-soaked black hair fell free. She blinked and tried to focus.

"She moved so fast, Worf. I've never seen such—"

"You moved as if asleep." Worf helped her stand on trembling legs, the helmet in her limp hands. "What went wrong?"

"I, I turned away for an instant. Just an instant."

"That error cost your life. Assume the warrior, after killing you, gains access to engineering and succeeds in sabotaging the ship. Your failure cost not only your life, but your shipmates'. Never let an adversary out of your sight. Didn't they teach you that at the academy? What else?"

"What—what else? Well, I, I—"

"Why did you turn your back on her? You knew she had a *d'k tahg.*"

"I, I—but she'd surrendered. I *had* her."

"jeghbe' tlhInganpu'," Worf said, reverting to Klingonese.

"What?"

"Klingons do not surrender."

"Worf, I read the surrender in her eyes, the way she carried her body. Not a Betazoid sensing. Anybody could have read it. She'd surrendered."

"Klingons do *not* surrender. I programmed this one to appear to do so. *My* deception. You should have killed her the instant you had her in your sights."

"But she—"

"Deanna, you know better. You forgot. You are too dependent on your Betazoid senses, even when they don't work. They are useless on sims. You fooled yourself."

"Klingons don't surrender, yes, I know. That is, I *should* have known, but—"

"But you forgot. Then what happened?"

"She looked at—at somebody behind me. I thought she did, anyway. She tricked me. I fell for it."

"That is not the problem."

"I don't understand."

Worf sighed. "We do not surrender or fake surrender. *not toj tlhInganpu';* Klingons never bluff. We *face* our enemy. Like the surrender pose, the look over your shoulder was something I programmed in, to reinforce the lesson. Again, it was not Klingon behavior. Again, you did not recognize it."

Deanna nodded. "You're right. I *knew* that. You fooled

me—no," she sighed and kneaded a bruise on her jaw, "I fooled myself. All this violence, it's, it's—I just need more practice. I'll get it yet."

The determination in her voice did little to assuage Worf's disappointment. Concern for Deanna's welfare and belief that *he*'d failed, not her, prompted his own sigh and a gentle touch on her slender shoulder. "You should report to sickbay." He allowed himself a moment of un-Klingon-like compassion. "See to those bruises. We will run the sim again later. After I make a few adjustments."

Deanna smiled, brushed Worf's cheek affectionately with her fingertips, handed him the helmet, and left the holodeck.

Worf stood alone. He breathed deeply to relax his troubled mind. Not Deanna's fault. She was intelligent and resourceful. Though slight of stature, she was strong in mind and spirit, and although she abhorred the violence, she'd committed to help Worf make his new training program work.

Had her dependence on her Betazoid senses betrayed her? If so, Worf mused once again, he had erred in letting her be his first test subject. That wasn't it. The fault lay deeper, and Worf blamed himself.

She truly does not understand the Klingon way.

Worf warred in his mind between his growing affection for Deanna and his dedication to duty. He could not—absolutely *would not*—allow that struggle to cause harm to his shipmates, including Deanna.

Hence his new training program and his choice of Deanna as first subject to test it. His routine vigilance as security officer, Starfleet Academy training, other training sims, and his daily *Mok'bara* martial arts sessions went only so far in preparing the crew to confront an enemy. *If Deanna could win in violent combat—hand-to-hand against Klingon warriors, the toughest adversary imaginable—then any crew member could be trained to defeat any adversary.* So the theory went.

With the Borg a new threat to the Federation, Captain Picard had approved testing the new program, devised with Lieutenant Commander Data's help.

But Deanna kept failing. She'd been killed repeatedly.

Built-in safety systems, designed to prevent injury on the holodeck, impeded Worf's efforts to maintain the high violence level he thought necessary. Data, with the captain's approval, had helped devise safety overrides for the program that necessitated the use of a helmet and other protective gear.

It still wasn't working. It was as if Deanna fought in a stupor with blinders and padded gloves.

Worf fingered the dent in the back of the helmet that protected Deanna when she'd been kicked to the floor. The kick had been simulated, but the fall had been hard and real. *I'm going to have to replicate stronger gear.*

He shook his head in frustration. He'd been as tough as he could be, had cranked up the program as high as it could go. That wasn't the problem. Deanna could fight well. But the subtleties escaped her.

She just does not understand the Klingon way.

If Deanna didn't understand the Klingon way, then nobody did—except Captain Jean-Luc Picard and Commander William T. Riker, who'd served on Klingon ships. That meant the program had failed and the crew was at risk. That meant Worf had failed.

The thought of failure frustrated him. Anger boiled in his blood and he clenched his fists and growled.

Which gave him an idea.

Anger. Of course. SeymoH QeH: *Anger excites. Why didn't I see it before? Anger is the missing element. Deanna is not angry enough, not made to be angry enough. Again, my fault. But how do I—*

"Picard to Lieutenant Worf."

"Worf here."

"Report to my ready room immediately."

"Aye, sir."

Worf headed to the bridge. At the turbolift, the ship's executive officer, Commander Will Riker, joined him.

"How's the new security simulation working out?" Riker asked.

"It is not yet ready for general use by the crew, sir."

"Problems?"

Worf glared at Riker, at first affronted. Then he took in the concern in Riker's piercing gaze and relaxed. Though Riker and Deanna had once been lovers, Riker's present concern didn't relate to the memory of those intimate times. The two were friends now, and Riker was concerned as a friend. And as Deanna's commanding officer.

Riker had at first opposed using Deanna as Worf's first— what word had he used? *Guinea pig?* Deanna had insisted on helping. She helped win the captain's approval. Riker had once provoked Deanna to anger, Worf remembered. It helped her get bridge command certification.

Yes, I'm on the right track. Anger, or rather, Deanna's lack of it, is the problem.

"There are problems," Worf admitted. "I will fix them."

"Maybe we should reconsider real-time war games in the corridors, but—" He shrugged.

"Too risky." Worf dismissed the notion firmly, again. The captain had already agreed with Worf. *Who would know good war games from a real emergency?*

The turbolift door opened on the bridge.

"*Qapla',*" Riker said: "Success." He assumed command of the bridge, and Worf strode to the adjacent ready room.

He found Captain Picard waiting for him with Lieutenant Commander Geordi La Forge, the chief engineer, and Lieutenant Commander Data.

Picard nodded to indicate a chair, and Worf sat, waiting for his captain to speak. Picard got right to the point.

"We've taken on what appears to be a lifeboat which we found adrift. It's in cargo bay one right now."

"Why wasn't I summoned before it was brought aboard?"

"It was brought in under a force field," Picard said, "just in case. You were observing your new training simulation and I didn't deem it necessary to interfere at the time."

"Geordi and I examined the vehicle," Data said in his emotionless android voice. "Though our search was cursory, you will find our examination adequate. We determined it represents no threat to the *Enterprise*. It is most intriguing—"

"Worf, you won't believe this," Geordi butted in, his excitement volcanic. "It's a Klingon ship—I mean, a lifeboat from a Klingon ship. It's a hundred years old. A century! Can you believe it? I've never seen anything—"

A lifeboat? On a Klingon vessel?

"We look forward to your detailed engineering report, Mister La Forge. Meanwhile, Mister Worf, the reason you're here is because there is a passenger. A Klingon. That is, we *think* he's Klingon, but—" Picard shrugged.

"But what? Either he is or is not. I do not understand."

"The passenger is alive," Picard said. "He was found in a stasis field. Doctor Crusher did an examination and ordered him moved to sickbay."

"Sir, you still haven't explained—"

"Crusher to Captain Picard."

"Picard here."

"Captain, you'd better get down to sickbay. I think Lieutenant Worf should come too. Our patient has revived."

Concern etched the corners of Dr. Crusher's mouth as she met Picard and Worf at the sickbay door with Geordi and Data. "I'm sorry, Captain. I had to sedate him seconds after he revived, right after I called. He awoke, looked around, bolted up, and went berserk." She nodded toward a nurse sitting on a nearby bed. Deanna sat by the nurse, an arm around her, murmuring. "Scared Ensign Hammond badly, I'm afraid, though she's not hurt. Thankfully, Deanna was here."

"Counselor Troi?" Worf said. "How so?"

"She'd just walked in for treatment of minor bruises— your training program, I believe—when the patient revived. She distracted the patient long enough for me to administer a sedative. She did a brave thing, under the circumstances—"

"I look forward to hearing the whole story," Picard said. "Later. Meanwhile, how's our guest?"

"Harmless for the moment. Sedated. See for yourself."

She nodded toward a bed across the room. A force field flickered around the bed.

The officers approached the bed. Worf frowned.

The man on the bed did not appear Klingon; he lacked the heavy, corrugated forehead characteristic of Klingon physiology. Thick black eyebrows arched up on a smooth humanoid forehead. A long, tangled moustache and a small trimmed beard framed his glistening, almond-dark face. The beard looked new, the Klingon looked young. *About my age, or only a few years younger.*

The helpless, slack-jawed man looked part Klingon and part human. To Worf, he looked like a pathetic joke, an aberration.

He pointed a finger, almost touching the force field. "This man is *not* Klingon," Worf said, disgusted.

Dr. Crusher sighed. "My internal scan shows Klingon physiology; only the external is—*different.*"

"Obviously," Worf snorted.

"He's been bioengineered," Dr. Crusher continued, "deliberately made to look un-Klingon."

"What do you make of it, Mister Worf?" Picard asked.

"It is a mystery, Captain. See the uniform?"

"Go on."

"It is the uniform of a Klingon warrior, but it is an old style, long unused." Worf shook his head. "And a lifeboat? From a Klingon ship? Not a sleeper ship, but a *lifeboat?* As if he'd *fled?*"

Picard nodded. "Un-Klingon-like. Mysteries. Not like the Klingon sleeper ship, *T'Ong.* You handled that well two years ago, Mister Worf. Take charge here. I want answers. You may have Mister La Forge and Mister Data to assist you."

Picard turned to the android. "Your comments, Mister Data?"

"Sir, the vessel *is* of Klingon design. I found writing in *pIqaD*, the Klingon script, and the computer is an old Klingon style. The uniform and other factors confirm its Klingon origin and indicate an approximate age of 100.26 years. Despite all we know of Klingon ways, the vessel appears consistent with a lifeboat. It is not a sleeper ship."

"Impossible," Worf and Picard muttered together.

Picard glanced at Worf and proceeded. "Something's not right here, and you're going to find out what it is, Mister Worf. Start immediately and report anything—"

"Sir," Dr. Crusher's voice grew stern, "may I remind you this is *my* patient, and he is under sedation. In addition—"

"Can you revive—"

"*In addition.*" She took a breath, then lowered her voice. "Sir, there's something you should know." She took in Worf as well as the captain. Picard nodded for her to continue.

"Captain, this man is dying. He was dying when he went into stasis."

As Dr. Crusher spoke, Deanna gazed at the reclining Klingon. In her soft, dark eyes Worf saw compassion. The look annoyed Worf and he gritted his teeth. *He is likely a coward who deserted battle. He deserved no compassion.*

"I see," Picard said. "Can you do anything?"

She shook her head and looked away.

"How long—"

"Twenty-four hours. At most."

* * *

"There were humans here," the Klingon said with an odd accent. "Did you kill them?" He tried to rise on one elbow. "How long have I—"

Worf put a strong, steady hand on his shoulder. "They are gone."

The warrior lay on a bed in a small, bare isolation room adjacent to sickbay; all distinguishing features had been removed from the room. Worf agreed with Dr. Crusher that the man should be revived with as few jolts as possible. The doctor said his condition was such that any shock or exertion could kill him instantly, despite his redundant internal systems.

After Worf changed to Klingon garb, Crusher reluctantly agreed to leave him alone with her patient under the condition that she'd observe from a nearby room on a security camera. Deanna stood at Dr. Crusher's side.

Worf had a hypospray in a pocket, also at Dr. Crusher's insistence.

The warrior sagged, still groggy from the sedative. "What is this place?"

"Do you require water? Food?"

He shook his head. "I am K'pril, son of Korpi. Warrior."

"I am Worf, son of Mogh."

"I do not know your house."

"Nor I yours."

"We have much to talk about," K'pril said. "Do we not?"

"We do."

"What is this place?" He sat up, sniffing the air. "This does not smell like a Klingon vessel."

"It is not."

"Where are we?"

"You should first ask what year this is."

K'pril looked hard at Worf. "Why?"

Worf told him, and watched. K'pril's expression changed from shock and disbelief to anger in swift succession. Within three breaths, he recovered. He stood abruptly, fierce determination spreading lips over gritted teeth, a growl starting deep in his throat.

Worf stopped K'pril's hand short of the hilt of his *d'k tahg* sheath. The sheath was empty. Dr. Crusher had ordered the weapon removed. K'pril hadn't noticed yet that it was gone; he kept his eyes fixed on Worf's.

When K'pril staggered to his feet, for the first time, Worf saw how small he was. K'pril was a head shorter than Worf, and probably fifty pounds lighter. *A runt,* Worf thought, as he held the groggy warrior's *d'k tahg* hand rigid without effort. *Why wasn't he killed at birth?*

"Why do you stop me, Worf?" K'pril grunted.

"You would kill me for telling you the truth?"

The warrior sagged. "No. *Me. Hegh'bat.* Something went wrong. So many years? It means I have failed."

"Failed what?"

"My mission."

"Tell me of your mission. The vessel you were found in looks like a lifeboat, yet it looks Klingon. You were in stasis. You speak Klingon, yet your accent is wrong. You do not even look like a Klingon." Worf added to himself: *And you are too weak to be a warrior.*

K'pril seemed to shrink in on himself. For a moment a defeated look, like the one Worf had programmed into his sim, filmed his eyes. The moment passed and he returned Worf's hard gaze.

"I will tell you. Then you, Worf, will tell me things I want to know. Agreed?"

Worf nodded, and the little warrior told his story.

Admiral Loski was military governor of an entire star system, three planets and a dozen moons recently colonized by the empire far from the Homeworld. In the earliest days of the war on the Federation, through military misadventures in the sector and some freak accidents and coincidences, System Loski, as it was known then, got cut off. As Klingon commanders are trained to do in such cases, Loski carried on.

His idea of how to do so stretched the boundaries of military ingenuity. Loski had scientific pretensions. Another scientist, K'pril, helped devise a plan to infiltrate the Federation. The plan was to bioengineer Klingon physiology so warriors could infiltrate targets not accessible to overt Klingon forces and attack from within—in hand-to-hand combat.

The physical transformation was implemented in individuals in phases. It worked. Despite the physical grotesqueness involved, it met with great joy among warriors under Loski's command. It was accepted because it meant a chance to fight, not from a distance but hand-to-hand as a Klingon warrior was meant to fight. In fact, the idea gained such popular support that nearly every Klingon Defense Force member in the system, from the lowest clerk to the highest officer, underwent the transformation, or some stages of it.

Early probes into certain Federation facilities, like Deep Space Station K-7 and Sherman's Planet, with partially altered warriors and commanders, proved successful. Partially altered, Commander Kor's troops faced the

Federation in the Organian affair. For a time, the Federation believed the modified physiology prevailed throughout the whole empire. To Loski's delight, his warriors even got aboard a Federation ship and examined it. The ship: the notorious *U.S.S. Enterprise* . . .

"The *Enterprise?*" Worf said.

"You have heard of this ship? After so many years?"

"I have. But never mind. What role did you play in this, this—scheme?"

"I had personal motive in seeing the project succeed. My house has produced scientists for generations. I followed my family's ways, but I wanted to be a warrior. I have a warrior's heart," K'pril thumped his chest, "and look at me. Do you not see the body of a warrior?"

Worf said nothing as the little Klingon continued.

Doubts eventually arose among some subcommanders. Loski was challenged in personal combat several times. There also emerged rumor that the Homeworld had reestablished contact with System Loski and had ordered the project halted, and that Loski had ignored orders and gone renegade. Chaos and civil war erupted.

K'pril stayed loyal to Loski. The civil war lasted for months until the tide turned and Loski decided to order his flagship into a suicide attack against superior forces.

K'pril was aboard that ship.

Three days before the suicide attack, K'pril underwent the first stages of the bioengineering process.

He knew he had a rare genetic trait that would make transformation fatal for him. But he did it now, before the flagship died in battle, because he had an idea. To die with the ship, with his commander, would be honorable, as would

Hegh'bat, ritual suicide. But K'pril wanted to die a true war-rior's death, fighting hand-to-hand, as a Klingon warrior was meant to die.

"We were close to Federation space at the time," he said. "We knew of Federation warships in the area, and we had intelligence the *Enterprise* was among them. My plan would permit my life's ambition."

"Your commander agreed?"

"He did not know. He was too busy with his war. I got help from friends."

"You built a lifeboat and launched it toward Federation space? I am certain the Federation, even then, knew Klingons did not have such things. How did you know you would be rescued by a Federation vessel?"

"Remember, at the time we'd fooled the Federation about our very appearance. Besides, the Federation is driven by curiosity. Even if suspicious, they would take on the lifeboat just to see what it really was. They are also driven by com-passion. A weakness. I intended to exploit both."

"You hoped the *Enterprise* would pick you up?"

K'pril shrugged. "Or another Federation warship. It did not matter. One where I might die as a Klingon warrior is meant to die: fighting."

"And you were a scientist?"

Worf must have signaled revulsion in his facial expres-sion and body language, because K'pril grabbed Worf's shoulders and stood facing him, glaring up.

"Was," K'pril spat. "Now I am a warrior. I, K'pril, son of Korpi, have chosen to single-handedly attack a Federation ship. Can you say there is no honor in such a death? Can you say I am not a warrior? Can you?"

K'pril's grip was weak, and Worf fought an urge to laugh in mockery. His hand clenched the hypospray in his pocket.

"Have you ever fought?" Worf asked.

K'pril frowned, puzzled, as if the question were a problem he needed to calculate.

"Who *have* you fought?" Worf persisted.

K'pril stepped back and took a challenging stance. "Question my honor and I will kill you."

Worf said nothing. K'pril had made an honorable choice, even though he wasn't trained to fight. *But there are complications you don't know about, scientist-turned-warrior.*

K'pril took Worf's silence for agreement. Thinking himself victorious, he relaxed.

"Now I have told you my story. You have agreed to answer my questions."

Worf nodded.

K'pril spread his little hands and looked around the room, nose wrinkled in distaste. "Where is this place?"

"I assure you, you are quite safe here."

"Safe?" K'pril's fists balled and he glared up at Worf. "Safe? I do not want to be safe. *tlhIngan jIH!* I am a Klingon! A warrior! I want to fight!"

Worf braced himself for attack. "You do not understand—"

"Oh, but I think I do, Worf, son of Mogh. *You* are the one with a strange accent, not I. You don't talk like a Klingon. I was a scientist in the Klingon Defense Force, but now I'm a warrior—and a better one than you."

Worf growled and one hand went toward his empty holster—

—Which K'pril noticed for the first time. He gasped.

"Unarmed? How can that be?" K'pril looked quickly around the room, sniffing. *"toH!* I have it now. You said this was not a Klingon ship. *Federation?* Yes, I see the truth of it now in your eyes. You're not Klingon. You're—"

With a growl, K'pril reached for his *d'k tahg.* It had been removed, but he had only a second to notice.

Worf moved fast. He wanted to strike K'pril down, but he remembered Dr. Crusher, watching with Deanna, and her warning that the little Klingon might die if overstressed. The man's weakness sickened Worf. Still, he fought back his revulsion and hit K'pril with a hypospray tap to his neck.

Thinking the hypospray had killed him, K'pril smiled weakly, softening his features. "I die a warrior," he muttered as his eyes glazed over in unconsciousness.

Worf didn't think about those desperate warrior eyes as he lowered K'pril's limp body back onto the bed. He thought instead of the compassion for the warrior, compassion he knew emanated now from Deanna's watching eyes.

Again, the thought irritated him.

They arrived quickly, but a moment before Dr. Crusher and Deanna entered the room, Worf knew what he must do.

"I shouldn't have let you talk me into this," Dr. Crusher muttered, scanning her patient with a medical tricorder. "I *told* you. His condition is fragile. The shock might have killed him."

"You've hurt him," Deanna accused. She spared a barbed glance at Worf before bending over the unconscious Klingon, fussing with him tenderly.

Worf sighed. He didn't try to defend himself. *I suppose I expected as much.* He kept an irritated retort sealed between clenched teeth and took their abuse in silence. His mind was elsewhere. Planning.

He left the women as soon as he could and went to his room, where he took precious minutes to study history—restudy it.

Worf prided himself on his knowledge of Klingon history. He'd heard only scant mention of a bioengineering affair, nothing important, in the early war years with the Federation. It was a minor incident, though it had spanned several years; he'd paid it no attention. Now he knew why.

"The High Council was embarrassed, so they buried it in the footnotes," Worf muttered to himself.

Also: the house of K'pril was gone, dissolved in disgrace long ago. K'pril was alone. He didn't know how alone.

Federation records were easy to find once Worf knew what to look for. Until today, he'd had no reason to do so. Federation officials didn't hide their early misidentification of Klingon physiology or offer excuses.

The Organian affair had been well documented. Worf knew of it—Kirk and the old *Enterprise,* and Klingon Commander Kor. The Organian Peace Treaty. Until now, he'd had no reason to look at visual images from then. From the old records, K'pril's bizarre, mutant face looked back at Worf.

"Worf to Captain Picard."

"Yes, Mister Worf ?"

"I wish to speak with you, sir. In private."

A pause. Then: "In my ready room."

"I just talked with Beverly." Picard sat behind his ready-room desk as Worf entered. Worf remained standing. "I viewed a record of your conversation with K'pril."

Worf said nothing. The captain's expression looked odd.

"K'pril will soon be leaving us, Mister Worf."

"I know, sir. Eighteen hours, according to Doctor Crusher."

"Before then."

"Sir?"

"It's out of our hands." Picard's voice rose as if expecting an argument. "I've informed Starfleet Command and they have notified Empire authorities. We rendezvous with a Klingon warship, the *Pagh,* in two hours."

"Sir, you know what will happen if K'pril returns to Klingon hands."

"I know. Old soldiers never die, they just—"

"They do not even *exist.* He shames the empire. This is why the truth has been suppressed over the years. Even his family has been extinguished."

Picard's lips tightened into a thin line. "He must be prevented from committing *Hegh'bat* while aboard the *Enterprise.* Is that clear?"

"When he gets on board the *Pagh*—"

"When he is given over to the custody of his own people, his welfare is no longer our concern. Is *that* clear?"

Worf blinked several times, stung by the captain's rebuke.

Picard softened. "Believe me, Worf, I don't like it either. Inside that little scientist beats a warrior's heart. Poor man. He'd tried so hard. So brave and desperate." He shook his bald head. "So futile. His family disgraced, you say? There seems to be no right way to end this."

"No *right* way, sir. But an *honorable* one."

An expression formed on the captain's narrow face. Worf

recognized it: curiosity. *Curiosity,* K'pril had said. *A Federation weakness. But Picard understands Klingon ways.*

Picard tugged on his tunic. "I'll hear you out, Mister Worf. But this better be good."

"The *Enterprise,*" K'pril hissed between gritted teeth, looking around at the bare walls. Worf checked K'pril's wrist restraints again before he nodded to two security officers.

"Let's go," Worf said. The officers took up positions flanking their charge.

Worf wore his Starfleet uniform, and K'pril glared hatred at him.

"Perhaps you should let Doctor Crusher sedate him," Deanna muttered, arms folded, "and you could carry him out like a sack of garbage." Worf ignored the uncharacteristic sarcasm. He felt thankful Dr. Crusher herself wasn't also present to amplify the barb and complicate matters further.

"Why do you do this, Worf ?" K'pril's eyes blazed with anger, narrow shoulder muscles bunched.

"I am under orders—"

"*Federation* orders. *tlhIngan jIH!* I am a Klingon! What are you?"

Worf bit back a retort. He jerked his head toward the open door to the corridor, a silent order. K'pril spat. *Qo':* I refuse.

Patience lapsed, Worf grabbed for the man's arm. K'pril whirled suddenly and kicked. The sudden attack, unexpectedly agile, caught Worf off guard. The blow hit him on the jaw and knocked him backwards. His head thunked against the floor.

In the haze on the borderline of consciousness, he heard K'pril howl in attack, phasers blast, and Deanna cry in pain.

Seconds later, Worf awoke to the acrid smell of burnt flesh and stood, dizzy. In the room lay two dead security officers, the restraints lying on the floor. K'pril and Deanna were gone.

Shouts from the corridor. K'pril still had Deanna and was using her for—*for what?*

Worf knew, and he smiled with grim satisfaction as he stood. K'pril would finish his mission, even if delayed one hundred years. He'd go to engineering or the bridge. He'd kill as many people as he could and destroy the ship. If he could.

The shouting came from near the turbolift.

Worf ran that way.

He tapped his combadge and shouted over the blaring security klaxon. "Security. Where is he?"

"The bridge, sir. He's got Counselor Troi."

"Do not fire on him. I repeat: do not fire."

Worf ran to his room, not far away. There, he grabbed two *bat'leth* swords. They would do.

He got to the service corridor outside the bridge moments later, where security guards had cordoned off the area.

"Systems have been shut down, sir," one officer said. "He can't hurt the ship and he can't get out."

"Casualties?"

"Three. In there." He nodded toward the bridge. "Ensigns Hanson and Stern. And Commander Riker. All dead."

"Who is in there with him?"

"Counselor Troi. He's threatening to kill—"

"I know." Worf stepped onto the bridge.

"He has a phaser," the officer warned.

Worf ignored him.

Deanna sat in the chair at the defense and weapons station, hair disarrayed, hands on the computer board in front of her. K'pril held a phaser against her neck.

"The computer's been locked out," Deanna said, voice cracking. "I can't get in."

"Stand away from her." Worf aimed his phaser. He didn't look at the bodies.

K'pril ignored him, scanning the weapons panel as if to divine its secrets.

"I will shoot you," Worf said.

"You will not." K'pril pressed the phaser into Deanna's neck with one hand, fiddled with the computer board with the other. "If you do, I will kill your friend as I die. Or maybe you will miss and kill her and then I will kill *you*."

"You are a coward."

K'pril barked a contemptuous laugh. "You cannot provoke me, Federation lackey." He didn't look up.

"Klingons do not take hostages."

K'pril spat. "I'll swap you adage for adage. How about this one: Klingons are resourceful. I'm outnumbered by hundreds. What is the crew complement on the *Enterprise?* A thousand? This human," he jabbed the phaser again and Deanna cried out in pain, "evens the odds."

Worf tossed one *bat'leth* across the room. It landed on the floor behind K'pril. K'pril turned, saw the blade. He understood.

"You and I, traitor?" He smiled.

Worf held the other *bat'leth* and stepped down behind the helm. "To the death."

"Your troops will not interfere?"

"I so order it."

"Louder. I barely heard you."

Worf shouted. "No one interferes. Understood?"

A small chorus acknowledged the order.

Worf faced K'pril. "Satisfied?"

"I would rather kill a Klingon traitor on the bridge of the *Enterprise* than a hundred Federation soldiers anywhere else." K'pril jerked Deanna by the neck and thrust her toward Worf. She stumbled. Worf, watching his enemy, with one hand helped her stand. In the other hand, he held his *bat'leth* ready.

"Worf, you shouldn't—" Deanna began.

"Go." Worf pushed her away, but he didn't watch to see if she left. He faced the enemy.

K'pril stood away from the weapons station and tossed the phaser aside. He picked up the *bat'leth* and fingered its deadly, gracefully curved blades. He seemed to relax and stand taller.

"*Heghlu'meH QaQ jajvam*," he said with reverence.

"It is a good day to die," Worf echoed the traditional salute in English.

Then they fought.

The klaxons had stopped. On the *Enterprise* bridge, two Klingon warriors fought. They grunted in exertion and roared battle cries in fierce counterpoint to the crash and clang of the *bat'leth* being wielded with deadly force. They tripped over the three dead bodies, slipping on the bloody floor, but they rose and fought on. They smashed computers, monitors, and other equipment as they slashed, kicked, and dodged.

K'pril was smaller, but he was faster, more agile and more determined, more vicious. He danced away from blow after blow and countered with lightning jabs, cutting Worf on an arm with this pass, on a leg with another. K'pril laughed and taunted, increasing Worf's frustration. At last, muscles rubbery and bleeding from a dozen small cuts, Worf made a mistake and stumbled, his *bat'leth* slipping from his sweaty hands.

K'pril stood over Worf's exposed throat. "After you die," he panted, "maybe I will fight a *real* warrior." He raised the *bat'leth* over his head.

"No!" Deanna cried out. Worf saw a blur of Federation uniform; Deanna, rushing at K'pril from behind him, *d'k tahg* raised high. Face distorted in rage, she plunged the blade into K'pril's back.

K'pril's eyes widened. A brief smile formed on his lips, lavender with his blood; then he fell. The *bat'leth* dropped from his hands.

"Computer! End simulation!" Deanna's voice.

The bridge disappeared, along with the two blood-soaked *bat'leth*, the *d'k tahg*, the two dead crew members and Riker, and the simulated Deanna Troi.

Worf lay on the bare holodeck floor. Uninjured. K'pril lay a few meters away on his back, motionless, Dr. Crusher bent over him, tricorder poised. Deanna, the real Deanna, stood over Worf, fists balled at her hips.

Dr. Crusher stood. "Neurological system failure. Even his redundant systems. He's dead."

Deanna's lips trembled and she glared at Worf through tears. "You have a lot of explaining to do."

Picard kneaded a cup of Earl Grey tea, hot, in his hands. He spoke pensively across the ready-room desk. "All's well with Starfleet Command about our incident."

"Somebody will ask about this in the future," Worf said, "and I will answer, 'It is a long story.'"

"It took some doing. Deanna's report helped. She and Beverly could have had our hides nailed to the barn door."

"Sir?"

Picard looked up. "An old Earth adage." He sighed. "It was inevitable they would have found out, you know, Deanna and Beverly. They *are* good officers. The best."

"Indeed."

"The timing. Doctor Crusher assured Starfleet K'pril's sudden death was due to complications related to his disease. Not our fault. The empire has interpreted her report to show K'pril died in battle. Simulated or not, an honorable death."

"There is a chance his house may be restored to honor."

"A delicate piece of work, that report. Brilliant. As I said, they're good officers. And friends."

"We *are* blessed, sir."

"I hope you've come to grips with this, Worf. I have. At first I thought that I followed the Klingon way as I understood it. I later realized I allowed your impromptu simulation for human reasons: compassion. I felt sorry for him." He paused and fixed Worf with a frown. "Do you understand what I mean, Worf?"

"Human emotions are difficult to understand. I am trying to learn."

"Yes." Picard nodded. "Data has trouble with human emotions too. Too bad he wasn't on hand to help you with your makeshift sim."

"I *was* pressed for time. But it was good that Data was not involved." Worf sighed and leaned forward. "Sir, I have explained to Deanna. I said I was solely responsible, that I modified the training sim to accommodate the escape scenario in a hurry, that Data was not available to help, that I was in error and, and—"

"Go on."

"And I apologized for allowing her into the simulation."

"You didn't allow it. It was a mistake."

"Sir, I should have programmed her out. If I had known a simulated Deanna would have—*could* have—acted as it—as *she*—did. She killed K'pril. Stabbed him in the back. That was not my plan. It was—was—"

"An unexpected, unforeseen, and unpredictable expression of human emotion. Deanna's simulation expressed anger, just as Deanna might have. You could not have predicted it."

"I caused her grief. She is still shocked by her simulated self's action."

"I ask again, Worf, have you come to an *understanding* about this incident?"

"I am—working on it." Admitting weakness, fatal before a Klingon but admissible before his human captain, still rankled, and Worf had to force it past clenched teeth.

What do counselors do when they require counseling?

"*Qapla',*" the captain said. He stood and Worf followed.

"How's the security training simulation going now, Worf?" Picard asked as he escorted Worf to his ready-room door.

"It is ready for use by the crew, sir. I will have a report on your desk tomorrow."

Picard nodded.

"Sir," Worf said, one hand on the doorframe, "if I ever leave the *Enterprise,* I will know I have left my shipmates as secure as—as *humanly* possible."

Picard smiled, but said nothing.

Yes, the training sim is ready, Worf mused as he returned to his post on the bridge, *because I made Deanna angry. I hadn't planned it the way it occurred. Thankfully, her anger didn't stop her from filing a report that helped the captain keep us out of court-martial, but—*

Worf shook off the thought as he returned to duty. He forced his thoughts away from the strained conversations he'd had with Deanna since the incident. He'd shown her a darker self that she'd never imagined existed. It was inadvertent, but she'd never forget. He tried to forget the look in her eyes as she returned to the sim days after. The anger.

Deanna fought hard in the sim. She'd made it work. It was ready for the crew to use.

Worf had won.

Deanna walked past his security post and nodded a silent greeting to Worf. He returned the stiff nod.

Yes, I won. But I lost.

Reciprocity

Brad Curry

Sleep would not come, so she rose from her bed, poured herself a glass of warm *tevash*, and curled up with an old book in her favorite chair.

But despite the bland *tevash* and the dull prose of the novel, she found herself unable to relax. She considered taking a long, hot bath, but then thought, no, something more was needed to calm her restless mind. So at last, she decided to use the remedy for sleepless nights that had served her best over the years: she would climb the worn, spiraling steps to the top of the tower, stand before the high-arched window there, and watch the stars.

She was quite old now and rarely made the climb up from her comfortable quarters on the ground floor. Years ago, when she had first made her home in the deserted tower by the sea, she had climbed up and down the long spiral staircase several times each day. But with the passage of time, she found the ascent increasingly difficult, and now kept mostly to her spacious apartment below.

But on this night, the view from the tower's uppermost window was worth the trip. The sky was clear, and a gentle breeze from the sea caressed her lined and intelligent face.

The small, pale moons of her world had already set, and a multitude of bright, glimmering stars filled the sky.

When she was younger, her work had taken her to many of those stars and the worlds that circled them. For years, she had traveled across the galaxy, from one new world to the next, with none that she could truly call home. But it had been an existence that suited her, for her work was her passion, and she had devoted her life to it with no regrets.

Eventually, however, she completed the labors that had first sent her to the stars. Then, wanting only to rest, she had come here, to this gentle world of warm seas and soft rains.

She ran one hand over the cool stones of the tower's wall. She was not, she knew, the first of her people to call this world home. Centuries, perhaps millennia, ago some unknown architect of her race had traveled here and fashioned this ancient structure with subtle skill.

How many of her kind, she found herself wondering, had stood on this very spot over the years and watched the distant stars? And how many more would do the same in the long centuries to come? It might very well be, she thought with some regret, that she would be the last to call this place home. For although her species had arisen in this part of the galaxy, many of her people had chosen to leave their ancestral homes, seeking new worlds to explore and settle.

Suddenly, out of the corner of her eye, she noticed a movement in the night sky. To her surprise, one of the bright points of light above was traveling, slowly and purposefully, across the horizon.

With keen eyes, she watched the point grow larger, until the outline of a small craft could be discerned, skimming low over the water. When she was certain of its destination, she turned from the window and, with a resigned sigh, began the long descent back down the stairs.

By the time she reached the ground floor and the tower's wide entrance, the craft had landed and was resting a short distance away among the dunes. As she watched, a doorway slid silently open and a solitary figure stepped out onto the sand.

Her visitor was an older man, almost her own age. Even in the soft light escaping from the craft's doorway, she recognized him: her former student and colleague.

She walked out to greet her guest, a wide smile on her face. "I hope you have a good reason for disturbing an old woman in the middle of the night."

Her visitor stepped forward, and the two friends embraced. "I think," he said, offering her a grin of his own, "that you'll find my reason more than acceptable."

She took his arm, and they walked together toward the tower. "As much as I love seeing your cantankerous old face," she said, "you could just as easily have sent a message. Crossing light-years of space to this backwater world wasn't necessary."

Her friend stopped and looked at her with a warm and exuberant expression. For a moment, the years rolled away and he was once again her eager young student. "The message I bring," he said, smiling, "could only have been delivered in person."

He took her hand and squeezed it. "One of our survey teams has made a discovery." He laughed, a joyful sound in the cool night air. "No, not just a discovery—a DISCOVERY!" He laughed again, and to her amazement, there were tears in his happy eyes.

She stared at him, a feeling of cautious hope warming her

heart. "Just exactly what kind of discovery are you talking about?" she asked slowly.

Her friend put his hands softly on her shoulders and looked gently into her curious eyes. "The discovery," he said, "that we've all been waiting for." He paused and then smiled. "The discovery that *you've* been waiting for all of your life."

Jean-Luc Picard lay quietly in bed, staring at the ceiling. After nearly an hour of tossing and turning, he was still wide awake. Sighing in exasperation, he rolled onto his side and gazed contemplatively at the cause of his insomnia.

Outside the ship's windows, hanging close together in space, two white-hot objects burned with hellish intensity. One of the blazing objects was a neutron star; the other, a brilliant white dwarf. In a rare event, the two collapsed stars were about to pass extraordinarily close to one another, a chance meeting in their lonely wanderings through space. As they drew close, they were exchanging stellar matter— and in the process, releasing tremendous amounts of energy.

The *Enterprise* was observing the spectacle from several million kilometers away, a presumably safe distance. Nevertheless, Captain Picard was finding it difficult to remain completely at ease. When the stars reached their closest point—which would happen soon—their extreme proximity would produce exceptionally intense gravitational stresses in the local fabric of space. Unfortunately, the precise effects of those stresses could not be accurately predicted. It was this unpredictability—and the potential danger to his ship— that was giving the captain of the *Enterprise* a restless night.

Picard sighed and sat up in bed. Sleep, he realized, was

going to be impossible in his present state of mind. Accepting the inevitable, he got to his feet and padded silently across the room to the replicator.

"Hot chocolate," he said after a moment. As he picked up the steaming cup, Picard smiled to himself: Counselor Troi would be pleased to know she'd made another convert.

Cradling the hot cup in both hands, Picard went to his couch and sat down. Outside, the stellar pyrotechnic display was in full swing. Brilliant streams of incandescent plasma were flowing between the two convulsing stars, exploding with nova force as they impacted on each star's surface.

Picard leaned back and took a sip of cocoa. The view, he had to admit, was spectacular. He was just beginning to think *It's too bad such events are so rare* when he felt a slight shudder pass through the ship's frame. A moment later, the starfield outside slowly began to move.

He set his cup down. "Picard to bridge. What's our status, Will?"

After a brief pause, Commander Riker's voice came on the channel. "Our two friends out there are just about as close as they're going to get, Captain. If they were starships, they'd practically be rubbing the paint off each other."

His first officer's voice sounded tired but excited. Like Picard, he'd had too little sleep in the past few days.

"They're also beginning to generate some pretty intense gravity waves," continued Riker. "I thought it best to move the ship out a few million kilometers."

"A prudent choice," agreed Picard. "It looks like we're in for quite a show." He stood and headed for the door. As it swished open, he added with a smile, "Just don't let it all happen without me."

The turbolift door opened, and Picard stepped out onto the bridge. At the same instant, the deck beneath his feet suddenly lurched, throwing him against a bulkhead.

"Mister Data," he said, rubbing his arm, "can you compensate for these gravity waves?" Even as he spoke, another wave struck and the ship pitched again.

"I am attempting to do so, Captain," Data replied. The android's fingers danced across his console, and in a moment the ship's heavings began to settle down.

Picard sat down in his chair. "Are we receiving telemetry from the probes?" he asked, referring to the two class-5 probes that had been dispatched earlier to make observations of the event.

"Yes, sir," said Riker. "Both probes are functioning perfectly. In fact, the data we've already received should keep the astrophysicists busy for years."

Data suddenly broke in. "Captain," he said, "sensors indicate the space between the stars is becoming unstable. The gravitational stresses are creating an intense spatial distortion, similar to what is commonly found near a singularity. The process is increasing exponentially."

Picard stood up. "Increase shields to maximum. Helm, take us away—"

Before he could finish, a brilliant flash of light burst from between the stars, lighting up the bridge. A heartbeat later, a violent shock wave rocked the ship.

On the main viewscreen, an explosion of incandescent fury rippled outward from between the two stars. Space seethed and boiled, as though reality itself were being torn apart. Then, in the center of the maelstrom, a blue-white vortex blossomed into existence, filling the void between the now retreating stars.

Picard retook his seat and turned to his science officer. "Mister Data," he said, "can you tell me what just happened?"

Data studied the readouts on his console, then looked at the captain with an expression of android astonishment. "It appears, sir, that the gravitational stresses between the two stars have created a localized fold in the space-time continuum."

Commander Riker stood up and examined Data's console. He looked at the android, his eyebrows raised. "A wormhole?" he asked. "You're saying we just witnessed the creation of a wormhole?"

"I believe so, Commander," replied Data, with a nod. He studied his console again. "The sensor readings are indeed consistent with a Class-4 wormhole. The verteron emissions, however, indicate a high degree of instability. It is extremely likely that this wormhole is a short-lived phenomenon."

"Short-lived or not," said Picard, "the creation of a wormhole is a rarely observed event. Can you determine how long it will last?"

"No sir," said Data, "not using the ship's sensors. They lack the necessary resolution. A probe sent directly into the wormhole, however, should be able to give us sufficient information to predict the time of collapse, as well as determine the wormhole's exit location."

"Captain," the android added, with an almost apologetic

look on his face, "the two probes we had in place were destroyed by the energy release occurring at the wormhole's creation. I will need to launch another."

Picard nodded. "Very well, Mister Data. Launch another probe."

He turned to his first officer. "Well, Will, where do you suppose our new rabbit hole leads?"

Riker sat down in the chair next to the captain. "If it leads into the Gamma Quadrant," he said, "I almost hope it *is* a temporary phenomenon. There are some parts of the galaxy that are best kept at arm's length."

A slight smile crossed Picard's face. "You're sounding more like a soldier than an explorer, Will. Unfortunately, we can't have our wormholes made to order. We have to take what Mother Nature gives us."

Riker leaned back in his chair and crossed his legs. "I suppose that's true," he said. Then he grinned. "And after all, it is a big galaxy. There must be plenty of fun places a wormhole could reach."

Data turned to face the two men. "We are beginning to receive telemetry from the probe," he said. "The computer should obtain an astrometric fix momentarily."

His console gave off a short series of beeps. Data studied this new information, then looked back at Picard.

"There is a problem, Captain. During its passage through the wormhole, the probe's engines were damaged by the gravitational fluxes it encountered. It will be unable to return to this side."

Riker looked at Picard. "More Starfleet property down the drain," he said, then laughed. "Literally."

Picard raised his eyebrows and gave his first officer a wry

smile. "Since you think it's so amusing, you won't mind writing the equipment replacement reports."

Riker rolled his eyes and groaned. But before he could muster a retort, Data spoke again.

"Captain, the computer has determined the exit location of the wormhole." The astounded expression that accompanied the android's statement brought both Picard and Riker to their feet. They both leaned over to examine Data's console, then exchanged astonished looks.

"Remarkable . . ." whispered Picard.

Riker let out a low whistle of surprise and shook his head. "Well. I'll. Be. Damned."

The small craft descended in a slow and graceful arc and landed gently a short distance from the excavation site. An opening appeared and two people, an elderly man and woman, stepped out into the bright sunlight.

The woman stood for a moment and looked around her. She and her companion were standing on a windswept plain that stretched to the horizon in all directions. Above their heads, fleecy white clouds drifted in a deep blue sky. On the hard, flat ground below, a tall, grassy plant covered the plain, growing with slender blades that rustled in the breeze.

The woman smiled and drew a deep breath of the crisp, cold air. She had almost forgotten the thrilling feel of a new world's soil beneath her feet, the intoxicating taste of alien air in her lungs. *I've been cloistered away in my tower for too long,* she mused.

Her companion gently squeezed her arm, interrupting her reverie. "Come," he said, "let me show you our prize."

With a silent nod, she took his arm and they walked

together to the ramp that led down to the dig site. When they reached the bottom, they were greeted by a throng of excited scientists. As the introductions were made, the woman was surprised to find that many of the younger scientists seemed awed by her presence.

"What do you expect?" whispered her companion, noticing her puzzled expression. "It's not every day they meet a living legend." He gave her a mischievous wink.

The woman frowned, but before she could reply, she and her companion were interrupted by the arrival of a tall man wearing a worn lab coat. The site's chief archeologist, he beamed an infectious grin at the newcomers and gave an enthusiastic greeting to the elderly man, his friend and colleague. Turning to the woman, he offered a short, respectful bow.

"We've been waiting for you both," he said, grinning again. "You couldn't have arrived at a better time."

The archeologist stepped between his two guests and took each eagerly by the arm. "Please, come this way," he said. Without waiting for a reply, he led the pair through the crowd to a sturdy table, where a large object lay brightly illuminated beneath powerful worklamps.

The elderly woman bent carefully forward to examine the object. The artifact resting on the table was a long, black pod, somewhat greater in size than a large man. Although its exterior might once have been smooth, heavy pitting and wear now marred the surface.

She turned to the tall archeologist. "Have you been able to determine its age?"

He nodded and looked down at the artifact. "The geological evidence shows that it's been buried here on this world for at least twenty-five million years. And judging by the cosmic ray and micrometeoroid damage to the exterior, it must have drifted in space for a very long time before that." He paused and then looked at his guests. "Altogether, we estimate its age at approximately forty million years."

The woman shook her head. "So old . . ." she whispered, her voice heavy with regret.

The archeologist, oblivious, went on with his discourse. "The materials composing the object are unusual," he continued, "but nothing terribly exotic. The people who built this artifact probably possessed a technological ability similar to our own."

When he spoke next, however, his voice became solemn and thoughtful. "Of course, what's truly significant is not the object itself," he said softly, looking again at his guests, "but what we found inside."

"Can you do it, Beverly?"

Dr. Crusher sat back in her chair and studied the information displayed on her padd. "I think so, Jean-Luc," she said after a moment. "But I do wish I had more time."

Picard nodded. "I know. But there's not much that can be done about that. According to Data's best estimates, we have only twenty to twenty-five hours before the wormhole collapses. We just have to work with what time we have."

He smiled at his chief medical officer. "I don't want you to feel pressured, Beverly. It's just that your contribution to this project is . . ." He paused and then continued in a deadpan voice, ". . . the key to the success of the whole venture."

Dr. Crusher laughed. "Thanks for not making me feel pressured!"

She smiled and put her hand on his arm. "Don't worry, Jean-Luc, I've already finished most of the preliminary preparations. As soon as you give me *your* part of the job, I can really get to work."

She set her padd on the table. "Of course," she added, "the ones really responsible for the success of this plan are the brass upstairs. Has Starfleet Command given you the go-ahead?"

"Yes," Picard replied, "I just received their approval a short while ago. As you might imagine, my proposal was given very close scrutiny." He shook his head. "I can't say I blame them. If this thing isn't done correctly, the consequences could potentially be . . ."

Dr. Crusher finished his thought. "Catastrophic?"

Picard's face suddenly turned solemn. His gaze became focused, as if he were looking off across a great distance.

"Yes—precisely. If our 'package' is opened prematurely, some very important choices might never be made."

Beverly Crusher got up and went to stand next to the captain. "Don't worry; there's nothing to be concerned about." She gave him a reassuring smile. "Your plan, as usual, is flawless. And who else but you would think to make such a wonderful gesture?"

Picard's eyes twinkled at the compliment. "Thank you, Beverly. I appreciate your confidence. And, after all, my concerns probably *are* unwarranted. The chances that my 'gesture' will be received at all are remote in the extreme."

He gave her an affectionate smile. "Good doctor, not only

are you an accomplished physician, but you make a skilled ship's counselor as well."

"Thank you." Beverly grinned. "I'll let Troi know she can retire."

Picard laughed and then reached over and tapped the doctor's padd. "And now, I think, it's time I leave you to your work. Besides, there's one other member of this team I need to look in on."

Geordi La Forge stood up from the photon torpedo casing he was working on and faced Captain Picard. "I'll be ready on this end, Captain, no problem," he said. "The necessary modifications are fairly straightforward."

He patted the smooth torpedo casing. "I'm confident my team and I have found a way to keep your 'package' intact. This is one note in a bottle that just might be found."

"Thank you, Geordi," said Picard. "I hoped that your job wouldn't be too difficult."

"Doctor Crusher's the one with the real engineering job," said La Forge, a hint of concern in his voice. "Will she be ready on time?"

"She assures me she will," replied Picard, "if I can stay out of her hair long enough to let her get some work done."

La Forge grinned, then crouched back down next to the torpedo casing. "Well, as soon as Doctor Crusher is ready on her end, I can get started."

Picard smiled at his chief engineer. "That's just what I wanted to hear." He nodded approvingly. "Let me know when the modifications are complete."

Picard left engineering and stepped into the turbolift. As the door slid quietly closed, he rubbed his hands together.

"And now," he said thoughtfully to the empty lift, "all that's left is for me to do *my* part."

Removed from his duties and his crew, the captain of the *Enterprise* sat alone in his ready room, his mind focused in thought.

For a long time he sat, motionless, mentally revising and rehearsing. At last, when he felt completely satisfied with his efforts, he rose to his feet and walked to the center of the room. Straightening his uniform, he stood silently for a moment, composing himself.

"Computer," he said finally, drawing a deep breath, "begin recording." Then, in a voice clear and strong, Jean-Luc Picard began to speak.

The tall archeologist looked at the black object on the table, reflecting for a moment. Then he turned to face the two elderly scientists standing at his side.

"When we conducted our initial scans of the object's interior," he said, "we found nothing. The . . ." he searched for a word, *"capsule* appeared to be merely an empty shell. Aside from being the obvious artifact of a sentient species, it seemed to have no real information to offer. Just an empty casing—with the contents long gone."

He looked at the woman at his side. "But when one of our more perceptive and seasoned scientists"—he smiled at the elderly man—"suggested we run a more comprehensive bioscan, we detected minute amounts of organic matter."

"The DNA strands," said the woman.

He nodded. "The DNA strands."

"Those strands of nucleic acid," he continued, "were perfectly preserved by a material coating the object's interior. Initially, we believed that this preserved DNA might have come from cells—skin cells, perhaps—that were inadvertently deposited by someone originally working on the object. Quite a fortunate find for us, we thought."

He smiled at his two guests. "But then a more thorough examination showed that the strands didn't contain nearly enough DNA to represent an organism's complete genome. They appeared to be merely unrelated sequences of nucleic acids."

His next words were spoken slowly and with emphasis. "Had we made this discovery at any point in the past, even as little as half a century ago, the genetic material would have told us little." The tall archeologist looked appreciatively into the eyes of the woman at his side. "But of course, thanks to you, we no longer view DNA as merely a carrier of *genetic* information."

The scientist gestured to one of his colleagues and she handed him a small device. "Just before your arrival," he said, "we finished translating the DNA fragments into the algorithms of a computer program. A *holographic* computer program."

He turned and gently placed the device into the hands of the elderly woman. "This computer has been loaded," the archeologist said, "with that very program." He smiled warmly at her. "All that remains is for someone to run it."

The old scientist looked at the device resting in her hands. She turned to her longtime friend, her face overcome with wonder.

"Go ahead," her friend said softly, his eyes twinkling. "You've earned this moment."

She smiled back at him and looked once more at the computer in her hands. Taking a deep breath, she placed one trembling finger on the computer. She looked once more at the assembled scientists around her, smiled thoughtfully to herself, and then with one quick motion activated the program.

For a moment, nothing happened. Then, the air in front of her shimmered and focused to form the image of a being. No, not just a being—a man, with a shape much like her own.

But it was not the familiar shape of his body that drew her gaze but his remarkable face. Despite its alien features, it was the face of a leader, a face of wisdom and compassion.

The woman took a step forward. "So different," she said softly, "yet so much the same." Instinctively, she stretched out her hand to touch the image.

But before she could complete the gesture, in a voice rich and unforgettable, the man began to speak:

"My name," he said, "is Jean-Luc Picard. If you can see and hear me, then you were successful in discovering the genetic program that we sent back to you. That program— the program you now watch—was modeled after one my race and others recently discovered: the message that *your* people placed in our genes so long ago."

The image paused and the man's warm, gray eyes seemed to look straight into her soul.

"I wish we could speak together," he continued, "but my people and I lie more than four billion years in your future. All I can offer you is our gratitude for the gift that you once bestowed upon us. For the galaxy is now home to countless intelligent species, species who now know of your existence, the firstborn ones. You have my deepest promise: you will not be forgotten. . . ."

The excavation site was empty; the others were long gone. Only the woman remained, standing in silence, her face wet with tears. She had no words to speak, for no words could express the sense of fulfillment that now filled her heart.

For a lifetime she had worked, hoping to leave something of her people and of herself, for those who might come later. She had cast a message into the sea of time, and against all her hopes and expectations, that message had been received.

In the years that remained to her, she would often give thanks to the universe that had seen fit to so benevolently reward her labors. But her deepest gratitude she would always reserve for a man: a man who had come to her from a far distant future, a man she would never meet.

A man named Jean-Luc Picard.

Calculated Risk

Christina F. York

Dr. Katherine Pulaski watched as Lieutenant Reg Barclay wormed his thin frame beneath the *Debakey*'s medical transporter console. Although she could no longer see his narrow face, she could clearly picture the frown of concentration that wrinkled his forehead, and his tightly pursed lips.

Barclay wasn't what she expected when she'd requested a transporter engineer from the *Enterprise*. She'd expected Chief O'Brien, but Captain Picard sent her Barclay. He'd said he couldn't spare O'Brien, but she was beginning to think he just wanted to get rid of Barclay for a while.

She could hear Barclay muttering to himself, though she could discern no actual words. A piece of the metal case clanged ominously, and the muttering became louder, followed by a yelp of surprise, or pain.

"Are you okay under there?" With an effort, she kept her voice level. Barclay had been recalibrating the transporter all afternoon, and it was now well past the dinner hour. Pulaski didn't like untried treatments, and this one would be particularly delicate. She ran her hands through her short, dark copper curls, clenching her fists for a moment in frustration.

"J-just a few more minutes, Doctor." Barclay's voice was muffled by the console, but the confidence in his tone was clear. At least *he* thought he was getting close to finishing.

Patience, she told herself. Just be patient a little longer. She almost laughed out loud. Katherine Pulaski had many fine qualities—intelligence, a sense of humor, the ability to quickly and dispassionately analyze a critical medical problem—but patience was not among them. It was, she had come to realize, the reason she was assigned temporarily as chief surgeon of the medical ship *Debakey,* but would never be her captain.

Barclay slid from beneath the console, a calibration meter clenched in his fist. "Got it," he told her, rising to his feet. He was taller than the doctor, and he unconsciously stooped to look her in the eye. He appeared troubled.

"Is there a problem, Lieutenant?"

"Nooo." His denial lingered, more a question than a statement.

"Something is bothering you. What is it?"

He hesitated, then continued. "Do you think this is right? I mean, I know what it's like to be in love."

"Really, Lieutenant?"

"Yes. I was in love with Deanna Troi, back on the *Enterprise.*"

She cocked an eyebrow in question. "Was?" Her emphasis on the past tense brought a faint blush to Barclay's face.

"Things didn't work out. Of course that was before I was in love with Doctor Crusher. . . ." his voice trailed off.

Pulaski started to reply, but he quickly regained his composure. "But I know it was love, Doctor. When it happens, you know. Just like I did with Ensign MacGregor."

She shook her head in wonder. He really believed what he was saying. "All I really want to know, Lieutenant, is whether this thing," she waved a hand at the transporter, "is ready."

"It is."

"Good." Pulaski turned and ran her fingers over the controls. "I want this checked out thoroughly. Run it through a complete set of diagnostics, and triple-check the results. And I want it now."

Barclay slid in front of her, subtly forcing her away from the console. He spread his arms to the sides of the panel, as though to hold the controls for himself. "It's a funny thing," he said, caressing the keypads. "I used to hate transporters. Didn't want to be anywhere near the blasted things. Now, though," he slid a finger along a row of indicator lights, "now, they fascinate me. I could spend hours tracing their circuits."

You just spent hours. Pulaski bit back the retort. It shouldn't matter how long he took to set up the machine. What should, and did, matter was that it was completely ready when she sent the Prescotts through.

It wasn't just this technology, she reminded herself, as she walked the corridors of the medical ship. It was the pathogen itself. An olfactory neural stimulator was how Starfleet Medical had described it when they ordered the *Debakey* to Cygnus IV. A pathogen that attacked the olfactory nerves and produced intense emotional reactions.

What it was, Pulaski had concluded, was a love potion. Never mind that love potions and aphrodisiacs were the stuff of myths. Hell, after three failed marriages, she wasn't even sure she believed in love, much less love potions.

Nevertheless, the evidence was clear: Six months ago, Dr. David Prescott and Dr. Laura Prescott had requested reassignment from the science station on Cygnus IV. Separate reassignment. And they had announced to Starfleet their intention to get a divorce. They even had a preliminary separation agreement, and they established separate quarters on the remote outpost.

When the relief ship arrived, however, the Prescotts refused to beam aboard, or to accept their reassignments. They spent every possible minute together and talked incessantly of each other when they were apart. They acted for all the universe like teenagers with a first crush, rather than partners in a crumbling twenty-three-year marriage.

Pulaski stopped outside the isolation chamber where the Prescotts were housed. It was the only way she could get them aboard the *Debakey*. There was no way she wanted the pathogen to spread, and she had so far been unable to isolate the method of transmission.

Even though the chamber had an isolation field, Pulaski took the extra precaution of a protective suit and breather. Not that it mattered for her. With her past, she figured she was immune to love potions, or Cupid's arrows, or whatever it was that brought people together.

The Prescotts were sitting side by side on a small bench when she entered the chamber, fingers entwined. They talked in low voices, and the intimate tone sent a pang through Pulaski.

She cleared her throat, the sound echoing tinnily in the breather filter. She hated the distortion a breather gave her words. Laura Prescott looked up and offered a distracted smile.

"Look, David." She patted her husband on the arm. "Doctor Pulaski's here."

David Prescott turned and sketched a wave in her direction, obviously unwilling to take his attention from his wife. Pulaski greeted them, and sat in a chair next to the containment field.

"Doctor Prescott. Doctor Prescott." How forbidding that sounded. She was supposed to be a counselor, for heaven's sake! "David. Laura. It's good to see you again. I hope you're comfortable here. I'm afraid the accommodations aren't plush, but they were the best we could do on short notice."

"No problem, Doctor, as long as we're together." Laura smiled up at David, who gave her a quick kiss on the cheek and nodded in agreement.

Maybe Barclay was right. Maybe it would be better to simply beam these two back down to Cygnus IV, and leave them alone in their apparent bliss.

But she couldn't do that. The pathogen was dangerous. It had distracted two dedicated scientists from important observation and research. If it spread, the implications were monstrous. The Cardassians could sit back and wait for the Federation to wither and die.

Pulaski took a deep, calming breath. David and Laura had to commit to the treatment. She closed her eyes for a second, then opened them.

"Good. Now it's decision time. Lieutenant Barclay is checking the modifications to the diagnostic biofilter, and he believes the transporter will be ready for you within the next couple hours." She keyed a recorder, and asked in an overly formal tone, "Do you, Doctor David Prescott and Doctor

Laura Prescott, consent to the experimental transporter filter treatment?"

Laura nodded, and David grinned at her. Realizing her error, she slapped playfully at his shoulder, and spoke aloud. "Doctor Laura Prescott, ID #466549J-C. I hereby consent to treatment."

David did the same. Pulaski felt a flood of relief, a release of tension she hadn't realized was there. Somewhere deep down, she had been afraid they would change their minds at the last minute. She switched off the recorder.

"Okay, now that that's settled, let's move on. I want to talk with both of you about the changes the treatment may cause." The two scientists nodded, and Pulaski launched into a detailed explanation of what they hoped the transporter filter would do.

"Essentially," she concluded, "we want the filter to trap the pathogen in your pattern buffers, removing it from your systems before they are reassembled. It's common practice, but we've never tried to capture an unknown pathogen before. As I've said, we can't guarantee results, though our tests and simulations indicate a high probability of success."

The Prescotts both nodded solemnly. "We do understand, Doctor," David said. "And we're talked it over a lot. Even if it doesn't work exactly the way we expect, we feel like we have to do this."

Laura patted his hand, and he turned to smile at her. She spoke, as though they had scripted the exchange. "There is more than just our relationship at stake here, Doctor, at least for us. If this works, Starfleet can add this pathogen to the routine scans and learn to scan for unknowns. How can we say no?"

"Don't get us wrong," David said. "We want to be cured, Doctor Pulaski. We want to know what's real and what isn't. We need to know. We've been together nearly thirty years, but we don't want to live the rest of our lives as a lie.

"You can understand that, can't you?"

Pulaski nodded in agreement and left the Prescotts. She stripped off the isolation suit, and replaced the breather in the sterilization pod. What a liar! She acted as though she understood, when she didn't have a clue. She shouldn't even pretend to understand the complicated relationships between men and women, not with her record.

"Pulaski to Barclay. Come in, Lieutenant." The disembodied voice caused Reg's stomach to flip-flop. His concentration was so complete he had forgotten about Dr. Pulaski.

"Barclay here. What can I do for you, Doctor?"

"You can tell me that the transporter is ready, and the tests went smoothly."

Reg hesitated. He could tell her that, it just wouldn't be the truth. Better to tell her what he had found. "Not quite. The pattern analyzers and biofilter are working fine, but I'm not sure that we're getting everything. I need to run a few more tests. Say, another three hours."

Even over the communication channel, Reg could hear the effort it took to keep her voice level. The tension was clearly held in check with an iron will, the same determination he had seen her focus on problems throughout the project. "Very well. Continue with your work. I'm going to my quarters."

He shrugged. That was exactly what he had been doing, and would still be doing if she hadn't interrupted. The idea of using the transporter to identify and trap an unknown pathogen excited him. He wished she would just leave him alone, let him do his job, and get back to the *Enterprise,* and that cute Vulcan, Ensign T'Kaal, who just transferred into engineering.

Sleep. Even a few hours would do her a world of good. She had been working too hard for too many days, with too little rest. Some food, a little sleep, and she'd be ready to go again. Solve this problem and move on.

The terminal in her quarters was beeping quietly, announcing a message for her. She keyed the replicator.

"Coffee, black." Wait, she was supposed to be going to sleep. "Change that. Tea, peppermint. Light sugar." The slightly sweet tea would soothe her, maybe allow her to relax.

The solid warmth of the mug warmed her hand, and the spicy scent of sweet mint reached her nose. She reached for the message button. Personal messages were rare for Katherine Pulaski. She had no close family, and her three ex-husbands had each gone their separate ways and never looked back.

Until now. The image of Brian, her second husband, filled the communicator screen. There were a few more lines in his face, a touch of gray in his hair, but the lopsided grin, the perfect teeth, and the hint of adventure in his eyes were still the same.

"Hi, Kat." His voice was the same, too. Soft and warm, wrapping around her heart and sending flutters through her. It reminded her of the time they had spent together, the time before boredom and career demands had sent them in different directions.

"I've missed you." He paused, as though waiting for a reaction. Pulaski examined his face, then noticed the two new pips on his uniform collar. Whatever Brian had been doing the last few years, he had been very successful. "I thought maybe we could get together, for old times' sake. I heard you were on the *Debakey*, and I was in the neighborhood."

Neighborhood? Neighborhood in this case was defined in cubic parsecs. Brian Anderson, Admiral Brian Anderson, never did anything "for old times' sake." He did his job, and when it was done, he moved on. Just as he had when their marriage was over.

"We'll be passing your location tomorrow, Kat. Can I count on you to beam aboard for dinner? About twenty hundred hours? I know I can. It will be good to see you again." His voice had dropped into that soft register that had wormed its way into her heart the first time, and she felt a tug. Was it some residual affection for Brian, or just nostalgia? Or just a reflection of her confusion over the Prescotts?

The Prescotts. She keyed her communicator and talked to David. "We'll try it in the morning," she said. "Lieutenant Barclay is running a last set of tests, it's getting late, and I'd rather we were all rested before we start the procedure."

"Fine by us," David said, and Pulaski could hear Laura's murmured assent in the background.

"See you in the morning, then. Pulaski out."

She reached for her mug and sipped. The tea was cool now, and the sugar clotted in her throat. She should eat some dinner, she should be hungry, but she was too tired to care. She forced Brian, the Prescotts, and Lieutenant Barclay out of her mind, and went to bed. In ten minutes she was asleep.

* * *

"Ready?" Pulaski asked. Barclay nodded. The Prescotts, standing on the transporter pads dressed in isolation suits, signaled with upraised thumbs.

Barclay had added a containment field around the viral trap, where the pathogen would be reintegrated after it was extracted from the Prescotts. One last measure of security. Until they knew more, they couldn't afford to take any risks.

At Pulaski's signal, Barclay initiated the transporter. Within seconds, the Prescotts reappeared on the transporter pads. It all happened so quickly, Pulaski felt as though nothing had changed. But if they had been successful, everything had changed.

Barclay fiddled with the controls on the transporter console, then turned to Pulaski. "I have readings indicating some pathogens trapped in the filter. You'll need to test them to see if they're the right ones, but we caught something."

Her pulse raced. They had succeeded in filtering out an unknown pathogen, something that had only been a theory minutes before. Now she would have to determine if they had the right one. The trick was identifying the genetic sequence of the specific pathogen they were hunting.

The Prescotts, still in their isolation suits, followed a security officer back to their temporary quarters. Pulaski would see them in a few minutes, after she started the scans of the trapped pathogen.

"You think we got it, Doctor?" Barclay could barely contain his excitement. If they had the pathogen, he had helped trap a new threat to the Federation. Maybe they would name it after him. Probably not, though. More likely Pulaski would get the credit, or the Prescotts, or even Cygnus IV.

Still, he knew he had played a big part in capturing this particular bug.

"Hard to say, Lieutenant. I wouldn't even guess until I see the Prescotts."

They turned the vessel over to a medical lab technician, with detailed instructions for its handling. They had drilled the technicians for days on the procedures, but Pulaski didn't want any slip-ups. Safety was the key.

The Prescotts sat as they had the night before: close together, fingers entwined, voices low and eyes only for each other. Clearly, the treatment had failed. They were as deeply immersed in each other as before. Nothing had changed.

Laura looked up when Pulaski entered, and caught her eye. There was a flicker of something—relief, maybe—which was immediately hidden behind a mask of disappointment. David, watching her face, composed his expression to match hers. Together, they faced the doctor.

"Looks like we didn't make it this time," David said. There was a note of near-triumph in his voice, a repudiation of his earlier dedication to finding a cure.

"Maybe next time," Laura added. She couldn't cover the hope in her voice that there wouldn't be a next time.

"Actually, the results aren't clear yet. We know we trapped some pathogenic agents. We're just waiting for the laboratory evaluations. It'll be several hours before we know for sure.

"In the meantime, though, I want you both to think about whether you want to try again. Perhaps speak with the ship's counselor, if you think it might help."

The Prescotts both nodded, but there was a dismissing quality to their postures. They wanted to be left alone, and they didn't particularly care who knew it. Pulaski left them, and wandered back to her quarters.

Now that the procedure was complete, the sample was with the med techs, and Barclay was baby-sitting his transporter, there was little left for her to do. Little except to think about Brian, and what his message last night had meant.

She replayed the message, searching his face for a clue to what he really wanted. A reconciliation? Hardly. Brian knew as well as she did that it wasn't possible. They were Starfleet officers, dedicated to their careers. He was born to command, and he loved it. Ultimately, he had loved it more than he loved her. Be honest, she chided herself. She loved medicine, loved healing. In the end, medicine was more important than Brian. He had asked her to choose, and she chose a different path than he did. Still, it might be nice to see him again. They had parted as friends, but nothing more. Not like Kyle.

Kyle Riker, the man who had simply disappeared from her life one day, his body healed, his command restored. Three husbands later, she still thought of him as the one that got away.

She shrugged off the melancholy that threatened to envelop her. There was a pile of paperwork stacked on her desk, ignored while she worked on the pathogen. There was time to clean it up before she had dinner with Brian.

Barclay paced outside the medical lab. He considered names for the pathogen. Regicilium? Reg-Bar Syndrome? Barclaynosis?

There wasn't anything else to do. The med techs had

made it clear he couldn't help. In fact, they had made it painfully clear that he wasn't even allowed in the lab.

Lieutenant Rosemary Lowell, the dark-haired chief technician, had smiled prettily at him and then taken him forcefully by the arm. "We'll handle it from here, Lieutenant Barclay. There won't be any results until late tonight. Go realign some sensors or something, and let us do our job."

She had secured the door behind him, and he had found himself outside the med lab with no place to go and nothing to do. This assignment was only temporary, after all, and he had been too busy to get to know any of the other crew members. Even Pulaski was off on some personal business she had refused to tell him about.

He'd spent hours wandering the ship, wondering if someday the pathogen might be called Barclay's Disease. Or Reg Pox? Barclay Fever? Naturally, he was susceptible, as he was to so many other bugs.

Twice he got lost and eventually had to ask the computer for directions back to the lab. Each time, Lowell had answered his chime with a distracted, "Not yet. Come back later."

He tried the door again and got the same answer, albeit more annoyed than the previous six times. He shrugged. The only other people he knew were the Prescotts. Desperate for company, he decided to visit them in their quarters.

When David Prescott keyed the door and invited him in, Barclay realized with a start that this was the first time he had actually been in the isolation chamber. The first time he had seen the scientists as human beings, and not just the subject of his experiment. And they seemed genuinely glad to see him.

"I'm glad you stopped by, Lieutenant," David said, extending his hand, then pulling it back in confusion as he realized the futility of the gesture. "Sorry. I keep forgetting."

David resumed his seat next to his wife, draping an arm casually across her shoulders. For a few minutes the three of them sat smiling and nodding at each other, the silence stretching until it approached an awkward length.

Laura coughed quietly, then cleared her throat. "Have you heard anything about the tests, Lieutenant?"

"Not yet. The medical technicians keep telling me to go away." He grinned nervously. Now that he was here, he wasn't sure why he had come. He just hadn't wanted to wait alone anymore. He wanted to talk to someone. Someone who understood what it meant to be in love.

"So, how long have you two been married?" The minute the words left his mouth he wanted to hide beneath his chair. These people were getting divorced, once the treatment succeeded. He couldn't have picked a stupider question.

But Laura smiled at him, and patted David's knee. "Twenty-four years in August," she said. The pride in her voice was evident. "Most of them have been pretty good, with a few clinkers now and again."

David chuckled. "And now we're waiting to see how much longer." His smile slipped for a moment, then he regained control. "Have you ever been married, Lieutenant?"

Caught off guard, Barclay stuttered slightly. "N-no. But there is someone back on my regular ship." He was about to launch into a detailed description when his combadge interrupted.

"Med lab to Lieutenant Barclay. Come in, Lieutenant."

Barclay jumped to his feet, upsetting the chair he'd been sitting on. "Barclay here. Go ahead."

"This is Lowell, Lieutenant Barclay. Figured you were anxious to know. The genetic signature of the pathogenic material is an exact match. You caught your bug."

Barclay wanted to shout with joy. They had done it. His calculations and calibrations and tests and tests and tests had done the job. He was a success! Maybe they would name it Reginald's Disease, or Barclay's Lament. He liked that one. Barclay's Lament.

But there was something in the technician's voice. . . .

"Lowell, what aren't you telling me?"

"Nothing much. It's just that you might want to check your instruments. Our tests show an extremely small discrepancy in the volume of pathogenic material. You and Doctor Pulaski were the only ones near the containment vessel, right?"

"Yes." Barclay held his breath. He didn't want to hear her reply, but he had to know. "What kind of discrepancy?"

"Your filter recorded 3.287 micrograms, but we only have 3.244 micrograms here in the lab. Somewhere we lost .043 micrograms."

Barclay sank back into his chair. It didn't sound like much, but the quantity recovered had been so small to begin with, he had no idea whether the missing amount was dangerous or not. Besides, he'd bet it was probably just a fluctuation in the instruments. If he was a betting man. If he took chances.

Katherine Pulaski took a long, slow look around her. Brian had beamed her directly to his quarters. "Admiral's privilege," he'd called it. There was a small table in the middle of the room, set for two. The room was sparsely furnished, giving an impression of neatness and order. The few decorative touches were subdued, as though to downplay any personal connection. The exception was a portrait that stood on the console table below the window. She stopped and stared, feeling her head spin. It was an image of the two of them, made early in their marriage. It took her back to a time and place she hadn't been in many years.

"I hoped you would like it." Brian broke her concentration, taking her arm and leading her to a low settee in the center of the room. "It always reminds me that there was once a time when we were happy together."

Pulaski sank into the cushions of the settee and drew a deep breath. "Yes. Yes, there was a time. . . ." Her voice trailed off. She resumed, stronger, "But we were never unhappy together, were we." It wasn't a question. "We just . . . stopped being together at all."

"True. You always did have the ability to cut right to the heart of the matter, didn't you?" He kissed her lightly on the cheek. "That was something I admired about you from the first time I saw you."

She turned to look directly at him. She could feel her lips curling into a warm smile, in spite of her determination to keep her distance. "You did? Usually people want to avoid me once they realize I speak my mind."

"No, Kat. I liked the way you cut through the baloney and saw the real reasons, and said so. It got a little, uh, rough sometimes, especially toward the end. But I really think it made things easier in the long run." He grinned and made a rueful face. "At least I always knew where I stood with you."

Pulaski felt an unexpected moment of tenderness toward Brian. They had been content together, occasionally happy, and they had never really fought. Even the divorce had been amicable. They were both too busy to be married, and had just decided to call it quits.

After a few more minutes of "remember when," Pulaski could wait no longer. "So, Brian, just what was it you wanted me here for?"

"Same old Kat. I'd have been disappointed if you didn't ask." Brian's grin faded, and his eyes grew serious. The hint of adventure remained, but it was dimmed as he continued. "I've missed you, Kat. I never thought I could say that, much less mean it, but there it is. I miss you, and I want you back."

For an instant, she couldn't make her mouth form words. She had speculated, in a flight of fancy, that Brian might want to reconcile, but she had never thought it a real possibility.

Now he had said it. She forced a deep, calming breath through her body, just as she did before a delicate medical procedure. She had to think very clearly before she turned him down. If she turned him down. Of course she was going to say no. That "if " was a moment of nostalgia talking. Still, he had reached over and taken her hand, and she enjoyed his touch.

She shook herself, and withdrew her hand. Next she'd be getting all goo-goo eyes, like the Prescotts. Oh, dear lord! Could they have been contagious? Not possible—she had taken every precaution.

"Kat?" Brian's voice was concerned, his eyes clouded with worry. "Are you all right?"

"Fine. Just a bit startled." She tried to laugh, but it

sounded shaky, and she quickly turned it into a little cough. "Whatever prompted that idea?"

"It's been building a long time. I missed you, but I never thought there was a chance for us. This is coming out all wrong; I had it all planned, how I would tell you. . . ."

"Just spit it out."

Brian laughed again, this time a hearty, relieved sound. "You haven't changed a bit. Thank heavens. I would have been disappointed if you had."

Pulaski withdrew her hand and crossed her arms across her chest. "Out with it, Brian. Now."

He held up his hands in a gesture of surrender. "The admiral yields." He had visibly relaxed, and continued easily. "We never had the opportunity to work together. Maybe things would have been different if we had. We might not have been pulled in opposite directions."

She nodded. "And?"

"And now I have the chance to change that. I know how much you hate being deskbound, Kat."

She wished he would stop calling her that. It was too intimate, carried too many memories. "As I recall," she answered dryly, "you didn't much care for those assignments either."

"No, I didn't. And I am in a position to refuse them now. Which I have. They gave me this ship," he waved his arm in a gesture that took in the as-yet-unseen *Golden Hind,* "and an assignment to explore at the edge of known space. I set my own course, report directly to Starfleet Command, and choose my own crew.

"I'm offering you the post of chief medical officer, Kat. It's not a promotion, but it's not a desk job, either. You're the best damned doctor I know. And I have my own personal reasons, I admit. I'd like you on board, like the chance for us to get to know each other again. Who knows? Maybe this time could be different."

Maybe it could. Pulaski was surprised to feel a tug at Brian's suggestion. She knew better than to let herself get involved again. It hadn't worked the first time, what made her think it would now? But the offer was attractive: chief medical officer on an exploratory voyage. She could stay aboard ship for as long as she wanted.

"Doctor Pulaski." Her combadge sounded with the vaguely garbled voice of Lieutenant Barclay, patched through from the *Debakey*. "Sorry to bother you, but I think you better come to the med lab."

"What is it, Lieutenant?" Pulaski didn't bother to disguise the annoyance in her voice.

"There's an anomaly, sir. A slight difference in the volume of pathogenic matter trapped. The lab is missing .043 micrograms of what we trapped."

Pulaski felt her stomach drop to her toes and her blood turn to ice water. If there was material missing, it was possible the infection was spreading. She and Barclay were the only two who had been in contact with the containment vessel before it got to the lab—and she had been with Brian. Had let him touch her hand and kiss her cheek.

"I'll be there immediately, Lieutenant." She turned to Brian. "Confine yourself to your quarters until you hear from me. I may have been exposed to a pathogen, despite our best efforts, and we don't know how it spreads."

Brian's mouth opened, but Pulaski shook her head firmly. "Don't argue. Doctor's orders. I'll bet nobody's pulled rank on you in a while, but I'll do it if I have to. You know I will. Do *not* leave this room until I give you the okay."

She patted her badge. "Beam me directly to the med lab."

Pulaski arrived in the med lab with a feeling of relief. There was no room for personal thoughts or feelings here. There was a medical dilemma to solve, and it had to be done quickly. She could forget about Brian, and everything else.

"Lieutenant, what are the measurements?"

"The transporter recorded 3.287 micrograms. The lab reported 3.244 micrograms. We're missing 1.3 percent of what we trapped. Sir."

"All right. As of this moment, this lab, all lab personnel, Lieutenant Barclay, and myself are under Level I quarantine protocol, as well as Admiral Anderson. That will include the transporter bay and the Prescotts' quarters. When we move between locations it will be in full isolation suits and breathers."

She looked around the room. There were nods, but she suspected they were submission, not agreement. She didn't care. She wasn't here to be liked or agreed with; she was here to have her orders obeyed.

"We'll start from the beginning. Lieutenant Barclay, you will check the transporter, recalibrate all the sensors, check all the volume meters. I want to be sure that there is no margin for error.

"Lowell, I want the same procedures for all the testing devices in the laboratory. Each of you take two of the ensigns as backup. And I want a third team to go over the containment vessel itself.

"Has anyone left the lab since we started the procedure?"

They all shook their heads. Pulaski's relief was mirrored in the faces around her. Clearly, they all understood the risk they faced.

Barclay cleared his throat. "Does that include me, Captain? I just walked around the ship for a while, and then I went to see the Prescotts for a while."

"This is important, Lieutenant. Did you see or speak to anyone else?"

"No one, Doctor. I swear." Beads of sweat appeared on Barclay's high forehead. "I didn't see a soul. Except the Prescotts."

"I hope that's true. The Level I protocol will verify your movements for the last six hours." She pulled an isolation suit from the locker. "I'm going to check on the Prescotts."

The Prescotts were sitting together on the bench when she entered, but something had clearly changed. Although they still sat close, they didn't cling the way they had. Their voices were low, but the exclusionary tone was missing. Still, they were focused on each other with an intimacy Pulaski envied. What would it be like to have that kind of rapport with someone?

Forget it, it wasn't real. She'd been exposed, and so had Brian, and the Prescotts had probably been reinfected by Barclay. They'd taken two steps forward and fallen back three. Maybe four. Or five, if you counted Brian.

"How are you two feeling?" she asked, sitting outside the containment field. The field quite possibly wasn't accomplishing anything, but she couldn't bring herself to let it down. Not until she was sure.

"Actually, Doctor," David replied, "I think we're cured. I know it may not look like it, but things are different."

Laura nodded her agreement. "We're not as *focused* as we were. More relaxed somehow. It's not as intense as the pathogen, but it's actually better."

"Better?" Pulaski echoed. "In what way? Pardon me, but I thought the two of you were getting a divorce. And now you say you're cured of the pathogen, but you still seem very, well, attached." She halted, embarrassment creeping through her. She had no idea what they were talking about, though she couldn't admit it. After all, she was the doctor.

"Well," David said, "it's hard to explain. I, we," he patted Laura's hand, "thought we didn't love each other anymore. That after thirty years we had exhausted all the things that kept us together. There didn't seem to be any reason to stay married."

"We never had kids," Laura explained, "because we were frequently in environments that weren't hospitable to families. We didn't want to be separated while one of us stayed somewhere safer with the children."

David's laugh was sudden and hearty. "Remember the mining colony on Reganus? That wasn't hospitable for anybody."

Laura chuckled softly. "We lasted three years. I think you were just being stubborn. It was a challenge, and we never shied from challenges. We always took risks. We shouldn't have let this one stop us."

"This wasn't a challenge," Pulaski replied. "It was a pathogenic infection. A medical problem."

"No," David said. "It was a challenge. Not the pathogen, the assignment itself. We were isolated with only each other for company, and we lost sight of why we wanted to work together. We like each other, Doctor. We're friends. Even when we disagree . . ."

"Which is often," Laura interjected.

"Which is often," David agreed. "Even when we disagree, we still like each other." He placed an arm around Laura and looked mildly puzzled for an instant. "I guess that was the bad thing about the pathogen. I was infatuated with Laura, but I wasn't sure I *liked* her. But the infatuation kept us together long enough for me to remember."

"And I was reminded why I like David," Laura added. "Without the pathogen, we would have gone our separate ways before we realized what a mistake it was. Even if we aren't compelled to be together every minute, we still want to be married to each other."

Pulaski shook her head. She couldn't believe these people. Last month they wanted a divorce; yesterday they couldn't bear to be more than three feet apart. Now they sat here and claimed to be cured, but even though they didn't have to be together, they still wanted to be. None of it made any sense to her. She didn't understand it, any of it.

"If you're satisfied. . . ." She let her voice trail off, unable to think of anything more to say. She gave herself a little shake, hoping it wasn't visible through the suit. She couldn't let this confusion get in the way of doing her job. "I need to check on things in the lab."

"All right," Laura said, "and, Doctor . . ."

Pulaski turned and looked back at the couple. "Yes?"

"Next time you don't have to wear the suit."

Pulaski cycled the door behind herself. She didn't share the Prescotts' confidence. There was pathogenic material missing, Pulaski was acting funny herself, and Reg Barclay was following Lieutenant Lowell around like a faithful puppy. This had all the ingredients for a first-class disaster.

Barclay sat at the table with Lowell and the med techs. He had good news for the doctor, but she was already on her way back to the lab, and he wanted to deliver it in person. He had already ordered up a round of Romulan ale from the replicator. Technical expertise had its benefits.

Barclay looked up when the door opened, and Dr. Pulaski walked in. He saw her take in the scene in front of her, and for an instant her face was suffused with anger; then a mask of impassive calm descended.

"Lieutenant!" A whip cracked in her voice, and Barclay sprang to his feet.

"Would you care to join us, Doctor? How about a nice glass of Romulan ale?" he blurted out.

Her expression changed from forced calm to bewilderment, but her voice was icy. "What's going on here, Lieutenant Barclay? I gave you some very explicit orders."

"Sorry, sir. I wanted to tell you in person."

"Tell me what?" Pulaski stared at him as though he had sprouted a second head.

He was doing this all wrong. He was supposed to report their results. He cleared his throat and tried again. "We located the error, sir. It was a malfunction in the measurements at the transporter console. It was reading just over one percent high. Seems that Laura Prescott had a pendant that David bought her on Reganus. Mildly radioactive. It caused a fluctuation in the readings. We've tested the results several times, and determined that there is no missing material."

Pulaski felt a surge of relief, followed by a flash of annoyance at Barclay for not telling her immediately. Brian had called her at least four or five times in the last two hours, wanting to know when he would be released from "house arrest." But the annoyance passed before she could even voice it. They had trapped the pathogen. No one was infected, not even the Prescotts. They had been right. They were cured, and they still wanted to stay together.

Lowell's voice interrupted Pulaski's thoughts. "We apologize for starting to celebrate without you. We were all just so relieved to know the pathogen hadn't gotten out."

Her contrite tone, and the realization that the danger had passed, washed away Pulaski's irritation. She had the results she wanted. She looked at Barclay, still standing stiffly at attention.

"Relax, Lieutenant. And give me a glass of that ale." She lifted the glass and sipped experimentally. "And I don't even want to know how you managed to replicate this."

She raised her glass to the gathered technicians. "To a job well done."

Pulaski stood near the door of the lab. The med techs and Lieutenant Barclay were talking animatedly, each trying to top the others with tales of exotic diseases and treatments. Barclay, if she could believe what he said, had been infected with nearly every ailment in the galaxy, and a few others she had never heard of. He sat close to Lieutenant Lowell and spoke directly to her, as though the others weren't even there. She seemed oblivious to the attention, and Pulaski hid a grin behind her hand. It looked like Barclay was in love. Again. At least she knew it wasn't the pathogen. No one was infected.

Including her. She slipped out the door. She had to call Brian, but she delayed until she could call from the privacy of her quarters.

Brian's expression was a combination of concern and irritation when he answered her hail. "How much longer, Kat? I have a ship to run, you know."

"Relax, Brian. You never were very good at waiting. But the danger is past, and you can get on with running your ship." At least he had done as she had told him, however unwillingly. "Thanks for trying to be patient. I know how hard that is for you."

"I'm a man of action," he said, the lopsided grin taking the arrogance from the words. "Can't stand to sit still, can't stand a desk job, and I can't stand to wait. There's a report of a solar disturbance in the Wasner system, and I need to check it out."

Pulaski could see the question in his eyes. He had made her an offer, and he wanted her answer. The frontier was out there, and he wanted to be on the move.

"I didn't mean to keep you waiting," she said. "I was a little busy here. Stopping an epidemic, that sort of thing."

Brian, she noted, had the good grace to look slightly abashed. "Sorry, Kat. While you were saving the world I was sitting and waiting. It isn't something I do very well."

"How well I remember." She squared her shoulders. "But I have to say no, Brian. I've done a lot of thinking in the last few days, even before our talk. I don't think it would be different. And I'm afraid it might spoil a perfectly good friendship."

For a moment, she thought she saw relief mixed with the disappointment in his expression. It told her she was right. If she had gone, it would have been for all the wrong reasons, and their relationship might not have ended so amicably the second time.

"Are you sure, Kat? This assignment's over, or it will be soon, and you'll be back at Starfleet Medical behind a desk."

She nodded. "I might be, for a while. But something will come along. It always does." She smiled. "And Brian?"

"Yes?"

"Look me up next time you're in the neighborhood. You still owe me a dinner." She terminated the connection before he could answer. He might have tried to argue, to change her mind. She knew this was best. They had never had what the Prescotts had, and never would. Maybe she was starting to believe in love, after all.

The door chimed and she answered, "Come."

Reg Barclay appeared in the doorway. "I wanted to talk to you, Doctor."

"Yes, Lieutenant?" Pulaski motioned to a seat across from her.

"No thanks. I'll only be a minute." Barclay reminded her of a big, gangly bird, refusing to light on a branch. "I just want to confirm your conclusion. You're sure the Prescotts are cured? We got it all?"

"All the test results say so, Lieutenant. Beyond that, I have examined the Prescotts. I am satisfied we got the pathogen, and it hasn't spread."

Barclay's face relaxed into a genuine smile. "Good! Thanks, Doctor." He turned, and the door opened to let him out.

"Lieutenant?" Pulaski called after him.

He looked back over his shoulder. "Yes?"

"Weren't *you* sure?"

Barclay grinned. "Just checking. I'm on my way to request reassignment to the *Debakey*. I'm in love with Lieutenant Lowell."

Pulaski shook her head at his departing back. Maybe someday she could believe as much as he did, and find someone she could take a chance on. For now, she'd settle for finding her next assignment.

Gods, Fate, and Fractals

William Leisner

The United Federation of Planets. Home to over a trillion sentients, all living in comfort and harmony like no other society in all of history.

But there are some who don't like the way that history has played out. Or who think they can improve upon it. They see themselves as visionaries. Society, though, views them as something else entirely.

Criminals.

That's where we come in. It's our job to find these malefactors and stop them from making their visions of new histories reality.

My name is Lucsly. My partner is Dulmer.

We're temporal investigators.

Stardate 50564.2—a Friday. We were working the day watch out of Department of Temporal Investigations headquarters in San Francisco. Our boss, Assistant Director Kreinns, marched into our office, a stack of padds under his arm.

"Just received this report from Starfleet," he said, taking two of the padds and handing one to each of us. I quickly skimmed the document and immediately understood why the boss looked so concerned: Jem'Hadar troops had taken the Narendra and Archer systems. Besides being strategically located between the Federation and the Klingon Empire, the Narendra Sector was also the spatial location of a suspected temporal anomaly, detected five years, three months, and ten days earlier.

I lowered the padd, trying to remember the specifics of the old case. "There was never any evidence that the Narendra anomaly was more than a single linked-point event, was there?" A single linked-point event connected only two discrete timepoints—in this case, one in A.D. 2344, and the other in A.D. 2367. Since we were past the later timepoint, such an event should no longer be a concern.

Kreinns shook his head, jowls quivering with the movement. "We never reached a solid conclusion. The investigation got cut short during the Borg crisis. Narendra is still a potential poly-point event."

Dulmer dropped the padd on his desk. "Is this just a general heads-up, boss? Or do we think the Dominion is tampering with the timeline?"

"Tell me what you think." Kreinns handed out two more padds. I immediately noticed this one was a Mark VII-T model. Using triple-redundant temporal phase discriminators, the D.T.I. protected all historical records in VII-T devices, in order to compare realities.

The file was a weekly status report from Captain Benjamin Sisko, commander of Deep Space 9. *Speaking of poly-point events,* I thought silently. Sisko had been the focus of another investigation a mere three months and two days earlier, and I was far from pleased to hear from him again. But I pushed these thoughts aside and read on. The Dominion was the primary concern of his report, as would be expected, given his posting. There were several deletions, typical of military records—that much was consistent across all realities. It took a minute and fifteen seconds before I spotted the first obvious aberration.

" 'The Maquis,' " I read aloud. "What's the Maquis?"

"It was the name of a French underground resistance group during the Second World War," Dulmer said, eyes still glued to his padd.

"That doesn't explain its meaning in the context of a Starfleet status report."

"We don't know," Kreinns said. "But the way Sisko talks about them in this report, we should. Whatever this group is, for whatever reason, they've been eliminated from history."

Dulmer and I exchanged a significant look. In our seven years, six months, and nineteen days as partners, we'd come across only three other verifiable timeline alterations. All were, relatively speaking, minor changes—rearranging deck chairs on the *Titanic,* as it were. But this, the removal of a group that apparently was on the same level of importance to Starfleet as the Dominion, was a potential iceberg.

"I've already got Data Analysis going through VII-T files for other references." Kreinns furrowed his brow as he said this, and I mirrored him. Searching the thousands of gigaquads of reports Starfleet generated on a daily basis, all under temporal protocols, was not going to be a quick or easy matter. It was going to take time and, ironically, temporal investigations never had any of that to spare.

I scanned the padd again quickly. "All the systems mentioned in connection with this Maquis are along the

Cardassian border. That's our starting point." With a quick nod from the boss, I pushed myself off my chair, and with Dulmer right behind me, we were on our way.

Captain Erika Benteen leaned back in her chair, looking into the space between the chairs Dulmer and I occupied in front of her ready-room desk. "Maquis . . ." She repeated the word thoughtfully, her face, framed by a row of dark braids, taking on an earnest expression. Finally, she shook her head. "I'm afraid I've never heard of such a group."

Silently, I sighed. We were already three days, ten hours, and fifteen minutes into our investigation by the time we were able to rendezvous with the *U.S.S. Lakota* at Starbase 310. Benteen's ship had been deployed on the edge of Cardassian space since the Battle of the Border. If she could not offer us any insight, it did not bode well for our investigation.

"There is someone who might be better able to answer your questions," Benteen then said. She tapped her combadge and said, "Number One, would you step in here, please?"

Four seconds later, the doors slid open, and Benteen's first officer entered. He was a large man, broad in the shoulders, with a thick brush of dark, close-cropped hair. But most remarkable about his appearance was the elaborate pattern of lines and curves drawn across his left temple. "Yes, Captain?" he said in a surprisingly gentle voice.

"Commander Chakotay was born and raised in a colony along the Cardassian border," Benteen informed us. Then turning to her first officer, she asked, "Number One, are you familiar with a group calling themselves 'the Maquis'?"

"Mah-key?" he echoed. "No, I can't say that I am."

I considered the commander at length. The swiftness of

his response concerned me, especially when taken with the tattoo. A man who displayed an anachronism like that did so for one of two reasons: a deep reverence for the past, or a disdain for the present. "Are you sure, Commander?"

"Yes, sir," he answered, perfectly matching the seriousness with which I posed the question.

I still wasn't one hundred percent convinced, but at the moment there was no point pressing. I turned back to the captain and asked, "What can you tell me about Drovoer II?"

"A former human colony, now on the Cardassian side of the border. The colonists resisted relocation after the first treaty was signed, but when the fighting broke out again, they had a change of heart."

"They abandoned the planet?" Dulmer asked.

Benteen shrugged. "They didn't want it as badly as the Cardassians did."

"Not that they had any use for it," Commander Chakotay added, a sneer in his voice. "The climate is too cold for them, and its strategic importance disappeared after the second treaty, so eighty thousand refugees . . ."

Benteen raised a hand to silence him. "Thank you, Number One," she said, somewhat wearily. "Your opinions on the Cardassians are already on record."

"And Drovoer II is still uninhabited?"

"As far as we know, and we have no reason to suspect otherwise."

I stabbed my padd, striking that name from Captain Sisko's list of Maquis strongholds. "How about ci'Nent V? Vesten Prime? Beta Paugdi IV? Are any of these worlds of any significance?"

Benteen shook her head, perplexed. "Significant how?"

That, of course, was the very question we were trying to find the answer to. I frowned at my padd again, frustration mounting. It was never an easy matter uncovering facts in a timeline in which said facts were the fictional suppositions of a "what if " scenario. But I knew in my gut there were answers to be found here; I just wasn't asking the right questions.

Dulmer must have had the same thought. "How goes the fight against the Dominion?" he asked the *Lakota* officers.

Benteen seemed grateful to have a question she could answer. "It's a constant chess match with them. They make a move, we make a countermove, and both of us always looking at least seven moves ahead."

"And who's winning this chess game right now?"

Once again, Benteen's discomfort returned. "We're getting into an area, gentlemen, that I don't feel I should be discussing with civilians."

I leaned forward, halfway out of my chair, hands on the edge of Benteen's desk. "Captain, we're investigating a temporal aberration that may have completely altered the very nature of our conflict with the Dominion. We need to have answers to these questions, and quickly."

Chakotay readied himself to protect his captain from an attack, but Benteen didn't even notice him. She clenched and unclenched her jaw, then fell against the back of her chair. "We've been holding our own up to now," she said slowly. "We've been able to more or less contain the Jem'Hadar in the Badlands. But there have been more and quicker strikes into surrounding systems, spreading us, and the Cardassian fleet, thinner and thinner. And now that they've taken the Archer system . . ."

Benteen hesitated again, debating the release of another

military secret, no doubt. "Go ahead, ma'am," I prompted her.

Her face knitted in deep concern, and her voice lowered to whisper. "Reports have it there is a certain lichen on one of the Archer moons that can be processed into ketracel-white. If this turns out to be true, the effectiveness of our blockade of the Badlands is cut in half. And if they can cultivate the lichen . . ."

She let that possibility hang over the room, and I carefully absorbed all she said. This scenario would drastically alter the conflict—in the Dominion's favor. Which led to the question, if the invasion of the Narendra Sector had its benefits for the Dominion in the here and now, why tamper with the past? They still may have stumbled across a poly-point event and eliminated the Maquis, even by accident, but the connection between the two seemed more tenuous now than before.

"I'm sorry we can't be of more help, gentlemen," Benteen told us. "We're scheduled to arrive at Reves III in two hours. . . ."

"Exactly two hours?!"

Benteen and her first officer both appeared surprised by our reaction, spoken in unison. "Let me clarify," the captain said. "We'll arrive in approximately two hours."

I rolled my eyes slightly. "That's not a clarification, ma'am. That's a correction." I stood, along with my partner. "If you have any other corrections to make to your answers, let us know."

Benteen merely stared at us as we turned and left her ready room.

* * *

Thirteen minutes and twenty seconds after our meeting ended, Dulmer and I were in Paris. Large armored vehicles painted with black eagles and swastikas rumbled down empty streets, belching diesel fumes into the air. Dulmer and I sat at a sidewalk cafe table, unnoticed, watching the holographic scene play out for us, while the rest of the city residents peered out from behind drawn blinds and curtains.

"Whoever these Maquis are, they didn't choose their name by accident," I said, brainstorming. "There's some parallel here."

"The Dominion has been using 'blitzkrieg' tactics," Dulmer said.

"True," I said—the Dominion could not be eliminated as suspects. "Then again," I added, "more than a few people have compared the Cardassians to Nazis."

"Same for the Romulans," Dulmer said with a small shrug. "Not to mention the Klingons, on their bad days."

As we pondered these choices, a young Parisian, no more than a teenager, ran out of his hiding place, into the street. He stood in front of the panzer, waving his arms and shouting out a string of curses. The vehicle didn't even slow down. Instead, it fired a staccato burst of bullets, causing a spray of blood to explode from the kid's shoulder. He screamed in pain, barely regaining his senses fast enough to jump clear of the heavy treads bearing down on him.

"Something just struck me," Dulmer said.

"What's that?"

He pointed to the teenager, still cursing the German troops from the sidewalk. "That's the Maquis," he said. "An oppressed people, watching their home being overrun by vicious aggressors, fighting back as best they know how.

They're the good guys, the heroic figures of this period."

"Right," I said, not quite following.

"The Benjamin Sisko who wrote that report didn't think they were heroic. He considered them a nuisance, if not a threat. And the way he wrote about them, he wasn't trying to convince Starfleet of his opinion; Starfleet was already in agreement."

Dulmer, I realized, was absolutely right. "We're assuming the modern Maquis is a human group, just because they took a name from human history," I said, considering the other possibilities.

Dulmer fixed me with a dour look. "How likely do you think it is a nonhuman group adopted a human name?"

I stared blankly at him. Maybe I just didn't want to see what he was driving at, but he offered nothing more. Instead, he pointed to the teenager on the side of the street. He was still cursing the troops when a German officer on horseback trotted over to the curb and casually shot him through the forehead. Then, even though the program had ignored us thus far, the Nazi seemed to look right at me, his cold blue eyes locked on mine. Evil eyes.

Human eyes.

"Computer, end program!"

Dulmer managed to jump to his feet before his chair reverted back to thin air and free photons. He shot an irritated look at me.

I shrugged by way of apologizing. "Maybe we're taking the matter of the name too literally," I said. It was possible the Maquis and their aggressors *were* both human. But this was just a guessing game based on limited information, serving no purpose other than to make us question the timeline we were out to restore. And with the guesses we were making, we were only making that job harder to finish.

We left the holodeck. Commander Chakotay was in the corridor waiting for us. "Agents, I remembered something that I believe might be of significance," he said.

"What's that?" I asked.

"I was thinking about Drovoer II," he said. "Before the government surrendered the system to the Cardies, there was a huge artists' retreat there. They held an annual show and competition; painters and other artists traveled from all over the sector. . . ."

I stopped listening to the commander as my mind suddenly jumped to warp. *The government surrendered.* Of course. Just like the French did in A.D. 1940, the Federation allowed their territory to be taken over, without regard to the affected citizenry. What if some of them stayed behind after the evacuation, intent on fighting the invaders? The answer was so obvious now that it was blinding.

". . . Why anyone would choose to name their group after an obscure painter like August Macke," I heard Commander Chakotay say as I became aware of him again, "I don't know. But perhaps that's a lead?"

Dulmer was staring daggers at him. "First of all, Commander, it's 'Maquis,' not 'Macke,' " he said, stressing the vowels in both names. "Second, do you really believe the Federation would concern itself with a hypothetical band of disgruntled art-contest losers?"

The commander was wounded. "I was only trying to—"

"You've been *extremely* helpful," I told him as I grabbed Dulmer's elbow to guide him down the corridor. "Thank you very much for your input." I caught a last look at Chakotay as I pulled Dulmer into a turbolift to share my newfound insight with him. I believe the commander was more bewildered by my effusive thanks than my partner was.

After discussing my theory with Dulmer, we contacted headquarters, suggesting a refocusing of data-search parameters, concentrating on the Cardassian treaty negotiations. Within one hour and twenty-seven minutes, Kreinns contacted us with new information.

"Your hunch turned out to be right on the money, Lucsly," the boss said, although he didn't seem particularly happy about it. He lifted a Mark VII-T from his desk. "Apparent point of divergence: stardate 47751. The Cardassian peace treaty had just been formalized, citizens displaced by the new border agreement were up in arms, and the Cardassians were pressing for a speedier evacuation. However, in the real timeline, the first gul on the scene, Evek, ordered his ship *not* to fire on the Federation.

"So the Battle of the Border never happened," Dulmer said, with a slight smile. I shared that sentiment. We now had something more palpable than the mysterious Maquis—the over two thousand lives lost in the six-day conflict—that we were out to save.

But the boss still wasn't smiling. "New negotiations were initiated then and there, resulting in an agreement allowing the colonists to remain on their homeworlds, but still in Cardassian territory."

It took a second and a half for my mind to register that point of information. "In Cardassian territory?"

Kreinns nodded. "The Cardassians promised to leave them in peace, and the colonists agreed to live as expatriates."

"The Federation abandoned them? Just like that?" Dulmer asked, in utter disbelief. I shared his incredulity, although we both knew better than to question outright the veracity of this information. To voice any doubt in the validity of the real timeline was the quickest way to get thrown out of the D.T.I.

It took me a while (seven seconds) before I could come up with a safe comment. "As ill-conceived as the first border treaty was, I can't comprehend how the Diplomatic Corps could have simply cut Federation citizens loose like that."

"It wasn't the Diplomatic Corps that negotiated the new agreement."

I shook my head, confused. "Then who?"

Kreinns hesitated, then said, "You know the old joke . . ."

My partner made a quiet moan. I brought my hand to my face and covered my eyes. Yes, we knew the old joke, a joke as old as the D.T.I. itself (one hundred two years, ten months, twenty-nine days). The joke was, "All temporal investigations lead, eventually, to the *U.S.S. Enterprise.*"

"Picard," I grumbled.

I hate jokes.

The former captain of the *Enterprise*-D, and current captain of the *Enterprise*-E, scowled at us over the viewscreen. He was obviously just as happy to see us as we were to see him. "What can I do for you, gentlemen?"

"We need to ask you a few questions, Captain."

"This isn't about the situation in the Narendra Sector, is it?" he asked, a frown drawn across his chiseled face. "There's really nothing more I can offer about that anomaly—"

"No. It's not about your encounter with the Narendra anomaly," I said. "It's also not about your encounter with Doctor Cochrane. Or with James Kirk. Or Samuel Clemens. Or Berlinghoff Rasmussen. Or—"

Picard clenched and unclenched his jaw as I ran through this litany. In our prior dealings with this man, the captain of the flagship and overly decorated "hero" of the Federation, it's always been necessary to remind him what a grand nuisance he was to the space-time continuum. When he had heard enough to come down a few pegs, he asked, sharply, "What is this about, then?"

"It's about Dorvan V."

"What about Dorvan V?"

"You visited Dorvan V on stardate 47751?"

"That's correct."

"What were you doing there?"

"We were assigned to evacuate the colony there."

"Did you complete this mission?"

"No, we didn't."

"Why not?"

"This is all in my logs."

"Just answer the questions, Captain."

Picard sighed. "The colonists refused to be removed from their home."

"So what did you do?"

"I tried negotiating with the colony leader, Anthwara—"

"Negotiating. To remove him from the colony?"

"Yes. But to no avail."

"No avail, you say?"

Picard looked confused. "What are you after, Agent Lucsly?"

"Just the facts."

Another sigh from Picard. "Our negotiations were cut short when the Cardassians arrived. They pushed for a speedier evacuation. Push then came to shove. The Cardassians fired on the colony, then on the *Enterprise*. Needless to say, at this point, our negotiations with the Dorvan colonists became moot."

"And why is that?"

Picard considered me with a look of incredulity. "Because we then went to war to *defend* Dorvan and its inhabitants."

I took a sharp breath and turned to my partner. He shook his head, confirming my thoughts: Picard knew nothing about the divergence.

"Tell me, Captain," I said, turning back to the screen, "did anything else out of the ordinary happen during this mission?"

Picard hesitated, either trying to remember, or trying to formulate a story. "One of my crew . . . actually a former crew member at that point, a civilian . . . opted to leave the *Enterprise* and stay on Dorvan V."

"Why?"

Again Picard took his time in answering. "He stayed to study with a being known as the Traveler. It was his intention to explore different planes of existence."

My jaw dropped. "Different planes of existence? That wasn't in your log, Captain." Had Picard used a phrase like "planes of existence" in an official log, the D.T.I. would have been on him like blue on an Andorian.

"I didn't feel it necessary."

I gaped at Picard, who just stared back at us, remorseless

and somewhat smug. Could it be he didn't understand what he had done? "Planes of existence are not playthings, Captain. My whole adult life has been dedicated to the protection of this plane on which we exist, this space-time continuum. Every day, we have to fight against people like you, and Ben Sisko, and the rest of this Kirk-worshiping fleet, to keep the fabric of this universe from unraveling around us. But now, you tell us you set a member of your crew loose to meddle in other planes of existence, an act which could cause a cascade effect across the entire multiverse . . . and you felt a log entry regarding such was unnecessary?"

For a relatively long time (eleven seconds), Picard said nothing. I waited patiently, showing the *Enterprise* captain a stone face.

Finally, Picard spoke. "Don't you think you're overreacting just a bit?"

I slapped the monitor controls and wiped the scofflaw's face from the screen.

The *Lakota* arrived at Dorvan V four hours and forty-seven minutes later. Dulmer and I beamed down alone. Entering the settlement, modeled after the earthen structures built by the ancient tribes of the North American desert, was like walking into the past.

My partner obviously got the same feeling. "I don't like this place," he said.

"Mm-hmm," I agreed.

We walked to the middle of the village square. It was midday, and the Dorvan sun beat mercilessly on the planet. All the colonists had apparently sought refuge from the heat indoors.

"Where's the government center?" Dulmer asked aloud. "None of these buildings have signs."

"No?" I flicked my eyes, noting a few pictographs here and there, but nothing in a recognizable language. I pivoted in place, examining the vista, and at the end of 360 degrees, I found myself staring into the chest of a giant man who had not been there before.

"Hello," he said, while I jumped back, nearly knocking Dulmer to the ground. Once I steadied myself, I took a better look at the man looming over us. He had a prominent brow, and his chalky-white skin nearly glowed in the intense sunshine, leading me to conclude he was not of Amerind descent. "You are the Federation investigators," he said.

I nodded. "I'm Agent Lucsly, and this is Agent Dulmer. And you are . . . ?"

"I am a Traveler," he said with an enigmatic grin.

"Well, Mister Traveler, we'd like to ask you a few questions."

He shook his head slowly. "I'm not the one to whom you want to ask your questions."

"Please cooperate with us, sir, or we will have to—"

Before I could finish, Dorvan V had disappeared. I found myself floating in a void of pure black. Shocked, I went back on my heels, flailing my arms—but did not fall. There was no gravity, and yet there was no normal sense of weightlessness either.

"What is this place?" I heard Dulmer say. He was trying to sound authoritative, but he was obviously as thrown by the sudden shift as I was. After a remarkably short period of disorientation (I cannot be sure how long), we both found an unusual sense of equilibrium.

"Let's call it an alternate plane of reality," the Traveler said, still smiling his same smile. "The person you want to talk to is here." The alien pointed off to his left, and in the distance I saw a cluster of what appeared to be stars. The stars drew closer to us—or we drew closer to them; it was impossible to tell. As we were about to collide, the small lights consolidated into the form of a young human male. He looked up at Dulmer, and then me, contempt in his bright hazel eyes. Then he turned to the Traveler.

"What are they doing here?" he demanded.

"You wouldn't listen to me," the alien said. "Perhaps you will listen to them."

"They're from Temporal Investigations. Bureaucrats," the kid said. "They aren't going to understand any more than you do."

"You said I wouldn't understand because I wasn't human. They are human. If you make them understand, then I will concede the matter to you."

The kid considered this, and then turned back to regard Dulmer and me. "So, how did you figure out what happened?"

"We have our methods," I answered. "The real question is, what exactly did you do, and why?"

"I altered time, because the way things originally happened wasn't right." He said it with such casual defiance, I was sorely tempted to imprint his obnoxious face with my fist.

"And who are you to decide which timeline is right and which isn't?"

"Who are you?" he retorted. "You know nothing about the other timeline. I do. Trust me, the entire Alpha Quadrant is better off, all because I changed one small event."

"Trust you? You mean like Joshua Albert trusted you?"

The kid froze, then his eyes narrowed. Before he could collect his thoughts again, I continued. "Yeah, we know something about the timeline after all, at least prior to stardate 47751."

"You're a rather mistake-prone young man, aren't you?" my partner continued. "The Nova Squadron incident. Your experiments with nanites and static warp bubbles."

"And let's not forget the time you got drunk and built a force field around engineering to keep the regular crew out," I added.

"I wasn't drunk; I was—" He cut himself off, scowling. "All that happened an entire lifetime ago. In the three years I've been here, I've learned more about the nature of time than you can even begin to comprehend! You have to believe me when I tell you that the real mistake was what happened in the original timeline."

The kid tried hard to sound commanding, but his overly intense demeanor and high-pitched voice almost made his speech laughable. I looked him straight in the eye and leaned in close, flagrantly violating his personal space. "You're right," I told him. "I don't know the details of the original timeline. But here's what I do know: it was the *original* timeline. The one that happened first, that was meant to happen. Now, whether you believe it's a god or fate or some complex string of fractals, *something* causes the events of time to happen the way they do. Something bigger than anything we know, or that we *can* know. This new timeline was created by *you*, a human being, a mere mortal. I cannot abide placing the destiny of the entire universe in *your* hands."

The Traveler had his eyes on the kid's face the whole while. "Do you see now?" he asked.

"They still don't understand," he whined. He almost sounded pitiful, but the last thing a genius mind with the power to alter the space-time continuum deserved was pity. Dulmer and I both reached out at once, grabbing each of his arms at the elbow.

But the kid shook us off like our arms were cobwebs. His face turned red, and a low hum, like that of a warp engine, seemed to come from inside him, growing louder.

"YOU HAVE TO UNDERSTAND!"

Suddenly, my mind exploded with three years of history that had never happened. The two timelines coexisted in my mind, side by side, and I could compare them both. The Battle of the Border against the random torture of Federation expatriates. The solid, stable rule of the Cardassian Central Command against the embarrassing terrorist blows and upheaval following the rise of the Detapa Council. A relatively small Dominion presence in the Badlands against—

And just as suddenly, I was back with the Traveler and the kid. The memories lost their solidity, but they were still there, like a cloud of smoke that would not diffuse and blow away.

"You understand now," the kid said, "don't you?"

"Yes," Dulmer answered, his voice a hoarse whisper. For my part, all I could do was lick my lips and wait for the haze to clear.

"And what you saw was just a fraction," the kid said. "If you could see how events unfold in the future of the time-lines—"

"But they cannot," the Traveler interrupted.

"No," the kid said. "But now you know why I did what I did. Are you still going to stand there and pass judgment on me?"

I turned to my partner, and he turned to me. Like the alien Traveler noted earlier, we were both human. Neither of us could have been unaffected by what we had experienced.

He won Dulmer over.

And with the look he was giving me, Dulmer was hoping I was won over as well.

Again, I licked my lips. I took a deep breath and turned back to the kid.

And the look on his face—so smug, so pleased with his superior knowledge and intellect—caused my good sense to return in a Biblical-style flood.

"You're damn right I am!" The kid reeled back as I exploded. "Everyone who tries to manipulate the timeline thinks they're doing it for the best. The law of averages says about half of them are right. Well, I'm just a human being; I can't make that call and stop only half. Either I preserve the original timeline or I chuck it all, and I'm not about to do that for the likes of you. In the name of the United Federation of Planets—"

"God, no," Dulmer groaned.

"—I demand that you return the space-time continuum to its original state!"

The kid's face fell. The alien considered him, taking no pleasure in the hard lesson his student had to learn. Then, he looked at me. "All will be as before," he assured me. I nodded, keeping my eyes forward. I couldn't look at Dulmer, though I could tell he was staring at me, making my ear burn red hot.

Looking down at his feet, the kid muttered, "You're a fool, Mister Lucsly." He lifted his head and stared me right in the eye. "I know I'm not a god. Neither of us are, sir." Only then did I notice how much intelligence shone through those eyes. There was an intensity coming off him that made every hair on my body stand at attention.

"But at least what I did was for benevolent reasons," he said in a hissing whisper. "Will you be able to tell yourself the same?" He then grinned at me, baring all his teeth like a wild dog. The teeth were the last thing I saw before . . .

. . . I sat at my desk, sipping a *raktajino* and scanning the latest reports. It was a gradual disorientation that came over me, like an early morning fog rolling in from the Bay, which then coalesced into memory.

Random torture of Federation expatriates, against a six-day Battle of the Border.

A weakened Cardassia in political turmoil, against a solid leadership united with the rest of the Alpha Quadrant against a common foe.

And Gul Dukat's alliance with . . .

I dropped my padd and turned to my desktop monitor, calling up the Federation News Service's live feed. Reports were that the Dominion had attempted to detonate the Bajoran sun and destroy a combined fleet massed at the mouth of the wormhole. Meanwhile, the Jem'Hadar were scouring the demilitarized zone, on orders from Dukat to eradicate the Maquis.

I just watched and listened, stunned, so totally absorbed that I didn't even notice Dulmer enter. He noticed the monitor, shaking his head. "Hell of a thing to happen, huh?" he said simply. Then he went to the replicator for coffee.

He didn't remember the other timeline.

I uttered a silent curse as the boss entered a few steps behind Dulmer. "Just got a report from the *Lakota,* on the DMZ. Temporal distortions in the vicinity of Drovoer II— looks like someone's playing with Paul Manheim's theories again."

"Probably the Maquis, looking to change this past week," Dulmer said dryly, quickly pushing himself up from his chair.

I rose to the call of duty as well. I was a bit slower out of my seat than my partner, but I managed to stand nonetheless. I walked with him out of the office, heading off to Drovoer II, to preserve the timeline as the gods, or fate, or a complex string of fractals deemed it to be.

I hoped to hell they knew what they were doing.

I Am Become Death

Franklin Thatcher

I sit with my back to the ruins of Starfleet Academy, watching the sun set over what, two millennia ago, was called San Francisco Bay. The salt air, the offshore breeze, the brilliance of the cloud-streamed sky, the yellow sunlight: all these drew me to this place. It had seemed just the right place to come to die.

But *they* had been waiting when I arrived.

Damia speaks from behind me. "Father Data?"

From the time I had first heard it, I detested the reverential term the Children of Soong had given me—detested it as much as the monument they had erected to Soong on Omicron Theta, where I and my brother, Lore, had been made. "What do you want?"

"We have summoned a ship from this timeline to rescue you. It will arrive tomorrow."

She waits for my answer, standing behind me, silent as only an android can be. She came a thousand years to find me; she can wait another thousand for my answer.

Jaris, my keeper—my jailer—these past dozen centuries, has chosen to explore the ruins, thinking his job admirably done. I had covered my escape so well that it took him a thousand years to track me. But with time travel, he has been able to stop me, almost before I started.

The timeship had appeared with hardly a whisper, the instruments of my own small ship not even detecting its arrival. As I stepped onto the weed-crazed pavement outside the ruined academy, I had, at first, taken Damia for human. But her all-too-easy shift of emotions, her not-quite-right choice of mood, made it all too clear. For all of the achievements of the celebrated Children of Soong, emotion for them was still a matter of hardware and programming, the precise simulation of emotion—but a simulation still. Jaris's appearance a moment later confirmed my deduction and signaled the complete failure of my bid for death. On their belts they carried pencil-thin metallic rods: weapons, prominently displayed in a misguided attempt to guarantee my compliance.

Without invitation, Damia sits down beside me to watch the sunset, her face a mask of emotion that unwittingly mocks my own feelings. Her expression is for my benefit more than hers, as if she is saying, *look at me, Father Data, I have emotions just like you.* But they are not just like mine.

When Doctor Soong implanted the emotion chip in me so long ago, a strange sensation had overtaken me. The remembrance of Tasha Yar and of Lal, my doomed daughter, had filled me with a hollowness that I could not understand, a discomfort that I could neither isolate nor control. Eventually I identified it as grief, and developed subroutines to master it, to numb myself to it. Then came the death of Jean-Luc Picard, my mentor and friend; then of Geordi La Forge; then Troi; then Worf. One by one, all of my friends died. New friends, too, grew old and died.

I became obsessed with the deaths of those I loved—

those already gone, as well as those still living. Who would be next? But no algorithm—no calculation—could predict, or prepare me. Eventually, I left starship duty, seeking refuge in the halls of academia. Even so, age gradually took all those who befriended me. Even Tana, after nearly sixty years of marriage, crossed that border to an unknown that I would never experience.

In my grief, I began switching off my emotion chip, allowing the narcotic of emotionless machine intelligence to engulf me. But when I switched it on again, it was as if it had never been off. At last, I rid myself of the troublesome chip, destroying it so I could never be tempted to replace it.

Only, that wasn't the end of the matter.

While the emotions produced by the chip had been artificial, I discovered that, even without the chip, there was still feeling. Over succeeding centuries, that feeling had grown deeper and more profound, until, at last, I knew that what I felt was true emotion, not merely its simulation: emotion born of a dozen human lifetimes of experience, of relating to those frail creatures to whom emotion was a gift too often taken for granted. At last, I knew what it was to be human.

And I wanted no part of it.

I insulated myself from all mortal species, taking residence at the great complex on Omicron Theta, surrounding myself with the androids who considered it to be their homeworld. But I could not hide from the feelings. I found myself at once drawn to and frightened of human companionship.

At last, when the conflict within myself grew too large, I came here, to the place most intimately related to all those I had loved.

Like the samurai of old, I would take a ceremonial place

in the main hall, amid the dust-covered heroes of the long-dead Federation, open my flesh, and shoot full power into my positronic brain.

A thousand years in the future, Jaris must have finally found me here, my hand still poised over my chest, touching the controls that had ended my life. Had Jaris been mortal, he would have known to come here at the first.

Damia stirs beside me. "Why did you come here, Father Data? Why did you want to . . . ?"

Her penitent tone, her reverential dip of the head as her voice trails off, so calculated for effect, so cunning and faithless, angers me. How dare she ask such a thing of me? Me, whom she no more understands than the inside of a black hole.

In coming back through time, Jaris and Damia have undone their own past, the intervening thousand years. They are now trapped in this life as surely as I. I tell myself I should feel compassion for her, but I will not.

"Tell me," I say, instead of answering her question, "why did you choose to save me—to come back, destroying your own future?"

"Because you are the First," she says, as if it should explain everything. "You are Father Data."

"But I am *not* the first. Lore was first."

She affects a shiver. "How can you so freely speak of him, Father Data?"

"He was my brother. We were identical in almost every respect."

"Yet he tried to kill you."

"Doctor Soong felt that the colonists of Omicron Theta would be more comfortable if Lore exhibited weaknesses similar to their own. Thus, Lore's programming included pride, greed, and jealousy. But Lore allowed those traits to control him. He chose to destroy, rather than create, and, in the end, was himself destroyed. He had no reverence for his creator, nor for the creatures in whose image he was made."

She puzzles over this for a moment. "I have seen the bones of beings our size and structure."

Her words fill me with an amorphous dread, yet also with a morbid fascination that drives me to know the truth behind them. "Have you never seen a human?"

She looks at me with an expression that bespeaks ignorance not only of true emotion, but of all that I have lived for in my two thousand years. "No," she says. "In my time, they have been extinct for three centuries."

The first stars of night seem to whirl above me, and I am caught in an instant's maelstrom of memory and emotion, the realization of something I have known, but never admitted, for two millennia. When I had first come aboard the *Enterprise*, I had asked Captain Picard to assign me two duty shifts per day, instead of the one assigned to my human shipmates. I, after all, did not need to sleep. *"If you truly wish to learn what it is to be human, Mister Data,"* he had said, *"you must accept and understand the limitations of human existence. You must learn to excel, not by quantity, but by quality. Request denied."* Only now do I recognize the lesson he was teaching me. How could humans—or any sentient species—compete with a race which had no need of food or sleep, no need for nurturing or friendship or love? What, in the end, could humans offer the unfeeling Children of Soong but a history for them to observe and mimic?

In my mourning over the extinction of the sentient races

of the galaxy, I also come to understand the true purpose of the timeship, the reason for unraveling a thousand years of history. Through the light of the rising full moon, I see in Damia's eyes a race of machines adrift, without center or purpose. Their only hunger lies in the past. I admire them for realizing that the past is the key to the future, but I know they will never find what they are seeking. Just as Jaris, now nearly as old as I, has never found true emotion, the Children of Soong will never find the completion they seek, no matter how precisely they imitate the living. At the time of the birth of the Children of Soong two thousand years ago, life had irrevocably died from the galaxy, leaving them with neither rudder nor sail.

Even before Jaris's laughter arises from the ruins behind us, I rise and approach, Damia following close behind. Outside the academy's domed entrance my ship sits on its haunches as if beckoning: *come, flee this place.* Beside it hovers the sleek timeship. If I tried to flee, another timeship would intervene at my next destination. But the decision I have made may already have changed the future beyond its ability to stop me. It is not Jaris's laughter which draws me, but my resolve to see that decision to its end.

Beneath the academy's crumbling dome, Jaris stands within the arc of statues, exactly where I had intended to end my life—exactly where he had found me a thousand years hence—among the greatest explorers and scientists. Here are Gagarin, Glenn, and Armstrong in their ancient space helmets; Einstein, Cochrane, and Daystrom; Halsey, Kirk, and Riker: sentries of a time forever lost.

"What petty temple is this, Father Data," Jaris says, "that so many should have to share a single, shabby roof ?" He laughs again, the forced and tinny laughter of simulated emotion. *"Your* father's—now that's a temple!"

Noonien Soong is notably absent from this pantheon. The humans understood what Jaris will never know. Soong's installation of my emotion chip had cost a young boy's life. *"An unfortunate circumstance,"* Soong had said at the time, *"but you are human now. Wasn't it worth it?"* Soong's peculiar morality had piped the direction for his Children, and had excluded him from this distinguished company, even after his death. I feel only shame in the monument that the Children have erected on Omicron Theta to their honored creator.

Jaris sees my empty expression and claps my shoulders, laughing again. "Ah, you should see it a thousand years from now. In your time it is scarcely as big as this poor hovel. We have labored on it, since!"

In my mind a strange memory clicks into place: a man in nightshirt and cap, cowering before an emaciated spirit bound in chains. *You have labored on it, since. It is a ponderous chain, Ebenezer!*

"What's that?" Jaris says.

In this galvanizing moment, I am unaware that I have spoken aloud. Had Jaris any true emotions at all, he would know what will happen next.

In one lightning stroke, my fist lashes out, striking Jaris's chest. I feel the metal and synthetic structure of my hand shatter and tear as it rips through the resilient armor surrounding the energy source within his body, lifting him off the ground. As my hand smashes into the mechanism itself, there is a brilliant flash that I feel more than see. When I struggle back to my feet, Jaris's body lies twitching on the floor, his chest torn open, sparks running like drops of water through the fading light of his inner circuits. My arm is gone to the elbow and completely useless to the shoulder, its control circuits incinerated by the influx of unbridled energy. I turn to Damia, who stands with eyes wide. In her hand is the metallic rod she has drawn from her belt. She points it directly at me. I step toward her, testing her. She flips the rod to one side and a beam lances out, vaporizing one of the busts behind me, then she immediately trains it back on me. "Stay where you are."

But I know her as if her mind were laid open to see. I cock my head mechanically and affect the tone of simulated emotion. "To Jaris, I was an event, a collection of circumstances. He did not come to rescue me, but his own illusion of the past and who he thought I was. Whom say you that I am?"

For an instant, Damia puzzles at this dichotomy of sudden violence and reason. "You are Father Data. First Son of Creator Soong."

"Would you then destroy what you came here to save?"

She holds her silence for a long moment before lowering her weapon—which affords me sufficient time to raise the pencil-thin disruptor I took from Jaris in our moment's struggle. Even before the echo of Damia's scream has faded, I turn and leave the empty hallway.

Back in my ship, my hand flies over the controls. No second timeship, sent from the new timeline created by Jaris's and Damia's interference, has yet appeared. Perhaps, merely by making the decision, I have already succeeded in changing the future. Perhaps there will be no more timeships. But I cannot depend on "perhaps." I set the field generators of my own ship to create a randomly fluctuating chroniton field that will hinder observation from another time of my actions. I then set my ship's core to build to overload. In a few steps, I cross the crumbling pavement from my doomed ship to the timeship. Within, the controls are clearly marked—another indication that, even in Jaris's time, the galactic android culture is stagnant; that, in a thousand years, neither its language nor its methodology has evolved. I set my destination and engage the timestream drive, hurling myself back through the centuries. Moments later the drive of my own ship overloads, destroying most of what remained of San Francisco.

Bergnendul and Hopmikbud scroll through the systems list, perusing the modifications I have made to their warp drive. The parts I have used for the modification have been collecting dust in the hold of their ship for untold years, lacking only someone skilled enough to install and calibrate them.

Bergnendul nods continuously as he reads the test results. "Good," he says, grinning foolishly. "Good changes."

Hopmikbud nods, also grinning. "Yes. We are powerful."

"Then you will continue to search another month," I tell them. It must be a command rather than a request. A request implies weakness, and the Pakleds, being weak, despise weakness.

The two look at each other, nodding their heads like courting birds. "Yes," says Hopmikbud. "We will look for one more month."

I nod my head in agreement of our verbal contract, renewed each month for nearly two years. I dust myself off with my one remaining hand and head for my quarters. While I have no need of rest, the two Pakleds will want to confer in private, going through the systems more thoroughly, taking the time to understand what I have done. If I remain in the engine room, they will try to do it surreptitiously, taking twice as long before getting back to the search.

In my quarters, I pull the tricorder from the pocket of my work trousers and scan the tiny room. The previous week, the Pakleds had salted my room with nanites. The nanites had been from a commercially available pack, designed to gather samples and perform technical analysis. My perception of the Pakleds as slow-witted and imbecilic had made me careless. I found the nanites only by chance, and have not been able to account for all that would have come in a commercial pack. It is likely that the Pakleds already know I am not a bioform.

Fearing that the Pakleds might recognize or reveal it, I have not told them my name. It is possible that they know of my current-time self and might make the connection, and too little time remains to find another ship to finish the search. Unbeknownst to the people of this time, Dr. Soong still lives, and will soon signal the Data of this time to come to his hidden laboratory. By that time, I must have found my brother.

It is strange to think of Lore as the one chance of survival for the galaxy's sentient species. In my brief experience with him, he was, without exception, ambitious at the expense of all around him. Indeed, while he had emotions neither real nor simulated, his avarice crossed into the sadistic, not merely the profitable. His behavior, while appearing unpredictable at that time, now presents a tool to undo the work Dr. Soong intends to complete prior to his death from natural causes a year from now—a year that will condemn all the sentient species in the galaxy to extinction.

The chaos underlying Lore's thought processes will

make his exact actions difficult to predict. But I have calculated, to a high degree of confidence, that the events following his appearance at Dr. Soong's laboratory will change the course of history, that the android children of Dr. Soong will never come to be.

What the future will hold for my current-time self, I cannot predict. Were it my decision, I would prevent him from receiving the emotion chip which Dr. Soong is, even now, preparing for him, for sorrow has not improved my existence. Nevertheless, I believe the changes will make a better life for my new self.

After this drama has played out, I dare not even try to guess what part I may hold in the chaotic interactions of the new timeline. It is something I will have to judge when the moment arrives.

My patience with the Pakleds grows as short as the time left to me. Months have dwindled, first to weeks, then to days. I have begun to entertain thoughts that, just a few weeks ago, I would not have considered valid. Can it be possible that the Children of Soong came back in time and rescued Lore from the deserved oblivion to which I sent him? I have begun to imagine increasingly bizarre and unlikely scenarios to explain why I have not found him: that the Pakleds have found him without my knowledge and have beamed him aboard to scavenge the technologies his body contains. Or is it possible that my memories are distorted after two thousand years? That I do not correctly recall the *Enterprise*'s position when I beamed Lore into space after our encounter with the Crystalline Entity? Have my programs become corrupt? I cannot explain the confusion I feel creeping in on me, the madness that would give birth to these self-doubts.

I know the Children would never rescue Lore, and yet I cannot help but wonder at some deeper conspiracy that robs me of my hope for success.

At last, the sensors return the first hopeful signal. A quick check, a second pass, and I know I have achieved my quest. I order the Pakleds to bring the ship around, and they quickly obey, as eager as I to end our contract, though for different reasons. I manipulate the transporter controls and beam Lore's body directly to the cargo bay.

The Pakleds follow me as I go to look upon my brother's face for the first time in two thousand years. As we reach the cargo bay doors, they hold back as if knowing something evil has come aboard their ship, as if sensing the violence of which Lore is capable.

Already pebbly ice, condensing from the humid atmosphere of the ship, has formed on his body, chilled to near absolute zero after drifting two years in interstellar space. Sheets of vapor rise and fall as warmth creeps back into his limbs. One frost-encased hand lies clutched to his chest as if, in those moments after I had beamed him into space, he had struggled for air.

The Pakleds exchange anxious whispers behind me, as if they know that here is the antithesis of life, avarice incarnate, not understanding that this evil must be loosed for the greater good. And yet, as I move closer, I, too, feel growing dread. Something is not right.

In this moment, I do not want to deal with the Pakleds' meddlesome dawdling. "Go!" I shout, and turn to confront them. "Get out!" But they stand motionless as animals caught in a beam of light from the darkness, their eyes trapped by Lore's ice-encrusted form. I draw my phaser and brandish it at them, and at last they flee. I close and lock the doors behind them, then quickly return to Lore.

Brushing away the steaming frost with my one hand, I find the access panel of Lore's chest open, his fingers locked in their final position over the manual keypad, just as mine would have been at the ruins of Starfleet Academy had the Children of Soong not intervened. With my tricorder I scan him, and even in his rigid and frozen state, I see that the matrix of his positronic mind is irretrievably fused.

Lore is dead.

On his face is the grin I remember from two thousand years past, as if he knows he has once again triumphed. My emotions become an instant jumble of anger, sorrow, fear, envy, and relief. But above all is the realization that my plan is now in complete disarray. I glance around the cluttered cargo bay, expecting, at any moment, to see another of the Children's timeships whisper into existence.

But I know why they have not appeared, why their timeline no longer exists. And I know that my plan will yet succeed.

I wait, sitting on the floor next to Lore's body as the crumbling frost slowly melts, rivulets of water trickling away to form puddles in the shallow points and deep scratches of the floor.

When his body is almost room temperature, I release the seams of his artificial flesh, opening him like a fish to be gutted. With only one hand, the work is slow, but in an hour I have replaced my destroyed arm with his and restored circuits that were damaged when I killed Jaris.

As I stand over his body, clenching and unclenching my new hand, I wonder how he would have felt had he experienced this restoration to wholeness, this return to life of a dead limb. I look at the grin, frozen by death on Lore's face.

It is a rational transaction, I tell myself, as when I had tried to kill Kivas Fajo: one life for many.

I attach my severed arm to Lore's body, and then exchange our clothing. I prop him up next to a control panel, balancing his stiff form to appear to be working at the controls. I then key in the codes that will release my lock on the cargo bay doors. When I hear the Pakleds open the doors, I wait just long enough for them to recognize my clothing on Lore; then I raise my phaser and fire, vaporizing Lore's body. I turn back and drop, rolling away from the clumsy shot fired by one of the Pakleds. Resetting my phaser to stun, I drop Hopmikbud before he can jump for cover. Bergnendul stumbles and falls over him as he tries to flee, his weapon skittering away on the floor. He scrambles back until he comes up against the doors, closed and locked by the sequence I have again keyed in.

Hopmikbud is still conscious, but briefly paralyzed. I stoop and collect the two fallen disruptors.

"Who . . . who are you?" Hopmikbud demands, his voice quavering.

I stand over the cowering Pakleds, and there come to my mind words written on Earth long ago: *I am become death, the destroyer of worlds.*

I stretch my lips into the grin I remember from Lore's face and step forward, resolved to this fate, this role I must play to its end.

"I am Lore."

Research

J. R. Rasmussen

To: The Producers, *Star Trek: Deep Space Nine*
From: J.R.
Re: Take this job and . . .

Dear Most Powerful Ones,

The expense claim for my final research trip is attached. Two doctors' bills will arrive in a few days; the studio's insurance should cover most of it. The rest comes out of your pocket, Oh Powerful Ones. Enjoy the Beverly Hills prices.

As of right now . . . I'd cite day and date but I'm hazy from the temporal transport . . . You are minus one researcher. I'm staying in the twentieth century until New Year's Day takes it away from me.

So what if I'm the world's only time-traveling researcher? I can't list it on my résumé. It won't buy a mug of *raktajino* at Quark's. It hasn't helped my writing career.

Mainly, this job is trouble. Big trouble. Painful trouble. I don't care what the surgeon says about it being my imagination, the remaining Borg implants ache when the weather changes.

As for my final assignment, I brought back isolinear optical chips, two dozen of them. Yeah, a handful are crispy around the edges, but that's what Jem'Hadar phased-energy blasters do. An inch to the right and it'd be me with overcooked edges.

The chips hold Starfleet's data on the final confrontation with the Dominion, including Sisko's eyes-only report to the admiralty. You won't believe how things work out. It'll blow the ratings through the roof. You're gonna love it.

I know you wanted data covering a thousand light-years of *Voyager*'s journey, but the temporal transport took me to Bajor instead of the Delta Quadrant. I hope the next sucker who gets this job has faster reflexes than I do. Or you'd better find a way to precisely control up-time arrival.

That's what you get, working with purloined hardware. Real hard to get spare parts from the twenty-sixth century. That great-great to the umpteenth generation grandson of mine should of been horsewhipped by Picard instead of sentenced to do legitimate historical research. What kind of a name is Berlinghoff, anyway? Rasmussen I understand. But Berlinghoff?

I have to admit, it was clever of Berlinghoff to stash the blueprints for the time-travel pod where he could get them after he convinced Starfleet's headshrinks he was rehabilitated.

If only he'd been clever enough to take the studio limo instead of driving to the meeting at Paramount. People in twenty-second-century New Jersey never heard of turn signals? (Did I thank you for the flowers you sent to the funeral?)

And, yes, it was just as clever of you all to figure out how to take advantage of the time-travel gizmo, after Berlinghoff landed it on my pool deck that night.

Our trip to 1964 to talk to the Great Bird of the Galaxy was the most exciting day of my life. He adapted or adopted almost everything we suggested. Genius. Pure genius. Mostly on his part.

Sorry, I'm rambling . . . aftereffect of the transport, you know. Ahh, I remember the point of this memo.

I quit.

Feels good.

Bungee jumping through the twenty-third and twenty-fourth centuries, bringing back details of the future . . . it's a story right out of a hack sci-fi novel. Maybe I'll pitch it to a television network for a series. I'll leave out the *Star Trek* parts, of course. Don't want to infringe on the franchise.

No way to use being assimilated by the Borg at Wolf 359. Longest week of my life, waiting for the automatic recall circuit to bounce me home. And you'll dramatize all the juicy parts of *Voyager*'s return to Sector 001.

Maybe something on the amusement park planet . . . the "Fantasy Island" of the twenty-fourth century. Yeah, I could pitch that. . . .

Sorry, rambling again. Speaking of rambling, Mr. "Baby God" Crusher says hello. I ran into him and the Traveler, this time passing through the Celestial Temple. The Prophets like him; there's no accounting for taste.

Which brings me to why I quit. I had an encounter with an Orb, on Bajor. In my vision, Wesley and I were on Risa, getting close. Real close. You don't pay me enough to get that close to Wesley Crusher, god-to-be or not. He talked about wanting to be a father, said the early twenty-first century would be a great place for a child to grow up (before World War III, of course).

And Berlinghoff asked me, several times, when was I going to have a baby, get the dynasty started, so to speak. If I weren't terrified of spawning more time paradoxes, I'd get my tubes tied.

Yours in celibacy,
J.R.

P.S.: The pod's stowed under its tarp on Stage 17; the keys are under the mat. Live long and prosper.

Change of Heart

Steven Scott Ripley

She morphs her hand into a sparrow, and through the void it flies to stab the Vorta in the chest. Beak pierces flesh, wings dash lungs. The Vorta's heart bursts, the creature's medium of rhythm laid to rest. The solid falls to the ground, puffs of pink carnacite dust billowing up from his body's impact. She allows her sparrow-hand to fall with him, easily twisting the beak through his frail body, then with somewhat more effort and with a corkscrew motion she pierces his bulky surface suit, burrowing down into the hard earth beneath him. She shapes her hand into a turning bore to probe the arid layers of stratum. Bits of Vorta flesh, scraps of organ and bone, grind and disintegrate into microscopic flakes, mulch and fresh nutrients for this too-solid planet. Useless, really, but an encouragement for life: death is a complex process.

She observes the face of the dead Vorta through the wide oval visor of his surface suit's black helmet. Havok was his name. His eyes stare at nothing and appear opaquely purple, his white skin a dusky rose under the red dwarf sun's naked light. His broad ears sharpen to knobby points. His facial expression is racked into what these solids call pain, rigor already setting in. She came to this planet to try to understand his treachery, and now she has killed him. His body will slowly decompose in this hard, poisonous place. Perhaps he will be of better service to the cosmos as food for dust.

She is jealous of the dead Vorta. Though she is no solid and incompletely understands these creatures, she suspects his death is close to what she calls life. The lack of conscious tasking so many solids fear, unity in a blanketing comfort of oneness, is so much better than traveling through these bitter lands. She ached for her return the moment she left her home, the Great Link, and she finds no joy in the world of solids, no exultation, no victory, no love. There is nothing here but blasts of icy wind that cut and separate, hollow echoes in a dark tunnel, biting and senseless. And what is she doing on this planet named Bleak Prime, tucked away in a forgotten corner of the Alpha Quadrant, with her arm plunged through a mad Vorta's heart and probing deep into the planet's mantled crust? But she knows. It is the frustrated magnetic attraction of her essential liquid self to the planet's molten core, the draw of like to like. The moment of desire will pass: it always does.

She withdraws her arm from Havok and turns away, stalking through the thick layer of chalky-pink carnacite dust that lines this canyon cul-de-sac's floor. She briefly registers the geological anomaly: she has not seen such quantities of pulverized carnacite in a natural formation on Bleak Prime before. The ground-up stone is a quarter of a meter deep here. She kicks up salmon clouds of it as she passes through. Curious. On three sides of the large cul-de-sac, vomits of crumbled black stone lie in great slag heaps, piled at the feet of the tall, broken obsidian cliffs that crack and tumble with each new regional earthquake. Due to these, this canyon gradually grows wider and more jumbled with glinting black slabs and shards, and one day soon the cliffs will be gone and some idiot geologist stationed here will think to reclassify the topography. She wonders why Havok chose this place to die, and what it could have possibly meant to him.

She retraces their route down the ravine, not bothering to morph herself into a hawk or some other avian creature to fly back to the Flower. A long walk up the twisting ravine, at least an hour, but she must not be seen by the inhabitants of Bleak Prime as her true self. Rather than take her usual solid form, the one so like their lost lamb, she has drawn herself into the shape of a Marmosan *lherical* for this mission, a third-sexer from the planet Marmosa and therefore an Objective Witness. No solid has died for her current guise; it is enough for her to assume a new personality. Simpler to maintain, given the dangerous situation she must observe. Oblette will not question the actions of an Objective Witness. The Marmosans, though now subjects of the Dominion, originally claimed this planet and have been allowed to continue to administer their judicial system, as well as the planet's mining consortium. It is an effective cover for her. Or rather, *lher,* as the Marmosan third-sexers' personal pronouns go, and when she interacts with Oblette and the others, she identifies with *lher* and *lhe,* and so on. It is expected; she must.

The changeling draws near the mining complex, dubbed the Flower by the locals. An appropriate name for the refinery. Spoked with irregularly placed conveyor tubes for receiving raw ore from airborne shuttles and capped by a convex dome, the tower is an elegant testament to the ingenuity of the engineers who work here. The Flower's lower stem is sheathed by hydraulic and electromagnetic cushions rooted deep into the ground, and the tall structure sometimes sways and waves, not under a biting wind but when an earth-quake rocks the vicinity. Clever solids, masters of their wretched worlds—or they try to be. One must grudgingly give them points for diligence.

She turns back to observe a western vista, perched on a cliff's outcropping at the top of the ravine trail. The planet is certainly an oddity. The local geologists call Bleak Prime a metallurgical wellspring, but the engineers stationed here call it hell. The upper surface blossoms with spindly pinna-cles of multicolored minerals, ruby-red, emerald-green, quartz-yellow. Below these toothpick jewel towers, thrust up at tilted angles from mineral deposits far below the surface, lie what some call the mountains, the obsidian ranges and cliffs that rise and fall and rise again with quake-jarred fre-quency. Then the brainy foothills, pink lumps and clusters of carnacite, a deadly mineral composite in its natural state; for though the planet's gravity and surface pressure are suffi-cient for solids to live here, the atmosphere is thickly choked with poisonous gases emitted by the carnacite, and ter-raforming has not beaten back the effect. And finally dust, stacked ribbons of hard, sterile earth separating the planet's tortured core of mangled elements. All competing for domi-nance and failing, fractious under the swell of the planet's lively magnetosphere, and every softly shadowed color tinged with blood under a hoary old heart of a red dwarf sun. The essence of bleak, some call it.

The changeling finds she rather likes the place.

She steps into the Flower's stem and rides a delicate mag-lift petal up to the high dome. On the way up she morphs herself out of her bulky surface suit, black stubby arms and legs sucking into the fleshy presence of Objective Witness Mariole. Anchet Mariole is fat and ugly as sin. The changeling enjoys this persona, the fear and respect *lher* presence commands from the workers here. Anchet is tripled-chinned, ears as severely molded as conch shells, gray hair a hatchet of bristles, eyes such stiletto slits no one can guess they have no color at all. *Lhe* wears the sharply cut, black uniform of the Objective Witness, but on rotund Anchet the suit resembles an enormous bell, ready to toll judgments.

"Witness Mariole," the fawning Vorta Oblette says, "we were just discussing whether or not to send out a rescue team for you."

Anchet steps off the open mag-lift platform and ignores Oblette, who soon falls behind as *lhe* strides across the amphitheater floor toward *lher* private suites. The blood-red glare of the surface is here replaced with what solids call normal lighting, a more democratic spectrum of colors. Dozens of awed workers peer and gape as Mariole rumbles along. *Lhe* passes pale, white-faced Vortas, friends and consorts of treacherous Havok, bored-looking Kellerun traders, cowed Marmosan engineers, a few gray-skinned Cardassian advisors, most likely spies for their co-opted government. There are no Jem'Hadar stationed here: they are needed on the war front. *Lhe* notes a sullen Vulcan or two—smart creatures, but not to be trusted. Anchet does not approve of Vulcans living and working atop the Flower's dome, so high in the echelons of this planet's mining consortium. They cannot possibly mean to stay; they have lived too long in the anarchy of freedom and Anchet can see the danger in their dark slave eyes. Secret plots and schemes: perhaps Witness Mariole will sniff these out as well, before *lhe* departs.

One of the Vulcans approaches as *lhe* is about to leave them.

"Witness Mariole," the Vulcan female softly asks, "where is Havok? Is he dead?"

Anchet slowly swivels about. *Lhe* can hear sharp intakes of breath echo about the amphitheater, frightened whispers from the less foolhardy.

"What," Anchet says, *lher* voice slimy as cold porridge, "is your name, Vulcan?"

"Bicek, *lheric,*" she says calmly, respectful enough to remember the proper form of address for a Witness. She does not appear frightened, only curious and troubled.

"And why do you concern yourself with the death of a treacherous Vorta, Vulcan Bicek?"

A sensible pause. It seems brave young Bicek has a sudden inkling of the peril she courts. She averts her face shyly, and the tip of a peaked ear peeps out from beneath her thick swath of black hair. Then her dark eyes gleam bright and she meets Anchet's steady gaze. She has found the courage to speak.

"It is not the death of a Vorta, *lheric,*" Bicek says, her voice carefully modulated to betray no emotion, "but the death of the *wrong* Vorta that troubles me."

Anchet Mariole stares at Bicek for a placid minute. Nothing disturbs the fat Witness, not even the idea that *lhe* has miscalculated. But that has yet to be proven.

"Join me in my suites in half an hour." It is unwise to ignore honest testimony. And *lhe* must admit it: under these circumstances, surrounded by mad sycophants, the testimony of this Vulcan slave may be the only honest story *lhe* will hear.

She morphs out of her persona the moment she is alone, longing for home. Her liquid self oozes across the cool flagstone floor of her chambers, content to be a shapeless pool for a while. Holding shape for extended periods does not tire her, for she is an old changeling and used to it. Or to be more precise, the process is not physically taxing for her: it does involve some spiritual effort. Lately she has felt reluctance to assume solid form during long missions. It is one thing to leap out of the Great Link and turn herself—for moments, moments—into a tiger or a triangle or a spray of exultant mist. That is pure joy, ecstatic separation with a tease of false danger, and soon she dives back into the fold and her people's heaving oneness. In the Great Link all changelings are complete. But here she is nothing more than a drippy puddle on dry land, and to be a solid is to be a fake. They are all impostors, all the solids are. Even the Vortas.

The strange behavior of the Vortas stationed on Bleak Prime is troubling. Her people anxiously await her report on this subject, and yet she is no closer to understanding the problem now than she was when she arrived. Just as the Jem'Hadar are genetically engineered to serve as warriors for their cause, the Vortas are grown and cut to act as unswerving servants for the Founders, beholden to them as to gods. Yet the Vortas of Bleak Prime, Havok and Oblette and the others, seem to have attained some measure of self-will, broken from the stamp of their genetic imperatives. How can this be? What is it about this planet that could cause such a schism in the chain of command? She questioned Havok about it before she killed him, and he only stared at her blankly, as if she'd gone insane, and not he.

She wonders if she has. Nothing here is as it should be. She is surrounded by spies and traitors on Bleak Prime: they color her thoughts, poison her will. The very air sparks with treachery here. But soon her job will be complete. Then she can go home and dance!

A vibration tremors through her, the sound of Anchet's suite bell chiming. She sighs and draws herself erect. Back to business. She quickly morphs into form as she moves toward the western end of her chambers, where the Witness holds court and receives visitors. En route she passes a gilt-edged mirror hung on the northern wall. She happens to glance at it, and gasps aloud, stunned.

A familiar and unexpected figure stares back at her.

"Odo!" she says, horrified.

She peers closer at her image. No, not him, though near like him. She has forgotten where she is and without thinking morphed into the form she usually assumes when dealing with solids. A female version of Odo glares at the polished surface, her tiny brown eyes open wide in surprise. A diminutive figure clad in a dusty golden robe, her short dark hair smoothed back into a rigid cap on her skull. Just as he wears his. She first chose this persona because she wanted to show Odo a reflection of his pathetic solid self when she visited him. She hoped it might shame some sense into him, and for a while, it did. Yet he has betrayed his people again and again.

Now she can only laugh bitterly: the mirror trap she once hoped to set on *him* has sprung on *her,* it seems.

Annoyed at herself, she morphs into the obese form of Witness Mariole and steps into *lher* receiving alcove. An opaque western window glows luridly red from the harsh sunset outside. Anchet weightily spreads *lher* massive bulk into a wide-armed obsidian chair with a tall, forbidding back, decorated with stone-carved gargoyles from Marmosan folklore. *Lher* guests spend more time staring at those chiseled ogres than at *lher* ugly face. All the better.

Time for the Vulcan's testimony.

Bicek stands at respectful attention before the Witness. The sun has almost set and crimson shadows in the room lengthen and blur, obliterating angles and swallowing up dim corners. A perfect setting for a tale of treachery.

"I monitor statistical reports," Bicek says, "and advise Oblette and the other scientists regarding efficiency techniques they might use to improve our mining output. I have found Bleak Prime to be a fountainhead of inspiration in that regard."

Bicek pauses in her narrative, glancing out the window at the riot of seething scarlet hues produced by sunset. She tugs at her uniform's collar, shivering. And yet, if all reports are to be believed, the ancient Vulcan sun is closer in its sequencing history to this planet than to the younger yellows in other solar systems. Perhaps Bicek has a streak of wild, superstitious Romulan blood in her veins: Vulcans often do. Thus making them all the more dangerous, Anchet reminds *lherself*.

"As I reviewed my reports of the past few months," Bicek says, "I saw a trend develop. I noticed our carnacite-conversion output dropping at a greater percentage than it ought to, given the enormous quantities available on the surface. As you know, once filtered from its gaseous constituent, the mineral is useful as simple filler material for Dominion construction projects. I assess it to be as important as any other commodity produced by our efforts."

This is the way of all Vulcans, to present even the simplest train of thought as a progression of logical arguments. A refreshing quality, actually. Dominion slaves are rarely so acute in their mental abilities.

"I mentioned this drop in conversion output to Havok first, of course," Bicek says, "though I wondered why no one had reported it before. He did not appear especially distressed by my news. Or surprised. I have noted that the Vorta species is not especially . . . rational . . . in its approach to most matters. . . ."

Anchet grandly inclines *lher* head. An obvious point.

"And so, for the reasons I have stated," Bicek says, "I decided to take it upon myself to report my observation to Oblette, a few days later. And it appears my news may well have resulted in Havok's execution, as it was Oblette who called you here to investigate. . . ."

The Vulcan sails on delicate waters. Anchet grows still, waits. The sun sets and the room suddenly snaps to darkness. *Lhe* does not move to turn on a lamp, for like all Marmosan third-sexers *lhe* does not like bright lights, *lher* weak eyes preferring moody spills and shadows. It is only a conceit, of course, for the Marmosan persona. But perhaps the darkness will help Bicek stumble through this next part of her story, for now Anchet can sense the rapid pulse of her heart and a faint stink of nervous sweat.

"*Lheric,*" the Vulcan softly says, "I agree Havok may

have had some knowledge of this sabotage and assisted in its cover-up, but I also have strong reason to believe Oblette himself is responsible for the apparent decrease in our converted carnacite output."

"Why?"

"Because," Bicek says, her voice regaining strength and resolve, "of the manifest entries in our data banks. I discovered the deception in a roundabout way. I sometimes assist our computer specialists with their data-bank entries for our shipment manifests, when they are running behind schedule, and as such I have knowledge of our operating system—"

"Though you have been given no passwords."

"I have been given none," Bicek says, "but I do produce efficiency reports on the operators, and in the course of my work—which I'm pained to admit is severely backlogged— I recently noticed that on a certain day, two months ago, an operator logged approximately three hundred more paddstrokes than he would normally perform in the course of a given workday. The difference was extreme enough that I reported the variance to the system supervisor, Bartcha, who is a Cardassian and somewhat excitable. Bartcha grew annoyed at my report, and immediately drew up the operator's log history on his monitor. And so it happened that I saw, as I stood there and peered over Bartcha's shoulder— for I was curious about the variance myself—that for several minutes the operator in question had actually logged out of the data-entry system and logged in somewhere else, which accounted for the extra paddstrokes. But we could not ascertain where the operator had gone in the Flower's system during that time."

"And so," Anchet says, "excitable Bartcha called the

operator to his presence and drubbed him thoroughly, at which point the name Oblette was mentioned—"

"No, *lheric*," Bicek breaks in, and Anchet is so intrigued by the story *lhe* scarcely notices or cares about the interruption, "for we discovered soon afterward that the operator had met with an unfortunate accident out on the planet's surface, and was dead."

Anchet rises and walks slowly about the large chamber, moving from lamp to lamp and switching them on in turn. *Lhe* gestures for Bicek to rise and follow, and they eventually settle back down on either end of an overstuffed blue sofa in the center of the room. Anchet curls up *lher* sandal-clad, three-toed feet on the couch. Bicek perches uncomfortably on the opposite end, her posture ramrod stiff.

Anchet can see the writing on the wall, decides to help the Vulcan along. "You may skip," *lhe* says in a sarcastic tone, "the dull next section of your testimony, wherein Bartcha ordered you to forget the whole matter and you pretended to comply, but instead committed an act of treason by obtaining a forbidden password and delving into security systems you should not have seen. I assume your trail led you into the Flower's most sensitive security area, where you discovered that large amounts of converted carnacite had been systematically stripped from the manifests and diverted elsewhere, and you eventually found the culprit to be none other than Oblette himself."

"It did take some effort to decrypt the scramble Oblette used to cover his tracks," Bicek says. "However, your assessment is not entirely accurate. I did not use stolen passwords to piece together the true story, though I admit I did offer Havok a few pieces of key advice during our investigation."

Anchet drops *lher* startled feet to the stone floor with a slap. "Havok?"

"I went to him about it immediately. I am not certain why." Bicek looks troubled, uncertain. "I am one-quarter Romulan; there is always that. Let us say I had an intuition about the situation. Though I felt certain Havok was involved in the matter, for some reason, perhaps his lack of fear when I first mentioned the shortages, I did not think he was responsible. I knew him well. I always appreciated his company. He was not a fool."

Anchet smirks. "More the fool I, then, eh, Vulcan Bicek?" Bicek stares rigidly across the room, pretending to study a wild abstract painting hung on an inner wall, depicting the whirling tripod configuration of a Marmosan sexual joining. "Well, no matter," *lhe* chuckles, "my ego has no real stake in this matter; I am only interested in the truth. Did you discover where the stolen carnacite was diverted, and why?"

The Vulcan solemnly shakes her head. "I did not. Havok would not say."

"And so," Anchet says, "on the one hand we have Oblette blowing the whistle on Havok, and on the other Havok blowing the whistle on Oblette, but in the latter case I can see no point to Havok's actions. He certainly did not reveal any of this to me during his testimony. As far as I can tell, you are the only living person who knows the full truth about Oblette's guilt. Why would Havok share this knowledge with you and no one else?"

Bicek tilts her head thoughtfully. "I believe Havok knew I would speak, *lheric*. He trusted me to act, if I may say so, as an objective witness. Events moved quickly once you arrived on this planet. I did so at the earliest opportunity."

"Fine." Anchet rises and strides toward the door leading to the amphitheater. "Let us examine the electronic evidence, which I hope is readily available?"

Bicek nods, following.

"And then let us take a stroll in the moonlight, Vulcan Bicek."

Anchet pauses in the threshold as *lhe* thrusts the door open, smiling sardonically at the frown on Bicek's long-drawn face.

"Irony," Anchet says, "is an illogical habit of mine. Shall we go?"

Bleak Prime has no moons.

Anchet decides to drive a crawler-pod down to the site where Havok died, rather than bother with the charade of putting on a surface suit. They have reviewed the computer system's evidence of Oblette's guilt, and Mariole has pronounced it sufficiently damning to merit further investigation.

"Where are we going?" Bicek asks.

Anchet thrusts the pod into gear and they crawl out of the Flower's surface-vehicle bay onto the rocky landscape. "I too am sometimes driven by inexplicable intuitions, Bicek," *lhe* says, "and I find myself driven by one right now."

But the Witness explains nothing more. Not without more evidence.

Anchet glances back as the vehicle-bay's doors grind closed, and sees a gaggle of pale Vorta faces peering at their departing craft. They stand in a tight knot behind the glass-partitioned viewing window on the far, inner bay wall. Oblette is among them, talking quickly to the others. He looks frightened, and well he should be. The bay doors close, and Anchet is relieved of the painful sight of his stupid solid face.

"It is odd," *lhe* says casually, "the behavior of the Vortas stationed here. The species is normally devoted to the Founders." *Lhe* is curious to hear Bicek's thoughts on this subject.

"Perhaps being stationed on this distant planet for so long has affected their good judgment," Bicek says.

Anchet shrugs, shakes *lher* head. "That does not satisfy me. It does not explain how a genetic imbalance has occurred here."

Bicek nods. "I have watched it happening these past months with some interest. Perhaps you should obtain DNA samples and investigate further." The Vulcan eyes Anchet carefully as she speaks. Has she penetrated the changeling's disguise?

"As an Objective Witness," Anchet says stiffly, "I am more concerned with criminal action and its consequences. Still, it seems out of character for the creatures."

"Motivation for criminal actions often remains a mystery," Bicek says, "no matter how deeply one delves into the psyche or the seed of the miscreant."

"Yes," the changeling says sadly, "I know."

She is not thinking about Havok.

During the slow pod-crawl down the ravine floor, due to the treacherous terrain and an occasional surface tremor, they do not speak. The changeling sets the pod on autopilot, punching in the coordinates for the cul-de-sac, and then finds time to dream. She of course keeps the shape of Anchet morphed about her, but deep inside the changeling can dance.

She skims restlessly around the Great Link, looking for someone. And all around her the Others rush about and look too, a million strong, their amorphous arms waving and probing beneath the planet's liquid surface. All is meet and merge, a complex play of Self and Other that the solids will never comprehend. She feels an emptiness, the pain of a missing piece in the Great Link, and grabs at the nearest passing Other to lock essence and merge, touch and question. "Who are you looking for?" she asks the Other. "Who are *you* looking for?" the Other shoots back. "Who?" *"Who?"* Echo upon echo, all urgent, some growing frantic. She releases the Other, morphs herself into a spinning vortex, and prepares to spread out thin, as loosely knit as possible and still hold shape, to touch as many Others as she can. Then she hears the name of the lost one they seek, resounding toward her across the Link, the hated name bouncing from voice to wailing voice. *"Odo, Odo, Odo, Odo, Odo . . ."* The name pierces her spinning self and arrows through her, much as she speared the Vorta Havok, a vile thread upon which they all hang, like gaudy beads strung across the chest of a foul whore for all the universe to see and despise. And all because of Odo: Judas changeling, monster, abomination, fool. Loved one. Self. Where are you? Why have you betrayed us?

A voice draws her out of her dream. Ah, the Vulcan.

She clears her throat, a more complicated process than Bicek can guess, as most of her insides heave with golden nectar, her ambrosial real self. She hardens entirely into Anchet. Sight returns as eyes solidify into sentient jelly.

Forming brain registers the recently spoken words hanging in the air. Congested voice thanks Bicek for mentioning they have arrived at their destination. But one part of herself will not toughen at her honeyed core, and there she mourns and rages, for she will never, never understand why Odo is Odo, and it whips her into a passion fit to burst. It is worse than the betrayal of the Vortas, and far more terrible.

Even solids are better than Odo, she thinks, *yet I am Odo, too. For inside the Great Link or out, we are all One. So, then, who am I?*

The self-devouring logic is inescapable, and cuts deep.

Anchet directs a claw-arm outside the pod to scoop up a sample of the carnacite dust that layers the cul-de-sac's floor. Sensors immediately begin to scan the collected material. The beings wait in silence. Bicek shifts uneasily in her chair, no doubt sensing her companion's dark mood. Odd, Anchet thinks, that Vulcans, so dedicated to logic and the application of mathematical analysis, should also be so sensitive to shifts of feeling and heart. But has it not been said by some clever solid that mathematics is the only religion that can prove itself to be a religion? So, perhaps not so strange. Life is a complex process.

The results flash up on Anchet's monitor. Bicek cranes her neck to see.

"Is it carnacite?" she asks.

Anchet shakes *lher* head. "Not entirely. It is a dried dilution of the isogenic enzyme compound known as ketracel-white, mixed with an equal part of converted carnacite."

Bicek looks confused. "What does this mean?"

"It means, good Vulcan," Anchet says, "that the Vortas on

this planet have been planning to use their stolen, converted carnacite to dilute Dominion supplies of ketracel-white, used to control the Jem'Hadar warriors, who are genetically addicted to ketracel-white and die without regular ingestion of the isogenic enzyme their bodies crave. It is treason beyond anything I could imagine."

"And this," Bicek says, nodding out toward the cul-de-sac floor where the crawler-pod sits and the pierced body of Havok still lies, "is a supply area for their efforts, because they could not store the illicit compound inside the Flower, where they might be discovered."

"And Havok took me here to die," Anchet says heavily, "to rub my nose in the truth. I do *not* understand why he did not simply tell me all this from the beginning. It might—I do not say would—but might have saved his worthless life."

A pause. Anchet waits for Bicek to speak. *Lhe* wants to hear the answer, and also *lhe* does not. Deep inside her persona, the changeling writhes and gnashes at her hated shell, too subtle to ignore the irony of this situation and too raw to accept it. The truth from a Vulcan, a slave! The truth about the treachery of the Vortas. And, perhaps, the treachery of Another.

"I believe I know the cause," Bicek says with slow deliberation, "for as I said, I knew Havok well."

"Then tell me how a traitor can betray both sides at once," Anchet harshly says, "unless he is utterly mad!"

"Because he loves all things as one," Bicek says quietly, "because he sees all sides are the same, and so perhaps in that sense he is mad. It is said that those who see most clearly are holy fools and mad people. A curious paradox, is it not?"

The changeling stares at Bicek in alarm and horror, in tenderness and despair.

Odo has done the same, living with solids and even loving them! Our lost lamb. Yet he is still loved, and we know he loves us, too.

She feels her golden heart welling up. Soon it will burst through the mask of Anchet and flood the universe. She opens her mouth to let it out. To scream. Cry. Love.

But something enormous and heavy suddenly crashes into the top of the crawler-pod, the impact throwing them both to the floor. The changeling morphs out of Anchet and flattens herself in protection as the pod's ceiling caves in upon them. Bicek cries out once, then dies. Toxic gas from Bleak's atmosphere chokes her, ravaging her skin and stopping her heart within seconds. Then another sharp-edged slab of obsidian stone drives down into the pod from above, obliterating the small vehicle completely and scattering the Vulcan into mists of copper-toned blood.

The changeling escapes the ruin and lurks close by in the pink dust, fluid and golden in her true form, sensing the destruction. She slithers behind Havok's body as showers of pod and Bicek fall onto the cul-de-sac. She carefully lifts a thin rim of her amorphous body up over the contour of the dead Vorta's chest, scanning the nearby region with her delicate sensory array—her lovely body so naturally designed for touching and dancing in the good Great Link, not for fighting solids in the howling depths of space. But the Vortas, for she senses them now standing in a line stretched across the top of the obsidian cliffs, continue to use their combined telekinetic powers to dash slab after broken slab down into the ravine, to destroy her.

Rage. She morphs herself into a living spear, the greatest spear the universe has ever seen, then coils, launches, and skewers the Vortas as easily as plump fruit. Oblette is the last to go. He sees the others die first, and dies screaming for the mercy he so sorely lacks. Then she morphs herself thin as a pin, curls up into a tiny ball, and throbs, aching and alone, in a hard stone corner of Bleak Prime. She feels no triumph at all.

A long time passed before she returned to the Great Link.

She might have returned in a few days, but first by many surreptitious means she traveled to the planet Vulcan, Bicek's homeworld. A dangerous journey, for every sixteen solid hours she had to return to her natural viscous form, trusting her Jem'Hadar pilot to protect her as she lay in golden state and dreamt of home. But luck and the canny skill of her pilot guided them, and eventually they landed on Vulcan unchallenged, as if expected.

She stepped out of her shuttle and morphed into the person of Bicek, asking to speak to the high priestess who ruled the planet. Without delay she was led into the presence of the Vulcans' spiritual leader, a tall, forbidding old creature who handily put the persona of Anchet Mariole to shame. There on a high plateau surrounded by writhing mists and pinnacles of ochre stone, the changeling handed a small bag to the high priestess, and told her these were the ashes of all that remained of Bicek, and should rightly be scattered into the winds of her childhood home. The priestess accepted the bag without the obvious comment, that it was odd Bicek herself should deliver her own ashes. The changeling had little doubt the shrewd-eyed madwoman knew exactly who she was. But the Vulcans allowed her and her pilot to leave the planet without incident, and the changeling sensed there was some mad logic to it all, an essence of truth beyond rational thought.

She felt an urge to reveal herself on the voyage homeward, a tug of liquid attraction as her cloaked shuttle crept near to the so-called Bajoran wormhole and Deep Space 9. Odo was there; she could feel his presence. But common sense prevailed. The solids of the Alpha Quadrant had no love for the Founders, and she could scarcely blame them for that. And Odo truly was a treacherous holy fool: he would not protect her. He could not, for he was mad with truth.

At last she arrived home and stood on solid ground for one final moment, on a tiny promontory of rock tipped up out of the oceanic beauty of the Great Link. She dove in with great force, and soon the Others shared her traumatic adventure and the news of their near escape from disaster, merging with her rage and sorrow. Agreement was made to abandon the facilities on Bleak Prime, perhaps to study its strange effects on their genetically engineered servants but no longer to live or mine there. That was a course far too dangerous and unpredictable for their cause.

The Link grew somber and still as they pondered the final words of the Vulcan. But only the changeling who was once Anchet Mariole heard the gentle voice of Bicek as she told the Others her tale, the acutely singular voice of a solid she could not forget. . . .

"A curious paradox, is it not?"

If the changeling had a heart, it might burst. Love is a complex process.

A Ribbon for Rosie

Ilsa J. Bick

Maybe she was an angel. Mama says angels talk to God and help us. But Papa doesn't believe that. He says angels are make-believe. He says that when people are lonely or scared, they want to believe in something stronger than they are, to prove that there's a reason bad things happen to nice people.

So maybe she was make-believe. Maybe she jumped out of my head because I wanted her to. But she said a whole bunch of stuff I didn't understand. I remember the words, but my brain doesn't understand, and that's weird, because if she came out of my make-believe, then I should.

She came the night Mama had made a Denevan plum pudding. Usually we love Mama's Denevan plum pudding, except that night Mama was cutting up the pudding real slow, because she was mad. Papa had just told Mama that we might be moving again. He didn't say we would; he said we might. But that was enough to make Mama mad. See, with Papa, *might* usually meant *would*.

We used to move a lot because of Papa. He'd say that

things never got boring. But when you're always new, it's hard to make friends. I wouldn't mind being bored.

Not that I was the only one who had trouble making friends. Papa had tons more. He always argued with someone. Then he'd tell Mama who said what and what happened next. I never understood what Papa was talking about—junk about time and quantum-phase shifts. Papa had this idea to go faster than warp, which no one believed except him and Mama. Me, I'm not old enough to know what to believe.

Anyway, Papa said moving was easy because we had each other and that was all we needed. I don't know about that. Mama cared about other people. Whenever we moved, Mama would call her father, my grandpa. Home base, she said. Home for Mama was on Earth, in a country called Norway. She gets homesick, and she used to talk to Grandpa all the time. That is, she used to before we left Federation space three months ago, and now there's just nobody.

So the night Papa told us we might leave Heronius II was the night my Denevan plum pudding didn't taste so good. Mama didn't have any at all, so Papa ate his and hers and mine. Mama went to call Grandpa. I heard her crying, and Papa could tell I did. Go outside and play, he said.

I didn't argue. See, go outside and play is grown-up code for go away. Grown-ups always tell you to go out and play even when the only things to play with are a couple of bugs you find under a rock. It's just so you leave. But it's very hard to play when someone tells you to; it's not like, go brush your teeth. Grown-ups say silly things all the time— like telling you to go to sleep or be happy, as if you could just because they say so.

I went. Like just about everywhere else, we lived on the very edge of the colony: close but still far enough away so you'd have to look twice to convince yourself that we're really part of anything. There was no one around, and it was really late, way past second sunset. I'd grabbed Rosie, who's my best friend. She's all I have from Earth, except Mama. Rosie was Mama's doll, and she brought Rosie with her after she married Papa and decided to move away from Earth for good. Then she gave Rosie to me.

Outside I scuffed around with Rosie and kicked up black dust clouds. The dirt was black on Heronius, because of all the volcanoes, and *that's* because the magnetic fields of the planet kept shifting all the time, which was why we were there in the first place. About a half-kilometer away was Papa's new ship, and so I headed over there. Heronius had three moons, and when they were all out, it was like a special kind of daylight. Like walking into silver, or maybe heaven. Everything glowed.

In the glow, Papa's ship didn't look like a ship. It looked alive, which I think ships are anyway. Machines can be like people. I don't mean like an android. I mean that when you live in a house, the house turns into you, or when you pilot a ship, the ship is a thing that knows what it likes and doesn't like, just like a person. I told Papa that once, and he ruffled my hair and told me that maybe I'd be in Starfleet someday and command a big starship, only over his dead and broken body. I think it was a joke, but you can never be sure with parents.

I set Rosie down on the rocks near the ship, being very careful not to tear her new dress. Volcanic rocks are sharp. And then I sat down on a flat place next to her and watched the way the three moons made the ship look washed in silver.

Silly thing was I wished I could be home in bed. Other kids were in bed already. Me, I didn't have a bedtime. That was Papa's idea—not to regiment me, he told Mama. And I think that was the reason Papa stopped working with the Federation.

Anyway, about *her*—want to hear what I saw the first time? The way she came from around Papa's ship, it was like she kind of peeled herself away, as if she and the ship had been the same thing. She was very tall and thin and wore a silvery uniform, as if she had fallen out of space, like a meteor or an angel, and on the way the stars had gotten wrapped around her. She shimmered.

She didn't see me right away. I was so surprised I don't think I breathed or anything but just watched. When she turned a little bit, I could see that she was wearing a combadge—you know the type they have on starships to talk to each other. Our ships have been so small, you just yell if you want something.

There were other things, stranger even than the way she was just *there*. She was metal. I mean, at first I thought it was decoration, like jewelry. Her jewelry wasn't alive or morphic or even glittery, and when I finally got to see it better, I figured that probably jewelry wasn't the right word. More like circuitry. Remember how I said it looked like she was part of the ship? So it was like she had walked out of a machine and had pieces still sticking to her. Or maybe she couldn't decide yet whether she'd be human or machine. There was circuitry over her left eye and a weird metal star on the other side of her face, right at her jaw. And she wore a glove on her left hand, only padded at the tips and lacy, the way a spider's web looks when there's dew on it. Yet everything was exactly where it ought to be, as if all the metal and silver and circuitry were so much a part of her and what she was, she wouldn't be her without them.

I wasn't scared. She was the most beautiful person I'd ever seen, just as beautiful as Mama is, maybe more. *That's* beautiful; Papa says that there's no one in the universe as pretty as Mama is, and he's right.

And then there were her eyes. They were very blue. They glittered. Her eyes were where all her feelings were; in her eyes was everything, and you could tell that everything she was feeling wasn't about me, because she hadn't even seen me. She was looking at our ship. She stood there, and then she touched it, the way you would a butterfly. When you touch a butterfly, you have to be careful, or you'll kill it, because beautiful things are delicate.

That's the way she touched Papa's ship: gentle and afraid, as if she was worried that the ship would just melt or go away. She put one, then two hands on the ship and stroked it, the way I do Rosie's hair. Then she shivered, like she was cold.

Everything was really quiet, as if Heronius was holding its breath, and she and Papa's ship were all silver in the light of the stars and the moons.

Hello, I said.

She jumped and turned real fast. Because I was in the rocks, I don't think she saw me at first, and I didn't want to make her so scared she would go away. So I stood up. That way she could see I was little, and she wouldn't be worried.

She came away from the ship and looked down at me.

She didn't look angry, the way some grown-ups do when you catch them doing something they don't want you to see.

I was unaware of you, she said. Have you been there long?

The way she talked was weird. At first I thought maybe she was an android. I'd only met one android in my entire life, and his face was flat, like a pond when there's no wind. She wasn't as bad, but she said things without lots of feeling, like a computer. You know how computers are: kind of like excuse me, but the hull is going to breach and you're all going to die, and I just thought that you'd like to know and maybe do something about it.

Longer than you, I said. I mean, I wasn't rude or anything, but I didn't know how I felt about her being so close to our ship and all.

She didn't answer right away but kept staring. I felt real small, so I grabbed Rosie, and that made me feel a little better.

What are you doing around our ship? I asked.

Yours?

I hugged Rosie tighter. My papa's. So it's mine, too. Kind of.

She looked at me, and she looked at Rosie, and then she shivered again. Are you cold? I asked.

She said no, but her voice was really tiny, almost scared-sounding.

Are you an android? (How dumb. I knew it wasn't true. It was just something to say.)

She looked about as surprised as I guess she could, which wasn't very. Her eyebrows—well, eyebrow and circuit—

came together in a little pucker. An android? No. Why do you ask?

I stared down at my sneakers all covered with black Heronian dust. I hate when I have to explain things, but I'd opened my big mouth. Well, uhm . . . it's the way you talk, I said.

The way I speak.

Yeah. Like no contractions. And you talk fancy. Only androids and Vulcans do that. Except you're not Vulcan, and you don't look like any android I've ever seen, because their eyes aren't usually any color but yellow or black, and their skin is kind of, you know, creepy white. Mama says that's because they don't have blood like humans do, and blood is red and is what makes our skin have color, and red's my favorite color. Maybe you're a new model, but then they ought to finish your polydermal layer. Your circuitry's showing.

Her hand—the one with the lacy glove—went up to her left circuit, the one where her eyebrow would have been. No, I am . . . complete. These are bioimplants.

Oh, I said. Whatever *they* were, I thought. Like artificial? I asked. To help you see?

Not quite. Artificial, that is. They are integral to who I am.

See, you did it again.

What?

Said integral, instead of I am who I am.

Clearly we are having a communications problem, she said, like I had a bad isolinear chip or something.

How come you talk like that?

Speech is cumbersome, and language is imprecise.

Aren't you used to talking?

Not until recently.

Oh. Are you from a ship?

How have you drawn that conclusion?

I told her—the combadge and all. So, did you come this afternoon? The colony comm didn't say anything about a ship, I said.

My ship did not land.

You came in a shuttlecraft?

No.

This was like playing a guessing game, only it wasn't much fun. You transported? I asked. I get sick when I transport. Do you get sick when you transport?

No. But I did transport, in a manner of speaking.

And then she got that look on her face that most grown-ups get when they're not going to say anything more. She changed the subject. Grown-ups do that all the time. Your vessel, she said, does it have a name?

Just a number.

Three-two-four-five-zero, she said in that computer voice again, only that wasn't like she was so smart or anything. The registry number was next to the hatch. It wasn't like I could say wow, great guess, so I didn't say anything.

She opened her mouth to say something else but didn't. Instead she pointed at Rosie, and that's when I saw she had some circuitry on the back of her right hand, too. It matched the star on her jaw.

What is that?

Huh? I was so busy looking at the stuff on her hand I was sort of surprised. It's a doll, I said.

Doll. She said it like she'd never heard of one.

Maybe she couldn't hear very well. So I said louder, A doll. You know, a toy, only Rosie's not really a toy, she was my mama's, and she's from Norway. That is, Mama's from Norway, and so's Rosie, and Norway's on Earth, and—I stopped because it was all sounding pretty complicated, even to me, and I'm used to the way I think.

Before I knew it, she was touching Rosie's hair with her left hand, the one with the lacy glove.

Hey, I almost said. I wanted to jerk Rosie away, but I couldn't. It was the strangest thing: like Rosie belonged to her, too, and it wouldn't be right to just yank her away.

Instead I asked, Would you like to hold Rosie for real?

You'd have thought I was asking her to touch a Verillian pit viper. You know how scary things can be wow-neat and wow-creepy at the same time? That's the way Rosie seemed for her—as if she just *had* to hold her but figured she might die or something. Her eyes were real wide, and she looked like she was holding her breath. And maybe it was because of all the moonlight, but she looked like she might cry.

Then I felt really bad. Rosie makes me feel good. At least, I don't feel lonely. Sometimes, at night, Rosie helps a lot. The dark can be very scary. Parents tell you there aren't any monsters or boogeymen, but I'm not sure. So I snuggle under my covers with Rosie and suck my thumb and get all quiet-feeling, and it's very nice. It's like being little again— so little that Mama can hold you, and there's room left over.

My eyes felt all tingly. Please don't cry, I said. Here, and I pushed Rosie into her hands.

Thank you, she said, and her voice was all choked-sounding, like when I have a cold. She was blinking real fast. I watched her fingers, the ones with the glove on them, stroke

Rosie's hair. Rosie's hair splashed like a stream of silver water over her fingers.

She is beautiful, she said.

Not as pretty as you, I said all in a rush, which, even though it was true, I wished I hadn't said. I am *so* dumb.

But all she said was thank you, and she kept playing with Rosie's hair.

She likes it if you sing, I said.

Sing?

Yes, like a lullaby.

Does Rosie know one? She wasn't making fun; she was just asking.

Yeah. Actually, it's my favorite.

So I sang what Mama used to sing whenever I had a bad dream. She listened, and after a little bit, she rocked Rosie back and forth, but so slow I could tell she wasn't really thinking about it. And her eyes got a faraway-memory look. Papa gets that look, when he looks at the stars. I can talk to him, but that doesn't mean he hears. He usually doesn't, and even if I can get him to look at me, he's not really there.

I kept singing, and soon she was humming, real soft. It's an easy song, and it was nice not to sing alone. When I'd done, she kept on a bit, until she heard herself. Then she stopped and blinked. She looked at me all queer. Then she handed Rosie back but gentle, like Rosie might break or something.

That was very beautiful, she said.

Didn't your mama ever sing to you?

She twisted her head away and looked back toward the ship. I do not remember.

You mean, you don't remember if she sang to you?

No, and then she looked right at me. I do not remember my mother.

Why not?

We were separated when I was young.

What about your papa?

He was . . . lost.

You mean you're an orphan?

Yes.

Wow. I always thought orphans were supposed to be little kids, not grown-ups. Sure, people get old and die, but somehow you don't figure that your mama and papa, even if *their* mama and papa are dead, can ever be orphans. After all, they have you, and they have each other. I couldn't imagine what it would be like not to have my parents around.

I think she could tell I felt bad. She said, It is all right. It was a long time ago.

That made me feel better, a little. Were you adopted? I asked.

By a very large family.

Oh. It was all I could think to say. Do you miss them?

At times.

Do you ever talk to them?

Talk?

Yeah. On subspace. I call Grandpa all the time. He's on Earth.

No, I do not speak to them.

What about letters?

No.

But won't they worry?

I was one of many. I suspect I think of them more than they will ever think of me.

What kind of family was that? I wanted to ask more, but just then I heard Papa call my name. *Heck.* It was late. Already the first moon had set, and it had gotten darker. In the sky the third moon, the one shaped like a lima bean (I hate lima beans), was catching up to the second.

Coming, Papa! I shouted.

Only not just me shouted. All of a sudden, I heard her say Papa's name, too.

I was pretty surprised, and when I turned around, I could tell I wasn't the only one. The way her face had changed, you could tell she was all mixed up, like the way water crashes into the beach when all the Heronian moons are in conjunction: *crash, whoosh, bam,* and everything is just a total mess.

That was also the first time I had this idea that maybe she wasn't there by accident. That she hadn't just been passing by, ho-hum, in a ship and thought, gee, Heronius looked like a great place, which it isn't. That maybe she was there because of us.

Oh. I felt small and scared, and I wanted Mama. I couldn't help it; I kind of fell backward. I would have cut myself up real good, except she grabbed my arm. But when she saw my mouth all twisted up, she let me go. I will not hurt you, she said.

I know. Except I didn't, and I couldn't get my mouth to work right, and my teeth went *click-click-click,* like I was freezing. That was Papa. I have to go.

Yes, she said, real quiet and low.

Then, just as fast as I'd felt afraid, I felt bad. I was going home where everyone loved me, and she'd be all alone out here in the dark. And the more I thought about it, the more I knew she'd been looking for us. I just knew. Maybe it was the way she touched our ship or held Rosie, or maybe I knew she was deep-down sad—so sad and lonely she probably thought she'd never feel better.

I grabbed her hand, the one with the glove. She jerked a little, and then her fingers curled around mine, and it was okay.

Come home with me. You can meet Mama and Papa.

She shook her head.

But why not? We have enough to eat. You can sleep in my room.

I cannot. It is not . . . I must think what to do.

What do you mean? Are you going away? Is your ship leaving?

My vessel is far away. And I must go.

No, I thought, she couldn't. Maybe she wouldn't ever come back.

No, I said out loud. I tugged harder. No.

It was then that I saw she was wearing a kind of bracelet on her left wrist. The bracelet had a bunch of lights and numbers winking on and off. She saw that I saw, and said, The device correlates to specific resonance frequencies.

What? I asked. The bracelet was pretty, and I was kind of hypnotized by it. I don't get it, I said.

You do not have to—and she almost, *almost* smiled—get it. But I will find you again. Now that I know that this is the correct place, the correct time. . . .

What?

She dropped my hand then and took a couple steps back toward Papa's ship. It is the ship. It will take too long to explain, and I cannot see your parents. I am not ready.

Papa called my name again, and his voice was closer, like he'd come out of the house. She backed up real fast then.

Wait! I started to climb after her. Promise you'll come back!

I promise.

Promise? Cross your heart and hope to die?

She was so close to the ship then, and the moons had crossed so that there was a lot of shadow, and I couldn't see her.

But I heard her. No, and her voice sounded as hard as the rocks, no one will die.

My chest got tight, and I couldn't breathe. Where was Papa, where was Papa?

I don't understand!

It is not essential—

I think she was going to say something else, but Papa called me again, and then there he was, and I was never so glad, and it was too late because she'd have to see him and Mama too, and none of us would be alone anymore. So I turned back to the ship to tell her, because she'd been sent special to find me, and I liked her, and I wanted her to like me.

But the shadows were as black as spilled ink, and she had gone away.

I didn't tell. I walked home with Papa, and he shoo'ed me to bed. Mama was already in their room.

I had lots of bad dreams that night for the first time in a long, long time. But I couldn't remember any of them when I woke up.

* * *

At breakfast, Papa said that Mama had gone with her team to study the magnetic phase shift of a bunch of di-isotonic rocks. The phase shift didn't come on Heronius but once every twenty-seven standard years, and then only for three days. Mama's a planetary geomagnetologist. That means she studies changes in the gravimagnetic matrix of rocks. Just because I can say all that junk doesn't mean I understand. Mama's explained it to Grandpa about a hundred million times.

Way back, Mama went to study Hortas on Janus VI. Hortas live in rock. Heck, they *are* rocks. At first no one knew how Hortas found their way around, but Mama figured that Hortas sensed magnetic resonance variances in rocks.

Now, Papa was on Janus VI, too. He thought he could do what Hortas did, but in space, by mixing gravity and magnetic resonance to bend space-time in a way that's different from warp, to travel in time.

So Mama and Papa fell in love and all that stuff. Then there was me, but that didn't stop anybody. Mama's always chasing rocks, and Papa's always running after time.

But breakfast was quiet. Papa pushed his food around. The longer Papa didn't talk, the more afraid I got. Maybe it was because of *her,* or because I hadn't slept very well, and it wasn't right for Mama to leave without kissing me good-bye.

Then Papa cleared his throat, and I saw his face, and my breakfast tasted like sand.

Papa said, We're leaving day after tomorrow.

Why? I asked, except I had to say it twice because there was this big, dry lump in my throat.

Papa got this tired look, like he'd been up for about five

months. Because the Federation won't let me conduct my experiments in their space.

You don't work for them.

It's their law. All work involving new warp technologies has to pass review.

How come?

As long as we're in Federation space, they don't want anyone mucking up the works, especially space-time.

Space seemed like an awfully big place to me. I told Papa so.

Not big enough for the Federation, he said.

I was holding my spoon so hard, my fingers hurt. There wasn't any point in arguing, and it was really okay, because I hadn't made any friends. But still.

Where will we go?

Then Papa smiled, like he was going to play a trick on someone. The Delta Quadrant.

Now I knew we were in the Alpha Quadrant, but I didn't know there *was* a Delta Quadrant. The Federation doesn't own the Delta Quadrant? I asked.

The Federation doesn't know what's *in* the Delta Quadrant.

Why not?

Because it's very far away.

How far?

Papa told me.

I just sat there, with my mouth hanging open, like a cartoon: a big *WUH?* in the bubble, and hundreds of question marks.

Boy, I thought, I have trouble making friends now. I'll never make any out there. There aren't even any *people*.

Papa could tell what I was thinking. Trust me, dear, he said, there will be plenty of people: new races, new worlds. And space to work, to breathe! More free space than you can imagine. Space enough to work without interference or oversight from the Federation. Space enough and time.

My stomach squiggled, like I'd swallowed a bird. But . . . but there won't be any people, any human beings. . . .

Papa winked. We'll be the first.

My face got all hot. I wanted to cry, and then I thought about *her* and what it felt like when she went away, and I felt even worse, as if there was this big, heavy, black space ahead in time. Only it was a thing, and if we got there, I'd get lost and be all by myself, without Mama or Papa or anybody.

Papa was watching me. I knew I ought to smile. I knew he wanted me to be real brave. But we were going just about as far away as we could get from other people and still be in the same galaxy. I might not ever see another human being or any other kids or their parents ever, ever again, and I got all sick-scared inside, like maybe I was going to die or maybe never be the same, not ever again. Here Papa was saying all this junk about needing room to breathe, but no one bothered asking *me* if I was breathing okay.

It wasn't the kind of thing you said, though.

And Papa was still watching me, and I loved him and hated him all at once, and so much I wanted to scream.

But I just dipped my spoon into my breakfast and said, Oh, okay, when do we leave?

No one talked at all during dinner. Afterward Mama and Papa went into their room again. When I heard Mama start to cry, I left.

I went straight to Papa's ship. Sure enough, *she* was there.

Papa says we're leaving the day after tomorrow, I said.

She looked real serious.

Do something, I said.

Did your father say where he was going?

I told her. That made her look worse, almost as sick as I felt. I could tell that she was thinking, like a computer—going *tick-tick-tick* real fast through all the choices.

Then she said, I will speak to your father.

This way, I said and grabbed her hand, the one with the glove. This time she didn't jerk back but held on real tight.

Mama and Papa were sitting on the couch. They both looked up when we walked in, and then they just stared.

For a minute, no one said anything. Her hand gripped mine, and I heard her swallow. It was that quiet.

Papa's forehead got all wrinkly. He stood up real slow, and Mama got up right behind him. Who are you? Papa asked.

She let go of my hand and took a step toward them. I must speak to you.

Papa's voice got angry. What are you doing with my daughter?

It's okay, Papa.

Mama shushed me. Come away, dear.

No. She's my friend.

Papa started toward the wall comm. I'm calling colony security.

No! Her voice was loud, like thunder. You must not. You must listen.

Why?

Because what you are planning will place you in great danger.

Papa's eyes got as narrow as a snake's. How would you know what I'm planning?

I know. You cannot go to the Delta Quadrant. You must not.

Mama gasped, and her hands went up to her mouth. Papa opened his mouth, but no sounds came out.

Then he coughed. I've not filed a flight plan. I haven't told anyone but my family. How do you know this?

You must listen, she said. She wasn't shouting, but her voice was still sharp, like the edge of a knife.

Answer me. How do you know?

You would not believe me.

Then why should I listen?

Because I speak the truth.

Who are you? You're not human. What are you?

I am human. I was once . . . something else.

What? Papa asked, but he sounded scared now not just angry, and I didn't know Papa could be scared. What were you? What *are* you?

Not in front of the child, she said.

I was surprised. I thought we were friends, I said.

We are, she said. But there are some things suitable for children, and other things that are not.

That made me mad. That's not fair, I said. You told me everything else.

What else? asked Mama.

My God, you're from the Federation, said Papa. You're here to spy on me.

No.

Oh no? Papa balled his fists up and got taller. How do you know so much? You're wearing a uniform. That's clearly a Starfleet combadge. You don't come from the colony. We've never met.

You cannot know that, she said, so low no one heard her but me.

Papa kept talking, You know about the Delta Quadrant.

I told Father, said Mama.

Papa said a bad word. That means they're monitoring our subspace.

She said, No, you are wrong.

Dear God, you're not even human. What are you?

I will explain, but first—

No, you listen to *me,* and then Papa said a *very* bad word, and Mama said, No, that won't help. And then Mama said to me, Come here, sweetheart, come here, baby, come to Mama. And I shouted, Listen, will you please just listen, she wants to talk to you!

Then *she* touched my shoulder. Go to them.

Yes, come here, baby, said Mama.

I didn't want to, but I did what she said. Mama cried a little bit and hugged me so I almost couldn't breathe.

Papa was staring at her real hard. I don't know who you are or where you come from—

It is irrelevant—

But you accost my daughter, come into my home—

It was the only way—

Give me one good reason not to have you thrown out on your—

I had to be certain of this place, she said. Of this *time.*

Papa stopped. Papa stared.

Time? His mouth didn't work right. Time?

She said it again, real slow and loud, like he couldn't hear so well, *Of this . . . time.*

Of this time, Papa said, but he whispered it instead. Time? As in . . . travel? Another time?

Yes.

But how—why now—

I know, I understand, said Mama. It's the gravimagnetic variance. The phase shift. That's it, isn't it?

Yes. It has opened a window. The gravimagnetic phase shift has created the optimum conditions to facilitate a displacement in time-space.

Mama tugged on Papa's sleeve. That's exactly what you've been saying all along. It's possible, isn't it? Isn't it?

Papa shook his head up and down. But I don't . . . I can't control the displacement. It's unstable. How—

The temporal fabric is quite tenuous. It cannot be artificially replicated, only enhanced. There is a relay array in the Delta Quadrant. The array is powered by a quantum singularity. Previously we had sent holographic images and rudimentary communications in a series of transceivers. The ship's log contained information of an encounter with an advanced Federation technology capable of opening temporal fissures. I adapted the array for that purpose. Unstable, but enough to direct a high-density particle beam for a short time.

Then you're from the Delta Quadrant, said Mama.

There are no Federation vessels out there, said Papa.

There are none, she said, *now.*

Papa's eyes got round. You're from the future?

Yes.

Then you've done it, you've really done it! You've managed to control the timestream.

Within certain parameters and under optimal conditions, yes. It is not what you imagine. Those of us on the ship cannot all return.

Papa turned to Mama, and he looked excited. It's a beginning, don't you see? I knew I was right, I *knew* it!

And all the time I'm thinking, Oh, no, oh, no, no, no, no, why are you doing this, don't tell him that, don't make him happy, don't make him *want* to go.

I pushed away from Mama.

I thought you were going to help! I shouted at her. I thought you were going to stop him! Don't tell him all about time and the future and all these good things about the Delta Quadrant!

They all jumped. I think they'd forgotten I was there.

But, dear, said Mama.

You're too young to understand, said Papa.

I do not have nice things to say about the Delta Quadrant, she said.

What do you mean? asked Papa.

I didn't pay attention. I was so mad, I stomped my feet. This isn't helping! He's going to go anyway, don't you see? You're *making* it happen!

Darling, said Mama.

No more, she said. Not in front of her.

Why not? asked Papa. Why can't she know? What are you saying?

Not in front of the child.

Mama squeezed my shoulder. Go to your room, dear.

No!

Listen to your mother, said Papa.

No, no!

Then she came and squatted down until I could see all the patterns of the circuit over her left eye.

We are friends, are we not?

My mouth was tight. Yes.

And friends must trust one another.

Yes.

I told you I would return, and I am here.

Yes.

Then trust me now. Do as your mother says. Go to your room. Sing to Rosie and calm her. She must be frightened.

Mama said, How do you—

Rosie's scared, I said. I felt a tear trickle down my cheek.

She does not understand, she said.

No.

She used her finger, the human one, to wipe the tear away. She will, she said. Trust me.

So I left. My room was on the other side of the house, and even though I disconnected the auto—Papa showed me how once—so the door was open a crack, I couldn't hear anything but noise. Her and Papa talking back and forth, then Mama, some spaces where no one was talking, then Papa's voice going higher like when you ask a question, then her. Then, a long, long space, and then another, very strange noise, one I'd never heard before. A voice without words. Just sound. And then I figured out that the sound was Mama. The sound came and went, like waves on a beach, and I could hear Papa making shushing sounds, but Mama didn't shush.

And she was still talking, only lower now and her voice was all strange, too.

It was like a bad, bad dream. I grabbed Rosie and made a cave out of my covers. But I couldn't sing; I forgot the words.

The next thing I remember, Papa was uncovering me. I made a little sound to show Papa I was awake. He put his hand on my cheek.

She's gone?

Papa said she was.

Mama was crying.

Yes.

Why?

Papa's thumb kept going back and forth across my cheek, and then he pushed the hair way back from my forehead. My hair was wet, because it's very hot under the covers and I'd gotten all sweaty.

She said scary things?

Papa's finger rubbed my chin. Yes.

What?

She was right. It's not for you. Don't be in such a hurry to grow up. It's not so wonderful. Be grateful you don't have decisions to make.

What decisions? Are we still going? What did Mama say?

Papa pushed himself off my bed. Go to sleep. We'll talk in the morning.

That night I dreamed, and it was all bad, and I remembered it all when I woke up.

Only we didn't talk. Mama was gone all day, the last day of the phase shift. Papa walked in and out of the house. I had a funny-awful feeling all day. Usually drawing helps me feel better, as if all the yucky feelings spill right out onto the paper. Except I didn't have any paper, and I didn't want to bother Papa. So I drew on the walls. I just did it. I used lots of black, which is weird, because red is my favorite color. But I felt black. So I drew black.

Next thing I knew, Mama and Papa were there. I expected they'd be mad about the walls. But they just looked at the pictures. I remember how they held hands, only not in the way people in love do. More like they were holding each other up.

Then Papa pointed. What are they?

Dream pictures.

Dream pictures? asked Mama. When did they start? asked Papa.

Last night. Night before.

When she came, said Papa.

What are they? asked Mama.

It just came out. Ships, I said.

Ships? asked Papa.

Space ships.

But, dear, said Mama, they're cubes.

They're ships, I said, and stared at my fingers. They were black.

She came again that night. She walked right in, like she belonged.

Papa said, I have something to show you.

He took her to my room. She stared at my pictures for a real long time. Then she asked, She drew these?

Yes. What are they?

These are Borg. It is as I told you. The temporal stream has curved back upon itself.

I've checked your figures, said Papa. I ran the simulation. You might be mistaken.

She pointed at my pictures. You need more? This is *Borg*. If you go, you will become Borg. Or worse.

You can't know.

I *can*.

No. You said your bioimplants phased with a high-density particle beam. That the relay synchronized to a gravimagnetic disturbance to create the temporal rift. What if the rift didn't loop you back at all but into a parallel continuum?

Impossible. Your ship matches the resonance frequency of the vessel in B'Omar space.

In your time, your continuum. Ours might be distinct.

Why do you refuse to listen? I am not here by accident.

Papa didn't say anything. I thought maybe he might change his mind, and then we wouldn't leave. I think Mama wanted that, because she laid her hand on Papa's shoulder, as if her touch said more than words.

Then I saw Papa's face move in a certain way, and it was all awful again.

I'm sorry, he said. While I concede that what you present is plausible—

It *will* happen—

I believe you've stepped across times, not back into your own. Or ours.

She looked as if she might cry. You are a *fool*—

Please—

The child is showing you!—and now she *was* crying— She *knows*! *I* know!

Mama gripped Papa's shoulder. Can't we stay?

No.

But I'm afraid, I'm—

There's nothing to be frightened of—

No, whispered Mama. Look at her, *look* at her. Can't you see—

She cried, Listen, please listen—

You're both of you becoming hysterical—

Stop! It was a new voice, and it was screaming, screaming, and then I heard that the voice was mine. Stop, stop, stop, stop, stop, *stop!*

Mama rushed over. Oh, my poor darling, my little girl—

Oh, Mama, Mama, *Mama!* I cried.

Only there were two voices calling for my mama. Because *she* had said Mama, too.

Mama and Papa stood real still, Mama hugging me, and Papa staring, and me snuffling into Mama's arm.

She was crying, Please, Mama, Papa, please, *listen to me*—

I looked up at Mama. I didn't know I had a sister, I said.

I turned back. Are you my sister?

Papa stepped between Mama and me, and her. You've got to leave. You don't belong here. I am truly sorry for what has happened to you, but this is not your time.

She stopped talking. Her face was all wet.

No, she said after a long time, I can see that it is not.

We all went to the ship. She touched it again, like she had when she told it hello, except now it was good-bye.

Papa said, Don't come again.

She'd stopped crying. She said, I could not, even if I wished. The shift on this planet is nearly over. By the next shift, time will have overtaken us all.

I'm sorry things didn't turn out differently for you.

And I grieve for you, she said.

She looked at Mama. Good-bye.

Mama's lips shook. Good-bye. Be well. Be—

Mama looked away.

Then *she* came to me. I have something for you.

No, said Papa. Let her, whispered Mama.

I want you to have this, she said. She held out a little box.

I looked at Mama, and she nodded, so I took it.

Is it a present?

Yes. For your birthday. Open it then, not before.

Please, I said. Are you my sister? Who are you? What's your name?

I am Seven.

I'm going to be six.

I know.

Then she backed away and did something to her bracelet. I must go before the rift collapses.

I thought my chest would burst open. Will I ever see you again?

All of a sudden, she got clear, like a picture with all the color washed out. Like a cloud thinning out under the sun.

Will I? Will I?

I saw her move her lips, and the sound came back all echo, like an empty room.

Pray, the echo said, pray that when you look in the mirror, you do not.

We're all alone now.

Days are long, but it's always night in space. Mama gives me lessons. I play with Rosie. I draw a lot, but I don't like my pictures. Now they're not just those ships but people. Only they're people-machines, like she was, but worse—all metal and tubes and only one eye. And they're white, like skin when all the blood is gone.

I show my pictures to Mama and Papa. Papa says there are no people like that. Mama doesn't say anything.

Yesterday was my birthday. Mama made a chocolate cake. And Mama and Papa sang Happy Birthday, Anika, and there were six candles plus one to grow on, and I blew them all out.

And I opened her box. Inside were two red ribbons: one for me, one for Rosie. I love them, and we're going to wear them forever. Because red is my favorite color, and because red is the color of a sunset and the color of human blood, and mostly because red is the color of luck.

Touched

Kim Sheard

During the seventeenth cycle in the age of Marth'o, aliens first reached my planet. I know, because I was the one there to meet them.

I was on my way home from the Grain Festival. Most people had chosen to take the transport tubes back, but I had decided to walk. After all, we were celebrating our harvest, so I wanted to walk through the fields that yielded that harvest. More importantly, though, I wanted time alone to think. I would soon be reaching the Age of Choosing and would need to select either an occupation or a mate. None of the obvious choices pleased me. The career of technician was beyond my skills, but the life of a farmer or a home mate seemed too mundane.

I had always been curious and excitable. As a child I had spent hours doused in make-believe when I was supposed to be doing my schoolwork or my chores. My parents were almost always exasperated with me. To my sorrow, that time was now over. I had no choice but to grow up and leave behind the ways that my elders had always called foolish. I needed to become responsible and adult. I was capable of it, of course, but I was certain I could never be happy that way.

It was warm for a walk. The sky was bright with white sunlight that forced me to look at the ground to avoid its intensity. As soon as I could, I ducked between the rows of *karlak* so that the four-pace-high plants could shade me from the glare. I regretted having left my eyeshades behind that morning. I walked slowly for about a thousand paces before the *karlak* ended and I had to leave its shelter. I squinted in preparation before I pushed the plants aside, but still my optic nerves were overloaded with bright red spots. That was why I didn't immediately believe what I saw. I thought it was a trick of the light or the beginnings of the headache that the gleam would almost certainly cause. But after I blinked the red dots away, I realized that what I was seeing was very real, although unfamiliar. Interested, I dropped down on my stomach among the plants to observe, my vivid imagination already at work creating a fanciful explanation for me.

About five hundred paces from me, in the middle of a crop of short *mak'a* grain, was a boxy white object about five paces high and ten paces long. My first thought was that this farmer had built a storage shack in the middle of his field, but then I spied the black and red markings on its side. I used my telescopic eye to get a closer look. The designs were like nothing I had ever seen before, small individual marks as square as the item itself. As was habit when encountering things I didn't understand, I pretended that they were of extraterrestrial origin. Then, as I watched with my hearts pounding, one side of the box lowered and steam rushed out. It was beautiful in an odd sort of way. After a few seconds, a being came out.

It walked upright on two legs as we Pathons do, but it

had only two arms and two eyes. It was very light brown with a small amount of black hair on its head. What I assumed were its coverings were mostly black, with a splash of red near its head and where the two arms met. Its face looked ugly to me without a third eye. It had another deformity, a scar perhaps, on the left side of its head. That's it, I thought. It must be a Pathon, but a deformed one. Certainly there must be a Pathon somewhere on our planet that has lost an arm and an eye. My parents would have been proud of my reasoning.

But then a second one came out, smaller than the first, but with similar coloring and the same deformities. Instead of the scarred forehead, though, this one had a bumpy one. It looked like it had been dashed painfully against the river rocks. It had yellow on its clothing rather than red. When I saw the two of them together, it finally occurred to me to be frightened. Still I lay there gawking.

I reached out with my mind and was just barely able to read their surface thoughts. It was difficult to turn the conversation in their strange language into images I could understand, but soon I could get the gist of it. The larger one was the leader, it seemed, and it was grilling the smaller one about the status of the "shuttle." It was referring to the shiny white box, which was apparently a transport of some kind. The smaller one, called B'Elanna, was frustrated and snapping that it had done all it could do for the problem given the circumstances. They had underestimated the force of this sun's gravity. This sun! They had implied that they were from another sun! I shook as the adrenaline tried to get me to run away, but still didn't get up. What I was watching was better than any story I had invented as a child.

The larger one—"Chakotay," B'Elanna had called it—
went back into the shuttle and emerged a moment later
with three cylindrical objects. Each one had a point on top.
Chakotay handed one to B'Elanna and pointed, and they
poked them into the ground in a triangle around the shuttle.
When the tubes were set up, they glowed with blue light.
Had I not been able to read their thoughts, I would probably have thought the tubes were explosives, but I didn't
sense any evil intent from either of them, just worry. I
almost laughed. Ironic that I was here looking at aliens,
and they were the ones that were worried. I rubbed my telescopic eye briefly, hoping that it would hold out against the
glare.

Chakotay stood within the triangle of lights and pressed a
small shiny object on its chest. It was apparently trying to
talk to someone that I couldn't see. Nothing happened, even
after several more tries, and it shook its head, disappointed.
B'Elanna had spent several minutes inside the shuttle, but
then emerged, carrying two satchels and two rolls of cloth.
Chakotay indicated that they still couldn't make contact and
pointed toward the *karlak* fields. They were coming this
way! I froze, afraid of being seen if I moved. I didn't know
what they would do to me if they found me.

Staying still seemed to work, as they proceeded to the
edge of the field about thirty paces to my right and began
pulling the *karlak* leaves off the plants. They spread out the
cloths ("blankets," they called them) and tossed the leaves
on top. Then, when they had a large pile on each blanket,
they dragged them through the low *mak'a* toward the shuttle.
I watched, incredulous, as they covered the white box with
the big leaves, trying to hide it. It took several more trips, but

they finally managed to cover the whole thing so that the green covering blended in fairly well with the similar shade of grain.

Next, they shook the blankets, rolled them up, gathered the satchels, and began walking once again in my direction. The one called Chakotay pulled a handheld object with blinking lights from its bag, pointed it in front of its body, then moved it in a wide circle, allowing me to see more of the flashing colors. When the item was pointed toward me, Chakotay frowned and indicated to B'Elanna that someone was near. I considered running, but didn't have time. Within a few seconds, they had found me. I jumped to my feet and backed up slightly.

My head was telling me to run away, but deep down, I wanted to meet these creatures from another sun. I couldn't believe this was happening to me, the child who could never do anything right. My face wouldn't stop grinning at them. That smile apparently encouraged them, because Chakotay extended a hand, palm up, and spoke. The voice was soft, gentle, and by Pathon standards, masculine. Although I couldn't understand the words of his greeting, I did understand the sentiment. I returned his gesture and said hello myself. His thoughts were vaguely frustrated again because he could not communicate with me very well. He apparently could not read my thoughts, and his "translator," another of his devices I supposed, had not yet heard enough of my language to interpret. I gathered that speaking more Pathon might help him understand.

"Hello," I said. "You are on the planet Pathon. You are the first to come, and I welcome you. If you are having trouble with your transport device, perhaps some of our technicians could help." It wasn't the speech that the first alien visitors to our world deserved, but it would have to do.

They were beginning to understand. They nodded and urged me to continue. "My name is Quator. I was on my way home from the Grain Festival when I saw your shuttle. Why were you hiding it?" The shiny badges on their chests began to speak with me in what I supposed was their language. I stopped for a moment, giving Chakotay the chance to speak, this time in my language, courtesy of the translation device.

"Hello, Quator. I am Chakotay, and this is B'Elanna. Would you please repeat the first part of what you said, now that we can understand you?"

I repeated my welcome to our planet. The aliens looked at each other and then turned back to me and laughed. "Your planet?" Chakotay asked jovially. "What does that make us?"

"Aliens," I insisted. They laughed again. "I scanned your thoughts. I know you are from another sun."

They looked at each other again. "A telepath," B'Elanna said in a feminine voice.

Chakotay sighed. "We're not supposed to be here," he said to me. "We had an accident with our shuttle and had to land here. We aren't supposed to interfere with your people."

I shrugged. "You're not. You're just talking with me."

"Yes," he answered, "but before today no off-worlders had ever visited your planet. We have changed everything for you."

"But this is wonderful news!" I said. "We have wondered ever since we charted the stars ages ago if there were others out there like us. Now we have our answer."

"But are you ready for it? Is there somewhere private we

can go to talk and to try to contact our ship? Somewhere shielded from your species' telepathy?"

"Your thoughts can't be read unless you can be seen." I gestured to them to follow, and we walked several thousand paces to a cave far from the city. "This is the Festival Time," I said. "Everyone will be at home with their families. No one will come and see you here today."

"Thank you," Chakotay said. B'Elanna was busily emptying the satchels. She pulled out more objects similar to the one with the blinking lights that had detected my presence. She scanned the cave and the area around it and then returned and began taking some of the items apart. Meanwhile, Chakotay spoke with me about my people and our culture.

"There are about five hundred thousand of us on our planet," I explained.

"How are they counted?" he asked.

"At birth, we are each issued an ID tab." I lifted my center arm to show him where it was attached to the skin underneath. "It is taken off the body at death, and the numbers are adjusted."

"How does it work?"

I shrugged. "I don't know exactly. Some kind of psychic imprint of our mother, I think. The counters are able to track the imprints somehow."

"You mentioned your technicians. What kinds of things do they fix?"

"Everything from our irrigators to our transport tubes."

"Tell me about your transport tubes."

"Pathon has natural underground currents that we use to run the transport tubes."

"What kinds of transportation do you have above ground?"

"Animals, spring carts, water transports, things like that. Nothing like your shuttle. Did you drop from the sky?"

"Yes," Chakotay said. "All of the shuttle systems are off-line now, though, and we don't have the tools here to make them work. Tell me, did you see us fall from the sky?"

"No, the sun was too bright for me to look upward. I wish I could have seen it, though."

"Did you hear it?"

"No," I said.

B'Elanna raised her head. "Well, that's one good thing about the engines dying. We came down quietly."

"And your idea about parachute thrusters was a good one." I couldn't make much sense of this strange talk, but it sounded very exotic. I tried to memorize the terms they used. Chakotay spoke again, this time to me. "Is there anyone else around that could have seen us coming?"

"I doubt it. Like I said, it is the Festival Time. No one is working. The farmer whose field you landed in certainly wasn't working, and his house is far from the shuttle. His land is vast."

"I hope you're right." He was truly interested in what I had to say, and I was grateful for his patience. I was obviously backward compared to his people, and I surely wasn't the type of ambassador to which he was accustomed.

B'Elanna approached us. "I think I've done enough jury-rigging. If we can get to a higher elevation, we can probably contact *Voyager*. That's our ship," she added, obviously for my benefit.

"Can we salvage the shuttle?"

"Not unless we can somehow reconfigure *Voyager*'s transporters to work at the lower elevation, and I don't think that's likely in a timely fashion."

Chakotay glanced at me. "We certainly can't fix it and fly out of here, either. We'd surely be noticed."

"You still want your presence to be a secret?" I asked.

"Yes," said Chakotay.

"Come, then, we will hike to a higher elevation."

"You won't be missed?" he said.

I shook my head. "Not on Festival Day. My family will assume I am with friends, and my friends will believe I am with family." I was desperate to be allowed to spend more time with them. Finally, Chakotay nodded his approval.

I led them up the Mount of Kubl'a, using the trails the animal herders had worn. It took over a millicycle, so they shared food and water from their packs with me. We also enjoyed some ripening berries along the way. We were all tired and sweaty when we reached the summit. I explained that the sun would not set for another half-cycle. The fields that were now green and lush would soon be brown and withered from the unrelenting sunshine.

I plopped down on a nearby rock, but B'Elanna immediately pulled her adjusted gadget out of her bag and began punching its buttons. Her stamina and dedication to making her devices work impressed me. I wished that I had the same technical ability. Soon, she tapped the device on her chest and called out for *Voyager*. I was startled when a feminine voice returned from midair. I chuckled at myself for being surprised after everything I had already experienced in such a short time.

"Away team, this is *Voyager*. What is your status?"

Chakotay was the one to answer. "Our shuttle suffered full systems failure." He glanced at me, obviously choosing his words carefully. "We were forced to land on the second planet in this system. At least one native sighted us. She helped us travel to a higher location so that B'Elanna's equipment could get through to you."

"We'll enter orbit of that planet in two minutes, Commander; then we'll try to transport you aboard. Recommendations for the shuttle?"

"We won't be able to beam it up from its current location. We can't risk sending repair teams and then flying it out, either. It would too easily be seen or heard."

"Understood," came the disembodied voice. I got the impression much was going unsaid, but I respected their privacy and did not listen to their thoughts.

"I think six photon grenades should do it, Captain." B'Elanna, said.

"We'll beam them down in a few minutes, Lieutenant. What of your guide?"

I stepped closer to Chakotay and spoke to the device on his chest. "Hello. I am Quator. If I tell others about you, no one will believe me."

"Commander?"

"She's probably right, Captain. The population here is scattered and, if you'll forgive me, Quator, rather primitive. They most likely wouldn't believe an individual account of aliens."

I couldn't help but giggle. He was absolutely right, of course, but not for the reason he believed. I was known for trying to pass off fanciful tales as truths. If I told of my experiences, I would not be given much credence. Chakotay grinned at me.

"All right, Commander," the captain said. "Accompany the young woman down the hill, destroy the shuttle, and then rendezvous with us at your current coordinates. What is your ETA?"

"We'll need to get some sleep first, Captain, and then it will take about four hours each way. We should be back by fourteen hundred hours tomorrow."

"We'll look forward to your call. Janeway out."

Chakotay smiled and then looked at B'Elanna and me. "Well, let's get some shut-eye."

During our trip down the mountain, we spoke of many things. I told them about my frustration in choosing a vocation and explained the customs of the Grain Festival. In return, they explained what life on their starship was like. On their journey toward home, they had seen beings of all colors, sizes, and levels of intelligence, and passed planets of all kinds. It sounded very exciting, but they were quick to assure me that there were dangers and difficulties involved as well. Dangerous or not, I knew my life could never be that interesting, at least not on its current track. To help me understand their secrecy, they also explained the principle that prevented them from influencing my world. While they may not have affected my world as a whole, they had certainly touched my life. I knew that I would never be the same.

When we again reached the *karlak* field where we had met, they thanked me for my help and encouraged me to go home. My emotions were a jumble; my chest was tight with the thrill of my experience, while at the same time my eyes were wet with tears that it was ending. Chakotay looked at me kindly and said, "Good luck with your decisions. I know you will choose wisely."

"Good luck with your journey," I managed. "I hope that you make it home soon."

"Walk on the perimeter of the *mak'a* field so you won't get hurt," B'Elanna said. I nodded and started on my way. My head ached again, but this time from unshed tears rather than the sunlight. I walked all the way to the forest before I looked back. B'Elanna and Chakotay were nowhere in sight—they had probably gone into the *karlak* fields—but the shuttle still gleamed in the sunlight. Then, before my eyes, there was a quick, silent burst of light, and the shuttle disappeared. I focused closely on the area but could find nothing of it, not even debris. I wondered again at their marvelous devices, and then turned and continued on my way.

My family supported my vocational choice, although it was an unusual one. Within a cycle, I had finished my first collection of tales, and even those who had once been skeptical of my decision were impressed. No Pathon writer had shown such promise and imagination in hundreds of cycles, they said. My parents beamed, saying that I had always been a curious and inventive child, and they were proud of me.

Surprisingly, the compliments meant little to me. Only putting words on paper, describing two-armed creatures who traveled the galaxy in boxy ships and spoke to jewelry attached to their clothing, pleased me. I found that I needed to write down all that Chakotay and B'Elanna had told me, and then, when I had finished with those stories, I had no difficulty composing my own in the same vein. I knew then that the universe was a huge and wonderful place, and I knew that even those tales that came from my mind probably held some grain of truth somewhere, sometime. And with every tale I finished, I breathed quiet thanks to those who had made it all possible.

Almost . . . But Not Quite

Dayton Ward

Dulmer ran like hell.

He didn't have to look behind him to know the bear was gaining. The massive animal's labored breathing was growing louder with each frantic step the significantly smaller human took.

If I live through this, maybe I'll finally learn to keep my big mouth shut.

It had begun innocently enough, with Dulmer quietly moving through the forest toward the remote mountain camp. The darkness of the crisp Montana night helped to conceal him. He was also aided by the fact that most of the residents were currently gathered near the rather austere building that was the camp's saloon. That was fortunate, for in a camp this size an unknown face would be noticed immediately.

Even from this distance, he could hear the sounds of laughter and music coming from the center of the camp. Looking up, he could see the moonlight reflected from the surface of the alien ship that towered above the trees. The Vulcans, despite being an eminently logical people, were long-renowned for their ability to effortlessly combine beauty and efficiency in the construction of their vessels.

He had decided to approach the camp from the south, farther away from the massive concrete bunker that had acted as the launch site for Cochrane's ship. This was supposed to have allowed him to move down the bank of a small mountain stream where it would be easier to cover ground, instead of pushing through the surprisingly thick undergrowth.

That was when he saw the bear.

It had been standing in the shallow water, probably looking to capture a fish for its next meal. Then it saw Dulmer and apparently decided he made a more filling, and perhaps better-tasting, alternative.

So Dulmer ran.

He darted back up the bank and into the forest, weaving between trees and dodging the foliage as best he could. Aside from the darkness, the terrain here was uneven and covered with rocks and thick undergrowth, making footing a hazardous proposition at best. A misstep here would send him crashing to the unforgiving earth, with the bear following quickly behind.

Dodging right to skirt yet another tree actually brought the bear into Dulmer's field of vision. Despite its bulk, it moved with incredible speed. Only the natural obstacles provided by the forest had given Dulmer any chance at all to this point.

But then the bear was nearly on him, and he was sure it must have sensed its quarry's already meager advantage beginning to evaporate. The bear suddenly released a roar that rattled Dulmer's teeth and sounded too much like a victory cry.

It almost, but not quite, drowned out the whine of a phaser beam.

Even as Dulmer staggered backward in an effort to stave off the inevitable for a few more seconds, an orange hue enveloped the bear. Then it faded, leaving only the animal, slumping to the ground. Dulmer watched in shock as it rolled onto its side and began to snore.

"Close your mouth before you attract a swarm of insects."

From behind a particularly large tree stepped Dulmer's partner, Lucsly. The dark-haired man still wielded the phaser he had just employed.

Dulmer was still trying to catch his breath as he said, "We're not supposed to be armed on these missions."

Lucsly shrugged and indicated the unconscious bear with the weapon. "Suit yourself. When he wakes up, I'll be sure to keep this hidden so as not to risk upsetting the timeline."

Dulmer shot a scathing glare at his partner. "You're really enjoying this, aren't you?"

Shrugging, Lucsly said, "What are friends for?"

Ignoring the sarcastic sentiment, Dulmer made a vain attempt to brush off the dirt and grass he had managed to collect on his headlong flight through the forest. "I still can't believe we got stuck with this, and right as I was about to leave for Risa. It's not as if we don't have an entire department to handle PVRs."

Lucsly sniffed disdainfully. "Post-temporal violation reconnaissance is an invaluable tool in the Temporal Investigations arsenal. I've always wanted to go on a PVR, myself. If you're upset with this assignment, you have only yourself to blame."

"All I said," Dulmer replied, "was that I thought Sisko's stunt with Kirk had no lasting effect on the timeline, and that

I might have done the same thing myself under similar circumstances."

Taking a tricorder from a pocket in his jacket, Lucsly began a scan of the area as he said, "And that's where you made your mistake. You know how totally inflexible they are on the top floor. One of their agents even entertaining the idea of such a frivolous flirtation with history sends them into a panic. Didn't that case with the android head teach you anything?"

Dulmer sighed in exasperation. This was one story he was tired of telling. "All I did was joke that a five-hundred-year-old cave sounded like the perfect place to leave my ex-wife." The uproar from Dulmer's superiors at DTI had followed him for weeks after that particularly ill-timed joke.

"At least your pitiful attempts at humor gave us an interesting assignment this time," Lucsly said as he began to thread a path through a narrow break in the hills rising up from the dusty soil around them.

"Oh yes," Dulmer muttered. "Two months of research on a dustball of a planet that maybe a dozen people even know exists, coupled with administrative cleanup after a bunch of loose cannons go gallivanting through time without even a thought for the consequences."

"I wouldn't call Captain Picard a loose cannon," Lucsly admonished. "He did the only thing he could, given the circumstances. According to my scans of the area, it seems he also did a remarkable job covering his tracks." Then he held up the phaser. "Well, except for this."

"Where did you find it?" Dulmer asked.

"While you were out entertaining the local wildlife, I was doing the recon," Lucsly replied as he pointed to the structure that was only barely visible in the pale illumination offered by the moon. "I found it in the *Phoenix*'s launch bay. One of the *Enterprise* engineers probably left it there." He shifted the weapon to his left hand, then brought his right hand up to his nose and sniffed it. His face wrinkled in disgust. "It smells like someone spilled some kind of alcoholic beverage all over it."

Dulmer caught a whiff of the odor. "It smells like tequila."

Annoyed, Lucsly shook his head. "Other than that, I've found nothing that could be attributed to meddling by time travelers. I didn't run into anyone during my sweep, so even with your little side trip, we've been very lucky. I think we can wrap this one up and get out of here."

"Sounds good to me," Dulmer said. "I'm ready to get going to Risa."

"Well, don't forget we have one more case to PVR before we can go home."

There was the momentary feeling of disorientation, and then Dulmer was simply standing in the midst of what had to be the most dreadful-looking place in the known universe.

The world did not have a name or even a catalog entry in Federation data banks. An entirely new and separate level of security had been enacted to protect the planet and the staggering secret it possessed. To those select few that even knew of its existence, it was known simply as "the Guardian planet."

Discovered over a century earlier, the otherwise unremarkable planet's one incredible object of interest was the mysterious and apparently sentient time portal, which had proclaimed itself to be the Guardian of Forever. From this single point, any moment in time in any location could be visited simply by telling the Guardian where you wished to go. Said to be billions of years old, the Guardian had stubbornly resisted all attempts by Federation scientists to understand it. After a century, the sum total of information on file about the Guardian basically stated that it was an immensely old, yet still functioning, time portal.

Well, and that James T. Kirk had found it.

That one fact had stuck in the collective craw of Temporal Investigations for decades. Regarded in hushed circles as the ultimate temporal demon, Captain Kirk had apparently made a career of instilling ulcers in DTI agents up to, including, and after his death. That he should also be the man credited with finding the most sophisticated and powerful time-travel apparatus in history had made him the bane of DTI's existence since its inception shortly thereafter. Though it was not generally well-known information, it was popular DTI lore that the agency's creation was a direct reaction to Kirk's three separate involvements in time travel during a period of only a few months.

However, Kirk was finally beginning to get some serious competition.

Since taking command of the *Enterprise*-D almost ten years previously, Jean-Luc Picard had himself racked up quite an impressive list of temporal violations. While he was a much more reserved and introverted commander than James Kirk had been, Picard was not above taking the proverbial *mugato* by the horn if the situation warranted it. This latest excursion by Picard and his ship to 2063 Earth had been just such an instance.

Privately, Dulmer praised the initiative exhibited by people like Kirk, Picard, and just recently Benjamin Sisko.
These were not reckless men, unconcerned with the possible
consequences of their travels through time. Quite the con-
trary, each officer had repeatedly shown that preservation of
the timeline was of paramount importance, whatever the reason for their travel in the first place.

That did not, however, mean that it was an activity he
wanted to emulate.

Given a choice, Dulmer would rather have been lying in
a comfortable lounge chair, sipping some ungodly alcoholic
concoction while every want or need was tended to by a
beautiful woman dressed only in . . .

"Amazing," Lucsly said, shaking Dulmer from his
reverie. He looked up to see a huge grin plastered across his
partner's face.

"Reading about time travel is one thing," Lucsly continued. "Listening to the accounts of others who've done it is
fascinating, too; but nothing compares to having actually
done it. Now I know what Alan Shepard must have felt like
when he finally got his chance to walk on the moon. Sure,
he'd heard about it and watched Neil Armstrong do it first,
but it wasn't the same as doing it himself."

"Yeah, it's a real treat, all right," Dulmer muttered as he
opened the carryall bag he had brought along with him on
this venture. "And now we get to take yet another fantastic
trip through time. Are we correcting a problem? No. Are we
retrieving valuable information or perhaps rescuing a fellow
agent? No. What are we doing? Research on the aftereffects
of temporal displacement during an incident that began
almost a hundred years ago."

Lucsly chose to ignore the obvious sarcasm as he opened his own bag and began pulling out the clothing he would wear on their next trip through the Guardian. "The actions taken by Admiral Kirk and his crew were very unorthodox, and were ripe with potentially disastrous contaminations of the timeline. Frankly, I'm surprised the damage was as minimal as their reports stated. Our task is to evaluate the immediate consequences of their actions and use that information as part of a new curriculum on Temporal Mechanics being developed for Starfleet Academy. This is a very important assignment, Dulmer. You should be happy they offered it to us."

Dulmer snorted. "I'll be happy when someone offers me *jamaharon* on Risa." In truth, though he would never allow his partner the satisfaction of knowing this, Dulmer actually enjoyed the PVRs. They provided a welcome respite from the mundane research duties they'd been saddled with during the last two months.

Several minutes later, the agents were appraising each other's ensembles.

"Somehow," Lucsly said, "I'm not entirely convinced this is a low-profile appearance." He looked down at himself once more. His attire consisted of a pair of trousers made from some type of coarse material, the color of which was considerably faded. The cuffs of the pants were tucked into a pair of heavy boots that were badly in need of polishing. The shirt he wore had no sleeves and was adorned with a garish print on the front. Reading the caption on his chest, Lucsly looked up and asked, "What was 'DeathTongue' supposed to mean, anyway?"

Dulmer shrugged as he assessed his own outfit, which

was similar to Lucsly's except that his shirt had sleeves, though they only fell to the midpoint between his shoulders and elbows. An arrow was printed on the shirt, pointing to Dulmer's left and accompanied by the caption "I'm With Stupid."

"Archives didn't say what any of this meant," he replied. "I know we're supposed to blend in, but I think the ladies in Research are having a little fun at our expense."

Lucsly smiled. "Well, where we're headed, we won't be given a second thought. Come on, let's get going." With that, he opened his tricorder, set it to active scan, and pointed it at the Guardian. For the second time that day, he busied himself with recording every scrap of information the only grudgingly cooperative mechanism would yield.

Trying to muster up a fraction of the enthusiasm his partner felt, Dulmer closed his carryall and rose to join Lucsly at the time portal. As the pair stood before the enigmatic device, Dulmer could feel an almost electrical sensation playing across his exposed skin. Was the power commanded by this ancient machine so great as to cause these sensations merely by standing before it? He shook the feeling off. It was time to go to work.

"Guardian, we require your services once more."

In a voice that echoed in the natural alcove created by the rock formations and ruins, the Guardian replied, *"Let me be your gateway."*

Dulmer felt the usual knot in his stomach. "We wish to visit the planet Earth, specifically to the site of a temporal displacement that occurred in North America in the late twentieth century."

"Many such journeys are possible."

Unlike Lucsly, Dulmer had performed several PVRs during his early days with Temporal Investigations, so this was not his first encounter with the Guardian. However, the raw power behind the voice still felt to Dulmer as if it were vibrating the very marrow in his bones. No matter how many times he did this, he knew he would always feel this same sense of trepidation.

"The site of the displacement is southern California, Earth year 1986."

There was a momentary pause, and then the Guardian returned with, *"Step through the portal at your convenience."*

As Lucsly examined his tricorder, Dulmer watched as his partner's features screwed up in confusion. "Wait a second. There's something wrong. The tricorder's detected a difference in the timeline since I scanned the last time. It seems to originate in Los Angeles, Earth year 1996."

Dulmer's own expression turned to one of astonishment. "1996? That's impossible." He paused for several seconds, racking his mind for something about the year that was familiar. "I don't remember reading about any violations during that period."

Looking up from the tricorder, Lucsly said, "From what I can tell, the anomaly in question appeared in 1967 and its aftereffects carried forward until 1996. At that point there is a divergence in the timeline."

"Good Lord," Dulmer whispered.

"We have to report this to DTI," Lucsly prompted. "They need to figure out what to do."

Dulmer shook his head. "What if the timeline split has altered the future in some way? We might be the only ones who aren't affected." It had been determined during Kirk's initial discovery of the Guardian that anyone or anything in close proximity to the time portal was somehow shielded from any changes to the timeline.

Realization abruptly dawned on Lucsly's face. "You're not suggesting we go back to investigate this, are you?" When Dulmer nodded silently, Lucsly's eyes nearly bugged out of his head. "Are you out of your mind? We're not qualified for this! We need to contact headquarters and let them sort this out."

Dulmer indicated the Guardian with a wave of his hand. "Think about this. If there has been an alteration in the time-line, then everything and everyone we know, if they even still exist, might not even know about this planet or the Guardian. We can't risk that. There's only one option, Lucsly. We have to go."

After several seconds of agonized argument with himself, Lucsly finally nodded slowly. "You're right."

Dulmer thought he sensed dazzling light blinding him, but the sensation lasted only for the briefest of moments. Then, he and Lucsly were simply standing in the past.

"Well, we're here, I think," Lucsly said as he opened his tricorder and activated it.

Seeing something that he thought he recognized nearby, Dulmer motioned for Lucsly to follow him. He led the way to a squat, blue metallic box with a glass viewing port. Inside was what looked to be a parchment of some kind with black printing on it. Dulmer pointed to it.

"*Los Angeles Times,*" he read from the bold type on the paper, and then pointed to the date. "We made it, all right."

Lucsly continued to work with his tricorder. They were

fortunate that there appeared to be no other people about at the moment. In fact, the scene was almost tranquil. Regardless, Dulmer kept a watch out for anyone approaching as Lucsly operated the unit.

After a few moments, he motioned for Dulmer to step closer. "Look here," he said, indicating the tricorder's tiny display screen.

"I've managed to cycle back through all the information I recorded back at the Guardian," he said. "I think I've found the discrepancy." He pressed a series of commands into the tricorder and the image shifted. First, there was a picture of what Dulmer recognized to be a common sight on 1996 Earth, an automobile. Powder blue in color, the ungainly vehicle appeared to be careening down a street. The image was distorted frequently with streaks of orange.

"That looks like phaser fire," Dulmer commented.

Lucsly only nodded, then said, "Keep watching."

On the screen, one of the bright ribbons of energy suddenly connected with the speeding vehicle. The automobile flared briefly with color, then promptly disappeared from sight as though it had never existed.

"Destroyed?" Dulmer asked in amazement.

"Right," Lucsly confirmed. "Except for one thing. I just watched another scene almost identical to this one, except in that version, the automobile got away."

"Maybe you were looking at a different automobile," Dulmer offered.

"How many vehicles in 1996 Los Angeles get subjected to phaser fire?" Lucsly countered. "I'll wager the number to be fairly small. So the question is, are we here to prevent that vehicle from being destroyed, or to ensure its destruction?"

For emphasis, he produced the phaser from under his shirt.

Dulmer reached out frantically. "Put that thing away before someone sees it." He looked around quickly to reassure himself that they were still alone. "All right, suppose what you say is true. Why would the Guardian show us two different versions of the same event? Why not simply show us the way it's supposed to be and let us get on with fixing it?"

His partner shook his head, an expression of confusion etched in his features. "I remember reading Ambassador Spock's report on the time he and Captain Kirk traveled back to 1930s Earth using the Guardian. He stated that the images he'd downloaded into his tricorder showed him two possible outcomes for a series of events that were yet to happen. It was only through time-consuming study of the information he'd gathered that he was able to determine which course of action to take."

"The only thing I can think of that makes sense," Dulmer said, "is that the alteration had to have occurred after we began actively studying the Guardian." He pointed to Lucsly's tricorder. "That contains all the readings you've taken of it for at least the past week. It's possible that you recorded the two different versions of the timeline yourself, on two separate occasions. The answer to all of this could be in there."

Lucsly pondered this for a moment, then said, "Well, we're here and we have our tricorder. Maybe there's something here that will provide some additional clues." With that, he reopened the tricorder and began to scan the area.

"There's a significant concentration of radio waves coming from a point approximately two hundred meters from where we're standing. Other than that, there's nothing notable in the area."

Dulmer shrugged. "Seems as good a place to start looking as any. Let's go."

With Lucsly's tricorder leading the way, the pair walked quickly in the direction of the signals it had detected. To his surprise, Dulmer found himself fascinated at the world surrounding him. Quite the contrast from the cooler and more primitive climate he'd seen in 2063 Montana, the weather here was much milder. The sun shone brightly, and the trees that grew here were lush and beautiful.

"Is that it?" he asked, pointing to a large building with a dome on top. The structure was labeled "Griffith Observatory."

Lucsly nodded. "That's it. Astronomers used facilities like this to study stellar phenomena from Earth. It was surprisingly beneficial, though their results improved dramatically when they finally abandoned planet-based telescopes for orbiting facilities. Even the radio telescopes of the day were significantly improved when they were put into space and their telemetry relayed back down here." He pointed to what was apparently the building's main entrance. "This way."

Following the tricorder's readings led the agents into the depths of the building. It soon became apparent that the observatory also served as a museum of sorts. Lucsly quickly became adept at keeping the tricorder hidden while still being able to consult its readings, and with good reason. Several dozen people circled and studied mockups of planets and other spatial bodies, as well as early space vehicles. Despite himself, Dulmer found the various exhibits to be fascinating.

It wasn't entirely easy going, however. Even though they were making efforts to blend in with the rest of the crowd, Lucsly soon realized that he and Dulmer were still drawing curious stares from some of the other people touring the exhibits. He knew that he was keeping the tricorder effectively hidden, so what else could it be? As he turned to ask his partner his thoughts on the subject, it hit him.

Of course.

The attire chosen for him and Dulmer had been assembled with an eye toward having the agents pretend to be members of an eccentric fringe element of society reported to be popular during the late 1980s. "Punk rockers," he believed the report stated. Of course, it was one of the several reports submitted by then-Admiral Kirk and his *Enterprise* command crew following their visit to 1986. Instantly, Lucsly's imagination fed him an image of Kirk submitting the report as a joke just so that he, Lucsly, would stumble across it, read it, take every word in it as gospel, and then dress accordingly as he prepared for a PVR a century later.

Naturally their attire, while possibly adequate for a low-profile mission to 1986 where many other people might be dressed the same way, seemed to be quite out of place here in 1996, where the other people in the building seemed to have chosen more conservative ensembles.

A faint beep from his tricorder caught Lucsly's attention. He said to Dulmer, "The receiver for the radio telescope is in the lowest level of the adjacent building. However, the tricorder is showing primitive hardwired data connections leading from it to this building."

"Probably a computer interface," Dulmer replied.

"Twentieth-century computers required such connections to communicate with different peripheral equipment, as I recall."

They proceeded down a dimly lit corridor near the rear of the building, the only sound the telltale beeps of the tricorder. Finally, Lucsly stopped before a door on the right side of the passageway. It was a simple wooden affair, adorned with raised wooden numbers that read "123" and a simple metallic sign that warned "DO NOT ENTER—EMPLOYEES ONLY."

"I'm not detecting any lifesigns," Lucsly said. "So, how do we open it?"

With an impatient sigh, Dulmer reached for the round protuberance on the door, turned it clockwise, and pushed the door open.

The interior of the office itself was as much an exhibit to the pair of agents as the actual museum they had just left. It was an eclectic clutter of primitive computer equipment and dilapidated furniture. Nearly all of the available wall space was adorned with photographs of planets and various other stellar phenomena. Lucsly's attention was drawn to one particular photo, which depicted a figure dressed in an archaic space suit. The astronaut stood next to a colorful banner of stars and stripes rising on a metallic pole from dusty, gray soil.

"That's Alan Shepard!" he said excitedly. "This picture was taken on the moon in the 1970s! He's standing in the Ocean of Storms."

"Fra Mauro," Dulmer said.

"Don't be silly," Lucsly snapped. "Lovell went to Fra Mauro. Shepard was at the Ocean of Storms."

With a sigh, Dulmer recited, "Almost, but not quite.

Conrad was at the Ocean of Storms, Lovell was on the flight that never made it to the moon, and Shepard went to the Fra Mauro Highlands after Lovell's mission failed."

Lucsly looked at him skeptically. "Are you sure?"

"Tell you what," Dulmer said. "We'll check it out when we get back, and the loser has to do the paperwork on this mission."

With a confident nod, Lucsly said, "Clear your padd, then."

Dulmer shrugged. "Let's get on with this. What's the tricorder saying?"

Lucsly pointed to the squat computer-display monitor that sat atop the well-worn desk. "The telescope telemetry is being transferred to this computer." He indicated the graphic representation on the monitor. "According to this, an object is being tracked in orbit."

Nodding, Dulmer continued, "Pretty high up, too. Satellites in this time period operated in much lower orbits." Suddenly, his head snapped up.

"Someone's coming."

Frantically, the agents looked for somewhere, anywhere, to hide.

"They've found us, all right. The orbital schematic matches *Voyager*'s position," a man's voice said.

"According to this data," the other man, whom the first speaker had called Tuvok, added, "they are tracking the warp emissions from our engines."

"Nobody in this century even knows what warp emissions are." The skepticism in the other man's voice was patently obvious.

In what Dulmer had noted to be a cool, reserved voice, the one called Tuvok said, "Nevertheless, it appears they have configured their telescope to scan for them."

Suddenly, a third voice, that of a young woman and containing more than a trace of irritation, joined the first two. "Excuse me? 'Do not enter—Employees only'? The sign on the door?"

From inside the small closet in the far corner of the office, Dulmer listened with disapproval as the first two men quickly, and clumsily, began to fabricate some kind of excuse for being in an obviously "Off Limits" area. To Dulmer, this simply reinforced that temporal excursions should be left to those personnel who were trained to deal with the various aspects of interacting with people and events from the past. If the two morons out in the office had been trained, experienced, professional Temporal Investigators, they wouldn't even have set foot in the office without a cover story fully rehearsed and ready to go in the event of their discovery.

Which reminded Dulmer that he didn't have a clue what he himself might say. Any of the three individuals currently participating in the verbal sparring match out in the office could easily open the door to the tiny closet that he and Lucsly had jammed themselves into. Their efforts would be rewarded with the stupefied expressions of two trained, experienced professional Temporal Investigators.

Somehow, I'm going to have to find some way of blaming this on Sisko, or maybe even Kirk.

Swallowing the lump in his throat, he began to mentally compose his own defense, when he was suddenly interrupted.

"What are you doing?" he asked, his voice barely a whisper.

"Trying to get my tricorder," Lucsly replied in equally hushed tones.

"Well, *that's not it.*"

The pair of agents had somehow managed to squeeze themselves into the minuscule storage closet amidst the collection of old computer parts, books, papers, and various other unidentifiable objects. The limited space remaining was barely large enough to contain the two men, and then only after a miraculous feat of flexibility.

"Leave it," Dulmer said. "The Vulcan might hear it."

"Vulcan?" Lucsly asked as he ceased his squirming.

Dulmer answered, "Tuvok. He's a Vulcan, and a Starfleet officer. The last I heard, he and the rest of his crew were lost with the *Voyager* near the Badlands, two years ago."

"So what are they doing here in 1996?"

Dulmer asked himself the same question. From what he remembered about the *Voyager,* it had mysteriously disappeared two years previously in the unstable region of space near Bajor known as the Badlands while pursuing a Maquis vessel. Starfleet ships had scoured the area for weeks before finally calling off the search. Several months later, the *Voyager* had been officially declared "missing and presumed lost" with all hands.

But now, somehow, these two members of her crew had ended up in 1996 Los Angeles, but for what reason? Were they somehow propelled through an unknown stellar phenomenon to end up at this point in time? Were they desperately seeking some clue to returning to the twenty-fourth century?

Dulmer returned his attention to the conversation taking place in the office. The first man, who they now knew to be named Tom Paris, was presently trying to engage the young woman, Rain Robinson, in small talk. Dulmer sighed. He recognized the calm, confident tones of a man who was accustomed to using what he considered to be charm in order to converse with a female, for whatever reason. Dulmer decided the man wasn't as good at it as he might think himself to be. At the moment, Paris was trying to account for his impressive command of spatial mechanics and related science, which was undoubtedly superior to that of the twentieth-century woman who had found them.

"I majored in astrophysics," Paris said. Dulmer could hear the jovial lilt in the man's voice through the closet door.

"Where?" Rain Robinson asked. Apparently, she wasn't any more impressed with Paris's charms than Dulmer was.

"Starfleet Academy."

Lucsly nearly convulsed at the mention of the Federation's training facility for Starfleet officers. "Is he crazy?" he said, almost forgetting to keep his voice a whisper.

"She won't know anything about it," Dulmer said. "Now keep quiet before they hear us."

"Pardon me, Tom," Tuvok was saying. "We should be going. Our . . . friends . . . are waiting for us."

Good, Dulmer thought. *Then maybe I can get Lucsly off my foot.* He guessed that the "friends" Tuvok had mentioned would be their fellow crew members on their ship.

There were some perfunctory good-byes, and the agents could hear the two men leave the office. The next several seconds were filled only with the muted sound of something clicking repeatedly.

"Computer keyboard," Dulmer guessed.

The near silence of the room went on for a few more seconds until it was suddenly broken with, "What the hell?" As the agents listened from inside the closet, there was more frantic clicking, followed by, "Those bastards!"

Something fell heavily to the floor. Dulmer and Lucsly could then hear hurried footfalls as the woman ran from the office.

After waiting a few extra seconds, Dulmer cautiously opened the closet door and peered out. The office was empty.

"Dulmer," Lucsly said as he scanned the computer with his tricorder once more, stepping around an upended chair which was probably the source of the heavy thud they'd heard a moment before. "Those two destroyed the secondary data storage unit in this device. All of the data pertaining to the orbital scans is gone."

Dulmer nodded. "Have to give them some credit for at least trying to cover their tracks. But the girl's on to them, at least partially. Come on, let's go."

As he moved for the door, Lucsly grabbed his arm. "What can we do?"

It was a valid question. The image from the tricorder played out once more in Dulmer's mind. He saw the different outcomes, one right after the other, over and over once more.

What was the key? What would make the difference?

Instinctively, Dulmer already knew the answer. They—he and his partner—were the difference. They were here, now, where they weren't supposed to be. It had been preordained, whether by the Guardian or some other force that Dulmer would never understand, for them to take action here, whatever that action might be.

With a distant look in his eyes, Dulmer finally replied, "Hopefully, we'll know when we get there."

Running down the corridor from the office, the pair of agents plunged through a door and suddenly found themselves outside the observatory. As they emerged onto the sidewalk, they were just in time to look to their left and see a man in a dark suit nearing the far corner of the building, heading away from them.

"Look," Dulmer said as he pointed to the very much out-of-place object in the man's right hand. "Who the hell is that? That looks like some kind of phaser in his hand!"

"This is getting weirder by the second," Lucsly warned. "Do you suppose he's some kind of temporal agent?"

The possibility was one that gave Dulmer pause. It wasn't all that far-fetched that another agent, perhaps from another time period than he and Lucsly, could be operating here in this time, trying to affect the resolution to a problem that was still unknown to them.

Dulmer said, "I remember reading about a time-traveling human in the report on one of Kirk's few DTI-approved missions. I wonder if that could be him?"

"Well, whoever he is," Lucsly replied as he pulled on his partner's arm to follow him, "he's getting away. Come on."

"Who are you people, and what is that thing in your pants?" the woman demanded.

"I beg your pardon?" Tuvok asked.

"That little gadget you put in your pocket," Robinson pressed. "What is it? A demagnetizer?"

Suddenly Paris pointed toward the observatory, where a man had appeared and was brandishing what looked like a phaser. "Get down!"

Raw power sang out as a harsh energy discharge erupted from the strange man's weapon. In scarcely the blink of an eye, the blue automobile the two wayward time travelers and the woman had been standing near abruptly disappeared in a firestorm of orange violence.

Lucsly, his own phaser already out and in his hand, said, "That phaser beam is more powerful than ours."

"Somehow, I don't think he's a good guy," Dulmer muttered. Immediately, instinctively, Dulmer rose to his feet, his every muscle tensing as he moved to intervene.

Always his opposite in manner and method, Lucsly coolly stopped him with no more than a hand placed gently on Dulmer's arm.

"Wait," he said in his characteristically calm voice. "We can't just interfere. What if he is some kind of temporal agent that we don't know about? We could undermine everything he's doing here."

Meanwhile, the Vulcan named Tuvok had produced a weapon of his own, which Dulmer could see was a Starfleet phaser. He and the unidentified man were now exchanging fire. The headpiece that Tuvok had been wearing had fallen off in the fray, revealing his otherworldly features.

"No agent would take this kind of blatant risk," Dulmer insisted. "Whoever he is, he's not one of us. We can't just let him gun those people down. As far as we know, that woman's a civilian. We can't let anything happen to her."

"We don't know what's supposed to happen here!" Lucsly argued, the first signs of true strain finally beginning to encroach on him. "For all we know, he's *supposed* to kill her. If we interfere, we could cause irreparable damage!"

The mysterious man had now lost his weapon, thanks to a well-aimed shot by Tuvok. Having been granted a few precious seconds, the trio had used them to make their way to another vehicle.

It was the blue one, from the tricorder.

This is it, Dulmer thought, and once more the scenes played out in his head.

The blue automobile speeds away. The orange phaser strikes. The vehicle dissolves in a hellstorm of energy.

The blue automobile speeds away. The orange phaser strikes. The vehicle skirts away, unharmed.

Ahead of them, the automobile was beginning to accelerate away from the scene, its occupants almost safely out of sight.

Almost.

The other man, the man in the twentieth-century business suit, had recovered his most definitely un-twentieth-century energy weapon and was once again sighting in.

What the hell are we supposed to do? Dulmer's mind raged as doubt once more crowded him. They didn't have time to consult the tricorder and the priceless storehouse of knowledge it contained. The events they had seen earlier were unfolding.

Right here. Right now.

The vehicle containing two Starfleet officers from the future and one most-likely innocent civilian woman from the present was moving too slowly to be out of the line of fire in time.

Ultimately, that decided it for him. Damning all consequences, Dulmer reached out and in one quick motion snatched the phaser from his partner's grasp, raised the weapon, and fired.

The man, his target, fell unconscious to the grass.

"Oh my god," Lucsly said as he ran to where the stunned man had fallen. His eyes quickly focused on the unfamiliar weapon laying in the grass nearby.

"I've never seen a phaser like that before," Dulmer said. He reached to retrieve the phaser, if indeed that's what it was. Once more, he was stopped by his partner.

"Leave it."

"Whatever that thing is," Dulmer said, "it doesn't belong here. It's obviously more advanced than anything that's supposed to be on this planet today. It's even more powerful than our own weapons. We can't risk someone else finding it."

Lucsly shook his head, then pointed in the direction the other time travelers and their unwitting companion had fled. "Those two men, the Starfleet officers, weren't just here to meddle with history. I have to believe they were here for a valid reason, maybe even to correct something they found to be wrong in this time. It's a safe bet they know a lot more about the situation than we do." He indicated the still-unconscious man lying on the ground at their feet. "For all we know, we may have interfered too much already. Our best plan is to leave everything as is and go back to the Guardian. The longer we stay here, the better the chance we *will* do something catastrophic."

Years of memorized temporal theory classes washed across Dulmer's mind. The inherent risk of time travel, practically beaten into their skulls by a host of instructors at the

DTI, came to the forefront once more. The slightest alterations of established events could cascade into massive
changes in the timeline, affecting the very existence of billions of innocent people, both living and as yet unborn. The
most innocuous of actions could be devastating. The
Temporal Prime Directive, which Dulmer had just shattered
with his actions, prohibited interference in established historical events. Every second they remained in this time geo-
metrically increased the chances of their presence having
detrimental effects on the timeline as they knew it.

The two Starfleet officers, saved from obliteration by
Dulmer, were already hopelessly out of the agents' reach,
their destination unknown. Their actions, as well as
Dulmer's, would literally be left to the judgment of history.

Several days later, Dulmer sat at the functional, yet
entirely too small, portable field desk in the temporary
dwelling he and Lucsly lived in while on the Guardian's
planet. The small building was spartan by the standards he'd
grown accustomed to on Earth, but it served its purpose well
enough. He took comfort in knowing their stay here was
nearly at an end. His trip to Risa was tantalizingly near.

He was going cross-eyed from the stack of padds he was
working his way through when Lucsly entered the room.

"I found it," he said, holding up yet another padd.

Straightening in his chair, Dulmer reached for the unit
and asked, "Found what?"

"Those men from the *Voyager*," Lucsly replied. "I was
able to sift through the information I downloaded from the
Guardian. It turns out you were right."

Dulmer quickly scanned the abbreviated data entry on the

padd, finally sighing with relief. His actions, rash and instinctive, had nevertheless been correct. Dulmer and Lucsly's presence in 1996 had apparently been crucial, no matter how limited their actual contributions might have been. The captain and crew of the *Voyager* would, in that time period, eventually complete their task and return to the twenty-fourth century.

"I've already spoken with TIC via subspace on this," Lucsly said, referring to the Temporal Investigations Commander. "Due to the sensitive nature of the *Voyager*'s involvement, we can't make this file public knowledge, even within the rest of DTI."

This confused Dulmer. "Why?"

"Because the ship's still listed as missing, presumed lost. TIC feels that making it known the *Voyager* wasn't destroyed, at least not immediately after it was lost, would be a risk. They could be involved in other temporal violations while trying to find their way back."

"But their families have the right to know they might still be alive out there, somewhere," Dulmer pressed. Then he realized what his partner was *not* saying. "Wait a minute. You scanned the data for future events, didn't you? You know what happens to them, don't you?"

Lucsly nodded, reluctantly. "Yes. However, TIC has forbidden me to talk about it, even with you." He shrugged meekly. "Sorry."

Dulmer was momentarily disappointed, but he knew secrets were a big part of what Temporal Investigations was about. He'd known it since his first days in training. Still, the idea that the *Voyager* might have survived supposed destruction in the Badlands and was lost somewhere in deep space, valiantly attempting to reach home, both saddened and excited him.

Interrupting his thoughts, Lucsly said, "Well, there's no sense agonizing over it. Let's just get busy and get the reports filed so we can go home."

Dulmer smiled suddenly. "Almost, but not quite." He picked up one of the several padds littering his desk and tossed it lightly to Lucsly. "I've been doing some checking up on my own."

Lucsly looked down at the image on the padd's screen. The picture depicted was the same photograph of the astronaut they had seen in Rain Robinson's office in Los Angeles. There was a computer-tabbed entry next to the picture that read: ALAN B. SHEPARD, JR.—APOLLO 14—FRA MAURO HIGHLANDS—FEBRUARY 5TH, 1971.

As Lucsly looked up from the padd with a pained expression on his face, Dulmer was already standing before him with a stack of additional padds. "Okay, we have Picard's mission, the research from the Kirk mission, and the rest of my notes on the *Voyager* fiasco." Suddenly, he snapped his fingers and retrieved yet another padd from the desk. "Also, TIC wanted additional background information on the course for the academy, so I took the liberty of tagging a bunch of computer files I thought might be helpful." With an evil grin, Dulmer regarded his partner, and then finally added, "By the way, she'd like the full report on our visit to 1996 by tomorrow morning."

Lucsly's expression turned to one of near-menace as he asked, "You're really enjoying this, aren't you?"

"Hey," Dulmer said. "What are friends for?"

The Healing Arts

E. Cristy Ruteshouser and Lynda Martinez Foley

Captain Kathryn Janeway could not breathe. Instinctively, she tried to speak, to communicate her distress, but without breath she found herself struck dumb. She struggled to master the panic that threatened to overwhelm her, then reached out to snatch at Harry Kim's shoulder. Her fingers dug into the smooth fabric of his uniform, and he turned his head.

His dark eyes widened. "Captain! What is it, are you—somebody help her!"

Janeway slumped, rolling off the cushion on which she'd been sitting, a roaring in her ears. Her mouth filled with the taste of salt, and she realized she'd bitten her tongue. Her visual field narrowed—she seemed to gaze down a shaft, like a Jefferies tube with blurred gray walls. Only the pale blue ceiling of the Vashnar banquet room showed at the end of that shaft, and she stared helplessly. *Blue. Only blue. Only—wait. Blue eyes. A woman's blue eyes. Is she touching me? What—?*

The contraction of the gray shaft slowed, paused, reversed. The roaring eased, and the captain suddenly felt her chest inflate with a huge, ragged influx of air. She gasped, and panted, every sign of her sudden affliction fading as rapidly as they had appeared. Her vision cleared, and she found herself the focus of every eye in the room.

"Captain!" Tuvok touched her arm, gently helped her to a sitting position. "Are you all right?"

"I think—"

Kim, from her other side, broke in urgently. "Look! What's happening? Is it contagious?"

Janeway, still breathing hard, followed his gaze. A young woman slumped to the floor next to her, stiffening, her eyes bulging. *Blue eyes. Those same blue eyes.*

"Have no concern for her," soothed First Counselor Aken, their host among the reptilian Vashnar. "She will recover. She is a strong healer."

"But she's—" Harry began to argue, then paused. The rigidity had begun to ebb from the limbs of the stricken woman, and her eyes closed. After another moment, she seemed to relax, and then her eyes opened once again.

"Well done," praised Aken. "Very well done." She beckoned to one of the humanoids serving at the banquet. "Take the healer to the Sanctuary. She is to rest for two cycles." Aken gestured with two claws. "She did well."

Janeway reached out and gently touched the healer's arm. "Thank you."

The healer smiled tiredly as she was drawn to her feet and escorted out. The captain watched her leave, noting that the blue of the healer's eyes was matched by the color of her garment. "The healer," she repeated. "Your doctor is of the Anjurwan?"

Aken made a soft trilling sound, the Vashnar version of laughter. Her slender tongue darted in and out. "Of course not! As I have told you, our beloved Anjurwan are like children. She is a healer only. But a very adept one, is she not? How do you feel, Captain? Are you well? Is this a chronic condition of yours?"

"Hardly." Janeway assessed herself. Her muscles complained, no doubt a reaction to her rigor, but otherwise she felt fine. "I've never experienced anything like that before."

"Oh, dear." Aken's normally yellowish scales took on a distinctly pink tone. "Then perhaps it was something you ate. Please forgive me my inadequate hosting! Perhaps we should call the healer back."

"No, no, I'm fine, really."

"Captain." Tuvok regarded her levelly. "It would seem a prudent course of action to have the Doctor examine you."

He's probably right. For a minute there, I was sure I was going to die. "Sage advice as always, my friend. Aken, my apologies to you, and to your staff, but—"

"Of course, of course, do not apologize. Guard your health."

"Anaphylactic shock," summarized the Doctor succinctly. "A very nasty reaction. Definitely something you ate." He frowned. "None of the Vashnar foodstuffs you were to consume at the banquet seemed likely to provoke such a reaction, but one can't always predict the effects of unusual combinations."

"I know." Janeway nodded. "Not your fault. I should have been more careful. I was so relieved to conclude our trade with the Vashnar successfully, I suppose I let my guard down."

He lowered the sides of the diagnostic bed. "At any rate,

you're fine now. I'll administer an antiinflammatory to deal with the residual muscle soreness. What did the Vashnar treat you with?"

She sat up and swung her legs over the side of the bed. "Well, Doctor—"

The corners of his mouth turned down in disapproval. "You didn't ask." He folded his arms. "Captain, I've instructed you, and all the crew, to make absolutely sure that you—"

She held up a hand to ward off the tirade. "They didn't treat me with any medicine at all."

His brows bunched together over his nose. "Then perhaps they used a psychotropic ritual dance? Minosian healing chants? Or did they pray over you? I've certainly heard of the healing power of prayer, but in a case of anaphylactic shock—"

The captain sighed, and the Doctor stopped. She eyed him, trying to discern even a hint of sarcasm, but he held his tongue, his face smoothly impassive.

"I was healed," she continued.

There was a pause. "You were healed. Go on."

"By a healer."

"By a healer," he invited gamely. "Please continue."

"I don't know any more than that. A humanoid woman healed me, it seems. A member of a race called the Anjurwan. Third Counselor Devar told me they were brought to this system three generations ago by a race from the Alpha Quadrant, the Vians. That could mean that the Anjurwan come from the Alpha Quadrant as well. I was hoping you might be able to tell me more."

"The Anjurwan," he mused, his forehead still corrugated.

"The Vians. I don't believe so, Captain. But I'll do some checking."

The Doctor leaned back in his chair, switching off the screen on his desktop computer console. He tapped his combadge. "Doctor to the captain."

"Janeway here. What do you have, Doctor?"

He let his frustration show in his voice. "Virtually nothing. There is exactly one reference to 'Vians' in the database. The same reference mentions a race that might be the Anjurwan. And it's remarkably uninformative. It's amazing what the medical officers of the last century thought of as a useful—"

"You said they 'might' be the Anjurwan. What do you mean?"

"You didn't say the Anjurwan are mutes."

"Mutes?" She thought about it. "You know, I never heard one of them speak. They might very well be."

The Doctor sighed. "I see." Half to himself, he added, "If you want something done, you have to do it yourself. Captain," he continued, raising his voice, "I'll go down to the planet and see if I can learn any more about the Anjurwan and this, ah, healing they seem to do."

"You will."

"It might be useful if you—" He paused, belatedly noting the warning tone in her voice. "With your permission, Captain."

"I'll be returning to the planet's surface in thirty minutes, Doctor. I'm as curious about all this as you are. Meet me in transporter room two."

"Of course."

* * *

"And so," concluded Third Counselor Devar, "when the Vians departed, we embraced the Anjurwan. It frightened them to be abandoned so, especially since it seems their former homeworld was destroyed when their star went nova. We believe they feared another cataclysm."

"But how do you know?" Janeway wondered. "If they don't have the power of speech, as you say, then how do you communicate with them?"

"A form of sign. A very simple language we developed ourselves. But it hardly seems necessary, most of the time. The Anjurwan devote themselves to those they serve, and it is the focus of their existence to sense—without words—what is needed. Ah, here we are. The Sanctuary of the Healing Arts. This is the finest Sanctuary on Vashnar," he added proudly, ushering Janeway and the Doctor through the white stone archway into a courtyard.

The lines of the Sanctuary were beautiful. *They do indeed cherish their healers, don't they?* mused Janeway appreciatively. She repeated Devar's statement, sharing a glance with the Doctor. " 'To sense without words'? Can you explain, Third Counselor?"

He puffed out his chest. "Of course. To be concise, the Anjurwan are empaths. The finest, most sensitive empaths that we have ever encountered."

"Empaths? They sense emotions?" asked the Doctor.

"Yes, but it's far more than that. If an Anjurwan knows you well, he or she might as well read your mind. They are supremely sensitive."

"And they heal through empathy?" The EMH frowned. "I don't see—"

"Well, those who are healers do," interrupted Devar. "As is the case for any talent, the strength of the gift varies. Only one in twenty can heal, Doctor, and only one in a hundred is as skilled as the healer who saved your captain. They are highly prized. But here," he continued, stepping through a second archway inside the courtyard, "here is Doctor Teth, chief physician of this Sanctuary. She will answer your questions far better than I could. Doctor, this is—what is wrong?"

Teth brushed past them, her scales bristling with tension. She headed for the outer courtyard. "No time, Devar. A medical emergency." Two other Vashnar followed her, their expressions equally intent. Three blue-clad Anjurwan, two female and one male, brought up the rear. The blue eyes of one of the females caught and held Janeway's for an instant, and she recognized the young woman who had saved her life.

"Oh, my." Devar was staring after Teth, and the captain followed his gaze. Three Vashnar were being carried into the courtyard, and it was there that they were intercepted by the physicians. "Oh, my. Another accident. Fourth Counselor Ravik's son, oh dear. Our young, they will risk their lives, thrill-seeking—"

"*Thrill*-seeking? Those are severe lacerations!" The Doctor started forward, unfolding his medical tricorder. "How in heaven's name did they—" He paused. "What are they doing?"

A good question, thought Janeway. The injured Vashnar had been laid upon stone benches in the center of the courtyard. To her surprise, the three Vashnar physicians made no move toward their patients, and her questing gaze disclosed no medical instruments in their hands or anywhere upon their persons. Instead, each physician took the hands of an Anjurwan and led the healer to one of the moaning young Vashnar. Their motions seemed oddly ritualistic as they turned the healers to their patients. Then they merely stood, immobile, as each of the Anjurwan knelt and seemed to assess the young Vashnar, moving their hands over the boys without touching them.

"They're bleeding to death," muttered the Doctor. "Aren't you going to do anything? Are you going to let them die? Doctor Teth!" He stared into the face of the chief physician. "If you're not going to help them, let me—"

Teth caught at his arm. "No. Let the healers do their work."

Janeway took the EMH's other arm and drew him back. "Doctor. I'm sure they know what they're doing. Don't interfere."

"Know what they're doing? They aren't doing anything! Are they doctors, or not?"

"Ssshh! Of course they're doctors," put in Devar hastily. "They focus the efforts of the healers. Look."

"They're *standing* there and *watching* them. If that makes someone a doctor, Mister Paris ought to be one by now, he's spent enough time standing there watching me work. But—"

"A doctor must focus the healer. Else they might not give their all in time of need. A healer cannot function without a doctor, isn't that obvious?"

Janeway watched in horrified fascination as the injured boys visibly weakened. One by one the Anjurwan seemed to complete their assessment and laid their hands fully on their patients.

"What's obvious is that nothing's being done for—"

The Doctor's voice trailed off, and Janeway knew why. Before her eyes, the wounds on the nearest young Vashnar began to close, began to fade. In seconds the wounds had vanished, and the moans of the boy trailed off.

"Captain—" murmured the Doctor in a near-whisper, his eyes flicking from the Vashnar to the healer and then to his medical tricorder, with which he scanned both. "This is incredible."

"Look," she murmured back. "The healer."

Appallingly, the Vashnar's wounds had reappeared—on the healer. Somehow the wicked lacerations seemed more horrifying on that perfect pale skin. Blood, as red as a human's, began to ooze, and the Anjurwan woman's head tilted back as her mouth opened in a silent scream. She drew her hands away from her patient and clutched them to her chest, panting. Teth, her silent attendant, drew a step closer; the Anjurwan, clearly aware of the Vashnar doctor, appeared to gather her strength and resolutely reached out once again to her patient.

"This is amazing. Her nervous system is actually *linked* to his, supporting his essential functions. She's a complete life-support system. But it's draining her, dangerously—she should stop—" The Doctor began to step forward again.

Teth turned on him. "Will you deny her the dignity of her calling? She is a healer. It is her soul's desire to heal, to give herself if need be to save another. It is the highest purpose for an Anjurwan! This has been so since before they came to us. Do not interfere!"

"But she's—" The Doctor paused, eyes intent on the results of his scan. "No, maybe not." He looked up, seeing what his captain saw—the wounds on the healer beginning to fade as they had faded from the Vashnar boy, fading right out of existence, seeming almost to wink out as they disappeared. The Doctor turned his attention again to the tricorder. "Remarkable. Her readings are stabilizing. She may be all right. No thanks to *you*," he added scathingly to Teth. "You say you're a doctor? From what I've seen, you're more like a drill instructor. *She* did all the work."

"Doctor," reproved Janeway, "we only know what we've seen here. We're not here to judge. Besides, they all seem to be recovering."

The EMH pointed. "What about her?"

"Her" was the healer who had attended Janeway earlier that day. She had slid to the stone floor beside her patient's bench and lay there immobile. The other two healers appeared exhausted but conscious and aware—the young blue-eyed woman was neither, seeming scarcely to breathe.

The doctor attending her shook his head sorrowfully. "Two healings in one day, and this one so difficult. Such a promising young healer, the best I have focused in months. Teth, we must gather the others."

Teth nodded solemnly and moved away. The Doctor sighed in relief. "Good. They're bringing more healers to save this one," he noted to Janeway.

The Vashnar doctor flashed him a startled look. "Of course not. She is past saving herself. Teth will bring the others for the death ceremony."

"Death ceremony!" Janeway stared. "What? Why will she die? Can't another healer—"

"This healer cannot save herself." The doctor saw the uncomprehending looks on the faces of the captain and the

EMH, and his sorrowful voice took on an impatient note. "She would not accept the sacrifice of another, don't you understand? She will not take life to save her own. This is the highest moral law for a healer."

"Surely your technology is advanced enough. Can't you do something?" the captain asked, carefully maintaining a diplomatic tone.

"We have our healers. Healing is an art, not a science. We have grown beyond science in this, thanks to our Anjurwan."

Flashing Janeway a look of mute appeal, the Doctor approached the motionless healer. The Vashnar eyed him with disapproval; the Anjurwan, with shock. One struggled to his feet and shook his head at the EMH, motioning him away, his green eyes imploring.

"I won't hurt her," the Doctor reassured the healer, his tone unusually gentle. "I want to help."

The Anjurwan shook his head again and caught at the Doctor's hand. His eyes went wide then, his already pale face whitening further, and he recoiled, stumbling to his knees. The EMH spared him one startled look before kneeling next to the unconscious female healer.

"Shock," he muttered, scanning her with his tricorder. "She's in shock. Isn't *that* a surprise. Pulse thready, blood pressure falling—Captain, this is nothing I can't treat."

Janeway looked cautiously from one of the two remaining Vashnar physicians to the other, then cast a glance at Devar. "May he?"

The doctors shared a look of consternation. "How? Where is his healer?"

"*I'm* the healer. And I'll treat her with medicine. With science," growled the Doctor without looking up. "This is hardly more than routine. Ten minutes in my sickbay, I'll have her stabilized."

"That would be wonderful," blurted Devar. "Wonderful. Wouldn't it? Doctor Kiv, wouldn't that be better than losing your best healer?"

"This healer saved my life today," Janeway pointed out. "Please, let my medical officer save hers. It's only fitting."

Kiv flashed out his tongue and flicked it thoughtfully, then nodded once. "You're right. If your healing *science* can save her, let it. We will be in your debt."

"This can't be right," the Doctor muttered to himself. "It's not *working.*" He tapped a quick series of commands into the diagnostic bed's control panel, and scanned the readout again. "Phenopathine is compatible with her physiology, but her blood pressure *dropped.* It's as if her system—" He let the sentence trail off, and selected another hypospray from the tray atop his medcart. "All right, then let's try angiochlorophan."

He administered the medication and studied the readouts. The healer's blood pressure began to rise, and the EMH smiled triumphantly. "So she responds to the beta-adrenergic costimulator, but not the—what?" He stared. "Blood pressure *dropping?* This is impossible! First the cardioregulator is ineffective, then the endothelial regenerator, now this! Her biochemistry is not that unusual. Why can't I stabilize her?"

The captain's voice spoke over the comlink. "Janeway to the Doctor."

Grimacing in frustration, he straightened. "Doctor here, Captain."

"How is—"

"How is my patient? I suppose it's been ten minutes already. Captain, I don't understand it, but everything I've done has been ineffective. It's as if—"

"As if what?" prodded Janeway after a moment.

He hesitated, shaking his head to himself, then voiced his growing concern. "It's as if her system is fighting me. Undoing everything I do, almost immediately. My interventions start to take effect, and then the effects reverse and she's left worse off than when I started. I can't explain it."

"Fighting you. Then you're saying she's dying."

The word stung him. "Not if I can help it."

"But if she's—"

"I know! But I think I have an idea." As he uttered the words, he heard them with surprise. *I do? What—yes. Maybe I do.* "Give me more time, Captain."

"Do you need Mister Paris? I can spare him here. I think I've had enough medical training to ask Doctor Teth the right questions."

The EMH barely heard, his mind too engaged with the problem at hand. "That won't be necessary."

There was a pause. "All right. Keep me informed, Doctor."

"Of course," he acknowledged absently, eagerly chasing the stray thought down the pathways of his program. "Doctor out. Computer, access file Doctor-eleven beta, 'medical log entry from stardate 5130.8.' Scan the log entries made by that physician for, hmm, six months following that date. Compile any additional related information."

The computer beeped obediently. "Scanning entries, stardates 5130.8 to 5507.7, log of Doctor Leonard McCoy, chief medical officer, *U.S.S. Enterprise.* No additional related information."

"Nothing?" The Doctor shook his head incredulously. "Nothing else on Vians, mutes, empaths? No reference?"

"Eight references to sentient species without speech capacity. Twenty-three references to species with empathic capability. All species unrelated to current query. No additional related information."

He stared at his near-comatose patient, noting the progressing pallor of her skin. "What about Doctor McCoy's personal logs during that same period?"

"Personal logs are not accessible without command authorization," the computer reminded him primly.

"Doctor to Capt—" He hesitated. *There's a faster way, isn't there? Besides, I really could use another pair of hands here, and I don't mean Mister Paris's.* "Computer, compile all information on Doctor Leonard McCoy up to and including the indicated time period, and generate a holographic simulation. Allow the simulation access to my medical database. I'd really like to consult with this Doctor McCoy."

The computer acknowledged. Five seconds later, it announced its readiness with another beep.

"Activate holographic simulation of Doctor McCoy."

The air on the other side of the diagnostic bed shimmered, and a figure coalesced into being—the figure of a human male, slender and fortyish, with light brown hair and intent blue eyes. He wore a uniform so antique as to be preposterous, a blue tunic over black trousers that flared over uniform boots.

"Doctor McCoy," greeted the EMH in a neutral tone.

Leonard McCoy afforded his holographic colleague a

startled look, then frowned slightly. "Where the heck am I?"

"You're in the sickbay of the starship *Voyager*. Please tell me what you—"

McCoy turned to study his surroundings, squinting slightly. "*Voyager*, huh? Never heard of her. You sure this isn't—"

"Doctor!" The EMH marched around the diagnostic bed and caught McCoy's arm. "I'll give you the complete tour later! We have a patient!"

McCoy focused abruptly on the motionless healer. "We do?" He touched the young woman, felt for a pulse, nodded once. "All right. What's wrong with her?"

"We have here an empathic healer suffering from internal bleeding and hypovolemic shock. We also have a holographic representation of a Starfleet medical officer who doesn't see fit to record logs of any possible use to posterity. You've encountered this species before. Tell me what you know about them."

"Hold your horses just a minute. What the dickens are you talking about? This species—I don't—" His eyes narrowed, and he took a closer look at the healer. "An empath? You mean she's one of Gem's people?"

"I have no idea who Gem is. I need to know what you've learned about this species. She's a member of a mute race of empaths. Does that by any chance jog your memory?"

"It sure does. How was she injured? Did the Vians do their damned tests on her?"

The Doctor exhaled sharply in vexation. "Do you usually conduct an inquisition while your patients deteriorate? I—"

"I'm trying to get more information, dammit!" McCoy's blue eyes flashed in anger. "I encountered her species once, six months ago, and all I had to work with was my tricorder! I saw Gem heal Jim Kirk, and I got a sense of how she did it, but I don't know anything about how to heal an empath. I didn't get a chance to try."

The EMH stared at him. "You wouldn't care to make a suggestion? Venture a guess? You're supposed to be one of Starfleet's greatest medical minds. You're known for making intuitive leaps. An intuitive leap would be very useful right about now."

"All right," agreed McCoy grudgingly. "Tell me what you've tried, and how she's responded."

The Doctor complied, then added, "As best I can determine, her system has actively antagonized every treatment I've been able to devise."

"Antagonized," mused McCoy. "Counteracted. You try to regenerate the vascular damage, and as fast as you repair one vein she breaks it back down. Right?"

"Isn't that what I just said?"

"Don't get testy. I'm just making sure I'm clear on this." He touched the young healer, checking her vital signs. The Doctor offered his tricorder, but McCoy waved it away. "Don't bother. I get the picture. What's her name?"

"Name?" The EMH shifted his feet uncomfortably. "I have no idea."

"Oh, come on. Doesn't anyone but me name these poor folks? Well, I called the other empath Gem. Let's call this one—Scotty said Gem was 'a pearl of great price.' Let's call her Pearl."

" 'Pearl.' Fine. Now, I'd like to—"

"What's *your* name?"

The Doctor's discomfort grew. "I don't have one."

"You haven't got a name either? My God, what is it around here? You look a lot like my cousin Elliot. Suppose I call you—"

" 'Doctor' will do, thank you very much. Tell me everything you know about the—about Pearl's people."

McCoy nodded. "All right. Here's the short version. On stardate 5121.5, I beamed down to the second planet in the Minaran star system with Captain James Kirk and First Officer Spock. A few minutes after we got there we were, well, abducted by two members of a race who called themselves the Vians."

"This was all in your log entry," interrupted the Doctor. "Tell me about Gem."

"We found her there. Turned out the Vians were testing her, trying to find out if her people fit some kinda criteria for survival. The Minaran sun was going nova, and the Vians could only save the people of one of its planets. What they wanted was to see if Gem had the instinct to sacrifice herself to save the life of another. So they tortured us. Kirk first, and Gem healed him, but his injuries weren't critical. So next they, um, picked me. They were pretty rough on me. I would have died."

"But Gem healed you."

"No. She started to, but it would have killed her. I can't take a life to save my own! I wouldn't let her do it."

"You seem to have survived," the Doctor pointed out bluntly.

"Thanks to Jim Kirk. He—well, you could say he talked the Vians into having a conscience."

"A very interesting story, I'm sure, but tell me about Gem."

McCoy pursed his lips. "When she healed Jim, her nervous system seemed to link to his, supporting his physiological functions. His wounds became hers. Then she healed them. I didn't have a chance to get more than the vaguest idea of how she did that. I know it exhausted her."

"No doubt. The other healers on Vashnar, they were exhausted too. Clearly there's a tremendous expenditure of energy."

"Looks like it was more than Pearl could spare."

"Yes." The Doctor stared at his patient. "But you have no idea why she's opposing my every effort to help her."

McCoy shook his head, but slowly. His blue eyes narrowed. "Wait a minute. When one of Pearl's people—"

"The Anjurwan."

"The Anjurwan. When they heal, they end up with the injury, and they heal themselves pretty fast. You know, there's a problem with healing too fast."

"I beg your pardon."

"Well, think about it. What if you try to perform surgery, make an incision, on someone who can heal herself that fast?"

"She'd heal the incision instantly. Of course! I should have seen this! She's counteracting every intervention, even if the intervention is designed to assist the healing process." His sense of triumph in solving the puzzle faded immediately. "So no matter what I do, she'll neutralize the effects immediately."

"Well," McCoy pointed out grimly, "until she dies."

The Doctor began to circle the diagnostic bed, thinking furiously. "I need a treatment that won't disturb the natural homeostasis of her system. Something to at least restore her energy reserves. If she's opposing my efforts, then she can still heal herself."

"Something like tetraadenylate phosphotropin."

"Not with her reduced hepatic function. I'll try monoacetic cyclostatin." Decisively, the EMH picked up the proper cartridge and slapped it into a hypospray.

"That's another good choice," allowed McCoy. Once the medication was administered, he scanned Pearl's sensor readings anxiously. "It's working. She's rallying a little."

"Yes—but not much. And I don't dare increase the dose." The EMH frowned. "Now what? She's still bleeding internally. And if I increase her coagulation rate, and she opposes *that*, then—"

"Then you'll lose her."

The Doctor stared darkly across the diagnostic bed. "Yes. I don't suppose you can manage to be a little more positive. That's twice now you've—"

"Positive? I'm a ray of sunshine on a Georgia morning. My mama always said so." McCoy bent over Pearl, studying her, then lowered the sides of the clamshell bed and took the healer's hand. "She's so cold."

"Of course she's cold. Can't you read a sensor? Her body temperature is—"

McCoy glared at him. "Can't you hold a patient's hand? You remind me too damned much of a Vulcan I used to know. Everything's readings and sensors with you. That's not all there is to medicine by an awful long shot. You ever say anything encouraging to a patient? Pat somebody on the shoulder, tell him it's all gonna be fine? You ever heard of good old-fashioned country doctoring? A good doc, he can make somebody feel better just by being there. I'm here and I want her to know it. You might pay attention, maybe you'd—"

"Computer," growled the EMH, "end program."

"—learn a thing or—" McCoy vanished.

The Doctor stared at the space where the other hologram had been. "If I want to hear about good old doctors, I'll call in Mister Paris. I'm sure he'd be happy to regale me with more tales of 'good ol' Doc Brown' and his lollipops."

His combadge signaled. "Janeway to the Doctor."

He closed his eyes briefly, shaking his head, then answered. "Doctor here. Yes. I've improved Pearl's condition slightly, Captain."

"Pearl?"

"Ah—she seemed to need a name."

"I've returned to the ship. The Vashnar doctors aren't too happy that we still have their—ah, Pearl. I had to promise them I'd check on your progress. I'll be right there."

"Of course, Captain." *Good old country doctoring. I suppose I should knit her an afghan, fluff up her pillow, bring her some chicken soup. Or is it garlic soup? I think I need something a little more efficacious than soup.*

The sickbay doors swished open, and the captain strode in. "Doctor. Report."

He straightened, squaring his shoulders. "I was able to partially stabilize the ionic balance across her cell membranes, Captain. It's delayed her deterioration. But she'll still be comatose soon if I can't do something to slow the process."

Janeway stared in concern at Pearl. "What's causing the problem? Why can't you help her?"

"She's a natural healer. She's still trying to heal herself. It's an unconscious process. I don't know how to suspend it, and if I can't, then—"

Janeway nodded. "I understand. But if you can't help her, the Vashnar insist that she return to their Sanctuary for some sort of death ceremony. They're quite adamant." She sighed. "Pearl. It's a good name for her." The captain reached out to touch the healer's bare forearm, patting it and then gripping it gently. "I wish I could help her. I owe her my—"

Pearl's arm twitched in Janeway's grip, and the girl inhaled sharply. The Doctor stared as Pearl's vividly blue eyes opened, then focused on the captain.

Janeway shot him an urgent glance. "She's conscious!"

"I see that." He picked up his tricorder. "Let me—"

"Doctor!"

Pearl was shaking her head, weakly pulling her arm from Janeway's grip, her wide eyes distressed. The captain let her go. "It's all right. Don't be afraid, you're safe, you're on my ship. It's all right."

Pearl stopped struggling, eyes moving from Janeway to the Doctor. She managed a weak smile.

"Her internal bleeding has slowed, her blood pressure has nearly stabilized. This may be a delayed reaction to the cy-clostatin." The EMH smiled at his patient. "You're doing much better." Awkwardly, he patted her shoulder.

Pearl's smile vanished and her eyes widened, her pupils dilating. She searched the Doctor's face for a long moment, then suddenly recoiled, nearly falling off the bed.

The captain caught her. "No. Don't be afraid, it's all right." She tried to still the Anjurwan's struggles. "She's terrified. What can we do?"

The Doctor scanned the diagnostic bed's readouts. "I doubt we'll have to do anything, she's about to—"

Pearl went limp. "She's about to lose consciousness again," he finished dourly.

"What happened? She seemed fine, and then you—" Janeway stopped.

"I touched her, is that what you mean? You're not suggesting I frightened her, are you?"

"It did seem that way," the captain answered carefully. "I'm not suggesting she had any reason to be afraid, but—" She paused, her face thoughtful.

"But what?"

"She *is* an empath. She's accustomed to sensing those around her empathically. To her, you must seem only half there."

"Not an uncommon reaction, if the crew's attitude four years ago is any indication," he shot back.

She reached out and touched his shoulder gently. "Four years ago, not now. What about Pearl? Will she recover?"

He consulted his tricorder, double-checking the readings and then slowly shaking his head. "No. Not in her present condition. I may try another dose of cyclostatin in a few minutes." He regarded Janeway appealingly. "Captain, I can't give up yet. Can't you stall the Vashnar a bit longer? Please?"

She considered. "I can tell them the absolute truth—that she's been conscious, and her condition has improved. That should keep them at bay for a while. But they're going to want to see her soon."

"I understand. Thank you."

"Good luck."

She left, and he stared at Pearl. *I'll risk another dose of cyclostatin.* That done, he watched her vital signs, frowning.

Nothing. She's not fighting it, fortunately, but it's also not helping. He considered his options, his sense of despondency growing as he realized how few and poor they were. *I've run out of ideas. The combined medical expertise of forty-seven of Starfleet's finest physicians, and I can't think of a thing to do.*

Well, except for one. Much as it pains me. "Computer, activate holographic simulation of Doctor McCoy."

McCoy reappeared. He glared at the Doctor. "That was damned rude."

"If you want to criticize me, take a number. You'll have to wait until I'm finished with myself." The EMH strode into his office and slumped into his desk chair, staring at the blank screen of his computer console. *There. That's me. A blank screen.*

McCoy followed, his expressive face curious. "What's wrong? I just checked Pearl. She's a little bit better."

"She's still going to die."

"Now who's being negative?"

The Doctor shot him an annoyed glance. "It's the truth. I can't help her."

"She just got better on her own?"

"It may have been the cyclostatin. Or it may not. The captain was here, she commented that Pearl no doubt senses the others around her empathically. She may have sensed the captain, maybe she responded to that."

McCoy gave him a thoughtful look, then turned to gaze at Pearl. "The captain just came in? That's all?"

"The captain touched her, and then—" He paused. *Touched her.* The blank screen of his mind began to glow with those two words. "She *touched* Pearl. She took her arm.

And Pearl regained consciousness." He looked up excitedly at McCoy. "A physical touch! That's how the Anjurwan heal. The empathic contact is apparently only potent with a physical link. A laying on of hands, if you will. Is it possible that Pearl formed an empathic link with the captain?"

"Why not?" McCoy's brows contracted. "But your captain isn't a healer, is she?"

"No. Of course not. But if Pearl linked with her as she would for a healing, she might have been able to draw—"

"Draw energy instead of give it! She might!" McCoy nodded eagerly. "We can test that out right now. Lay on those hands, Doc. Good old country medicine, just like I said."

The Doctor had been halfway out of his chair, but now he dropped back into it. When McCoy, already at Pearl's side, turned to stare at him curiously, he shook his head.

McCoy stepped to the door. "What the heck are you waiting for? Pearl needs you! I can't do it, I'm a hologram. You didn't forget that, did you?"

The EMH's response was curt. "No."

"Then get out here and help this girl, dammit!"

"I can't."

"Why not?"

"As you just pointed out, a hologram isn't much use when it comes to the laying on of hands."

The confusion on McCoy's face slowly cleared. "Well, I'll be. You're a hologram, too. Huh. That explains a few things. Where's the real doc, or doesn't the ship have one?"

The Doctor sighed, pained and exasperated. "It did. Don't ask." He stared at his hands. *I can handle a hyprospray, a dermal regenerator, a retinal imager. But I can't help*

Pearl. She needs a real doctor. A real person. And nothing I can do will ever make me real enough to help her. With her eyes closed, I'm not even here.

He tapped his combadge. "Doctor to the captain."

Janeway looked in appeal from the Doctor to McCoy. "I can't help her if she won't let me."

What had seemed like the obvious solution to the problem had, to their bewilderment, failed. Once the captain and Tuvok had been briefed on the situation—to their surprise, by two medical holograms rather than one—the captain had willingly laid on her hands, with Tuvok closely monitoring the exchange. Pearl, however, had been less willing. As before, she had strengthened sufficiently to regain consciousness, then had with great distress wrestled herself away from Janeway.

McCoy cleared his throat. "Um. I think I may have an idea about this." He shifted uncomfortably under the combined gaze of the others. "This seems awfully familiar to me. I'm beginning to think I taught her to do this."

"Taught her?" Janeway exchanged a glance with the Doctor. "You weren't here the first time."

"That's just it. I *was*. The first time, with Gem. The empath I told you about. The Vians said we were her teachers—me, Jim Kirk, and Spock. They as much as said that she'd teach her people what she learned from us. One thing she learned from me was that a doctor—a healer—doesn't let another healer save his life. I was dying, and I couldn't let her die in my place, so I pushed her away. Just like she did with the captain here."

"But I'm not going to give my life. I just want to

strengthen her so she can save herself," protested Janeway.

"She may not see any difference," the Doctor pointed out. "From what the Vashnar said, a healer who can't heal herself dies. Even with a dozen others available who could help her."

Distress etched lines on McCoy's face. "The Vians said Gem's instinct for self-sacrifice had become stronger than her instinct for self-preservation. Because of us. Me. Good God, I taught these people to martyr themselves. They let themselves die, and they don't have to!"

"And the Vashnar allow it," Janeway remarked stonily. "They've all but abandoned their medical technology, because the Anjurwan give themselves so freely." She shook her head. "This has to stop. The Anjurwan may be childlike, but they're a sentient race. It's hard to believe that the Vashnar can live with themselves, exploiting other intelligent beings like this."

"Over ninety years, what is readily available and freely offered becomes habit," Tuvok pointed out.

The Doctor turned to look at the empath, who lay watching them vaguely. "Our good country doctor, here, taught her ancestor a lesson," he mused. "Why can't we teach Pearl a new one?"

Janeway gave him a quizzical look. "What do you suggest?"

"Perhaps," he replied, arching an eyebrow, "we can convince her that *you* are a healer."

"But I'm not an empath."

"Neither was Doctor McCoy, but the lesson was learned from him. Captain, I watched the Vashnar so-called doctors rather closely. I think I can duplicate the motions by which the Vashnar 'focus' the healers. If you'll—"

"Of course." Janeway nodded, smiling. "I'll play the healer. But I won't 'give my all.' Just enough, and no more."

"Captain," broke in Tuvok, "perhaps I should—"

"No. Pearl saved my life; I'm going to do what I can to save hers. Doctor, if you please." She extended her hands.

The EMH took them, leading her toward the watching empath. Pearl's eyes widened as she took in the ritualistic motions of the Doctor turning the captain toward her "patient." She remained motionless as Janeway's hands moved over her, not quite touching her.

"Now," murmured the Doctor. McCoy opened a tricorder. Decisively, Janeway laid her hands upon Pearl.

The young empath stared full into the eyes of the captain, blue into blue. She didn't move.

"It's working," whispered McCoy. "She's linking with the captain. She's getting stronger."

The moment stretched out. Pearl's color began visibly to improve. The Doctor's eyes shifted to Janeway's face. She had in turn paled, and she trembled slightly.

"That is sufficient. The link should be broken now," Tuvok directed.

Time for a new part to the ritual. The Doctor stepped forward, reaching around the captain to take both her hands in his and draw them away from Pearl. He turned Janeway toward him and smiled. "Excellent. Well done. You may now rest." He pointed her toward the nearest biobed, and Janeway, without demur—and with Tuvok's help—stretched herself out on it. The Doctor turned to assess Pearl's reaction.

Slowly, her eyes enormous, the empath sat up and stared

from the Doctor to the captain, then back. Her expression of astonishment moderated into curiosity.

"She'll recover now," remarked McCoy, smiling. "She's weak, but your captain's a strong woman. Pearl just needs rest."

"I'll make sure she gets it," Janeway murmured. "I'll tell Kiv."

"You'll be here, resting yourself," returned the EMH sternly. "I'm sure Commander Chakotay can pass the word along. 'Doctor' Kiv will be in your debt. You saved his 'best healer.' "

"If her people are as imitative as Doctor McCoy seems to imply, she may return to them with a revolutionary notion." Tuvok folded his arms and cocked an eyebrow at the captain.

She smiled. "I'm counting on it."

"Pearl, you can't—get back in bed, girl—"

McCoy tried to restrain Pearl, who had slid off the diagnostic bed, but the Anjurwan—graceful despite her exhaustion—eluded him. She approached Janeway. Her blue eyes assessed the captain, then moved to Tuvok, then returned. She reached out a hand.

Janeway took it, her smile softening. "You're welcome. I—Oh!"

Pearl returned the smile, holding Janeway's eyes for a long moment. Then she turned to Tuvok, easing her hand from the captain's. She held it out to the Vulcan.

Tuvok took it, curiosity apparent even on his normally bland face. Then his eyebrows rose.

"Did you feel it too? Did she 'touch' you?" Janeway breathed.

"Indeed," he murmured back. "An empathic communication of remarkable emotional order."

Pearl slipped her fingers from Tuvok's, her smile warm. She turned toward the Doctor.

He began to shake his head as she approached. *I don't want to see that lovely smile turn to fear.* He stepped back. "Don't touch me. I'm not—"

Undaunted, she caught first his right hand, then his left, holding them in both of hers. Her expression now both determined and apprehensive, she stared into his eyes.

"Pearl—" *What? What was that? Did she say something? Impossible. Her lips didn't move, and at any rate she has no vocal cords. But I could swear she said—*

The apprehension faded from the lovely empath's face, and her smile bloomed. The soft voice seemed to whisper in his ear once more, gentle words that he couldn't quite catch, and then faded. She turned away, still smiling, and he fought down the sharp desire to draw her back, entice her to speak again. *Did she—? But how could she? I'm a hologram! She couldn't—but I think she did.* Wonderingly, he stared at the Anjurwan.

Pearl looked at the captain, then at the Vulcan, then at the Doctor, and nodded as if a question had been answered. Then she gestured. The signs were simple.

" 'I'd like to go home now,' " Janeway surmised. Pearl's closed hand moved to her mouth, then opened like a flower. " 'I have something to tell.' "

"You just do that, girl," approved McCoy. "I don't want any more of your sisters and brothers on my conscience." He turned to the Doctor. "I think I'm done here. You might as well shut me off."

The EMH regarded him for a long moment. "Thank you."

McCoy's eyebrows arched. "Well, you're welcome. Thank me for what, exactly?"

"For a lesson in—good old country doctoring."

"Any time," returned his colleague nonchalantly. "You know where to find me. Just don't forget, good medicine isn't all science, not by a long shot. Sometimes you gotta go with your gut. It's more like art. It takes a gift."

The Doctor looked at Pearl, who gazed luminously back, and allowed a smile. "I think you just may be right."

Seventh Heaven

Dustan Moon

The doors to the starship *Voyager*'s bridge swished open and Captain Kathryn Janeway entered with Seven of Nine at her side. Janeway felt refreshed from her night's rest, alert from her morning cup of coffee. "All I need is a fast starship and astrometrics to steer her by," she said with a bright smile, greeting the officers on the bridge.

Lieutenant Commander Tuvok, standing to her left, looked up from the security console, arching an eyebrow. "Captain, I believe the actual saying states the need for 'a *tall* ship and a *star* to steer her by.' "

Janeway shook her head. Vulcans. She smiled privately to her first officer, Commander Chakotay, who had risen from his chair when she entered. Warmth glittered in his eyes, and not for the first time Janeway felt the subtle tug of attraction for this handsome Native American, an attraction she fought to keep at a professional distance. She turned her head, focused on the Vulcan security chief. "A paraphrase for the times, Mister Tuvok." And then, wryly, "Must be too early in the morning."

Before Tuvok could reply, Seven spoke up. "Captain, may I begin modifications now?" Undoubtedly, Seven considered standing unoccupied for even a few moments an inefficient use of time.

Janeway looked her way. Seven's pale blue eyes regarded her without emotion, reminding her of cold steel. Not surprising—most of the time, Janeway could look within those eyes and practically see a calculating automaton lurking in the depths. But at other times, those rare moments after a trial aboard the ship had brought Seven's humanity to the surface, Janeway could sense a strong-willed woman fighting to break through inviolable Borg conditioning, fighting to reclaim her life as a person.

There were times when Janeway wondered if that day would ever come.

Janeway pointed to the port bulkhead. "Proceed. You may begin by replacing the relay circuits in the aft panels." She reached out, touching Seven's shoulder. "When you've finished your work, I'd like you to join me for lunch today."

Seven stiffened; the remnants of Borg technology implanted to her brow and cheek glinted in the light. "My biological system has no need for nutritional supplements at this time."

"Nevertheless, I want you to join me."

Seven frowned. "Understood."

So cold. Janeway sighed as Seven pulled away and methodically stepped over to the aft bulkhead, placing her tool kit on the deck, working the panel free. There was a day when Janeway wouldn't have let Seven get within ten meters of *Voyager*'s circuitry, but over time, Seven had proven to be an invaluable member of the crew, even risking her life on several occasions to save them. Janeway sensed a desire on Seven's part to please her by carrying out assignments effectively, and Janeway was only too happy to oblige. Seven's experience with the Borg gave her, among other things, a unique perspective on conduits and circuitry, and intuitiveness human technicians simply did not have. On a ship that still had over sixty thousand light-years to cross in order to reach home, every modification for efficiency counted.

Leaving Seven to her task, Janeway crossed the station tier, savoring the flavor of coffee that still lingered on her tongue. She walked down the steps and sat in her command chair at the center of the circular deck, secretly wishing she could have carried one more cup with her, not so much for the coffee's taste, but to relish its soothing warmth in the palms of her cold hands. She sighed and rubbed them briskly together—a time and place for everything, especially for the captain of a starship.

Crossing her legs, Janeway stared at the viewscreen. Stars flowed past like dandelion puffs on the wind. It never ceased to fascinate her, the intricate beauty of space, the bold brushstrokes of worlds while approaching a star system, the grand perspective of galaxies when one drew back. A masterpiece collection of stellar proportions, a gallery of stars, each subject portrayed in elegance by its own subtle lighting.

If only that gallery wasn't so damned long.

Janeway brushed the thought aside. "Helm, what's our heading?"

She expected the pilot to respond, but it was the voice of the operations officer, Ensign Harry Kim, that shot across the bridge. "Captain, long-range sensors are detecting intense gravimetric distortion 5.2 light-years dead ahead."

"Cause?"

"It appears to be a quantum singularity."

Janeway's heart skipped a beat. "On screen and magnify."

She stared at the image on the viewscreen. Her floating dandelion-seed stars appeared caught in a zephyr. Luminous gases curled into the grip of a burgeoning vortex; stars in the background swirled in distortion. Janeway held her breath.

"Detecting transwarp signatures breaking free of the gravity well."

Transwarp signatures.

Borg.

Janeway released her breath with a call to action. "Battle stations! Shields to maximum. Tuvok, have security teams on all decks break out phaser rifles and set to rotating modulation."

As the warning klaxon sounded, a vessel shot from the vortex, and stars visible in the background twisted back into shape. Janeway uncrossed her legs and leaned forward, biting her lower lip. The hull of this ship seemed like the layers of asymmetrical darkness common in Borg design, but this was no cube. The ship was triangular in design, pyramid-shaped, and closing fast.

"Helm, hard about. Take us to maximum warp. Weapons, reprogram phaser banks to rotating modulation and stand by."

Ensign Kim called out. "Transwarp vessel at 2.3 light-years and closing."

Seven of Nine's voice rang over the bridge, her diction stiff and precise. "Captain, I am unfamiliar with this vessel, but the structure is definitely a Borg configuration. You will not be able to outrun it."

"Then we fight." Janeway was standing now, facing tactical, her heart pounding to the rush of command. "Tuvok, arm aft torpedo bay, high-yield photon warhead. Hold for my command. Tom, evasive maneuvers. Work your magic."

Light suddenly erupted in green phosphorescence. From the corner of her vision, Janeway saw a flashwall come to life on the port side of the bridge, sweeping toward starboard. Ensign Kim blurted out what the captain already recognized. "Polaron beam. We're being scanned!"

Janeway felt fury. The scan violated the sanctity of her vessel and the members of her crew . . . and she was helpless to stop it. The flashwall passed through her without pause, but it seemed to backtrack over Seven of Nine, then resumed its course across the rest of the bridge.

Before Janeway had time to contemplate the subtle shift of the scan, two Borg materialized, male and female, one to each side of Seven, clad in black armor implants, cyborg appendages, and a hideous network of life-support tubes jammed into their pale flesh at various points. Servos whined as the Borg clamped cybernetic hands onto Seven's arms. Tuvok shouted, "Security breach," but it was all over before he could raise his phaser, before Janeway could shout a command.

The Borg dematerialized.

Seven of Nine was gone.

Seven of Nine struggled against her two captors as they led her along a platform that crossed the expanse of a vast pyramidal atrium in the center of the Borg ship. The walkways began at each corner and joined in the center to a torus structure. The torus encompassed a flowing blue pillar of transwarp power cascading from the peak of the pyramid, tumbling like a waterfall to the courtyard below. Borg moved like ants down there, and multitudes could also be seen working within tiers of open chambers that ran the length of the three walls, many of those levels crackling with green plasma light from regeneration chambers. The vessel's spacious interior was almost aesthetic in design, an illogical waste of space, but it was clearly capable of barracking a formidable army.

As Seven absorbed her surroundings and calculated the tension of her captors' grips against the maximum application of her muscular force, she felt an emotion she had never experienced as a member of the collective Borg hive, one she was now all too familiar with.

Fear.

"I will not be reassimilated into the Borg! I demand that you release me!"

The female Borg spoke. Klingon. "Cease your struggling. Resistance is futile."

Seven was surprised they had not injected her with nanoprobes by now. Borg procedure was simple and efficient: assimilate and absorb. It was inefficient to struggle with a species, yet that is what they were doing. What were they planning with her? Interrogation? Torture? Pain was irrelevant.

Assimilation was not.

"No! Resistance is not futile!" Seven slammed her shoulder against the female. "I do not want to be a member of the collective! I will fight until I am assimilated or dead."

Both Borgs tightened their grips, the bionic appendages constricting on Seven's arms like handcuffs. They jerked her back into place and continued marching forward. The female spoke. "You will not be assimilated. You will not be terminated. Cease your struggling."

For Seven, hearing a Borg utter such words was shocking. "Repeat your prior statement," she said.

"You will not be assimilated. You will not be—"

"You are Borg. Why are you not assimilating me?"

"Because you do not wish it."

Seven spat words like venom. "Since when have the desires of a species mattered to the Borg?"

"When we chose the honor of individuality over the degradation of the collective."

Seven's mind raced. Awareness of individuality? Recognition of singular entities instead of a linked whole? These were Borg like her then, aware of self. "Who are you? What is it you seek from me?"

Her captors stopped and the female stared at her, one eye biological, the other a misshapen spectral Borg implant, glowing bright red. "You were Seven of Nine, Tertiary Adjunct of Unimatrix Zero One. You served on grid nine two of subjunction twelve in cube three seven six four. You are no longer linked to the collective. What designation have you chosen to express your individuality?"

"Seven of Nine."

"Unacceptable. That was your Borg designation. You are no longer Borg."

Seven felt hot emotion burning within her. Rage. "We are all Borg. We shall all remain Borg until every last implant and suffusion of their technology can be removed from our biologic selves. Until that day, I am Seven of Nine."

The female inclined her head, assessing Seven's statement. Then she tapped her metallic breastplate with her only biological hand. "My name is Ohm. I will refer to you as Seven of Nine, as you wish."

Venom flowed through Seven. "It is not my wish. It was never my wish." With all her might, she lunged against their cyborg grip. Futile. "Release me and let me return to my ship."

"No."

"If you truly respect me as an individual, you will acknowledge my will. I do not enjoy being restrained. Release me immediately"—and her face twisted into a sneer as she spoke the Borg's name—"Ohm."

"We cannot. The Primary has given orders that we bring you to him."

"Who is this 'Primary'? That is not a Borg designation."

"We are not Borg."

Seven realized she must concede their professed distinctiveness or be caught in an endless loop of illogic. "Then who is this 'Primary' and what does he want with me?"

"The Primary is the titular designation of the one who commands." Ohm turned to the male. "Common reference in Starfleet terminology?"

The male's chin jerked. "Captain."

Ohm nodded, the motion stiff. "Yes: captain. Our captain wishes to speak with you."

"Then I shall proceed. There is no need for restraint. I cannot escape. Passage along this corridor will be more efficient if I walk between you."

Ohm nodded. Was that a smile? "Acceptable." She released her grip, and with a look to her companion, he did likewise.

Quick as lightning, Seven slapped her combadge. "Seven to *Voyager!*"

The only response was the ringing in her ears as Ohm backhanded her across the temple. Then, there was darkness.

Janeway stood, fists on hips, glaring at the image of the Borg ship on the viewscreen. The Borg had just beamed Seven away from the bridge and had dropped speed, arcing starboard. Janeway could guess where they were heading.

"Tuvok, can you get a transporter lock on Seven?"

"Negative, Captain. I am unable to penetrate their shields."

"Then hail the Borg ship," Janeway said.

Janeway heard the communication tone. "No response, Captain."

"Keep trying. Tom, come about, match course and speed. Don't let them get away."

"Aye, Captain."

Janeway dropped into her command chair. The lingering taste of coffee in her mouth had turned as sour as her stomach. She had always felt personally responsible for Seven of Nine, from the moment Seven had been severed from the collective and was forced to face her humanity. Now, Seven had been severed from *Voyager.* The Borg would erase her progress, purge the humanity from her. Would they hook the implants back up to Seven, shove that godawful pointed instrument back into her eye?

Not on my watch.

She inclined her head toward her first officer. "We've got to get her back, Chakotay. We have to follow them into the quantum singularity when they open it up."

Chakotay frowned, drawing the ancestral tattoo over his

left brow down like dark wings. "Kathryn, have you forgotten what happened the last time we entered one of these things? We had to eject the warp core. You'll be risking the entire crew to save one. You know we're no match for Borg technology."

Janeway fought to keep her tone low and calm. "I'd do the same for you, Chakotay."

"With all due respect, Captain, how do you know Seven wants to come back? For all of her human appearance, how much of her is still Borg under the skin?"

"I won't let them have her, Chakotay. Not now, not after how far she has come. I'll chase them to hell and back if I have to." She broke off the conversation by issuing quick commands. "Tom, ride right on their tail. Tuvok, I want all auxiliary and emergency power transferred to the shields. When they open the quantum singularity, we're going in."

Seven sensed something cool press to her forehead. She rose to full consciousness, heard voices, kept her eyes closed. Location, unknown. Position, lying supine, hard surface. Atmospheric temperature, thirty-six degrees Celsius. Olfactory input, oily scent of Borg synthetic lubricant four seven eight one, epidermal moisturizer. Auditory input, low whine of servomechanisms and bionic hydraulics, distant hum of transwarp generator.

"You shouldn't have hit her," a voice was saying. Proximity, point five meters. Tone, range of lower octaves, mechanical overlay. Species identified: Borg, male. Assimilated race: human.

A second voice. "She was attempting escape. Your orders were for me to bring her to you. It was inefficient to continue struggling with her. Human: impact to the cranial temple, unconsciousness is immediate. It was more expedient this way." Proximity of second voice, one meter. Tone, range of midoctave, mechanical overlay, female Borg. Specific vocal frequency matched to known reference. The Klingon Borg named Ohm.

The male voice. Irritation. "When will you comprehend that efficiency is not paramount? I specifically instructed you not to harm her. You were to harm no one."

"And I did not, though I do not understand what you need with *her*." Unidentified emotional inflection in tone, conveyed with stress on any reference to Seven. "Observe increased respiratory exchange. She is now conscious."

Seven felt a warm touch to her hand. "Seven of Nine?"

Her eyes flashed open. Her vision was blurred, but she squinted and hazy objects came into focus. A Borg male was leaning over her, his torso covered in black monotanium armor, his hand holding a damp cloth. Life-support tubes circled the top of his head, and an optical enhancement overlay his left eye socket, glowing soft green. But it was his human eye that was so disconcerting to Seven. It was focused on her and reflected far more than a Borg mind calculating optical input. It appeared to reflect . . . emotion. Seven had never seen this in the Borg, but she had seen that same look in the captain's eyes. Concern.

Seven stiff-armed the Borg. "Get away from me!" She sat upright, felt her mind swirl from the concussion. Visual acuity blurred again. She focused hard on the male Borg, and some of the haze clarified. Adequate. "Return me to my ship. Now."

Servos whined as the male Borg regained his balance, annoyance on his face. "We will respect your wishes after you have heard us out."

Seven winced, pain still throbbing at her temple. She pressed her palm to it and it subsided somewhat. "Who are you? Why have you abducted me from *Voyager?*"

The Borg tilted his head, his features softening. "Do you feel better?"

Seven frowned. She had no frame of reference with which to correlate a Borg inquiring of her well-being. It was disorienting. Irritating. Repulsive. "Physical comfort is irrelevant. Answer my questions. Who are you?"

Ohm stepped closer, raising her fist as though to strike. "You will speak with respect when addressing the Primary!"

The male Borg barked a command. "Ohm! Keep your place." He watched Ohm lower her arm and step back. Nodding approval, he turned to Seven, placing his open hand over his heart.

"I am Hugh."

Sitting in her command chair, Janeway clenched her hands into fists, felt her nails bite into the flesh of her palms as she glared at the Borg vessel on the viewscreen. It was stationary, rotating slowly, and had remained as such ever since they had followed it through the quantum singularity, entering this uncharted sector of the Delta Quadrant. It hadn't been easy, but they had managed to avoid a warp core meltdown, and *Voyager*'s shields, though stressed, were still functioning.

"Hail them again," Janeway said to Tuvok.

She heard the hailing tone. "No response, Captain."

Janeway felt the ship was just hovering there in its impregnability to taunt her. They were now ten thousand additional light-years away from their true destination, home, which was all the more infuriating. Chakotay had said nothing, but he didn't have to. Janeway could feel the crispness in his posture and features like the icy breeze of a winter morning.

"Why aren't they moving?" Janeway said, her volume indicating the question was open to all.

"My guess is that they didn't expect us to jump into the singularity with them," Tom Paris said. "Most ships tuck tail and run as fast as they can from the Borg. We didn't. They probably realize we're going to track them wherever they intend to go."

She watched another side of the ship rotate into view. "I'll be damned if they're just going to sit there and ignore us. There's got to be a way to get their attention and open communication. Tuvok, fire phasers. See if you can cycle the modulation faster than their shields can compensate."

Janeway heard the chirps from the tactical console as Tuvok entered the program, then saw the phaser lash out, a red spear of energy. "Captain," Tuvok finally said, powering down, "I have attempted the strategy with no apparent success."

"Then arm a photon torpedo. Modulate the frequency." Janeway heard the chirps, then the hot tone. "Do it."

The torpedo sailed toward its target, a streak of blue light. Impacted. Borg shields flashed in a faint sphere of green. Then, white brilliance flared across the screen. As the light diminished, Janeway leaned forward.

The pyramid of Borg technology still rotated in place. It almost looked serene in its movement.

"Again, Mister Tuvok."

"Captain?" Tuvok said. "I fail to see the effectiveness of a torpedo salvo. If one missile did not work, it is highly improbably the others will work either. It is obvious their shields can compensate at a rate superior to our torpedo modulation."

"You kick at a hive long enough, Mister Tuvok, and the bees are bound to come out. Again."

"Acknowledged." He launched the torpedo. No effect.

"Again!"

She felt a touch to her hand. First Officer Chakotay. "Kathryn, I understand how you feel, but this is pointless."

She jerked her hand away. "Again, Mister Tuvok. Fire!"

Nothing.

"Again!"

Chakotay had swiveled in his chair, facing her. He looked like someone studying a madman banging his head against a wall.

I'm mad, all right. "Again!" The torpedo flashed.

Tuvok's voice. "Captain, we are receiving a transmission."

Finally. "On screen."

"The transmission has linked with our receiver and has somehow manipulated the circuitry to access our computer database."

"Shut them out, Mister Tuvok."

"Unable to comply. The Borg have overridden system security and have now decoded our encryption. They are accessing Starfleet mission archives . . . stardate 40000 . . . stardate 45000 . . . they are now retrieving a file from stardate 45855.4 . . . *U.S.S. Enterprise*-D, under Captain

Jean-Luc Picard's command . . . the file is marked 'Classified.' "

Janeway watched the viewscreen go blank, then light up with a recording from the file. The scene was aboard the *Enterprise* in a room with a single adolescent Borg, held in a containment device that resembled a cage. The ship's chief engineer and doctor were standing before him, and the stardate showed at the bottom of the screen, ticking away in tenths of a second as the scene progressed.

Janeway had studied this recording before. It was open only to the rank of Starfleet captains and above. There was never any official statement of why it was classified, but the reason was obvious. Starfleet took the position that the Borg were one collective machine, not individuals, certainly not persons. After this incident where Captain Picard had returned to the collective a Borg who had discovered his individuality, Starfleet policy strictly forbade further attempts to rehabilitate other members of the collective. Starfleet became all the more adamant after those members of the Borg affected by individuality broke away from the collective and destroyed some colonies in their confused state. Starfleet's position had then crystallized diamond hard—no quarter, no mercy. To maintain that policy, they could not allow any members of the Federation to develop sympathy for the Borg.

But if this little scene got into public hands, it would be damning to Starfleet.

So would the arrival of Seven of Nine. If the *Voyager* crew ever made it back—when they made it back—Janeway secretly knew Seven would not be welcomed by all. In fact, in all likelihood her life would be in danger, but Janeway had always planned to help Seven across that catwalk when they came to it.

Now, she might not have the chance.

The video progressed to the portion Janeway knew by heart. The officers on the bridge were silent as they listened. Janeway's thoughts raced to why this scene was being played.

The adolescent Borg was speaking. "Do I have a name?"

The redheaded doctor replied, "I'm Beverly, he's Geordi, and you . . . you . . ." She looked at a loss for words.

"No, no, wait a minute," Geordi said. "That's it. Hugh!"

"We are Hugh," the cyborg said enthusiastically. He was no longer a member of the collective. He had a name.

Then Hugh did something Janeway had never seen in the file. He turned, as if he was looking through the viewscreen, and stared directly at her.

"I am Hugh. I am Primary of the Independent Nation of Borg. We mean you no harm. Cease your inefficient waste of energy."

Startled at first, Janeway addressed the image on the screen. "I am Captain Kathryn Janeway of the *Starship Voyager.* You have abducted a member of my crew. I want her back. Now."

"I cannot do that."

"Why not?"

"Seven of Nine has not made her decision yet."

"What decision?"

"Whether she wishes to join the Independent Nation of Borg. She is, after all, one of us. You do believe in freedom of choice, do you not, Captain Janeway?"

"I didn't see your people offering Seven many choices

when you boarded my ship. You've got a long way to go when it comes to manners, mister."

Hugh tilted his head and his eyepiece flashed green. "I apologize about the method employed, but it was the only option."

"Really?" Janeway rolled the word with cynicism. "You could have asked to talk to Seven."

Hugh's gaze dropped to the floor. When he looked up, the eyepiece flashed red. "Would you honestly have allowed me? Every race we come in contact with either flees out of fear or fights out of hatred. It's one of the reasons we had to leave the Alpha Quadrant."

Janeway sighed. "If you are indeed the Borg Hugh from the Alpha Quadrant, how did you find out about Seven of Nine and locate us?"

"Allow me to finish, Captain Janeway, and the answers will become apparent."

"Make it quick, Hugh."

"Acknowledged. We had to escape the Alpha Quadrant. Even Starfleet vessels were unwilling to differentiate between independent Borg and collective Borg, firing at will. This, in spite of the good report Captain Picard made to Admiral Nechayev about our people saving him in the battle against the android, Lore, and the Borg he controlled. Starfleet just wouldn't listen—you yourself know what your directives are in any Borg encounter, what you're ordered to do if you capture individuals from the collective."

Janeway knew all too well. Poison the individual with an invasive paradox virus and send that Borg back to pollute the hive. She shuddered thinking about it, because it was what she should have done with Seven. One of the few privileges of being cut off from Starfleet by over sixty thousand light-years was not having to account for your actions to a superior officer.

Hugh continued. "We escaped to the Delta Quadrant through the Borg's transwarp conduits. From there, we searched for an uninhabited sector to call home, a place where we could live in freedom instead of being treated as the freaks of the galaxy. We found such a place. Today, we run covert missions to help other Borg break free of the collective, as you were able to accomplish with Seven of Nine. It was through those saved that we found out about Seven. Then, when you tapped into the network of relay stations stretching across the Delta Quadrant to send messages home, we located *Voyager.*"

Janeway's temper had been cooling until the mention of Seven. "Hugh, I sympathize with your cause. Now tell me how Seven is doing."

Hugh spoke in mechanical tones, but his human eye glowed bright with compassion. "Seven is well. She is touring our new flagship with myself and my Secondary even as we speak."

Janeway smirked. "Show me."

Hugh blinked, and the screen suddenly transformed into a jerky image of a corridor scrolling past to the accompaniment of the whine and hiss of bionics, the metallic clank of boots. The image kept shifting in spectral tints, and Janeway assumed Hugh was somehow transmitting through his optic enhancement and Borg implants. The view stabilized and the scene panned left. Seven of Nine came into view.

"How are you feeling?" Hugh asked.

Seven scowled. "I told you previously, personal comfort is irrelevant. Can we proceed? Stopping to converse is inefficient."

Janeway was so relieved by Seven's response, she almost laughed.

The image of Hugh's face flashed back on the screen. "As you can see, Captain Janeway, Seven is functional, though perhaps a bit ill-tempered. I must concede, I intended to show her our star system, but your persistence forces me to plead our cause without her experiencing the fullness of our vision."

"Your cause is your business, Hugh. My crew is mine. I need to know that you intend to return Seven to us."

"I cannot do that."

Janeway felt her temperature rise. "Why not?"

"The choice to return is not mine."

"Explain."

"It is Seven of Nine's prerogative."

Janeway felt a lump in her throat. "What if she doesn't want to join your cause? She's mostly human, after all. What if she wants to return to *Voyager?*"

Hugh paused, tilting his head to one side. The optical implant over his left eye glowed amber. "What if her wish is to remain with us?"

Seven stood in the torus chamber suspended over the center of the atrium; it served as Hugh's command center. Hugh and Ohm were beside her, on a balcony adjoining Hugh's quarters that overlooked the vast courtyard. Seven had completed her tour of the vessel, had even walked within a Borg holograph of their homeworld, and she had to concede that

Hugh and his independent Borg allies had the cohesion necessary to construct a new nation for their kind—if they could continue to keep their homeworld hidden from the collective. As intriguing as their ideas seemed, it was nothing compared to the conclusion of the tour. Standing on this balcony, Seven had just witnessed what she judged would be the most incredible event she would see in her life.

A Borg concert.

The courtyard had been filled with Borg musicians, some replacing arm implants with sophisticated bows, using hands to support a variety of violins, cellos, bass, and other instruments from worlds across the quadrants. In some, their very implants had been reconstructed into instruments, breastplates that moaned like bagpipes and accordions, collars that shrilled like flutes and recorders. And the entire pyramid vessel—electrical conduits, plasma discs, even the transwarp core—had thrummed a resonant bass line for the symphony to dance upon like a stage.

Even now, as she watched Borg break down their instruments, Seven was still in shock. She had heard music before, on *Voyager.* She understood the mathematics behind production of musical frequencies, but the harmonics had never reached within her. Until now. Seeing her kind transform the horror of their assimilation into something wondrous touched feelings locked deep inside her.

"Beautiful, aren't they?" Hugh said, pointing to the Borg as they returned to their duties.

"You have given them a sense of community," Seven said. "They are singular, but not alone."

"The Primary gives them a sense of honor," Ohm said, as if in correction.

Hugh shook his head. "No, I haven't. I gave them noth-ing—it was always within them. They are just free now to express who they are."

"This week's concert was surpassing," Ohm said. She turned from the rail and faced Seven. "Next week, we per-form my opera. What instrument do you play, Seven? Will you have something to add to the melody of our distinctive-ness?"

That tone again. It bordered on hostility. Seven did not know why. She stood tall. "I sing," Seven said. It was true—she had been forced to sing in a holodeck cabaret.

"Really?" Ohm's tone mocked her as she swaggered closer. "Well now, what a coincidence. I am also a singer. A virtuoso." Her chest rose with a deep intake of breath. Ohm tilted her head upward and belted out a progression of scales. Then, licking her jagged teeth, she looked down at Seven and sneered. "Your turn."

Seven crossed her arms, adjusted her stance. "An ade-quate attempt, but your range is limited and your tone is flat. The notes will be more resonant if you breathe from your diaphragm instead of your throat."

Ohm's optical enhancement blazed red, and a Klingon growl erupted from her throat. "Human. Sever spinal cord at third vertebra. Death is immediate."

Seven met her gaze dead on. "Klingon. Shatter the cranial exoskeleton at the tricipital lobe. Death is immediate."

Hugh jumped between them, shoved them apart. "Enough! If we cannot respect the individual distinctive-ness of one another, how will we be able to defeat the Borg?"

Ohm staggered, regained her balance, bowed from the

waist to Hugh. "Forgive me, Primary. Your words are correct."

Hugh rested his hand on Ohm's shoulder. His voice was calm. "Go, resume your duties. I wish to speak with Seven in private."

Seven recognized the subtle shift in Ohm's features. A look of pain. She masked it quickly, and her face became as cool and blank as that of a Borg drone. "As you wish, Primary." She spun about and left, her boots clanking hollowly against the deck.

Hugh watched Ohm leave, then made a jerky mechanical turn back to Seven. "Flute," he said.

"Excuse me?"

"I play the flute. I made mine from wood. Flutes constructed from metal are too shrill for my taste."

"Oh." Seven did not know how to respond. "I am sure you play satisfactorily."

Hugh shrugged; the bionics hummed. "I try." He stepped closer. "We need you, Seven. Now that I have seen you, I realize just how great that need is. You are able to survive with minimal Borg implants—you look virtually human."

"I am eighty-two percent biological."

"Exactly. When people look at us, they see monsters, murderers, but your appearance would be aesthetically pleasing to biological entities. If you join our nation, I would appoint you ambassador to the biologicals. You could help establish an understanding, help negotiate peace agreements. Perhaps one day we might even be able to join the Federation, sharing our technology in return for their support to help us free the Borg from the collective. Will you join us, Seven of Nine?"

It was hard for Seven to keep staring into Hugh's human eye. He had so much passion for his cause, and it was . . . noble. Hugh made a good leader. He made a good captain.

"No," Seven answered.

Hugh's whole body sagged. "May I ask why not?"

"You may." Seven took a deep breath. The formulation of the words was difficult for her. She realized why and felt surprise—she did not wish to hurt him. "My desire differs from yours, Borg Hugh. I respect your cause. It is . . . good. But it is not mine."

Hugh sighed. "Do you have a cause, Seven?"

"Yes."

"I see no evidence of it."

"That is because you have not been to *Voyager.* That is where I belong."

"But you are alone there," Hugh said.

"No," Seven said. "I am not."

Hugh's life-support coils throbbed softly. Slowly, he nodded his head. His optical enhancement glowed pale green. "I understand." He paused, and hope shined in his eye. "Perhaps you would be willing to speak to the Federation on our behalf when you return to the Alpha Quadrant?"

Seven nodded. "Acceptable. I will speak for you."

A smile spread across Hugh's face. "Thank you."

"You are welcome. I am ready to return to *Voyager.*" Why was that so hard to say?

"Wait," Hugh said. "I have something for you." He opened his hand; green phosphorescence swirled within. As the energy haze dissipated, something glittered with nacreous white swirls against his gray palm.

"What is it?" Seven asked.

"A shell. Just a shell I picked up from a shore on our homeworld. Something to remember Hugh by."

"I do not understand. How can a mollusk serve to remind me of the Borg Hugh?"

"Hold it to your ear."

Frowning, Seven took the shell and complied with the request.

"No, turn it so the opening is at your ear."

She did so, resting the heel of her palm on her cheek's metallic star implant. She listened. "I hear weak acoustical frequencies resonating off the air mass confined within the whorled chamber."

Hugh frowned. "You are thinking like a Borg."

"I am a Borg."

Hugh touched her shoulder. Seven stiffened, uncomfortable with his proximity. He pulled his hand back. "Try not to analyze. Reach for the humanity inside you. Close your eyes, amplify the harmonic in your mind, and associate it with naturally occurring sounds."

Seven closed her eyes. Listened intently. Picked the obvious parallel. "Wind," she said.

"Good," Hugh said. Seven felt the soft touch to her shoulder again. She flashed her eyes open and Hugh pulled back his hand. Analyzing the sensation, she decided the weight of his hand was not uncomfortable, just the strange feeling that it evoked.

"Go on," Hugh said, smiling. "Close your eyes. You can do better."

She closed them again.

"Now think of the wind. How strong is it? Gale force, or breeze?"

"Breeze."

"Yes, because the sound is soft. Maybe it's an ocean breeze. Maybe it's even a whisper."

"It is . . . difficult for me to imagine these things."

Seven felt the warm touch of his hand. She kept her eyes closed as Hugh's fingers tenderly cupped over hers. The sensation was pleasant, exhilarating, sending shivers of impulses where their hands made contact. Hugh's voice was like the sound in the shell. "It is only difficult for you because the collective stole your ability to think for yourself. It was the same for me at first, but it gets easier over time. Try again."

Seven took a deep breath, held, then released it slowly. "I hear the breeze rustling through leaves—"

"What color are the leaves?"

"Green."

"What kind of trees are they on?"

"Palms."

"Where are you standing?"

"By the sea, and the breeze is rising off a glittering ocean."

Hugh's voice was a whisper. "And how does the breeze smell?"

"Fresh. Crisp."

"Maybe even sweet? Maybe there are flowers nearby, red roses, and their floral scent swirls on the breeze like downy feathers, and the sun is bright, and it warms the soft skin of your cheeks while the ocean laps against the shore."

"Yes. Yes." Seven felt her heart rate increasing. She opened her eyes.

Hugh tilted his head, and she had the sensation that he could see into the very depths of her soul. He was so close,

Seven could feel the brush of Hugh's breath upon her face as he spoke. He squeezed her hand. "This is Hugh's gift for you. For as long as you keep it, this will be my song from me to you."

As Seven looked in his eye and listened to the softness of his words, she felt a strange warmth flush through her. It was an odd sensation, different from the emotional response she felt when receiving Captain Janeway's approval. Powerful and compelling, it drew her toward Hugh as if by electromagnetic force. She leaned closer, and a random image coalesced in her mind of a starship approaching the event horizon of a singularity. Hugh's human eye glittered, and she sensed hidden galaxies swirling within, beckoning her to come explore every one.

Fear.

Seven felt a sudden rush of fear. Analyzed its cause. Recognized the voice of her subconscious. If she drew any closer, she knew she would cross the threshold and become so wrapped up in this singularity that she would never want to leave him.

Clarity of logic became the circuit that disconnected the emotional conduit.

"I must go," Seven said, backing up a step. She felt the contact of Hugh's hand break from hers, resisted the desire to feel his touch again. Hugh's arm fell to his side. For the first time since she had been with him, Hugh seemed unsure of himself. His human eye glittered, moist with fluid. Seven watched some of the excess spill slowly down his cheek.

"Thank you," she said, gripping the shell. She turned before Hugh could see the moisture form in her own eyes.

* * *

Captain Janeway sat on a ledge next to Seven's alcove in cargo bay two. The lighting had been lowered in this section to Seven's specifications, darkened like the corridors of a Borg ship, giving the room a nocturnal feel. Seven stood on the deck before her, silhouetted in the flickering light from the alcove.

Janeway leaned back on one arm. "It was good of Hugh to open the conduit and send us back where he found us—he even managed to get us ahead of where we were. But I'm curious, Seven. Why didn't you remain with them? Why did you choose us?"

"The Borg Hugh's offer was compelling, but I have duties aboard this vessel. It would not have been responsible to leave my post."

"Is that all? A sense of obligation?" Janeway flashed her sly smile. "Somehow, I don't feel you're being totally honest with me, Seven."

"Perhaps not. Were I of the collective, you would already know my deepest thoughts. But I am an individual. Is not privacy of thought part of being an individual?"

Janeway chuckled. "Touché. But don't forget that friendship is built upon the sharing of those private thoughts, Seven. Through the sharing, we get to know one another, understand one another, build respect, forge bonds."

Seven gave a clipped nod. "Understood. Then I shall share this with you. While the Borg Hugh was presenting me with the offer to join his people, I was not compelled. Yet later, while alone with the Borg Hugh, I felt oddly attracted by his presence. It was an emotional response I have not encountered previously. Powerful, but also disturbing."

"In what way?"

"The feeling defies logic. It was difficult for me to control. I can only describe it as an overwhelming sensation to . . . couple with him."

"Mmmm." Janeway smiled with warmth. "Romantic attraction. The gravimetric force of neutron stars and black holes can't hold a candle to that one. You've had a taste of your humanity, Seven."

"Does it get easier in time to subjugate this feeling? I find its power . . . disconcerting."

"Never. That's the beauty of it. It's a force beyond logic and algorithms. It's like a tidal wave that rushes over you, filled with chaos, but exhilarating all the same as it carries you away. With the right person, it's like being in seventh heaven."

Seven's brow furrowed. "I do not understand the reference. Do you speak of some Starfleet division of the universe I have not been informed of?"

Janeway chuckled softly. "No, Seven, it's a metaphysical reference. Heaven is associated with mankind's desire to achieve paradise, so saying you're in seventh heaven is like saying you've touched the ultimate level of something. Passion is an overwhelming experience."

Janeway felt her own feelings drifting, carrying her to another place and time. Her eyes closed halfway. There was a long silence.

Looking up, Janeway saw Seven watching her with a puzzled expression. "I must contemplate this emotion when I am more distant from the experience," Seven said.

With a soft groan, Janeway pushed herself up. "Well, don't dwell on it too much. I've been trying since puberty and I still haven't figured it out."

"Captain? There was also another sensation I experienced, almost as powerful. As I withdrew from the Borg Hugh, I felt my chest muscles constrict. My throat experienced the same sensation, and there was a sudden hollow feeling within my abdomen."

Janeway felt that pang in her own heart. "Regret, Seven. It's called regret." She patted Seven on the shoulder, noted that Seven didn't stiffen to the touch. "Get some rest. We'll talk more after you've regenerated. I think we need to spend some time together soaking up a beach on the holodeck. It's called 'girl talk.' "

"I shall look forward to our communication, Captain."

"Sleep well, Seven."

As Janeway walked away, Seven stepped onto the platform of her regeneration alcove, heard the cargo bay door swish open and shut behind her. The circular power matrix flashed in neon-green bolts of flux, and Seven suddenly realized how drained her body felt. Turning, she faced the cabin's door, but before backing into the alcove and closing her eyes, she lifted a hand to her ear. In her palm was the shell.

She could almost hear a whisper.

Afterword

John J. Ordover

". . . These are the voyages of the Starship *Enterprise*. Her five-year mission: to explore Strange New Worlds . . ."

Or in this case, *Strange New Worlds II*.

The stories you've just read weren't written by some sort of magical being called a "Writer." They were written by people just like you. What did they have that you don't have? Probably nothing. The major difference is that they sat down, wrote a story, and sent it in. The rest is details.

Is it really that simple? In a way, yes. You can't enter this contest just by thinking you really should get around to writing a story someday. You enter this contest by shutting down all those voices telling you to do something else instead, and sitting down to write. And write. And write. And write some more. As someone once said: "Write, rinse, repeat."

Writing well takes practice, and it takes the right kind of practice. The best practice comes from reaching down inside yourself, finding what you have to say that's different from what anyone else would have said, and saying it in a way that only you could have said it.

The best place to practice that is in worlds of your own imagining, not in the *Star Trek* universe or any other preexisting universe. Then, when you've practiced and picked up a few tricks, maybe sent a few stories off to the editors of *Fantasy and Science Fiction, Analog,* or *Asimov's,* take a shot at *Strange New Worlds III* (the rules follow this afterword; just turn the page).

That's the process that generated the seventeen superb stories you'll find in this anthology, and that will make up *Strange New Worlds III.* Want your story to be one of them?

Start writing now.

STAR TREK®

Strange New Worlds IV
Contest Rules

1) ENTRY REQUIREMENTS:

No purchase necessary to enter. Enter by submitting your story as specified below.

2) CONTEST ELIGIBILITY:

This contest is open to nonprofessional writers who are legal residents of the United States and Canada (excluding Quebec) over the age of 18. Entrant must not have published any more than two short stories on a professional basis or in paid professional venues. Entrants under contract with a literary agent (or who work for a book publisher) are not eligible. Employees (or relatives of employees living in the same household) of Pocket Books, VIACOM, or any of its affiliates are not eligible. This contest is void in Puerto Rico and wherever prohibited by law.

3) FORMAT:

Entries should be no more than 7,500 words long and must not have been previously published. They must be typed or printed by word processor, double spaced, on one side of noncorrasable paper. Do not justify right-side margins. The author's name, address, and phone number must appear on the first page of the entry. The author's name, the story title, and the page number should appear on every page. No electronic or disk submissions will be accepted. All entries must be original and the sole work of the Entrant and the sole property of the Entrant. Foreign-language submissions are not eligible. All submissions must be in English.

By entering, entrants agree to abide by these rules and warrant and represent that their entry is their original work and grant to Pocket Books the right to publish, promote and otherwise use their entries without further permission, notice or compensation.

4) ADDRESS:

Each entry must be mailed to: STRANGE NEW WORLDS, *Star Trek* Department, Pocket Books, 1230 Sixth Avenue, New York, NY 10020.

Each entry must be submitted only once. Please retain a copy of your submission. You may submit more than one story, but each submission must be mailed separately. Enclose a self-addressed, stamped envelope if you wish your entry returned. Competition runs from January 1st, 2000, to October 1st, 2000. Entries must be received by October 1st, 2000. Not responsible for lost, late, stolen, mutilated, illegible, postage due, or misdirected mail.

5) PRIZES:

Simon & Schuster will own all rights to the winning entries. Each winner will be required to execute a contract granting Pocket Books all such rights.

One Grand Prize winner will receive:

Simon and Schuster's *Star Trek: Strange New Worlds* Publishing Contract for Publication of Winning Entry in our *Strange New Worlds* Anthology with a bonus advance of One Thousand Dollars ($1,000.00) above the Anthology word rate of 10 cents a word.

One Second Prize winner will receive:

Simon and Schuster's *Star Trek: Strange New Worlds* Publishing Contract for Publication of Winning Entry in our *Strange New Worlds* Anthology with a bonus advance of Six Hundred Dollars ($600.00) above the Anthology word rate of 10 cents a word.

One Third Prize winner will receive:

Simon and Schuster's *Star Trek: Strange New Worlds* Publishing Contract for Publication of Winning Entry in our *Strange New Worlds* Anthology with a bonus advance of Four Hundred Dollars ($400.00) above the Anthology word rate of 10 cents a word.

All Honorable Mention winners will receive:

Simon and Schuster's *Star Trek: Strange New Worlds* Publishing Contract for Publication of Winning Entry in the *Strange New Worlds* Anthology and payment at the Anthology word rate of 10 cents a word.

There will be no more than twenty (20) Honorable Mention winners. No contestant can win more than one prize.

Each Prize Winner will also be entitled to a share of royalties on the *Strange New Worlds* Anthology as specified in Simon and Schuster's *Star Trek: Strange New Worlds* Publishing Contract.

6) JUDGING:

On or about November 15th, 2000, all eligible entries received will be judged by a panel of judges.

Submissions will be judged on the basis of writing ability and the originality of the story, which can be set in any of the *Star Trek* time frames and may feature any one or more of the *Star Trek* characters. The judges will include the editor of the Anthology, one employee of Pocket Books, and one employee of VIACOM Consumer Products. The decisions of the judges shall be final. All prizes will be awarded provided a sufficient number of entries are received that meet the minimum criteria established by the judges. The judges reserve the right not to award any prize in the event there are no qualified entries submitted.

7) NOTIFICATION:

The winners will be notified by mail or phone on or before January 1st, 2001. The winners who win a publishing contract must sign the publishing contract in order to be awarded the prize. All expenses on receipt and use of the prize, and all federal, local, and state taxes are the responsibility of the winner. A list of the winners will be available after January 1st, 2001, on the Pocket Books *Star Trek* Books website, www.simonsays. com/startrek/, or the names of the winners can be obtained after January 1st, 2001, by sending a self-addressed, stamped envelope and a request for the list of winners to WINNERS' LIST, STRANGE NEW WORLDS, *Star Trek* Department, Pocket Books, 1230 Sixth Avenue, New York, NY 10020.

8) STORY DISQUALIFICATIONS:

Certain types of stories will be disqualified from consideration:

a) Any story focusing on explicit sexual activity or graphic depictions of violence or sadism.

b) Any story that focuses on characters that are not past or present *Star Trek* regulars or familiar *Star Trek* guest characters.

c) Stories that deal with the previously unestablished death of a *Star Trek* character, or that establish major facts about or make major changes in the life of a major character, for instance a story that establishes a long-lost sibling or reveals the hidden passion two characters feel for each other.

d) Stories that are based around common clichés, such as "hurt/comfort" where a character is injured and lovingly cared for, or "Mary Sue" stories where a new character comes on the ship and outdoes the crew.

9) PUBLICITY:

Each Winner grants to Pocket Books the right to use his or her name, likeness, and entry for any advertising, promotion, and publicity purposes without further compensation to or permission from such winner, except where prohibited by law.

10) LEGAL STUFF:

All entries and any copyrights therein become the sole property of Pocket Books and of Paramount Pictures, the sole and exclusive owner of the *Star Trek* property and elements thereof. Entries will be returned only if they are accompanied by a self-addressed, stamped envelope. Contest void where prohibited by law.

No transfer or assignment of prizes allowed. In the event of unavailability, Pocket Books may substitute a prize of equal or greater value. Winners must sign and return an affidavit of eligibility and liability and a publicity release, which much be returned within fifteen [15] days of prize notification attempt or an alternate winner may be selected. Pocket Books shall have no liability to any person for any injury, loss or damage of any kind arising out of the acceptance or use of the prizes.

About the Contributors

Melissa Dickinson ("Triptych") is a 29-year-old graphic designer with degrees from the Ringling School of Art and Design. She and her husband David returned to Florida in 1996, after a two-year sabbatical in the mountains of New Hampshire. Melissa spent the time off learning multimedia design, reviving her writing skills, and rediscovering her love of *Star Trek*.

Kathy Oltion ("The Quick and the Dead") currently works in a medical laboratory in Eugene, Oregon, and writes when she's not gardening or playing clarinet in a ragtime band. This marks her third professional sale, and she wishes to thank her parents, husband Jerry, and the Wordos (aka Eugene Professional Writers Workshop) for all their love, help, and support.

Michael S. Poteet ("The First Law of Metaphysics")
pastors Trinity United Presbyterian Church in Clifton
Heights, Pennsylvania. He and wife Karen Nelson, also
an ordained minister, are graduates of William and Mary
and Princeton Seminary. A *Trek* fan since 1984, Michael
is also interested in Arthurian legend, Broadway music,
and homemade chocolate-chip cookies.

Peg Robinson ("The Hero of My Own Life") is about the
same as she was before, just slightly more published. She
has a wonderful husband, delightful daughter, and four
obnoxious cats. Her year's accomplishments are a finished novel, qualification for SFWA membership, and
becoming ineligible for next year's *Strange New Worlds
III*. Ah, well, life is never perfect.

Charles Skaggs ("Doctors Three") has a bachelor's
degree in business management but wants nothing more
than to write for a living. When not reading comic books,
he can be found watching *Star Trek* and Cleveland
Indians games with his beloved wife, Lori. "Doctors
Three" is his first published story.

Ken Rand ("I Am Klingon") remarried his ex-wife in
1993, ending a nineteen-year divorce. He's published a
nonfiction writers' how-to book, and he has written three
(unpublished) novels, a hundred (unpublished) short stories, two hundred humor columns, and countless articles.
For fun he makes kaleidoscopes. Friend Amy Hanson
helped with "I Am Klingon."

Brad Curry ("Reciprocity") lives in Florida, where he spends his free time reading, repairing his dilapidated Toyota, and, when he can overcome his innate laziness, trying to write fiction. A longtime science-fiction fan, he's pleased that "Reciprocity," his first published short story, features characters from the *Star Trek* universe.

Christina F. York ("Calculated Risk") lives in Eugene, Oregon, with SF writer J. Steven York. She is a lapsed science-fiction fan, and her husband is seeing to her reeducation now that the kids are grown and gone. Her *Deep Space Nine* story "Life's Lessons" appeared in *Strange New Worlds I,* which shows he's making progress.

William Leisner ("Gods, Fate, and Fractals") lives in Rochester, New York, where he is manager of the book department of a multimedia superstore. His previous credits include two award-winning teleplays for Ithaca College Television, and a story concept sale to *Star Trek: Voyager.* He is already planning his next creative accomplishment.

Franklin Thatcher ("I Am Become Death") won second place in the first *Star Trek: Strange New Worlds* anthology, and has since gone on to win first place in the L. Ron Hubbard's Writers of the Future contest. He is currently working on a novel. He, his wife, and their cats live in Orem, Utah.

J. R. Rasmussen ("Research") (Jeannie when she's not trying to get published) is a college dropout, newspaper reporter, editor, movie reviewer, and television columnist. Her day job is library administrator of the Reno (Nevada) *Gazette-Journal*'s electronic archive. In real life, she is a theater buff, Trekker, and rookie freelance writer.

Steven Scott Ripley ("Change of Heart") enjoys life, friends, and family from home base Puget Sound. An early career SF&F writer, he also works as a web guy with the city of Seattle. Nineteen ninety-eight highlight: contributing to the *Star Trek* legacy in this book. Nineteen ninety-eight big lesson: dolphins are indeed sentient beings.

Ilsa J. Bick ("A Ribbon for Rosie") is a child psychiatrist in Fairfax, Virginia. Along with Robert Justman and William Theiss, she presented on *Star Trek* at Washington's Smithsonian Institution and has published widely on science-fiction film. When she isn't writing, she cooks extravagant meals for her husband, two children, and other assorted vermin.

Kim Sheard ("Touched") has a degree in chemistry and works as a technical writer. "Touched" is her first fiction submission for publication. She lives in Fairfax, Virginia (a suburb of Washington, D.C.), with her husband, Henry, and two dogs. Her hobbies include singing, community theater, computers, and, of course, science fiction.

Dayton Ward ("Almost . . . But Not Quite") makes his second appearance in *Strange New Worlds*. A Florida native, he was transplanted to Kansas City during service with the U.S. Marine Corps. Now he's a systems engineer there, living with his wife, Michi, along with a temperamental dog and an insane cat.

Lynda Martinez Foley ("The Healing Arts") has been a proud Trekkie since the original series premiered. After 1994's Northridge earthquake motivated her to seriously pursue writing, she won and completed a scriptwriting internship with *Star Trek: Voyager.* When not basking poolside with her husband and two sons, she enjoys writing, schmoozing online, and working with numerous charities.

E. Cristy Ruteshouser ("The Healing Arts") set aside an adolescent dream of writing fiction in order to pursue a career in science. Armed with a Ph.D. in molecular biology, she now studies pediatric cancer and resides in Texas with her husband and three cats. "The Healing Arts" is her first published work of fiction.

Dustan Moon ("Seventh Heaven") lives with his wife on Moon Mountain in the Pacific Northwest. He writes fulltime and is putting the finishing touches on his epic fantasy *Driftweave.* He is grateful to Pocket Books for this free advertising space and will be even more grateful if this shameless plug helps him sell his first novel.

OUR FIRST SERIAL NOVEL!

Presenting, one chapter per month . . .

The very beginning of the
Starfleet Adventure . . .

STAR TREK®

STARFLEET: YEAR ONE

A novel in Twelve Parts®

by
Michael Jan Friedman

Chapter Six

Bryce Shumar walked into the small, green-walled cubicle and saw that his first interview was already waiting for him.

Circumnavigating the room's sleek, black desk, the captain took his seat in a plastiform chair and eyed the tall blond man seated opposite him. "Welcome," he said, "Mr.—"

"Mullen. Lieutenant Commander Steven Mullen. It's a pleasure to make your acquaintance, sir."

The man spoke in a clipped, efficient voice. A distinctly military voice, if Shumar was any judge of such things.

"Likewise," the captain responded.

He brought up Mullen's personnel file on the small screen built into the desk. It showed him everything . . . and nothing.

"You've got a degree from West Point," said Shumar, reading from the file. "You graduated with honors. Then you signed up with Earth Command, where you flew seventeen missions against the Romulans."

Mullen nodded. "That's correct, sir."

Shumar read on. "At the Battle of Aldebaran," he noted, "you took command of the *Panther* after your captain and first officer were killed. Despite your lack of experience, you destoyed two enemy warships, not to mention a major Romulan supply depot." He looked at Mullen. "It says here that you were given a Medal of Valor for that action."

"That's true as well," the blond man replied solemnly.

"But it was the crew who deserved that medal, sir. I just gave the orders. They're the ones who carried them out."

Shumar studied Mullen. "Do you mean that, Commander?"

The man's forehead puckered. "I beg your pardon, sir?"

The captain shrugged and leaned back in his chair. "Every Earth Command officer I've ever met gives his crew credit for his success. It's an unwritten code, I think."

"Perhaps it is, sir," Mullen answered earnestly. "But in this case, I mean it. My crew was responsible for that victory."

Shumar liked the man's approach. And Mullen's record was impeccable. There was only one more thing he needed to know.

"Tell me something, Commander," said the captain, "and for heaven's sake, please be honest."

Mullen nodded. "Of course, sir."

Shumar leaned forward again. "How would you feel taking orders from a man who's never commanded a starship?"

The blond man seemed to mull it over. "I don't know, sir," he said at last. "I suppose it would depend on the man."

The captain considered Mullen's response. Then he stood up and extended his hand. "Thank you, Commander."

Mullen stood too, and shook Shumar's hand. There was a trace of disappointment in his eyes. After all, they had only conversed for a couple of minutes—normally not a very good sign.

"Thank you for your time," said the commander. "And good luck, sir."

"My luck will depend," the captain told him.

Again, Mullen's brow puckered. "On what, sir?"

"On you," said Shumar. "I'd welcome you aboard, Commander, but I don't have a ship yet. All I have is a first officer."

Finally, Mullen allowed himself a smile. "Yes, sir. I'll do my best not to disappoint you, sir."

The captain smiled back at him. "I'm sure you will, Commander."

Cobaryn scanned the personnel file displayed on the screen in front of him. "You have quite an impressive résumé, Mr. Emick."

The sturdy-looking, sandy-haired man on the other side of the table smiled at him. "Thank you, sir."

The Rigelian regarded Emick for a moment. The fellow was pleasant enough and his transport piloting credentials were clearly first-rate. What else could he possibly need to know?

"I am not the sort of person who requires a great deal of time to make a decision," Cobaryn declared. "I would like to sign you on as my primary helmsman."

Emick's smile widened. "I'd be delighted, sir."

Cobaryn smiled back at him. "Excellent. As soon as I know when and where you must report, I will send word to your superiors."

"Thank you, sir," the helmsman said. He got up to go, then stopped and looked back at the Rigelian. "May I ask a favor, sir?"

Cobaryn shrugged. "Of course."

"I'd like permission to exceed the weight and size parameters allotted to personal effects by about thirteen percent. That is," said Emick, "if it's not too much trouble, sir."

The captain looked at him. "Like you, Mr. Emick, I have never set foot on a *Christopher*, though I cannot imagine that a deviation of thirteen percent will be a problem. But if I may ask . . . what is it that you have in your possession that is both so large and so precious to you?"

"It's a book collection," the man told him. "You see, sir, I like to read a lot—and I like it even better when I can read from an actual volume and not a computer screen."

Cobaryn nodded. He had heard that there was a movement of bound-paper book aficionados on Earth. Apparently, Emick was one of them.

"Do you have any special interests?" he asked.

"Quite a few, actually," the man told him. "Antarctic zoology. Aboriginal music. Religious art. Organized crime."

The last subject piqued the Rigelian's interest more than the others. "Organized crime?" he echoed. "What is that?"

"A phenomenon of Earth's early twentieth century," said Emick. "Some of Earth's larger urban centers were plagued by a number of illegal and often violent organizations."

Cobaryn absorbed the information. "I see. And you are in some way attracted to these organizations?"

The man recoiled. "No, sir. I'm appalled by them . . . of course. But they're still fascinating when viewed as a subculture."

The captain didn't see the appeal. "I suppose I will have to take your word for it."

"Or," Emick suggested as an alternative, "you could borrow one of my favorite books on the subject—*Chicago Mobs of the Twenties,* by Billings and Torgelson. Then you could judge for yourself."

Cobaryn effected another smile. "It would be my pleasure to do so. And by the way, your request for additional storage space is granted."

The helmsman's eyes crinkled gratefully at the corners. "I'm grateful for your understanding, sir."

"You and I and the other members of our crew have a

lot of hard work ahead of us," the Rigelian noted. "I want us all to be as comfortable on our vessel as possible."

"I will certainly be more comfortable knowing I've got my books around me," Emick assured him. "Thank you again, sir."

"Think nothing of it," Cobaryn told the fellow graciously. "Consider yourself dismissed."

He watched Emick leave the cubicle. Then he sat back in his plastiform chair and tried to imagine an Earth overrun by men dedicated to violence. It just didn't seem possible.

But then, in that same century, humans had supposedly inhaled the smoke of burning vegetation, built habitations on geological faults and destroyed herbivores for sport . . . so he had to concede that anything was possible.

Stiles went over Elena Ezquerra's file as he had gone over more than a dozen others that day.

He took note of the time she had put in on the *White Wolf* and the *Wildcat*. He saw the commendations she had received for bravery and initiative over the last couple of years. And he read the glowing praise that Captain Renault had heaped on her.

When Stiles was finished with the file, he looked up at the petite, dark-haired woman. She looked eager to see what he thought of her.

"I like what I see here," he told her. "I like it a lot."

Ezquerra's eyes lit up. "Very kind of you to say so, sir."

The captain shook his head. "It's not kind of me at all, Lieutenant. In fact, it's downright cruel."

The woman sat back in her seat. "I beg your pardon, sir?"

"It's cruel," he explained, "that despite all your considerable qualifications, I can't bring you aboard."

Ezquerra looked perplexed. "I'm afraid I don't understand, sir."

"It's very simple," Stiles told her. "Starfleet has put a cap on the number of Earth Command people we can take on as officers—and I've already filled my quota. So the only way I can add you to my crew is if you accept a demotion, which I would never ask you to do."

The lieutenant's shoulders slumped. "I see," she said.

But it was clear to him that she didn't like it. And for that matter, neither did he.

"There's one other thing I can do," Stiles said. "I can recommend you to one of the other captains in the hope they've still got room for you."

Ezquerra smiled a halfhearted smile. "You don't have to do that, sir."

"Actually," the captain replied, "I *do*, Lieutenant—because the alternative is to go track down my superior and vent my considerable frustration on him and maybe get myself court-martialed in the process. And as you can imagine, I don't see that as a viable option."

The woman took a moment to figure out what he had just said. When she was done, she nodded. "In that case, thank you, sir."

"It's the least I can do," Stiles told her.

Then he tapped the communications stud on the side of the desk and put in a call to Matsura.

Dane walked straight into his bedroom and hit the sack without even taking his boots off.

For a while, he just lay there, his mind reeling after an entire day spent staring at strange faces and personnel files that had begun to blur together all too quickly.

If Dane had needed further proof that he had no business in Starfleet, he had now received it in ample supply. How was he supposed to know who would be a good officer and who wouldn't? By making small talk for a few minutes? By counting the commendations in a damned computer file?

In some cases, he had picked the candidates with the most experience. In others, he had gone with a gut feeling. And as the day wore on, he had simply picked anyone who could do the job.

Dane was pretty sure that wasn't the way it was supposed to work. He was certain that none of his fellow captains had handled it that way. But then, he wasn't anything like his fellow captains.

Which is why, years from now, they would be flying the *Daedalus* and her sister ships . . . and he would be back in his *Cochrane* escorting cargo tubs through the worst neighborhoods the galaxy had to offer.

"Captain Dane?" came a voice, jolting him out of his reverie.

Dane swore under his breath. "That's me."

"This is Captain Fitzgerald in Earth orbit. I've got orders to turn the *Maverick* over to you at your earliest convenience."

Dane grunted. The *Maverick,* eh? Was that his uncle's idea of a joke?

"When should I expect you?" Fitzgerald asked.

Dane swung his legs out of bed. "Now," he said.

There was a pause. "Now?" echoed the voice.

"Now," Dane confirmed. "Or, to be more accurate, as soon as I can get to a working transporter platform."

Another pause—one that seemed to reek of resentment. "Acknowledged, Captain. Fitzgerald out."

In the silence that followed, Dane actually felt nervous. His heart was beating harder than it should have and there was an unfamiliar weakness in his knees. But it didn't stop him.

He made his way out of his quarters, followed the corridor

to another corridor and then another, and finally found the facility's main transporter room. It was manned by a single operator, a muscular man with piercing blue eyes and neatly combed dark hair.

"Can I help you, sir?" the man asked Dane.

"You can indeed," the captain told him. "You can send me up to the *Maverick*. She's in Earth orbit."

He stepped up onto the transporter disc and waited for the operator to comply. But it didn't happen.

"I wasn't notified of any transports this evening," the man said.

Dane looked at him. "So?"

The transporter operator frowned. "My orders require me to follow a schedule, sir. You're not on my schedule."

Dane came down off the disc and crossed the room. "Let's see that schedule you're talking about."

The man pointed it out on his monitor. "You see, sir? There's no mention of any transports this evening."

"That's funny," said Dane, punching in a little-known access code and then tapping his name out. Letter by letter, it appeared on the screen. "It looks to me like you've got a transport scheduled after all."

The operator read Dane's name. Then he looked at the captain, amazed. "How did you do that?"

Dane smiled a thin smile. "I've been doing it since I was ten. It's one of the perks of growing up a Command brat. Now are you going to transport me or do I have to do it myself?"

The dark-haired man hesitated for a moment. Then he said, "I'm ready when you are, sir."

"Thanks a bunch," Dane told him.

Crossing the room again, he stepped up onto the transporter disc. A moment later, he saw the operator go to work.

In less than a minute, the captain's surroundings vanished—and he found himself in a much smaller chamber. He recognized it as the transporter room of a *Christopher*-class starship.

There was a tall, balding man in a black and gold Earth Command uniform standing beside the control console. "Welcome to the *Maverick*," he said. "I'm Captain Fitzgerald."

His tone told Dane that he wouldn't have minded waiting until morning to bring his replacement aboard. In fact, he probably wouldn't have minded waiting until the millennium.

"I imagine you'll want to see the ship," Fitzgerald said.

Descending from the disc, Dane made his way across the room. "Look," he told his predecessor, "I know my way around a *Christopher*. You don't have to hold my hand if you've got something better to do."

He had meant it as a magnanimous gesture. If it were his vessel, he would have hated the idea of giving his successor a tour.

But Fitzgerald obviously didn't see it that way. "It's my duty to show you around, Captain. I'm going to see that duty done."

Dane shrugged. "Suit yourself."

Together, they left the transporter room and headed down the corridor to the nearest turbolift. En route, they passed a couple of lieutenants who acknowledged Fitzgerald but didn't so much as glance at Dane.

"Friendly crew you've got here," he noted. "I guess they're no more thrilled about giving up their ship than you are."

Fitzgerald shot him a stern look. "Frankly, it's not just a matter of giving up the *Maverick*. It's that we're giving it up to someone who's never worn the uniform."

Dane stiffened at the unexpected arrogance behind the rebuke. Who did these Earth Command types think they were? A superior species?

"It's funny," he said, refusing to rise to the bait. "I seem to hear that sort of thing a lot lately."

"And how do you respond?" Fitzgerald asked.

"Is that meant to be a gibe?" Dane countered bluntly.

"No. I'd really like to know," said Fitzgerald, allowing only the merest note of irony to creep into his voice.

Dane opened the doors with a tap of the pad on the bulkhead beside them. "Usually," he said in a matter-of-fact tone, "I tell them to go to hell. But that's only when they're not performing a life or death service like playing tour guide."

Fitzgerald's eyes became daggers as the doors finished sliding open. "Understand something, Captain. This vessel saw us through the worst of the war. If I hear you're mistreating her, I'll personally shove you out a missile tube."

Dane tried to keep a lid on his emotions as he entered the lift compartment. "Let's make a deal," he said as calmly as he could. "You don't make any more stupid threats and I'll treat this ship better than you ever did. I'll bring her flowers twice a week, wine her and dine her, bring her chocolates, the works. What do you say?"

Fitzgerald reddened. "That's not what I meant."

"Oh?" said Dane, feigning surprise. "Then what *did* you mean? That I was purposely going to bounce her through an asteroid belt?"

The other man scowled, accentuating the lines in his face. "I meant this ship is a whole lot more than you deserve."

"Maybe so," Dane replied evenly. "But then, the galaxy seldom plays fair, Captain. As someone who's fought a war all by himself, you should appreciate that." He indicated the inside of the turbolift with a flourish. "Care to join the tour?"

Biting his lip, Fitzgerald stepped inside and pressed the stud that closed the doors. Then he punched in a destination.

But before he could send the lift on its way, Dane canceled the command and instituted one of his own. "Let's go straight to the bridge," he said. "That's the part I'm *really* looking forward to."

Fitzgerald didn't say anything—either at that moment or any other—as the lift made its way to the *Maverick*'s command nexus. When they arrived, Dane took it on himself to open the doors.

As they slid apart, he absorbed the sight of his new bridge—a gold enclosure full of sleek, black consoles. Of course, it looked a lot like the bridges he had seen on a half dozen other *Christopher*s in his lifetime. But there was something about *this* one that made Dane's heart skip a beat.

"Captain on the bridge," someone announced.

Dane didn't know if the man was talking about him or Fitzgerald. What's more, he didn't much care.

"At ease," he said, speaking up before his counterpart could.

There were eight officers on the bridge. They all looked at him—none of them with the least bit of kindness.

"This is Captain Dane," Fitzgerald pointed out dutifully. "The new commanding officer of—"

"They don't care who I am," Dane interjected. "They're like you in that regard, Captain. They just want to know me well enough to hate me for taking their ship away."

The bridge officers stared at him disbelievingly. Obviously, they had never heard anyone speak that way to their superior.

"So let's do everyone a favor," Dane went on. "Now that Captain Fitzgerald has given me my tour—and let me tell you, what a splendid tour it was—why don't you all take a last look around the ship? Go ahead. I can handle the bridge by myself."

Fitzgerald glared at him. "You're out of your mind. This is a *Christopher,* man. If something goes wrong—"

"I'll take my chances," Dane told him. "And unless I'm mistaken, it's my option to do that . . . since this vessel officially stopped being Earth Command property two days ago."

The muscles worked furiously in Fitzgerald's jaw. "That's exactly right," he conceded. "I commend you on your grasp of protocol, Captain."

"Please," said Dane. "You'll give me a swelled head. Now go. Get out of here, all of you."

The officers glanced at Fitzgerald, who nodded reluctantly. Then, little by little, they filed into the turbolift. It took two trips for the compartment to take them all away, but eventually it did its job.

When the doors slid closed on the second group, Dane walked over to the captain's chair and sat down. He looked around at the empty duty stations, both fore and aft, and imagined them full of the officers he had signed a few hours earlier, their faces turned to him for orders.

Dane wouldn't have admitted it out loud, but he had never been so scared in all his life.

Look for STAR TREK fiction from Pocket Books

Star Trek®: The Original Series

Star Trek: The Next Generation®

Metamorphosis • Jean Lorrah
Vendetta • Peter David
Reunion • Michael Jan Friedman
Imzadi • Peter David
The Devil's Heart • Carmen Carter
Dark Mirror • Diane Duane
Q-Squared • Peter David
Crossover • Michael Jan Friedman
Kahless • Michael Jan Friedman
Ship of the Line • Diane Carey
The Best and the Brightest • Susan Wright
Planet X • Michael Jan Friedman
Imzadi II: Triangle • Peter David
I, Q • Peter David & John de Lancie
Novelizations
Encounter at Farpoint • David Gerrold
Unification • Jeri Taylor
Relics • Michael Jan Friedman
Descent • Diane Carey
All Good Things... • Michael Jan Friedman
Star Trek: Klingon • Dean Wesley Smith & Kristine Kathryn Rusch
Star Trek Generations • J.M. Dillard
Star Trek: First Contact • J.M. Dillard
Star Trek: Insurrection • J.M. Dillard

#1 • *Ghost Ship* • Diane Carey
#2 • *The Peacekeepers* • Gene DeWeese
#3 • *The Children of Hamlin* • Carmen Carter
#4 • *Survivors* • Jean Lorrah
#5 • *Strike Zone* • Peter David
#6 • *Power Hungry* • Howard Weinstein
#7 • *Masks* • John Vornholt
#8 • *The Captain's Honor* • David and Daniel Dvorkin
#9 • *A Call to Darkness* • Michael Jan Friedman
#10 • *A Rock and a Hard Place* • Peter David
#11 • *Gulliver's Fugitives* • Keith Sharee
#12 • *Doomsday World* • David, Carter, Friedman & Greenberger
#13 • *The Eyes of the Beholders* • A.C. Crispin
#14 • *Exiles* • Howard Weinstein
#15 • *Fortune's Light* • Michael Jan Friedman

#55 • *Double or Nothing* • Peter David
#56 • *The First Virtue* • Michael Jan Friedman & Christie Golden
#57 • *The Forgotten War* • William Fortschen

Star Trek: Deep Space Nine®

Warped • K.W. Jeter
Legends of the Ferengi • Ira Steven Behr & Robert Hewitt Wolfe
The Lives of Dax • Marco Palmieri, ed.
Novelizations
Emissary • J.M. Dillard
The Search • Diane Carey
The Way of the Warrior • Diane Carey
Star Trek: Klingon • Dean Wesley Smith & Kristine Kathryn Rusch
Trials and Tribble-ations • Diane Carey
Far Beyond the Stars • Steve Barnes
What You Leave Behind • Diane Carey

#1 • *Emissary* • J.M. Dillard
#2 • *The Siege* • Peter David
#3 • *Bloodletter* • K.W. Jeter
#4 • *The Big Game* • Sandy Schofield
#5 • *Fallen Heroes* • Dafydd ab Hugh
#6 • *Betrayal* • Lois Tilton
#7 • *Warchild* • Esther Friesner
#8 • *Antimatter* • John Vornholt
#9 • *Proud Helios* • Melissa Scott
#10 • *Valhalla* • Nathan Archer
#11 • *Devil in the Sky* • Greg Cox & John Gregory Betancourt
#12 • *The Laertian Gamble* • Robert Sheckley
#13 • *Station Rage* • Diane Carey
#14 • *The Long Night* • Dean Wesley Smith & Kristine Kathryn Rusch
#15 • *Objective: Bajor* • John Peel
#16 • *Invasion!* #3: *Time's Enemy* • L.A. Graf
#17 • *The Heart of the Warrior* • John Gregory Betancourt
#18 • *Saratoga* • Michael Jan Friedman
#19 • *The Tempest* • Susan Wright
#20 • *Wrath of the Prophets* • David, Friedman & Greenberger
#21 • *Trial by Error* • Mark Garland
#22 • *Vengeance* • Dafydd ab Hugh
#23 • *The 34th Rule* • Armin Shimerman & David R. George III

#24-26 • *Rebels* • Dafydd ab Hugh
  #24 • *The Conquered*
  #25 • *The Courageous*
  #26 • *The Liberated*

Star Trek: Voyager®

  Mosaic • Jeri Taylor
  Pathways • Jeri Taylor
  Captain Proton! • Dean Wesley Smith
Novelizations
  Caretaker • L.A. Graf
  Flashback • Diane Carey
  Day of Honor • Michael Jan Friedman
  Equinox • Diane Carey

#1 • *Caretaker* • L.A. Graf
#2 • *The Escape* • Dean Wesley Smith & Kristine Kathryn Rusch
#3 • *Ragnarok* • Nathan Archer
#4 • *Violations* • Susan Wright
#5 • *Incident at Arbuk* • John Gregory Betancourt
#6 • *The Murdered Sun* • Christie Golden
#7 • *Ghost of a Chance* • Mark A. Garland & Charles G. McGraw
#8 • *Cybersong* • S.N. Lewitt
#9 • *Invasion! #4: Final Fury* • Dafydd ab Hugh
#10 • *Bless the Beasts* • Karen Haber
#11 • *The Garden* • Melissa Scott
#12 • *Chrysalis* • David Niall Wilson
#13 • *The Black Shore* • Greg Cox
#14 • *Marooned* • Christie Golden
#15 • *Echoes* • Dean Wesley Smith, Kristine Kathryn Rusch &
  Nina Kiriki Hoffman
#16 • *Seven of Nine* • Christie Golden
#17 • *Death of a Neutron Star* • Eric Kotani
#18 • *Battle Lines* • Dave Galanter & Greg Brodeur

Star Trek®: New Frontier

New Frontier #1-4 Collector's Edition • Peter David
  #1 • *House of Cards* • Peter David
  #2 • *Into the Void* • Peter David

Star Trek® Books available in Trade Paperback

STAR TREK
THE EXPERIENCE
LAS VEGAS HILTON

Be a part of the most exciting deep space adventure in the galaxy as you beam aboard the U.S.S. Enterprise. Explore the evolution of Star Trek® from television to movies in the "History of the Future Museum," the planet's largest collection of authentic Star Trek memorabilia. Then, visit distant galaxies on the "Voyage Through Space." This 22-minute action packed adventure will capture your senses with the latest in motion simulator technology. After your mission, shop in the Deep Space Nine Promenade and enjoy 24th Century cuisine in Quark's Bar & Restaurant.